DEATH OF A WAITRESS

"Do you see Teri Jo so you can ask for the check?" Alberta asked.

Helen looked up and saw Teri Jo walking toward their table. She waved her hand, but before she could scribble in the air, which everyone understood was the universal, and unspoken, way to ask for a check, she noticed a look of utter fear consume the waitress's face. When Teri Jo fell to the floor inches from their table, that same look transferred to the faces of each of the four women.

They weren't horrified because Teri Jo had fallen.

They were horrified because a butcher knife was jutting out of her back . . .

Books by J.D. Griffo

MURDER ON MEMORY LAKE

MURDER IN TRANQUILITY PARK

MURDER AT ICICLE LODGE

MURDER AT VERONICA'S DINER

Published by Kensington Publishing Corporation

J.D. GRIFFO

**A Ferrara Family
Mystery**

MURDER
AT VERONICA'S
DINER

KENSINGTON BOOKS
www.kensingtonbooks.com

KENSINGTON BOOKS are published by

Kensington Publishing Corp.
119 West 40th Street
New York, NY 10018

All Kensington titles, imprints, and distributed lines are available at special quantity discounts for bulk purchases for sales promotion, premiums, fund-raising, educational, or institutional use.

Special book excerpts or customized printings can also be created to fit specific needs. For details, write or phone the office of the Kensington Sales Manager: Attn.: Sales Department. Kensington Publishing Corp., 119 West 40th Street, New York, NY 10018. Phone: 1-800-221-2647.

Kensington and the K logo Reg. U.S. Pat. & TM Off.

First Printing: December 2020
ISBN-13: 978-1-4967-3093-0
ISBN-10: 1-4967-3093-3

ISBN-13: 978-1-4967-3094-7 (ebook)
ISBN-10: 1-4967-3094-1 (ebook)

10 9 8 7 6 5 4 3 2 1

Printed in the United States of America

For Melisa. And our special orange vinyl banquette at The Brass Rail, the best diner in Allentown, PA.

Acknowledgments

Thanks again to everyone at Kensington Books and my agent, Evan Marshall, for their continued support and belief in me as a writer. And special thanks to all the great Jersey diners I grew up on, especially the Plaza Diner in Secaucus. Your disco fries and egg creams are legendary—you are still missed!

PROLOGUE

Un incubo non rovinerà la mia giornata.

When Alberta jolted awake, the first thing she did was clutch the gold crucifix hanging around her neck. Her action was a physical reflex, but the cross itself was an emotional touchstone. For over forty years the simple but cherished piece of jewelry, which was a gift from her parents on her twenty-first birthday, had always been a source of solace and comfort. This morning she needed it to give her strength.

She wasn't overwhelmed by stress and there were no major issues in her life that she needed to confront and sort out, yet for some unknown reason, Alberta had one of the worst night's sleep she'd ever had. Restless, consumed with ominous dreams, and culminating with Alberta waking up startled and gasping for breath, desperate to escape the clutches of a nightmare.

"Dio mio," she cried.

Her voice was shrill and tight, like she was being strangled, and in a way she was. Not by the hands of a violent attacker, but by her own unconscious fear. Something had penetrated her sleep, something unwanted and nefarious had gotten inside her brain and contaminated her mind, and even as Alberta lay awake in her bed, it wouldn't slither away. Stubbornly, it maintained its residence and Alberta could feel her heart still pounding in her chest, thumping loudly like a determined predator banging on a locked door. Her immediate surroundings, however, were the complete opposite, and their appearance belied the inner turmoil she was experiencing.

The early morning sun peered through the large window opposite Alberta's bed and cast a glorious glow throughout the room. The blue hydrangeas that decorated her bedspread, the same flowers that flourished in her backyard, appeared to blossom in the sunshine. At the foot of her bed, Lola, her beloved black cat, was curled in a ball, sleeping, and purring contentedly. The white stripe of fur over her left eye rose and fell with each breath. Lola appeared entirely unaffected by Alberta's abrupt rising.

Surveying the room for a sign that something was out of place, Alberta wondered if there had been an intruder in her home during the night. Perhaps someone had broken in and her nightmare was real. Could her sleeping mind, aware of an invasion, have become so frightened that it forced Alberta to remain asleep? Her eyes canvassed the room with more scrutiny, but she found nothing that was in disarray, nothing that looked suspiciously changed from the night before, and nothing that caused her any alarm. Until she looked to the right.

Hanging on the wall over her writing desk, where she

paid her bills and wrote out her Christmas cards as well as the occasional letter to a relative still living in Italy, was a painting of a country village in Sicily. It was a family heirloom; it was also the source of her nightmare.

In the background of the painting were two small houses and a larger square-shaped church that seemed to emerge from the side of a hill. A cross rose from the top of the church, modest yet foreboding, and seemed to judge the village from its vantage point. A narrow dirt road started at the entrance to the church and ran down the vertical length of the painting, separating the two houses, while all around a lush green landscape pulsated with life, except for a small portion on the left, where the bank of a river could be seen. For all its realistic depiction and natural beauty, the main focus of the painting was the couple in the foreground.

The young man in the painting was barefoot and virile; his left hand, the closest to the viewer, was at his side, and dangling from his grip was a bouquet of colorful wildflowers. He was smiling, his eyes filled with mischievous delight, caught mid-saunter through the field, lackadaisical but with a purpose, because on the other side of the dirt path was a beautifully dressed young woman.

She was walking toward the house on her side of the road, so she was only seen from behind, her long black hair cascading down her back and in startling contrast to the powder-blue dress she wore. However, her profile could be seen as she looked at the young man, and it was enough proof that the young man's impish smile was warranted. Her right eye was fully open and hopeful; her lips were closed, but in the beginning stage of her own smile, and her shoulders were high, as if she had just gasped for breath at the sight. It was a scene that usually made Alberta smile, but this morning it sent a chill down her spine. In a flash, the details of her nightmare rushed back to her and Alberta knew her bad dream wasn't arbitrary, it was an omen.

According to Ferrara family folklore, the painting was a gift as part of the courtship between Alberta's maternal great-grandmother, Viola, and her suitor, Marcello. The two had grown up in houses alongside each other, just like the ones depicted in the painting, and played as children in the fields and the nearby river, while the villagers watched with knowing silence as friendship developed into curiosity and, ultimately, into love.

Their marriage was inevitable, but Marcello, being the romantic that he was, courted Viola as if she were disinterested and aloof. He brought her gifts, wrote her songs, baked terrible-tasting desserts—an element of the story that made Alberta feel even more connected to her ancestors since she too was a terrible baker—until he finally presented her with the painting that hung on Alberta's wall instead of an engagement ring when he proposed marriage. Any other girl would have scoffed at him and demanded a ring, but Viola didn't care about shiny objects, all she wanted was Marcello. Even though Marcello didn't want anyone other than Viola to be his bride, his family had other ideas.

Thanks to the war and the devastated economy it left in its wake, Marcello's family had lost the little money they had and, like most families in the village, were poor and without prospects. When a rich man's daughter from Calabria, who was visiting family nearby, fancied Marcello, his family saw it as an opportunity to turn their backs on poverty. Marcello was forced to leave the village and travel back to Calabria with the rich girl's family and, unable to break the news to Viola in person, he left without saying a word. Later, Viola was told that Marcello was killed in an accident, but everyone in the village knew that Marcello had simply chosen his family over Viola.

Lies don't linger long in a small Sicilian village, so Viola must have known the truth about her young suitor, but for whatever reason she never let go of the painting. Alberta always felt it was because, despite Viola having married a very good man with whom she had four children, she could never let go of her first love or the only physical link that connected the two of them.

When Viola's granddaughter, Annamaria, was going to throw it out decades ago, Alberta asked if she could have it. The painting wasn't a masterpiece, nor did it depict a joyful memory, but Alberta wanted it nonetheless. Up until now it had never given her a bad feeling.

Inexplicably, she had dreamed about Viola and Marcello. Not about the love that was evident between them in the colors of the painting, but the anger and vengeance that lurked just outside the confines of the frame. She dreamed about what happened after Marcello fled, or more judiciously, was forced to flee the village, and Viola's reaction was far from subtle. Within Alberta's dream world, Viola unleashed a fury onto Marcello that was filled with deep-rooted and unresolved pain and anguish.

The details of the nightmare were bad enough, but worse than that, Alberta didn't know if she was victim or voycur. Was she observing Viola get her revenge, or was the vitriol somehow directed at her? Would she soon be on the wrong end of someone's fiery display of repressed emotions? Or would it be someone close to her?

Sitting up in bed, Lola finally waking up to stretch

long and slow, Alberta looked at the painting and declared, *"Un incubo non rovinerà la mia giornata."*

One nightmare wasn't going to ruin her day. Although
she meant every word that she said and believed it to be
true, she would find out very soon just how wrong she
was.

Her day was about to go from bad to worse.

CHAPTER 1

Ciò che Dio fa è ben fatto.

A few hours later as she sat across from her sister, Helen, in a booth at Veronica's Diner, Alberta couldn't shake her misgivings. Apprehension clung to her stronger than the scent of Emeraude had clung to her Aunt Nancy's skin. Her father's baby sister doused herself with so much of Coty's light citrus-smelling perfume that being in her presence was like being drenched in orange juice. Alberta swore the last time she visited Nancy's grave she practically choked on the scent of the perfume wafting up from the earth.

"Berta, what's wrong with you?" Helen asked.

It took Alberta a moment to realize her sister had questioned her and another moment for her to respond. "Nothing."

As Alberta said the word she shook her head back and forth so quickly while waving a hand wildly in the air that it looked like she'd had a sudden seizure. Helen dismissed the idea that her sister could be in the middle of a medical emergency, and knew it was much more likely that Alberta was attempting to convince Helen that she was fine. Unfortunately for Alberta, her attempt was unsuccessful.

"Don't lie to me," Helen snapped. "Something's wrong with you. You've been anxious since you picked me up."

Taking a sip of her coffee, Alberta rolled her eyes. "Why must you always be so dramatic? Nuns are supposed to be low-key and submissive . . . *sottomesso*."

"I am no longer a nun, so I don't have to act like I'm still in a convent," Helen replied. "Plus, I was never *that* kind of nun."

"Yes, Father Sal's filled us in on the stories of your glory days," Alberta said.

Helen glared at her sister, and Alberta wasn't sure if it was because she mentioned Father Sal, her sister's longtime nemesis recently turned frenemy, or if it was because she was waiting for Alberta's calm veneer to crack. Whatever the reason for Helen's stare, it unnerved her.

Alberta averted her eyes to the left so she wouldn't have to make contact with Helen and saw Father Sal sitting at the counter, a folded tweed jacket on the stool next to him. For a moment she thought she should escape the booth and join Sal, but her sister's voice startled her. When she placed her coffee cup in its saucer it clanged so loudly it could be heard throughout the diner.

"I know what it is," Helen said. "You're still jealous that Veronica is a better cook than you are and it's gotten you *ansiosa*."

"I'm not anxious," Alberta declared, wiping up the

spilled coffee from the table with a napkin. "And Veronica might bake a better pie than me, but if you ever say she's a better cook than me again, I'll never make another tray of lasagna, so help me God."

It was Helen's turn to pause and take a sip of her coffee. When she placed her coffee cup down on its saucer it was as if she was placing it on a layer of cotton. She reached for her pocketbook on the bench to her left, placed it in her lap, and fished for an item until she found it. After decades of seeing her sister without a stitch of makeup on her face, it was always jarring for Alberta to see Helen *gussy herself up* as she called it. It was even more jarring when the lipstick was several shades brighter than what she normally wore.

"*Santi numi!* What color is that?" Alberta gasped.

"Bubble gum pink," Helen replied, applying the lipstick to her top lip and then placing a napkin in her mouth to wipe off any excess color.

"Don't you think it's a little *youthful*?" Alberta asked, trying not to sound as judgmental as she felt.

"I do," Helen replied. "Which is precisely why I bought it from Tabby."

"Who?" Alberta asked.

"Tabby, the salesgirl at the drug store," Helen replied. "Her real name is Tabitha, but she said everyone calls her Tabby. I told her that's a cat's name and she laughed. She's kind of a *stolto*, but a whiz when it comes to cosmetics. She said the pink would complement my gray hair, and by golly she was right."

"It clashes with your glasses," Alberta said.

Helen took off her glasses and compared the color to the blot of lipstick on the napkin. "You're wrong," Helen said. "Blessed Mother blue and bubble gum pink are a perfect combination. And stop trying to change the subject, Berta. Why are you anxious?"

"I'm not," Alberta protested.

"You are so," Helen said. "Your foot keeps tapping the floor like you're Ann Miller's understudy."

Alberta ran her fingers through her own chin-length hair, which was dyed jet black, and tucked it behind her right ear. The mannerism was a holdover from her youth and a telltale sign that she was about to finagle the truth. She didn't like keeping secrets, especially from her sister. They were both too old to start telling lies to each other, or to anyone for that matter, but she also didn't want to hear Helen articulate in her own blunt way how stupid Alberta was to be nervous and apprehensive because of a bad dream.

"I think I had too much coffee," Alberta fibbed as she took another sip, this time making sure her hold on the coffee cup was secure. "It's very good here, but it's stronger than mine."

Snapping her pocketbook shut and placing it once again to her side, Helen eyed her sister suspiciously and replied, "You drink espresso like it's water. And you did that thing with your hair you always do before you tell a fib."

"What thing?" Alberta asked.

"The thing you've been doing since you learned how to lie," Helen answered. "You tucked it behind your ear. Fess up, Berta. What's going on with you?"

Family saves the day, as Alberta was always fond of saying, and this morning was no exception. Before she had a chance to answer, Jinx and Joyce walked into the diner and interrupted their conversation. Thanks to her granddaughter and sister-in-law's timely arrival, she had avoided surrendering to her sister's interrogation.

"Sorry we're late, Gram."

"Actually we're *fashionably* late," Joyce corrected.

Jinx and Joyce looked at each other and started giggling like schoolgirls. Alberta and Helen, not in on the inside joke, stared at them like disapproving schoolmarms, which only made the latecomers laugh harder, until Jinx finally managed to stifle her laughter long enough to speak.

"Scoot over, Gram, and I'll explain."

Dutifully, Alberta slid down the vinyl bench so Jinx could sit. When she did, Alberta noticed two things. First, the teal color of the bench clashed with Jinx's red outfit almost as horribly as Helen's makeup and second, she needed to go on a diet. Her five foot four inch frame was not built to house more than 150 pounds. And Alberta was definitely tipping the scale at a higher number than that.

On the other side of the bench Helen wasn't being as cooperative. Instead of sliding over to the end of the booth, she slid her arm through the handle of her pocketbook so it hung in the crook of her elbow, and stood up to let Joyce sit down.

"If I didn't know you loved me so much, Helen, I'd swear you were testing me," Joyce replied. Slightly taller than Alberta, but much thinner, Joyce had no problem sliding into her seat until she was leaning against the wall.

"I don't want to test myself," Helen replied as she sat down on the bench close to the aisle. "At my age I like to have as direct a route as possible to the ladies' room."

Looking at Alberta with complete sincerity, Jinx asked,

"Do you want to switch places with me, Gram? I have no problem holding it in."

Not sure if she wanted to slap her granddaughter or laugh in her face, Alberta replied, "Thank you, lovey, but I'm not as old as my sister. I still have authority over my own bladder."

Shrugging her shoulders, Helen said, "Until the day comes when you have to make a number one, but you're playing bingo and you're wedged in between two women who use walkers and the nearest bathroom is two flights down. Mark my words, Berta, that day is right around the corner."

"*Basta!*" Alberta cried. "I want to know why Jinx and Joyce were late."

"I thought it was high time I gave Jinx access to the Joyce Perkins Ferrara Museum of Fashion History," Joyce said, beaming with pride.

"Also known as Aunt Joyce's closet!" Jinx squealed. "Gram, have you ever visited?"

"On many occasions," Alberta replied. "Each time I'm stunned by the sheer size of the closet. *Madon!* That thing is huge."

"I think the appropriate word is *ostentatious*," Helen said. "Another would be *unnecessary*."

Ignoring Helen, Joyce grabbed the coffeepot sitting in the middle of the table and filled her cup. "Also too, another word would be *none of your business*."

"That's more than one word," Helen said.

"I have explained this to you many times, Helen," Joyce started. "I earned every item in that closet."

As one of the few African-American women working on Wall Street in the 1970s, Joyce had been a trailblazer. She had to work twice as hard as her male colleagues just to ensure that she wouldn't get fired. Her natural aptitude for understanding and expertly navigating the financial markets along with her strong work ethic ensured that she would climb high up on the professional ladder. At least as high as a woman of her ethnic background could climb back then.

She was never going to blend into the demographic landscape, so she took a different route and chose to stand out. Instead of adopting a masculine wardrobe like the other women working in her industry, her outfits all had a distinctly feminine touch. The only concession she made was to keep her hair cut very short, which she still did. Joyce loved that her no-frills hairstyle helped showcase the dangling earrings she often wore, like the gold hoops she sported now, which were her favorite.

"I worked my butt off for years," Joyce continued. "I helped pay our mortgage, I helped put our boys through college, and I built a huge nest egg, I deserve every dress, pantsuit, shoe, and accessory that is hanging in that closet of mine."

"I think calling it a closet really is a disservice, Aunt Joyce. It's more like a guest house, and I'm so happy to be your guest," Jinx declared.

"Any time, sweetie," Joyce said. "I can fit into most of the things from my heyday when I walked the runway on Wall Street, but even I have to admit that not all my clothes are age appropriate for a woman of my age."

"Which works for me because that means I get to wear them!" Jinx shouted. "Like this Joyce Ferrara original."

"It's actually a Pucci, but who's keeping score?" Joyce corrected.

Jinx opened up her red leather jacket to reveal a long-sleeved silk blouse in the fashion icon's signature brightly colored, psychedelic design, paired with leather pants in the identical shade of her jacket. With her long black hair falling in waves just below her shoulders, her shimmering green eyes, and the chiseled bone structure of her face, Alberta thought that her granddaughter could be a supermodel. In Joyce's hand-me-down, she certainly looked the part.

"And check out these shoes," Jinx squealed.

She did a high kick to show off a t-strap black platform shoe that added at least three inches to her 5'8" height. While Jinx's kick was an impressive display of physical dexterity, the heel of her shoe came dangerously close to sending an elderly man directly to the emergency room.

"Careful, lovey," Alberta said. "Your outfit is beautiful, but you don't want some innocent man to become a fashion victim."

Jinx wasn't sure if her grandmother was trying to make a joke, but she found the play on words hysterical and once again let out a high-pitched squeal. This time the sound was overshadowed by a loud crash coming from the kitchen. It sounded like every piece of cutlery within a ten-mile radius of the diner had fallen onto a metal floor.

"*Caro signore!*" Alberta declared. "What was that?"

"Just a typical morning at the diner," Joyce answered.

Helen looked over to the front counter and the door on the left that led into the kitchen. She looked as anxious as she claimed Alberta had only moments ago.

"What's wrong, Helen?" Alberta asked.

"Probably nothing, but the diner is much busier than usual this morning," Helen said. "Looks like they might be short staffed."

Craning her neck to get a better view of the activity all

throughout the diner, Joyce agreed. "You're right, Teri Jo is running around like a headless chicken."

"She works very hard, that one does," Helen commented.

"I don't know how she does it," Jinx remarked. "I'm at least ten years younger than she is and I'd have a heart attack if I had to run around the way she does."

"Especially in those shoes you're wearing," Joyce added.

"Who's Teri Jo?" Alberta asked.

"That would be me."

All four women turned to the waitress standing at the head of the table, three with a look of recognition, one with a blank stare. Alberta was the only one of the group who didn't know who Teri Jo was.

"I'm so sorry, honey," Alberta said. "I don't think we've ever met before."

"Berta!" Helen yelled. "Teri Jo brought us our coffee when we sat down. You were the one who ordered eggs Benedict for all four of us."

Embarrassed, Alberta's face started to turn red. Before it looked like her flesh was on fire, she remembered that being honest is usually the best recourse when you metaphorically shove your foot into your mouth. "I'm sorry, dear, I didn't sleep well last night and I'm still a little foggy."

Clutching her small order pad and pen, Teri Jo laughed, but it was more like an intake of breath with no energy or truth behind it. Alberta looked at the waitress's face and it was apparent to her that she wasn't in the mood to laugh; in fact, Teri Jo looked just as tired as Alberta felt.

She had lines around the corners of her mouth and several on her forehead. The skin underneath her eyes was taut, but darkened, and her eyes themselves, while not bloodshot, had small red veins etched into what had once been a pure white surface. Her hair looked just as damaged.

A short pixie haircut like the one Mia Farrow and Twiggy made famous back in the '60s only worked if it accentuated petite facial features and if the hair was shiny and healthy looking. All Teri Jo's cropped cut did was highlight the weariness in her face and the brittle quality of her hair. Instead of a woman in her late thirties, she looked like a teenage boy after a night of carousing.

Teri Jo must have felt she was being studied because she started to click the end of her pen, which only drew Alberta's attention to the awful state of her fingernails and cuticles. The waitress was definitely in need of a makeover, but before she could make an appointment with an aesthetician, she needed to make it through the morning rush.

"Are you alright?" Helen asked. "You seem a bit worried."

Teri Jo scrunched up her forehead, creating even more lines, and swallowed hard before answering. "I'm fine. One of the waitresses called out sick, so I'm on my own and we've been having plumbing issues with the bathrooms," she explained. "It hasn't been a great morning."

Helen grabbed the woman's hand, and even though she flinched, Teri Jo didn't pull away. "Remember what I told you to do when things get hectic," Helen said. "Take a deep breath, let it out, and everything will feel a lot better."

Smiling her first genuine smile, Teri Jo looked directly

into Helen's eyes. "Thank you, Helen, you always know the right thing to say."

Teri Jo followed Helen's orders and took such a deep breath it was as if she was trying to inflate her skinny limbs. She exhaled and although she didn't look any less thin than a moment ago, she smiled triumphantly. Her energy renewed, she went into waitress mode, grabbed the coffeepot, and filled up everyone's cup before placing it back down in the middle of the table. "I'll go check on your eggs and make sure Luis hasn't burned them to a crisp."

After she left, Helen noticed all three women staring at her. Instead of asking them why they were staring, she folded her hands in her lap, and stared back.

"Since when has anyone said to you that you always know the right thing to say?" Alberta asked. "Seriously, Helen, who are you?"

"I'm just a girl, sitting in a booth at a diner, giving another girl a little advice," Helen remarked.

"You never cease to amaze me, Aunt Helen," Jinx said, pouring some milk into her coffee. "Though with your history of public service as a nun, a teacher, and a counselor, I shouldn't be surprised to see you reach out to help a stranger."

Helen grabbed the small milk pitcher from Jinx and replied, "Teri Jo Linbruck is hardly a stranger; she's the hardest working waitress here. We've gotten to talk quite a bit when I come in during the week and it isn't so busy."

"It looks like she could use someone to talk to," Alberta said. "And you, Helen, look like you have more to say."

Once again three heads turned to face Helen, but this

time instead of remaining silent, she replied, "I think she's lying."

"About what?" Joyce asked. "Look around, Helen, this joint is jumping. I think it's more crowded than I've ever seen it."

Helen didn't follow Joyce's instruction, but nodded in agreement. "You're right, it's very busy, but . . ." Helen paused and seemed to finish her sentence silently. After a few seconds she decided to share it with the rest of the group. "Teri Jo hasn't had the easiest life. She's confided some things to me, so I've gotten to know her fairly well and I get the feeling that there's more to her than being frazzled by a busy breakfast rush."

The women wanted to barrage Helen with questions about Teri Jo and her difficult background, but at that precise moment the waitress appeared at their table with four plates of eggs Benedict. She balanced three plates expertly on one arm and held one in the other, which she placed in front of Jinx. She doled out the rest of the plates until she placed the last one in front of Helen. Just as she did, Helen turned her head to the right and sneezed into her arm.

"*Salute*" Teri Jo said.

"Thank you, dear," Helen replied. "Before I forget, do you need a ride later to the animal hospital for our volunteer session?"

"No, I . . . can't go today," Teri Jo said. "I have some errands to run."

Pulling a tissue out of her pocketbook, Helen blew her nose. "That's too bad. The animals always seem to calm you down."

"I'll try to make it if I get done early."

"Teri Jo!"

The shout didn't emanate from their table, but from somewhere in the kitchen. By the harsh sound of his voice, Luis, the cook, clearly needed assistance ASAP.

"I better see what trouble I'm in now," Teri Jo declared before dashing off.

"Poor thing," Alberta said, cutting into her eggs. "She really is running ragged. Hopefully the rush will be over soon."

After they all took the last bite of their breakfasts and stopped talking for more than a few seconds, they realized the din in the diner had gotten louder. The morning rush was far from over and it sounded as if it was only getting busier.

When Teri Jo rushed over to their table they expected her to start taking their plates away, but instead she placed a box in the middle of the table next to the coffee-pot.

"What's that?" Helen asked.

"One of my errands," Teri Jo replied. "I'm supposed to deliver this, but I'm never going to get out of here on time. Could you please do me a favor and deliver it? If I don't I'm going to get into trouble, and I've had enough of that already with this crazy morning."

Helen reached out and grabbed Teri Jo's hand. Again, the waitress was instantly resistant to the touch, but forced herself to allow the connection to continue. "*Ciò che Dio fa è ben fatto*," Helen said.

"Each day brings its own bread?" Joyce translated.

Not looking at her sister-in-law, but continuing to hold her connection to Teri Jo, Helen elaborated. "It literally means 'What God does is well done.' Don't worry so much about the future."

Teri Jo smiled, although it looked like she was about to cry, and said, "I'll try to remember that."

The women sat in silence for a while, each wondering what could have Teri Jo so upset, but also grateful that Helen appeared to be a source of comfort for the woman. A beep went off that interrupted their thoughts.

"I'm sorry, I have to leave for an appointment. I have to interview someone for an article," Jinx said, checking her phone. "I swear I don't think I'd remember anything if I didn't set an alarm to remind me."

"Do you see Teri Jo, so you can ask for the check?" Alberta asked.

Helen looked up and saw Teri Jo walking toward their table. She waved her hand, but before she could scribble in the air, which everyone understood was the universal, unspoken way to ask for a check, she noticed a look of utter fear consume the waitress's face. When Teri Jo fell to the floor inches from their table, that same look transferred to the faces of each of the four women.

They weren't horrified because Teri Jo had fallen, they were horrified because a butcher knife was jutting out of her back. Teri Jo wouldn't have to worry about her future any longer—she no longer had one.

CHAPTER 2

Felici sono quelli che sono chiamati alla sua cena.

The first one to reach Teri Jo was Helen, but when she got to the woman's side there was nothing for her to do. Teri Jo's body was unmoving and lifeless, the butcher knife sticking straight up from the center of her back. The only movement was coming from the blood that still seeped out of her wound, staining her white shirt a deep red and spilling down the sides of her body. Instinctively, Helen grabbed Teri Jo's wrist to feel for a pulse. Even though she didn't find one, she didn't let go.

Alberta knelt next to her sister. She knew she couldn't do anything to help, she just wanted to be near Helen so she would know she wasn't alone. Alberta knew it was exactly what Helen was doing for Teri Jo. The woman's soul might be lingering within her body for a few moments—who really knew what happened at the time of death—and Helen wanted to make sure that Teri Jo knew she would not leave this world without a witness. More personally, Helen wanted Teri Jo to know that she left someone behind.

Jinx and Joyce knelt on the opposite side of Teri Jo's body, so it was as if the four women were creating a human blockade to separate death from life. All around them people were screaming, shocked by the sight. They overheard several people calling the police and an ambulance, not that the latter would do any good, but the fact was that all around them was activity and action. They wanted to make sure none of it disrupted the unmoving body lying in front of them. Teri Jo wasn't just a person who should be respected; her corpse was also a crime scene that couldn't be contaminated.

Jinx looked up and saw Alberta looking around the diner, her expression calm but her eyes darting from left to right. Jinx was impressed at the sight. Her grandmother was turning into a real detective after all. She was kneeling before a dead body with a knife sticking out of it, but she wasn't freaking out or screaming, she was searching for a murderer.

Suddenly Jinx realized that the person who killed Teri Jo was probably inside the diner right now. In the past when they found a corpse, the murder had taken place hours before, but this time they saw Teri Jo stumble and fall to her death. Her wounds were fresh, her blood still alive with life as it rushed out of her body. Which meant her killer was most likely a few feet away.

"Nobody move!"

Jinx's voice cut through the chatter and immediately the diner became silent. No one spoke, but everyone turned to face Jinx. Now that she had a captive audience, she needed to exert her authority.

"Where's Veronica?"

A timid voice was heard from somewhere near the front of the diner. "I'm here."

"I need you to lock the front door and don't unlock it until the police arrive," Jinx ordered.

"Smart thinking, lovey," Alberta said.

She was beaming with pride that her granddaughter had taken such wise and decisive action, but thought it best to internalize her emotions so Jinx could maintain her power among the diner patrons.

"I've already called the police," Veronica announced from her position at the front door. "And someone said an ambulance is on the way."

"We won't be needing an ambulance," Jinx replied.

When Veronica heard the news she gasped and burst into tears. She stood alone against the glass door, one hand clutching her stomach, the other covering her mouth. She was the owner of Veronica's Diner and Teri Jo's boss, and at the moment she was in shock.

From within the crowd, Father Sal emerged and walked over to Veronica. When he reached her he put his arms around her, and the woman latched on to him as if his strength was the only thing keeping her vertical.

Alberta looked to where he had come from and saw that his thick, black-framed eyeglasses were on the counter and the red-and-black plaid jacket he'd bought for a recent trip to a ski lodge was draped over a stool. It clashed horribly with the tweed jacket the man who sat on the next stool was holding. Alberta vaguely recognized the man, but she knew she had seen him in town before because she remembered the black tinted glasses he was wearing; they reminded her of the glasses that are worn after a cataract operation. She was glad Father Sal was able to comfort Veronica. After a moment she realized he could also comfort Teri Jo.

"Helen," Alberta whispered. "Father Sal is here. Should we ask him to administer last rites?"

Without answering her sister, Helen turned around and saw Sal with his arms around Veronica but looking in her direction. Alberta watched as Helen and Sal locked eyes, and she noticed Sal close his eyes and nod his head very slightly. It was clear that they were silently communicating with each other. Helen turned back around and without letting go of Teri Jo's hand, she took out the rosary beads she always kept in her pocket. Instead of starting to pray, she made a bizarre request.

"I need some olive oil," Helen said.

She didn't shout, but her voice was filled with such purpose that three people ran into the kitchen. They didn't need to, because Luis came out of the kitchen with a bottle of olive oil and handed it to Helen. Before leaving he genuflected and made the sign of the cross, tears falling from his eyes at the sight of Teri Jo lying motionless on the floor.

Helen pointed the bottle at Alberta, and she intuitively knew that Helen was asking her to unscrew the top, which she did. Holding her index finger at the top of the bottle, Helen quickly said a Hail Mary, then turned the bottle upside down so some oil spilled out. She placed the bottle to the side and got to work.

Teri Jo's head was turned to the left so it was facing Helen, which meant Helen didn't need to move Teri Jo's body in order to make the sign of the cross on her forehead with the now-blessed olive oil. Up until that point, Alberta wasn't sure what Helen was doing, but now, mesmerized, she watched her sister perform last rites on her friend. It was one of the most humbling moments Alberta had ever experienced. The rest of the patrons in the diner must have felt the same way because no one spoke, they were all watching Helen.

"'Through this holy anointing may the Lord in his love and mercy help you with the grace of the Holy Spirit'," Helen said. "'May the Lord who frees you from sin save you and raise you up.'"

Alberta remembered that at this point in the ceremony the person receiving the anointment had the opportunity to confess any sins or recite the act of contrition. Teri Jo wouldn't have that chance. She would have to let Helen do all her talking for her.

Slowly and quietly, Helen began to speak the Lord's Prayer. Although she started the prayer alone, by the time she had finished, everyone in the diner was speaking and praying along with her. It was the first time in decades that Alberta had seen her sister cry, and the sight of her older sister, someone Alberta considered to be a bastion of strength and fortitude, weep openly, broke Alberta's heart. She fought the urge to reach out and hug Helen, because she knew her sister still had work to do.

Clearing her throat, Helen continued. "'This is the Lamb of God who takes away the sins of the world. Happy are those who are called to His supper.'"

"*Felici sono quelli che sono chiamati alla sua cena,*" Alberta repeated in Italian.

And happy are those when the police finally arrive.

At six foot four inches tall and built like a recently re-tired halfback, Vinny D'Angelo usually created a certain buzz when he walked into a room. At least until everyone got over the shock of his physical appearance and realized underneath his chief-of-police exterior, he was nothing more than their old pal Vinny.

"Vinny! Thank God!" Alberta cried. "Get over here."

"Where else do you think I'd go, Alfie?" he replied.

Alberta heard the high-pitched sound of his voice and was reminded that the rest of the town might consider him a gruff, professional cop, but to Alberta he would forever be the boy she babysat more than half a century ago when they both lived in Hoboken, New Jersey.

"What happened?" Vinny asked.

Alberta gestured to Teri Jo's body, the knife standing at attention in the center of her back, surrounded by blood, and replied, "I think it's rather obvious."

One by one the women kneeling around Teri Jo rose. Vinny extended his hand to Helen and she gratefully took it. When Vinny felt the olive oil on Helen's fingers and saw the open bottle on the floor, he knew immediately what she had done.

"Thank you," he whispered.

Helen nodded, and along with Joyce retreated back to the booth they were sitting in when all the pandemonium let loose.

Tambra Mitchell, Vinny's lead detective, started to put black tape around Teri Jo's body. This would reinforce the fact that no one should come close to the corpse and also preserve the outline of the body when it was finally taken to the morgue. Jinx stepped out of the way and walked away from the booths to join Vinny and Alberta.

"Tell me what happened," Vinny ordered.

"We really don't know, Vin," Alberta said. "One minute Teri Jo was serving us eggs Benedict, and the next she was falling to the floor with a knife in her back."

Breathing deeply through his nose, Vinny surveyed the room and noticed where Helen and Joyce were sitting. "Were you in that booth?"

"Yes," Jinx replied. "But we didn't see anything."

"Nothing?" Vinny questioned. "The dead body is a few feet away from where you were eating."

"I know," Alberta agreed. "But the diner was extremely busy, so Teri Jo was doing a lot of running around, and we were so engrossed in our own conversation we didn't notice much."

"Someone must have seen something," Vinny said.

"Well, we did see Teri Jo moments before she died," Jinx said.

"What did you see?" Vinny demanded.

"We were getting ready to leave and Aunt Helen was about to ask her for the check, when Teri Jo started walking toward our table and suddenly fell to the floor," Jinx explained. "By the time we got to her side she was dead."

Eyeing the front door, Vinny suddenly grew pale. "No one ran out of the diner? Or left just as you saw Teri Jo fall?"

Alberta and Jinx looked at each other and color drained from their faces as well. Whoever killed Teri Jo had to have done so in the diner. She hadn't left, so that meant the murder, literally, had to be an inside job. But if it was an inside job, that also meant the murderer could have escaped during the commotion created when they found Teri Jo's dead body, simply by leaving through the front door. No one would have noticed anyone leaving because everyone was looking at the dead body and away from the door.

"You really don't want us to answer that question, do

you, Vin?" Alberta asked. "Because the answer is, we have no idea."

Shrugging his shoulders, Vinny sighed. "You're right, I didn't want you to answer that question."

"Chief? What do you want me to do with the customers?"

Instead of turning to face Tambra, who had asked the question, Vinny turned to look around the room at the faces of the customers. He recognized every single one of them. They were all townies, longtime residents of Tranquility, people who had never seen the inside of a jail cell, let alone a courtroom. How could one of these people be a cold-blooded killer brazen enough to commit murder in a crowded diner during the day? Only one way to find out.

"Line them up for questioning and call in for reinforcements," he instructed.

"Will do," Tambra said.

"Jinx," Vinny said. "Do you think you and Joyce could help Tambra corral everyone so they can be questioned until some other officers get here?"

"We can," Jinx replied. "But please note that at some point I will call in a favor."

Shaking his head, he looked at Alberta and said, "I see the apple hasn't fallen very far with this one."

"I was nothing like that when I was her age, and you know it," Alberta replied.

Before they could continue their reminiscing, they were reminded of what they were doing at the diner in the first place. By the diner's owner.

"Vinny, whatever you need, please know that you have my full cooperation."

Veronica had stopped crying, but she looked like she could start again at any moment. Alberta didn't know the woman very well, since she didn't frequent the diner nearly as much as Helen and Jinx did. Since Joyce had lived in Tranquility for many years, she had known Veronica the longest even though she normally ate at fancier restaurants when she did eat out. This really was the first time Alberta had been in Veronica's presence when she wasn't placing an order. She thought it best to make the most of it and observe the woman's every move.

Unfortunately, thus far the only thing she'd seen Veronica do was cry and try not to cry. Which made perfect sense when one of her employees had just been murdered in the establishment that she owned. Why then was Alberta's sixth sense tingling? Maybe it was because she had learned not to trust anyone. Even the dead.

"Thank you, Veronica," Vinny said. "For now, please don't move anything or clean up. We need to wait for forensics to get here and for the ambulance to take the body away."

"This is just terrible, Vinny," Veronica blurted. "Who would want to kill Teri Jo? Everybody loved her."

Everyone may have loved her, but someone killed her, and the aftermath of that had to be dealt with. Looking past Veronica, Vinny saw that the medical examiner and an ambulance had arrived and he knew that it was going to be difficult for Veronica and many of the others to watch them work on Teri Jo's body.

"I think you should go to the other side of the diner with Tambra and help her keep the folks in line so they can be questioned," Vinny suggested.

"Whatever you think is best," Veronica said. "You have to find out who did this, Vinny, and bring him to justice."

Long ago Vinny had learned not to offer false hope, just a mere nod of the head. It always reassured the person on the receiving end and made them feel as if the murder would be solved in record time. Alberta was not so gullible.

"You don't think you're going to find who did this, do you?" she asked.

"First I have to figure out why someone would want to kill Teri Jo," Vinny replied. "She hasn't lived in Tranquility her whole life, but ever since she moved here she's been a model citizen."

"Helen mentioned that Teri Jo had a difficult past," Alberta offered. "Maybe some of that difficulty followed her here."

Vinny raised his eyebrows at the news. "I didn't know that, but I'll look into it. Right now, I have to get to work."

As Vinny greeted the medical examiner, Alberta joined Helen, who was still sitting at the booth. The moment Alberta sat down across from her, Helen said, "We have to find out who did this horrible thing, Berta. It'll be our most important case."

Alberta didn't answer immediately, having been thrown off-kilter by the conviction in Helen's voice, but Helen wasn't taking silence as an answer. "Promise me."

Unlike Vinny, Alberta wasn't going to get away with simply nodding her head. "Yes, I promise," Alberta replied. "We will find out who killed Teri Jo."

An hour later, after they had been interviewed by the police and reinforcements had come to help out Tambra with interviewing the rest of the patrons, the four women gathered their things so they could finally leave. As they were walking to the door, Helen turned back toward the table.

"Where's she going?" Joyce asked.

"She must've forgotten something," Alberta said.

She had forgotten something very important indeed. It was the box that Teri Jo had asked her to deliver because she was going to be too busy the rest of the day. Technically, that was no longer the case, but Helen had made a promise and she planned on keeping it.

Her pocketbook hanging from one arm and the box tucked underneath the other, Helen didn't stop, but kept walking to the front door. "C'mon, ladies, let's get out of here before one of these cops gets a brain and stops us."

No one had to speak, but they all knew it was official. The Ferrara Family Detective Agency had found its next case.

CHAPTER 3

Attenti alle aringhe rosse.

Later on that evening, the Ferrara Family Detective Agency would officially face their first roadblock.

"It's closed," Alberta said.

"The front door is wrapped up in pretty yellow police tape," Jinx added. "With very clear instructions not to enter."

"Do you think Vinny had them put that up specifically for us?" Alberta asked.

"No, Gram, I think it's standard practice," Jinx replied. "It was wishful thinking on our part that we'd be able to scout out the diner for clues after hours."

"*Che peccato*," Alberta said.

"It is a sin," Jinx translated. "The diner looks so sad all closed up and dark, it's lost all its charm."

Under the tutelage of its namesake owner, Veronica Andrews, Veronica's Diner had been a staple in Tranquility for the past decade. It was centrally located, open for business almost twenty-four hours a day, and while it was known for its delicious breakfast offerings, the rest of the menu earned high praise from townies and visitors alike. But what made Veronica's Diner an attractive attraction was the building itself.

Built in 1955, the architecture was classic and a relic from another time period, so it easily stood out among a sea of more modern buildings. Rectangular in shape with rounded corners, the front door was made of glass, and a series of large windows flanked either side. Just below the windows to the foundation were rows of silver paneling, the original aluminum updated at some point during the diner's life to a more durable material. The main body of the building was painted bright white, and at one point there was neon piping all around the roof, but that too was lost to history, and now it was simply painted fire-engine red with a cotton-candy-blue stripe going through the center. The red, white, and blue décor screamed, in a not so subtle way, that this was an all-American establishment.

Standing proudly atop the one-story structure was the name of the diner in a vintage font that immediately transported the viewer to a past filled with soda jerks and waitresses on roller skates. VERONICA'S was written out in in blue script and DINER was printed in red, both in neon, and the *i*'s in both words were dotted with a starburst to create an undeniable visual appeal. The interior was just as charming.

All throughout the diner the floor was a black-and-white checkerboard that if looked at for too long could produce a dizzying effect. The color of the booths and the bar stools alternated between orange and teal, but were all made of the same vinyl. The tabletops were lined in aluminum and were the same color scheme as the seats, though some were a more neutral white or gray, once again the product of having been refurbished over the course of several decades.

A long bar led to the kitchen, a front dining area, and rows of booths all along the sides. The interior design was accented in chrome and bright colors along with black-and-white photos hanging on the walls that depicted life from the 1950s. The cumulative effect inside and out was upbeat, hopeful, and safe. In just one morning it was all ruined.

"Like you said, Gram, *che peccato*," Jinx repeated. "We should've known the place would be hermetically sealed, now that it's a crime scene. I mean, this isn't our first time at the rodeo."

"Since it isn't our first time, I have a backup plan," Alberta announced.

"You do?"

"Of course I do," Alberta replied. "What grandma-turned-amateur-detective doesn't have a backup plan?"

Jinx couldn't help but laugh. A year ago her grandmother didn't know a thing about crime solving, and now she was acting like Miss Marple's Sicilian cousin. "Would you like to share this backup plan with your partner?"

Taking a small flashlight out of her purse, Alberta shined the light in Jinx's eyes and said, "Follow me, lovey."

Alberta led Jinx around the left side of the diner and down the narrow path that brought them to the back. The diner was located on the corner of Main Avenue, so parking was in the front and on the right. There was another building on the left, and behind the diner was an alleyway that separated the diner from a building that faced the intersecting street, Lanza Lane.

"If we can't get inside the diner, maybe we'll find some clues back here," Alberta said.

"Good thinking, Gram. If nothing else it'll give us the lay of the land," Jinx replied. "I've never been back here."

"It doesn't look like anyone comes out here much," Alberta said, shining her light along the stretch of the alley. "It could use some tidying up."

"Remember, you're not here as a grandmother, but as a detective," Jinx said. "So let's detect."

Unfortunately, there wasn't much to detect. All they learned was that there was a door that appeared to be a back access to the kitchen and another door that they surmised went to the bathroom. Two failed attempts to open the doors helped them easily deduce that they were locked. To the right of what they believed was the bathroom door was a window.

"Do you think anybody could crawl through that window, Gram?"

"Oh, *Madon*, I don't think so," Alberta replied. "Well, a kid, yes, but an adult? Maybe a woman, not one as big as Aunt Patty, but like you possibly."

"What about a man?" Jinx asked.

"Someone like Sloan might be able to wrangle himself through, but definitely not a man as big as Vinny," Alberta declared.

"I wouldn't describe your boyfriend as a little guy."

"Sloan isn't little, but let's face it, he's not as big as Vinny," Alberta said.

"Agreed," Jinx replied. "And don't think I didn't notice you didn't freak out or deny that Sloan is your boy-friend."

"Lovey, I've learned in life that there are some things you just can't fight," Alberta said, smiling girlishly.

"Like the fact that we're not going to learn anything more out here," Jinx said. "I mean, I'd love to try and see if I could fit through that window, but if we contaminate this crime scene any more than we have, Vinny will seriously lose his mind."

"*Dio mio*, you're right," Alberta agreed. "Let's call it a night."

Just as Alberta was about to turn the corner, she lost her footing and fell. Luckily she was still on grass and not the pavement, so she didn't hurt herself. She did, however, find a clue.

"Look at this," Alberta said, flat on the ground but waving for Jinx to join her.

Kneeling next to her grandmother, Jinx was just as in-trigued with what she saw as Alberta was. It was a fig-urine of a Swiss girl on a swing. What it had to do, if anything, with Teri Jo's murder, they had no idea, but be-cause there was a chance it could provide them with some information in their investigation, it was a clue worth re-trieving.

Jinx took out a plastic Ziploc bag from her back pocket and used it like a glove to retrieve the figurine without getting her fingerprints on it. Holding the Swiss miss in her hand with the Ziploc bag as a barrier between the girl and her fingers, Jinx smoothed out the bag, zipped it shut, and shoved the potential piece of evidence in her pocket. They were now free to leave, but couldn't because they were standing face-to-face with the diner's owner.

"Veronica!" Alberta shouted. "Fancy meeting you here."

The diner owner looked even more worn-out than she had earlier in the day. She was still wearing the same outfit and she hadn't attempted to freshen up her makeup. She may have looked disheveled, but she was still a boss and used to being in charge.

"What are you doing here *behind* the diner?" she asked.

It was a very good question and Alberta had a very good answer, even if it was a total fabrication.

"We stopped by to see if you could use some company, but then we heard a noise and thought there might be looters in the back, so we came to investigate."

Veronica's demeanor didn't change a bit, and Alberta got the impression that she didn't believe a word of Alberta's story. But then Veronica's expression softened and she appeared touched by their apparent thoughtfulness.

"That's very nice of you," Veronica said. "I'd invite you in for a cup of coffee, but as you can see, we're momentarily closed for business."

"Why don't you come back with us and have something a bit stronger than coffee?" Jinx suggested.

Veronica wasn't the only one surprised by Jinx's invite, but then Alberta realized its brilliance. Lure one of the people who was closest to the murder victim to an unfamiliar location while she's still emotionally vulnerable and interrogate her to see what secrets she might spill. It sounded like the perfect way to spend an evening. Luckily, Veronica agreed.

"I would like that very much."

"Perfect!" Alberta said. "We'll take my car so you can relax on the ride home."

"I'll text Aunt Helen and Aunt Joyce to meet us there,"

Jinx added. "It'll be a regular girls' night, and I have a surprise for everyone too."

Alberta almost stopped in her tracks. They'd started the day with an unexpected homicide; she didn't think she could survive another bombshell. When they arrived at Alberta's house with Helen and Joyce already sitting around the kitchen table, it was revealed that Jinx's surprise was harmless, but no less shocking.

"It is high time that we introduce something new to our little gatherings," Jinx declared.

Alberta felt her chest tighten because she thought Jinx was going to suggest Veronica become part of their inner circle. How could she even think of something so severe like that, without seeking the approval of the rest of the family? *No,* Alberta thought, *Jinx wouldn't be so* sconsiderato.

Jinx wasn't thoughtless, she was being thoughtful. In a rather nontraditional way.

"Henceforth and heretofore," Jinx started, "I hereby banish flavored vodkas from our in-house menu."

"What are you talking about, Jinx?" Joyce asked. "We love our flavored vodkas."

"When paired with the appropriate Entenmann's dessert, of course," Helen added.

"I know, but we've run out of new flavors to try, so we need something new," Jinx explained.

"We could build our own bootleg dispensary like Grandpa Joe's brother did," Alberta suggested.

"His wife made him shut it down when two goats and a llama died from drinking that swill," Helen reminded her.

"He had a llama?" Jinx asked.

"Doesn't everyone?" Helen replied.

Closing her eyes, Jinx shook her head a few times before continuing. "My plan doesn't involve any illegal activity, just some creativity. I've created a new signature drink for us, and keeping with our detective personas, I'm calling it a Red Herring."

All the women including Veronica applauded Jinx's revelation, and the applause only grew louder when she pulled a pitcher filled with some kind of red liquid out from the refrigerator.

"Remember what they say," Helen said. *"Attenti alle aringhe rosse."*

"Whoever said *beware the red herring*?" Joyce asked.

"The same person who said beware of granddaughters pulling strange things out of your fridge," Alberta said. "When did you put that in there?"

"This morning on my way to meet you for breakfast," Jinx confessed. "You had already left and I put it toward the back. There's so much stuff jammed in there I knew you'd never see it."

"The key to a happy home is a filled refrigerator," Alberta claimed. "Wouldn't you agree, Veronica?"

"I don't know much about a happy home," Veronica confessed. "But as a restaurateur, which is the fancy way to say that I own a diner, I concur."

Before Alberta could question Veronica further about the unhappy state of her home life, Jinx started pouring glasses of Red Herring for everyone.

"What exactly is our new signature drink comprised of?" Joyce asked.

"Vodka, prosecco, cranberry juice, some orange juice, and a splash of tomato juice," Jinx proudly explained. "With a mint garnish to make it extra fancy."

"It sounds . . . complex," Helen admitted.

"And maybe a little too heavy on the juice," Alberta added.

"Also too, it's delicious," Joyce declared. "Try it, ladies. Trust me, you'll like it."

The rest of the women took sips of their Red Herrings and the vote was unanimous, they all loved Jinx's new concoction. Even Lola seemed intrigued. The cat bounded into the kitchen from whatever corner of the house she was investigating, jumped on the table, and circled the pitcher, purring softly.

"It looks like your drink's gotten the seal of approval from your cat as well," Veronica said.

At the sound of the woman's voice, Lola abandoned all thoughts of trying to sneak a taste of whatever was inside the pitcher, and instead wanted to sneak a few cuddles from the stranger at the table. As usual, Lola ignored manners and decorum and leapt from the table into Veronica's lap.

"Lola!" Alberta cried. "That is no way to treat company."

"On the contrary," Veronica said. "I'm what is commonly known as a cat lady. My little girl, Ziti, passed away six months ago. I've been meaning to go to the shelter to adopt another cat, but I've been so busy at the diner I haven't had the time."

"Teri Jo told me you had a cat," Helen said.

Just like Lola, Helen often ignored manners and decorum. While there was nothing wrong with Helen bringing up the recently deceased woman's name, it came without warning and shocked the rest of the them into silence. Since Veronica was their guest and the subject of Helen's comment, the group waited for her to speak first.

"I can't believe she's gone, and in such a tragic way," Veronica said. "It seems impossible to me, I can't figure out what happened. I only hope the police can find out who's responsible so this nightmare can be over."

"Do you have any children, Veronica?"

It sounded as if Alberta had adopted Helen's blunt way of talking, but she only made her comment because of the way Veronica was holding Lola. The cat was cradled in Veronica's arms and being rocked like a baby. It took a few seconds, but Veronica finally understood the reasoning behind the question.

"No, I unfortunately wasn't able to have children," Veronica confessed, bouncing Lola gently in her arms. "Which is why my first husband left me."

"*Maledire*," Alberta said. "I'm so sorry to hear that."

Smiling wistfully, Veronica replied, "It is what it is, I got over it a long time ago. But life has a funny way of working itself out."

"Because Teri Jo became like a daughter to you?" Helen asked.

She hedged a bit, but Veronica finally agreed. "Something like that."

"I got to know Teri a little bit this past year, and she was very grateful for the job and the opportunities you were going to give her," Helen offered.

"I'm glad to hear that," Veronica said. "It's all so bittersweet right now though."

"What opportunities?" Alberta asked, ignoring Veronica's attempt to change the subject.

"I was grooming Teri to become the new manager," Veronica reluctantly replied. "But now, well, I'll just continue to handle most of the day-to-day operations like I've been doing. I'm not sure how much longer I'll be able to do it, though. It's exhausting, running your own business."

For some it's also exhausting staying in one position

for too long. Without warning, Lola jumped out of Veronica's arms and ran over to the front door. An unusual action even for Lola, until the women realized the cat wasn't acting ill-tempered, she was merely curious.

"Did you hear that?" Jinx said.

"I did," Alberta replied. "There's a noise outside."

Just as Alberta was going to open the door leading to the backyard, Joyce shoved a broom in her hand.

"What's this for?" Alberta asked.

"In case there's an intruder," Joyce explained.

"So I can sweep him off the porch?"

"No!" Helen cried. "So you can bash him in the head with it!"

"Jinx, grab Lola so she doesn't run out," Alberta ordered. "The rest of you stay right behind me."

No one questioned Alberta, not even Veronica. They all followed her command, which was further testament of Alberta's growing role as leader. She was also a sixty-six-year-old woman who was fully aware of her limitations. When she yanked open the door, she swatted the air with the broom and screamed.

Once she screamed, they all screamed, including Lola, but, of course, no one knew why they were screaming since there was no one standing in front of them trying to break in.

Alberta flicked on the lights to the backyard and they still couldn't see anyone lurking in the bushes or even trying to get away by jumping in Memory Lake and swimming to the opposite side. Whoever or whatever made the noise was no longer there.

"Maybe it was an animal. There are lots of deer this time of year," Jinx suggested. "Our screaming must've scared it off."

"To be on the safe side, I'm going to stay the night," Helen declared. "You shouldn't be alone, Berta."

Closing the door and putting away the broom, Alberta scoffed at the idea. "Don't be silly, I'll be fine."

"Do I need to remind you of what happened in this town this morning?" Helen asked. "I'm staying."

Giving up, Alberta threw her hands in the air. "*Bene! Resta se vuoi.*"

"I think it's time I should go," Veronica said. "I've had far too much excitement for one day, but thank you so much for inviting me. It was good to spend time with people who knew Teri Jo."

"You're welcome to come here anytime," Alberta said, accenting her words with a hug.

"Come with me, Veronica," Joyce said. "I'll drive you and Jinx home."

The women exchanged good-nights, but all goodwill evaporated when Alberta and Helen were left alone in the house.

"*Attenti alle aringhe rosse,*" Helen muttered.

"Are you still talking about Jinx's drink?" Alberta asked. "I thought it was tasty."

"Not *that* red herring, I'm talking about Veronica," Helen clarified. "There's something not right about her."

Alberta couldn't disagree, as she had also gotten strange vibes when she was in Veronica's presence earlier in the day. However, after spending a few hours with her and getting to know her a little better, she had dismissed her earlier misgivings.

"What exactly are you talking about, Helen?"

"She lied to us," Helen said. "Teri Jo told me Veronica was never married."

CHAPTER 4

Una cena con qualsiasi altro nome.

So now there were two mysteries afoot: Who killed Teri Jo Linbruck? And why was Veronica Andrews a liar? Could the answers to those questions possibly be linked? Could a murder and a lie be connected? Or could Alberta and Jinx be imagining things in order to speed up their investigation? Grandmother and granddaughter needed a reality check, which was why they were waiting, somewhat patiently, in Vinny's office to discuss their case.

"I let Alberta and Jinx wait inside, Chief," Tambra said as Vinny was about to enter his office. "I didn't think you'd mind."

"Why would he mind, Tambra?" Alberta shouted. "We've always been like family and now we're like colleagues!"

"Come on in, partner!" Jinx yelled.

"If you suddenly find yourself filling in for the meter maids, Tambra," Vinny said, "don't be surprised."

"Methinks the chief of police protests too much," Alberta said. "That's from the Shakespeare."

"I know it's from *the* Shakespeare!" Vinny shouted, slamming the door behind him as he entered his office. "I took creative writing classes in night school. I'm not just a man in blue, you know."

"You, um, don't wear a uniform, Mr. D'Angelo," Jinx commented. "And technically your sports jacket is more of a gray-blue."

Vinny glared at Jinx before slowly lowering his hulking frame into his well-worn chair. He folded his hands in front of him, exhaled slowly, and, much calmer, changed the subject.

"To what do I owe the honor of this visit from you two soft-spoken ladies?"

"Ah, *Madon*! You know why we're here, and we're not soft-spoken," Alberta cried. "What's wrong with you? I thought you got past being irritated by our interference."

"Gram meant to say 'by our help,'" Jinx corrected.

"That too," Alberta said. "So why the *brutta faccia*?"

"I don't have an ugly face," Vinny protested.

"Jinx, give the man a mirror," Alberta replied.

Exasperated, Vinny stretched his neck so his head tilted from side to side and then leaned over his desk. Automatically, Alberta and Jinx leaned forward in their chairs, hoping to be on the receiving end of an early breakthrough in their case, since they were certain Vinny was going to share some confidential news. They were disappointed to learn his news was old.

"A woman's been murdered," Vinny announced.

"Another one?" both women shrieked.

"No! Teri Jo."

"We already know that," Alberta said. "That's why we're here, to discuss the case."

"That's the problem," Vinny replied. "There is no case. We've come up empty."

Alberta looked at the chief of police sitting across from her and marveled that a man so physically imposing could also be so emotionally vulnerable. Vinny truly had not changed much from the quiet, introspective boy she used to babysit. She needed to give him a pep talk like in the old days.

"Vin, it's only been twenty-four hours," Alberta said. "When have we ever solved a case that quickly? These things take time."

Rubbing his face with his hands, Vinny sighed heavily. "I know all that, it's just that I hate the start of a murder investigation. It never gets easier."

"Which is what makes you a terrific chief of police," Jinx said. "Your empathy."

"Empathy doesn't solve cases," Vinny replied. "Clues do, and we don't have any. There were no fingerprints on the murder weapon, and the butcher knife was a very common brand."

"It wasn't from the diner?" Alberta asked.

"No, we checked the inventory and nothing was missing," Vinny explained. "Plus, the knife wasn't commercial grade, just a plain old butcher knife."

"Why buy an expensive model when the cheap version does the trick?" Jinx asked rhetorically.

"So much for empathy," Vinny commented.

"Sorry about that," Jinx said. "I speak before I think . . . a lot."

"You're a Ferrara," Vinny said. "I expect nothing less."

"Stop flattering us, Vinny," Alberta said. "We need to focus."

Duly admonished, Vinny went on to explain that they had interviewed everyone in the diner and no one saw Teri Jo get stabbed or even saw her walking around with a knife stuck in her back until she collapsed on the floor. Since there were no security cameras in or around the diner, they couldn't rely on videotape to fill in the blanks.

More than half of the diners didn't know the victim's name, and the other half only knew her on a superficial level, so even though Teri Jo had been living in town for quite some time, she hadn't made any friends. Most frustrating was that no one who was interviewed said anything that could be held against them. No one seemed to have a motive to commit murder, even though one of them must have.

"The killer had to be in the diner waiting for Teri, and at some point stabbed her when no one was looking," Vinny deduced.

"Or the person was lurking outside," Alberta said.

"No, she was murdered inside the diner," Vinny corrected. "At no point did she leave."

"That's true, but maybe the murderer did," Jinx mused. "There's a window in the back."

"How do you know that?" Vinny asked. "There's no reason to go back there. The parking lot is in the front and on the side. There's only an alleyway in the back."

"You know how we know," Jinx said. "We were snooping around the back, but before you have a seizure and blood drips out of your eyes like a bad guy from a James Bond movie, we didn't disrupt anything, we just looked around."

Instead of having a seizure, Vinny laughed.

"I know I'm not going to stop you and your cohorts-in-crime from doing what you're going to do," Vinny confessed. "But could we please work together and share clues and information?"

"Of course," Alberta and Jinx answered simultaneously.

Of course, they were also lying simultaneously because they weren't going to tell Vinny that Veronica lied to them about being married, and Jinx wasn't going to show Vinny the Swiss girl on a swing figurine that was currently in her purse. They did, however, want information from Vinny.

"How well do you know Veronica?" Alberta asked. "Is there a man in her life?"

Vinny thought a moment before responding. "I don't know her as well as some of the other businesspeople in town, and as far as I know she's single. Then again, I'm not as fascinated by someone's private life as some people are."

Ignoring Vinny's jab, Alberta continued her line of questioning. "When did Veronica move to Tranquility?"

"She's relatively new, past ten years maybe," Vinny replied. "I believe she came here when she bought the diner."

"It wasn't always Veronica's Diner?" Jinx asked.

"No, before that it was called Godfather's Diner," Vinny explained. "It was owned by a company. Can't remember the name, but I never had any trouble with them."

They were interrupted by a knock on the door and turned around to see Tambra standing in the doorway.

"Sorry, Chief, but you have to leave to get to that town council meeting," she announced.

"Thanks," Vinny replied. Walking to the door, he added without turning around, "You ladies know your way out."

"But this is becoming like a second home to us," Alberta joked.

Vinny's voice echoed through the police station as walked outside. "Get out of my office!"

"Let's go, lovey," Alberta said.

"I think we should stay to, you know, show Vinny who's boss," Jinx asserted.

"Trust me, down deep, he knows," Alberta said. "But even though Vinny doesn't know anything about the company that used to own the diner, I know someone who does."

"Who?"

"Sloan," Alberta replied.

"Of course! Your man comes to the rescue," Jinx said with a beaming smile. "You go talk to Sloan. I have to get to work before Wyck lets Calhoun take the lead on this one."

"Your editor would never give such a juicy story to your rival," Alberta protested. "You've paid your dues."

"Oh, Gram, you know nothing about the newspaper business," Jinx said. "Go pump your boyfriend for information and I'll talk to you later."

Thirty minutes later, Alberta was at the Tranquility Public Library waiting for Sloan McLelland, the head librarian and her *boyfriend*. She still found the word difficult to say. Not because it didn't define her relationship with Sloan, but because he was the first real boyfriend she ever had in her life.

As the youngest daughter in a strict Italian family, growing up in northern New Jersey at a time when women were not only known as the fairer sex but the inferior sex by many as well, Alberta hadn't been able to make a lot of her own choices. She was no different than the rest of the girls on her block, her state, or in the country. They were all, to some degree, controlled by the men in their lives. And Frank Ferrara was controlling.

He was also loving, a good provider, funny, and a wonderful father, but he was a control freak just the same. When it came time for Alberta to date, Frank had the final say on who was worthy of his daughter's hand, and very few passed muster. It didn't help that her older sister, Helen, had very little interest in boys when she was a teenager, having already decided to enter a convent when she graduated high school. As a result, Frank didn't have any experience navigating the tumultuous waters of a daughter's romantic life when Alberta came of age, so instead of letting Alberta go out in the world and sail uncharted territory on her own, he kept her safely docked at harbor. He thought he was protecting her, but he was only stunting her growth.

When Sammy Scaglione came into Alberta's life, he was the first man her father truly approved of, primarily because he came from around the corner and technically had been part of Alberta's life since her birth. He was familiar and Italian, so what could go wrong? Alberta went from first date to wedding night in record time. Of course, she and Sammy dated, but they each knew where the relationship was leading, and that outside forces were pushing them toward the altar whether they wanted to land there or not. Their families, friends, even society at large expected them to get married, so how could they disappoint everyone? Alberta may not have disappointed those around her, but she surely disappointed herself.

Now as a single woman in her mid-sixties, she was experiencing what it was like to be a girlfriend for the first time. It was frightening, exhilarating, and a new experience every time she was in Sloan's company. She loved every minute of it.

By the huge grin on Sloan's face it was evident that he did too.

"What a wonderful surprise to see you in the middle of the day," Sloan said.

He kissed Alberta on the lips, which was her wonderful surprise in the middle of the day, and then ushered her into his office.

"Do you want some coffee, tea, or perhaps me?" Sloan asked, his grin growing wider.

"Don't get salty on me, Mr. McLelland. I'm here on official business," Alberta said, trying hard not to smile in response.

"Well then, Miss Ferrara, please have a seat and tell me why you're here."

Sloan sat in the chair behind his desk, and for the second time that day Alberta sat across from an important man in her life. This man, however, was different. More than that, he made her feel different. He hadn't spoken out of turn when he addressed her by her maiden name; he looked at her as Miss Ferrara, not Mrs. Scaglione. He wasn't interested in the woman who was married for decades to a man who she was never truly in love with, or the woman whose identity was defined by being some man's wife. Sloan wanted to get to know the woman she was when she was single, then and now.

Staring at Sloan and silently remarking at how un-Italian

he looked, his WASP-y features, sandy-colored hair, and trim physique, Alberta felt her heart flutter. Part of it had to do with how attractive she found Sloan and how attractive such a feeling was for her to have. But it was also hearing her maiden name spoken aloud after so many years of being Mrs. Scaglione. Who was this Miss Ferrara? Did Alberta even remember?

Shaking her head to free herself from such ruminations that might never be resolved, Alberta concentrated on the reason she had come to the library.

"What do you know about Godfather's Diner?"

"*Una cena con qualsiasi altro nome*," Sloan replied.

"Someone's been brushing up on his Italian," Alberta remarked. "A diner by any other name might be a totally different kind of diner. What was Godfather's Diner like before it became Veronica's Diner?"

"They used to douse everything in garlic, even the eggs Benedict," Sloan replied. "You know those Eye-talians."

"Watch it, buster," Alberta said good-naturedly. "Garlic is good for what ails you."

"But not necessarily before nine a.m.," Sloan said. "Now that Veronica's taken over, the diner and the food on the menu are so much better."

At the mention of another woman's excellent cooking, Alberta's expression immediately changed from playful to perturbed. Sloan knew what he had to do.

"Not nearly as good as your cooking, though," he said quickly. "No one's that much of a magician in the kitchen."

"Well saved, Sloan," Alberta said. "But do you like Veronica as much as you like her food?"

Sloan thought for a moment before replying. "I don't like or dislike her, actually. It's been hard to get to know her since she's come to town. She keeps to herself mainly."

"Does she have a boyfriend?"

"Not that I know of."

"Can she be trusted?"

"Do you think Veronica killed Teri Jo?"

Another facet of Sloan's personality that Alberta appreciated was that he was blunt and straightforward. Unlike in her relationship with Sammy, she didn't have to guess as to how he was feeling or what he was thinking. Sloan didn't lie to her or conceal things from her out of some misguided protection; he treated her like an equal.

"I haven't decided yet," Alberta replied. "I do get a strange *sensazione* . . . a weird vibe from her, but it might be because Helen doesn't trust her and Helen's got good instincts about people, so I need to do some digging."

Taking the cue perfectly, Sloan said, "Then let's dig."

Alberta watched as Sloan typed away at his computer, searching the Internet for clues to Godfather's Diner and both its origin and demise in Tranquility. Once again she thought of her husband, and wondered if she'd ever watched him with such pleasurable intent. Before she could answer, Sloan cheered.

"Found something! Godfather's Diner was owned by a company called Third Wheel, Inc.," Sloan announced. "There's no other information except that it's incorporated in Delaware."

"Let's go to Delaware," Alberta declared.

Laughing, Sloan replied, "The company isn't based there, it's only incorporated there for tax purposes."

"*Madon!* Sometimes I'm a *stunod*."

"How many times do I have to tell you, you are not a *stunod*?" Sloan chastised.

Alberta shrugged her shoulders. "Old habits."

"Let me see if I can find out where Third Wheel is located," Sloan said.

Just as he was resuming his Internet search, a loud *ping* reverberated through his office, signaling that one of them had received a text message. When Alberta looked at her cell phone and gasped, Sloan knew no one had reached out to him. Whoever had reached out to Alberta, however, hadn't shared news accompanied by a smiley-face emoji.

"What's wrong?" he asked.

"I got a text from my home security company," Alberta said. "Someone's broken into my house!"

CHAPTER 5

Fai attenzione a un estraneo con regali.

Only when they pulled up to 22 Memory Lake Road and saw a police car parked in front of Alberta's house, did Alberta start to panic. This wasn't a false alarm, someone had indeed tried to break into her home. Maybe they were still there.

Sensing Alberta's fear, Sloan went into full-on boyfriend mode. He didn't try to convince Alberta she was worrying for no reason, he didn't placate her or treat her like an overemotional woman. He grabbed her hand, looked her in the eye, and said, "Let's find out what's going on."

Together they walked around the side of the house, confident but cautious, not entirely sure what or who they were going to find. When they entered the backyard they were stunned by what they saw.

"Lola!"

Alberta's cry didn't startle her cat because Lola was too preoccupied taking in all the sights she had only seen through the barrier of the kitchen window. Plus, she was nestled in Tambra's arms, so she was safe and secure while feeling the soft wind against her fur and smelling the sweet scent of the hydrangeas and roses that were so fragrant it made her nose twitch. She was in heaven, while Alberta was in shock.

"What is Lola doing outside?" she asked.

"When I got here, I found her lounging near the lake," Tambra explained, running her fingers up and down Lola's coat.

"How did she get there?" Sloan followed up.

Instead of answering, Tambra pointed at Alberta's kitchen window, or what was left of it.

"Someone threw a rock into your kitchen and busted the whole window," Tambra said. "It gave Lola just enough room to come outside and investigate who the culprit was, but she must've gotten lazy and plopped down to take a nap. Don't worry, we checked her out and she's fine, no cuts or bruises anywhere on this gorgeous little girl."

Tambra lifted Lola into the air and the cat seemed to relish the opportunity to see even more of the outside landscape. She purred louder and not very happily when Alberta grabbed her and cradled her in her arms.

"*Dio mio!* Thank God you're alright."

"Did you find who did this?" Sloan asked.

"No, the only one here when we arrived was Lola," Tambra replied. "Once the security company knew we were here they were able to unlock the house remotely and let us in. We did a complete search, and it doesn't look like anyone got inside. All they did was throw a rock through your window, which was taken back to headquarters to check for fingerprints."

"*Dio onnipotente*." Alberta sighed. "I can't believe someone would do this."

"And got away with it," Sloan added. "I trust there will be a cop outside to watch the house for the next few days."

"No, that's not necessary," Alberta scoffed.

"On the contrary, I think it is," Tambra said. "I've already arranged to have a cop parked in front and do some walk-bys in the back around the lake. Do I think the vandal will be a repeat offender? Not really, but it is a necessary precaution."

"If you say so," Alberta said. "Thank you."

"It's what we do," Tambra replied. "Now that I know you have your very own security guard, I can leave you to get your house back in order."

"I guess I have to call to get that window fixed," Alberta said.

"The security company already did that for you. They said it's in your contract," Tambra conveyed.

"I had no idea I even had a contract with them," Alberta replied. "So much for paying attention to the details."

Tambra smiled. "In my line of work you learn the devil is always in the details."

A few hours later, Alberta's kitchen window was back to its original state and all but Lola seemed to be happy with the restoration. Once Helen and Joyce arrived, Alberta convinced Sloan he should go back to the library and catch up on the work he abandoned when they got the distress call. As the three women sat around Alberta's kitchen table, life returned to normal, except that Lola wouldn't stop pawing at the newly minted window.

"Now that Lola's gotten a taste of the outdoor life, she may not want to stay confined to one space any longer," Helen surmised as she won her third game of solitaire.

"Sounds like another lady I know," Joyce remarked.

If Helen understood that Joyce was comparing Lola's frustration at being trapped inside with Helen's recent departure from the convent, she played dumb. However, she was not yet ready to play deaf.

"Remember that sound we heard outside the other night?" Helen asked, shuffling her cards loudly. "It wasn't an animal, there was someone out there stalking the joint."

"I have a stalker?" Alberta cried.

"Join the club," Helen remarked, ironically turning over the ace of clubs.

"Wait a second," Joyce said. "Maybe the stalker's stalkee wasn't Alberta, but Veronica."

"What?" Alberta asked. "Do you really think that could be true?"

"Absolutely not," Helen declared.

Although Joyce protested that it could be a possibility, given that there was a murder at Veronica's Diner the same day they heard a noise in Alberta's backyard while Veronica was visiting, Helen adamantly rejected that scenario.

"For that to be true, the person who threw the rock had to follow Alberta, Jinx, and Veronica on the drive from the diner to Alberta's house, because there would be no other way of knowing Veronica would be here," Helen laid out. "Plus, we didn't hear a car pull up and there's no way the person could've seen them at the diner and walked over to Alberta's in that short amount of time."

"When she's right, she's right," Alberta said.

"Which is most of the time, thank you very much," Helen replied, winning her fourth straight game.

"So whoever was out there the other night and whoever threw that rock through my window was after me, and not Veronica," Alberta summed up.

"Which doesn't mean Veronica is completely innocent," Helen commented.

"You don't trust her?" Alberta asked.

"Not in the least," Helen answered.

"Also too, did you hear that?" Joyce asked.

The ladies stopped talking, and just as Alberta was going to tell Joyce she didn't hear anything, they all heard a sound that made them jump.

"He's back!" Alberta screamed. "Give me the broom!"

Joyce grabbed the broom and handed it to Alberta, who positioned herself in front of the door. Running to her left, Joyce picked up Lola in one arm, and then a frying pan that had been resting in the drainer next to the sink, in the other, while Helen stood on Alberta's right, raising a ladle defiantly. The women might not be dangerous, but they were armed. When the door burst open they were grateful to see a friendly face.

"*Ah mannaggia!!*" Alberta shrieked. "Vinny, I could kill you with my bare hands! You scared the bejesus out of us!"

Unable to hold in his laughter, it took Vinny a moment to control himself so he could speak. "I'm sorry, I didn't mean to startle you, but I'm glad to see that you're taking self-defense classes."

"Shut up, Vin, or I'll clobber you with this ladle," Helen declared.

"No need for that, I wanted to bring you this."

Vinny placed a sundial on Alberta's table. It got the women even angrier than when they thought there was a stalker trying, yet again, to break into the house.

"Watch it, Vin," Helen snapped. "We're old, but we're not *that* old."

Even Lola was miffed. She turned up her nose at the sundial and leapt from Joyce's arms, landing on the floor before scampering toward the fridge.

"It's not a gift," Vinny replied. "It's what was thrown through the window. It must've been on your property."

"It was!" Joyce exclaimed. "I bought it for you, Berta, when you first moved in here."

"That's right," Alberta confirmed. "But it doesn't make sense that someone would use the sundial, because it's nowhere near the window. I kept it by the lake, and it was hidden by the bushes. I almost forgot it was there."

"If the person came around the lake instead of from the front street, they could have easily passed by it," Vinny deduced. "It was probably just some kids making mischief."

"I'm sure you're right," Alberta said.

She stole glances at Helen and Joyce, and with her eyes told them that she didn't believe a word of what Vinny was saying. There was no way the incident was random; it was deliberate and it was meant to get Alberta's attention. The frustrating part was that she had no idea what she was supposed to pay attention to.

"Regardless, I'm keeping a patrol car outside for the night so you can rest easy," Vinny said.

"Thanks, Vin, I appreciate that," Alberta replied. "Do

you want something to eat? I have leftover veal cacciatore."

Vinny peered into Alberta's refrigerator, and although he was strongly enticed, he turned down the invitation. "I'd love to, but I'm trying to lose a few pounds. I'm on a new diet, no eating after seven p.m."

"That, Vincenzo Hugo D'Angelo, is cruel and unusual punishment," Alberta said.

"A midnight snack isn't quite the same before seven," Helen added.

"Also too, you look fine, Vinny," Joyce finished.

"Thanks, but as much as my stomach's begging for some veal cacciatore, I'm maintaining my willpower," Vinny declared.

He shut the fridge door and turned to leave, but his willpower proved to be more stable than his balance, and he teetered back and forth until he pressed his hand into the door jamb leading into the living room to prevent himself from falling over.

"You see what diets do!" Alberta cried. "They make you light-headed. Are you alright?"

"I'm fine," Vinny said, slightly embarrassed. "It's this whippersnapper's fault."

He turned his back to the ladies, bent down, and when he got back up to face them, they saw the reason for his near fall was none other than Lola. Vinny held the cat in his arms and Lola, belly up, stretched in all directions, looking like she was luxuriating in a hot bath.

"Miss Gina Lollobrigida!" Alberta shouted, using Lola's full name so the cat knew she was in trouble. "You have been causing much too much trouble lately. What am I going to do with you?"

Lola's smug purr was not the response Alberta was

hoping for, but knowing her cat the way she did, it was the response she expected.

"*Irrispettosa*, this one is," Alberta said. "No respect whatsoever."

When Alberta tried to take Lola from Vinny's arms, the cat, sensing she might get yelled at again, leapt into the air, landed on the side table to the left of the entrance to the living room, and expertly shifted direction to the right as she jumped to the floor and disappeared out of view. She escaped, but she left some ruins in her path.

When she jumped on the side table, she knocked into a box, causing it to teeter from side to side. Vinny proved he was in full control of his body and twisted around to catch the box before it fell to the ground. Gingerly he placed it back onto the table.

"Sorry, there was almost another casualty in Lola's wake," Vinny joked.

"Don't worry, that's mine," Helen said.

The women knew she was lying, but they also knew they needed to keep her secret. After Vinny left, Helen grabbed the box from the side table and shook it softly to make sure that whatever was inside of it wasn't broken. When she didn't hear the sound of shattered glass or any other telltale noise that would indicate an item was demolished into bits and pieces, she was relieved. She didn't know what was in the box, but it was important. It was also the final link to her friend.

"That was good thinking, Helen," Alberta said. "I forgot that box was there."

"I did too, until Vinny reminded us," Helen confessed, placing the box in the center of the kitchen table. "It must be important if Teri Jo gave it to us with explicit instructions to make a special delivery."

"It could also be dangerous," Joyce advised. "*Fai attenzione a un estraneo con regali.*"

"Teri Jo wasn't really a stranger, Joyce," Alberta said, translating the phrase. "And we're not entirely sure this box is a gift."

Whatever it was, it was mysterious. The women sat around the table in silence and stared at the box as if it was going to do a trick. They half expected something to jump out or, God forbid, for the box itself to explode. They hadn't heard any ticking sounds, so if there was a bomb inside that was set to blow up, it would have done so already.

Nothing about the box was interesting. It was an ordinary cardboard box about sixteen inches all around, blank except for a white label with a name and address handwritten on it. From what Helen knew of Teri Jo's handwriting from seeing her scribbles on her diner checks, the writing on the label was not hers; someone else had filled in the pertinent information. The writing was large, with each letter rounded, while Teri Jo's was more like chicken scratch. She could have overcompensated to make the address legible on the label, but it was more likely that someone else wrote it. But who? And who was it to be delivered to? And was it a coincidence that Teri Jo handed them the box moments before she was murdered?

"I don't know how, but this box has got to be linked to Teri Jo's murder," Helen stated.

"This is one instance where I hate to agree with you, Helen," Joyce confessed. "But I have no choice."

"Then, ladies," Alberta said, "there's only one thing for us to do."

"I'm afraid to ask what that is," Joyce said.

"Isn't it obvious?" Alberta asked. "We have to carry out Teri Jo's last wish and deliver this box."

CHAPTER 6

Il tempo può essere sia un amico che un nemico.

As had become the norm when the Ferrara ladies went on a road trip, either for fun or while investigating a case, Helen was the chauffeur. She wasn't the best driver in the group, but the rest of the ladies knew that it gave Helen a sense of purpose to be behind the wheel. Plus, she did have the biggest car.

Her beige Buick LaCrosse was roomy, got great gas mileage, and its traditional-looking exterior blended in with the rest of the cars on the road. When trying to go undercover, it was always good not to stand out. Although when the four Ferraras traveled in a pack, it wasn't always easy to blend.

Sitting next to Helen in the front seat, Alberta rested her arm on top of the package that lay between her and her sister, and wondered to herself where this trip would lead them. Would it be a clue to finding out who killed

Teri Jo and possibly why? Or would it be a dead end? For all they knew, Teri Jo could have been a Mary Kay saleswoman on the side and the box merely contained an assortment of cosmetics and beauty products.

In the back seat, Jinx and Joyce were discussing the different ways Jinx could approach her reporting on the murder for *The Upper Sussex Herald*. Since she was, in fact, given the plum assignment as lead reporter on the case, she was able—to a certain degree—to dictate the editorial. Her boss, Wyck Wycknowski, who was the editor-in-chief, of course had the final say, but Wyck was a firm believer in giving the reporters on his staff who had proved themselves free rein to control the narrative of their stories. That meant Jinx, for the first time in her career, could really take control of how she presented her work. Sometimes freedom creates uncertainty, and Jinx wasn't sure what style would be best.

"I've already done the first-person approach, so I don't want to repeat myself," Jinx said. "What about if I adopted a straightforward, hard-nosed journalistic style? That might get noticed."

Joyce smoothed down the brim of the brown fedora she held in her lap and scrunched up her face. "I think it might get noticed for the wrong reasons," Joyce said.

"What do you mean?" Jinx asked.

"For all its in-depth reporting, *The Herald* is a small-town paper whose readers live in a small town," Joyce replied.

"That doesn't mean they're small-minded," Jinx protested.

"I never said that, and you should never confuse the two," Joyce said. "But it's like my mother used to say, it's not what you say, it's how you say it."

"Meaning the information in my articles isn't as important as the tone I use to write the articles?" Jinx asked.

"Correct," Joyce replied. "When I was working on Wall Street I had to learn how to make my voice heard among the throng of white men who liked to shout at the top of their lungs."

"What did you do?"

"I got to know the individuals who made up my audience and adapted to each man's style," Joyce explained. "Even though they all yelled, they all yelled differently. Some men's shouts were filled with passion, some yelled for attention, others screamed because they were afraid to use their real voices. Once I figured out their motives, I knew how to respond to them in the most persuasive way."

"That's brilliant, Aunt Joyce!" Jinx squealed. "No wonder you made a mint in the stock trade."

Laughing, Joyce placed the fedora on her head, making sure the brim slanted rakishly over her left eye. "I made a mint because I was damn good at my job, and so are you. Don't you forget it."

"Thank you, I appreciate the support," Jinx replied. "And I think I know the approach to use."

"What is it?" Joyce asked.

"The subject of the story really isn't Teri Jo," Jinx replied. "It's the residents of Tranquility."

"Because they bore witness to her murder," Joyce surmised.

"Exactly!" Jinx cried. "Teri Jo was murdered surrounded by her small-town neighbors. Why not put the small town front-and-center in my reporting?"

"*Meravigliosa!*" Alberta said, turning around to face

Jinx. "That's a marvelous idea. Wyck was smart to give you this assignment."

"Thanks, Gram. Small-town paper or not, I plan on making my mark in this world, just like the three of you have."

Alberta smiled and was delighted to hear the conviction in her granddaughter's voice, a strength she'd never had at Jinx's age. Although Alberta didn't feel as if she had contributed to society as much as Helen and Joyce had, she wasn't going to contradict Jinx. Helen, however, did feel the need to point out a discrepancy stemming from Jinx's comment.

"I don't think we're in a small town anymore," Helen observed. "This looks nothing like Tranquility."

The women looked around and realized Helen was right. The trip to Dover, New Jersey, had only taken thirty minutes, but when they entered the town it was clear that they weren't in Tranquility any longer.

There was nothing at all wrong with Dover, but it was a city whose crowded landscape was primarily filled with brick, concrete, and high-rise buildings. So far they hadn't seen one park and very few trees. It reminded Alberta and Helen of Hoboken, where they grew up, although Dover was larger and more expansive.

"It's hard to tell, but it seems safe," Alberta said.

"I think you're right," Joyce agreed. "It's like any city in the world, just a little rough around the edges."

Helen made a left on East McFarlan Street to enter Berry Street, which was their destination, and the women immediately surveyed the area. The row of narrow, semi-detached houses on either side were nearly identical and all seemed to have been built in 1940s, when such construction was popular. Some looked as if they could use a bit of tender loving care and a good power washing, but most were respectable looking and none appeared to be abandoned.

They parked across from 1352 Berry Street and they all stared at the house they would soon visit. Helen turned off the engine and said, "C'mon, ladies, let's do this for Teri Jo."

Alberta was about to knock a third time when the door finally opened, its inside chain lock still intact. Oddly, there was no one behind the door for her to greet.

"Hello."

When she heard the tiny voice she looked down and saw that someone had opened the door, but the little boy was only about three feet tall.

"Hi, sweetie," Alberta said, her voice automatically rising an octave. "Is your mommy home?"

The little boy didn't answer, only stared at Alberta and the women, his black eyes intense and curious.

"We're looking for Inez Rosales?" Jinx said, bending down so she could be eye level with the boy. "Is that your mommy?"

"Yes," he replied. "But the Snowman took Mommy away."

Any chance they had of questioning the boy any further was ruined when an older woman pushed him out of the way and appeared in the small crack of the opening.

"What do you want?" she asked.

The woman looked to be about thirty-five years old, and while her words were tinged with a Spanish accent, her English was perfect.

"We have—"

Before Jinx could finish her sentence, Helen interrupted her. "We wanted Inez to know that Teri Jo passed away."

The woman stared at Helen quizzically. "Who? We don't know any Teri Jo."

"I think Inez does," Alberta said. "Where exactly is she?"

"Arturo told you what happened," she replied. "You have to go."

Jinx stepped forward and pressed her hand on the door, preventing the woman from pushing it closed. "This is my card," Jinx said, holding her card in the open space above the chain link. "Please use it if you hear from Inez or if you need our help."

Slowly the woman released the chain link from the door and opened it to reveal that the little boy was still next to her, clutching at her leg. She took the card from Jinx's hand and examined it, her whole demeanor softened, and it appeared that she was ready to invite the women in. They were wrong.

The woman looked from one Ferrara to the other and then slammed the door in their faces.

An hour later, a fresh pitcher of Red Herrings in the center of Alberta's kitchen table, surrounded by several varieties of Entenmann's cakes, the ladies pondered the recent turn of events.

How were Teri Jo Linbruck and Inez Rosales connected? Why did it appear that the woman, who they assumed was a relative of Inez's or at least a close friend, was afraid of them and seemingly fearful in general? And where was Inez and who was this Snowman? The women had a lot of questions, which was typical at the onset of an investigation, but in this instance there was the possibility that they had already been given the answers.

"Ah *Madon!*" Alberta cried. "The solution is staring us right in the face."

Pointing to the box next to the pitcher, they all realized she was right. Whatever was inside the box, which was so important to Teri Jo that she requested they hand deliver it to Inez, was the key to unlocking the mystery of their connection. With the recipient not only missing, but possibly taken somewhere against her will, there was definitely an urgency to finding out what was contained within the cardboard.

"I know it isn't a huge moral dilemma, but the box isn't addressed to us," Joyce said. "Do we really have the right to open it?"

"Technically, it could be considered tampering with the mail," Jinx replied.

"No, lovey," Alberta said. "For us to tamper with the mail there needs to be a stamp on the box, and there's only an address."

"And since it was given to me and possession is nine-tenths of the law, technically, the box is mine," Helen said.

Digging through her pocketbook, Helen pulled out her car keys and dragged the serrated edge across the top of the box until the lid popped up. She dropped her keys onto the table and proceeded to pull out the contents of the box, which were covered in bubble wrap.

Slowly, as if handling an Egyptian artifact, Helen laid the item on the table and turned it over multiple times until the bubble wrap was gone and all that remained was the item itself. She placed it upright, but it was still shrouded in mystery.

"Why in the world would Teri Jo give Inez an antique clock?" Helen asked.

Standing in the center on the table was a pedestal clock, made of walnut, with intricate carvings on the top that weren't quite gothic, but softer and more rounded in their overall appearance. At the apex was a large bird about to take flight. It was hard to tell exactly what type of bird it was, but since the wings were quite large it more than likely was a depiction of an eagle. The numbers on the face of the clock were roman numerals and were made of white ivory. The base of the clock was a flurry of more walnut carvings, leaves, flowers, and vines. It was a beautifully crafted piece of functional art. But it gave the women even more questions than they originally had.

"This doesn't make any sense," Helen said. "Teri Jo was a waitress, why was she delivering an expensive clock to a stranger?"

"You're wrong, Helen," Joyce corrected. "It makes perfect sense. The Tranqclockery is right next door to Veronica's Diner."

"The Tranqclockery?" Alberta asked. "What's that?"

"It's the clock store with the cute name," Jinx said. "I've been meaning to go in there, but I kind of forget it's still around."

"Most of us do," Joyce confirmed. "The store is a relic from another time and it's been here for decades. Nowadays, it's only open for business a few hours a week, and Owen mainly does clock repairs."

"Who's Owen?" Alberta asked.

"Owen O'Hara, the owner," Joyce replied.

"An *Irishman*?" Alberta said. "Do we like him?"

"He's a bit of an eccentric and a loner, but a nice man," Joyce said. "He is friends with Father Sal, and I believe he was with Sal at the diner the morning Teri Jo was killed."

"Yes, I think I saw him with Sal," Alberta said.

"I didn't, but if he was having breakfast with Father Sal, how nice can he be?" Helen asked.

As they passed the clock around the table so they could inspect it, Joyce filled in more details about Owen's history. He was in his late fifties and had lived in Tranquility for a very long time, but wasn't a townie, having moved there as an adult to open the store. Joyce didn't really know how he was able to keep the store up and running because the novelty wore off quickly, and even though she popped into the store from time to time, she never noticed any new merchandise on his shelves. The stock he did carry, however, was top-notch and probably the most affordable antique clocks in the area.

"Teri Jo must have been doing Owen a favor by delivering the clock to Inez," Alberta surmised.

"That has to be it," Jinx agreed. "I mean, I understand there can be coincidences, but this is a no-brainer. The two places share the same alleyway, they have to be connected."

"I don't know if that's the whole picture," Helen said.

"Why not, Helen?" Joyce asked.

"I don't mean to generalize, and I absolutely don't mean this in a prejudicial way, but the little boy and the woman who answered Inez's door weren't wealthy and their neighborhood is far from exclusive," Helen explained. "Do you really think Inez ordered an antique clock from the Tranqclockery?"

The women found it hard to disagree with Helen's comment, but there was another explanation.

"What if she was having a family clock fixed?" Alberta suggested. "Maybe the clock is an heirloom that was passed down from generation to generation and Inez wanted to get it fixed to restore it to its former glory. It could have been broken."

"That would be more realistic than if she was buying a new clock," Joyce said, "but remember the clock Aunt Carmela gave to me and Anthony when we got married?"

"*Dio mio!*" Alberta cried. "The one Mama brought back for Carmela when she visited her sister in Sicily. Carmela wanted you to have something from the homeland. It was so beautiful."

"Beautiful, but expensive," Joyce said. "I had Owen fix it a few years ago and it cost me four hundred dollars. I have to agree with Helen that I just don't see Inez or that woman who answered the door being able to afford that much money to repair a clock."

"Hold on a minute, this clock is broken," Jinx said.

It was Jinx's turn to dig into her purse, and when she pulled out the Swiss-girl figurine still in its Ziploc bag, they understood that Jinx was connecting one clue to another. She explained to Helen and Joyce that Alberta found the figurine when they were snooping behind the diner. She couldn't prove it, but she was rather certain the figurine came from the Tranqclockery.

"This little Swiss Miss fits perfectly on this little horizontal edge that's protruding out from the carving on the base of the clock," Jinx said.

"I hate to burst your bubble, Jinxie," Helen said, "But why would Teri Jo want to deliver a clock to Inez that hadn't yet been fixed?"

Deflated, Jinx replied, "Must you always be the voice of reason, Aunt Helen?"

"We all have crosses to bear," she replied.

"I guess it's possible that the figurine fell off when the clock was being transported from the Tranqclockery to the diner," Alberta said.

"That's a longshot, Berta," Joyce added.

"Then we're back to square one with no idea what this clock means," Jinx said.

"It's like Grandma used to say, *Il tempo può essere sia un amico che un nemico,*" Alberta said, then translated when she saw Jinx's confused expression. "Time can be both a friend and an enemy."

Immediately Jinx's expression changed from one of confusion to clarity.

"An enemy that would throw a sundial through your kitchen window!" Jinx squealed. "A sundial is a type of clock, isn't it? Maybe whoever threw it into the house was trying to point us toward the Tranqclockery."

"He couldn't have left a note on my front door?" Alberta asked. "He had to break my window?"

"People, like God, work in mysterious ways," Helen said.

Clutching the clock in her hands, Alberta replied, "It looks like this mystery is leading us right to Owen's front door."

CHAPTER 7

In bocca chiusa non entrò mai mosca.

The front door of the Tranqclockery was, unfortunately, a dead end.

"*Dannazione!*" Alberta cried. "It's closed."

"I thought it might be," Joyce said. "I told you Owen keeps crazy hours, but you insisted that we try."

"I thought we would make good use of our alone time since Jinx had a date with Freddy, and Helen had a date with one of those reality TV shows," Alberta said.

"Your sister is obsessed with those things, and for the life of me I don't understand it," Joyce confirmed, then added, "Also too, tonight is the finale."

Standing in front of the Tranqclockery, a store that Alberta had driven past countless times since she moved to Tranquility, she was amazed that she never knew it existed before. She'd been to the diner many times, she even snuck behind it, and still was unaware that there was a clock store close by. But in her defense, the store could easily be missed.

Located on a side street and not on the main drag or one of the other avenues that cut through the entire town, the Tranqclockery was a small one-story terracotta building that was smaller than Alberta's own Cape Cod. A huge oak tree and several overgrown bushes dotted the storefront, obscuring almost the whole left-side window from the view of pedestrians and drivers. The lettering that spelled out the name Tranqclockery in an old-fashioned gothic style was brown. Set against the terracotta, the letters and the store itself were practically invisible at night.

There was also a very important intangible reason for why Alberta and many other residents forgot about the Tranqclockery's existence—the simple theory of supply and demand. If you weren't in need of a clock store, the fact that there was one in your town wouldn't register in your brain. The other theory of Murphy's Law also came into effect: The moment the clock store was important to Alberta and she wanted to pay it a visit, it was closed.

"I guess we'll have to try again tomorrow," Alberta said.

As she and Joyce were about to cross into the diner's parking lot adjacent to the front of the Tranqclockery, they heard a door slam. Since the diner was still closed due to the police investigation, that could mean only thing: The Tranqclockery was open for business.

They ran back up the steps to the front door and waited for the lights to turn on, but after about a minute they realized they must've heard wrong.

"Foiled again," Joyce said.

They trekked back to the parking lot, but something in the side window of the clock shop caught Alberta's eye and she made a right turn down the alleyway. When Joyce saw what Alberta was doing, she followed her, careful to walk gingerly to make as little noise as possible. In their brief career as amateur detectives, they had learned it was best to act stealthily and whenever possible hide in the shadows and observe. Which is exactly what they did.

Their view was partially obstructed, but through the window they could see what appeared to be two men having a conversation.

"Is that Owen?" Alberta asked.

"No, but that sounds like him," Joyce replied.

Owen was standing just out of view and was shrouded in darkness, while the other man was standing with his back to the window, so they couldn't see his face. All they could tell was that he had slicked back, jet-black hair, was dressed in a dark business suit, and when he went to shake Owen's hand he turned slightly to reveal a long scar down the side of his left cheek.

"He looks dangerous," Alberta whispered.

"Looks can be deceiving," Joyce whispered back.

When Alberta saw the man with the scar move forward, presumably to the back door to leave, she turned and dashed to the front door.

"Why are we going in the opposite direction?" Joyce asked, running after Alberta.

"If we catch them at the back door it'll look too obvious, like we were casing the joint," Alberta said. "We'll look more like real customers if we're at the front door."

Alberta pressed the doorbell and could hear the sound echo throughout the store.

"You realize that you, me, and your sister are growing more alike every day, don't you?" Joyce asked.

"What are you talking about?" Alberta replied.

"We must be the only three women on the planet who still use the word *joint*," Joyce declared. "At least to describe an establishment."

Oblivious to the word's other meanings, Alberta replied, "How else would you use the word?"

Impatient, Alberta pressed the doorbell again, this time letting her finger linger longer on the bell. She then added her own voice to the sound of the chime.

"Owen!" Alberta cried. "We need to speak with you!"

When the door finally opened, Owen didn't have to say a word to make it known that he was not happy to have customers. His glare spoke volumes.

Even though Alberta had seen Owen at Veronica's Diner the day of Teri Jo's murder and was reminded by Joyce that they had crossed paths a few times during the past year, she felt as if she was looking at him for the first time. Maybe he was like his store and she hadn't noticed him before because she didn't need him. Now that she did, she made sure she observed him much more closely.

Standing about five ten, Owen was thin, no more than 170 pounds, and completely bald. At one point his hair had been black because his eyebrows were very dark, in contrast to his shimmering green eyes. Appropriate for an Irishman, Alberta thought. What wasn't appropriate were his manners.

"I'd rather not shake your hand," he announced. "There are more germs on the human hand than there are in a dog's mouth."

Alberta dropped her right hand awkwardly and remembered an old Italian phrase—*In bocca chiusa non entrò mai mosca*—which translated to *It is wise not to speak when it is not necessary*. In other words, even though she knew Owen was lying since she'd just seen him shake Scarface's hand, she thought it best to keep quiet about that fact. If she made Owen defensive, she might never get any information out of him.

"I think you know my sister-in-law, Joyce Ferrara," Alberta said.

"Of course," Owen replied. "Joyce and I go way back. How have you been? Still painting?"

"I'm doing very well, Owen, and still painting every chance I get," Joyce replied. "I don't think you've been formally introduced to Alberta, but you've probably seen her face in *The Herald* once or twice."

Unconvinced, Owen glared at Alberta once again until he finally recognized her face. "Why, yes, I most certainly have. You're Tranquility's very own Charlie Chan. Except female. And Italian. But just like Charlie, solving unsolvable crimes."

Blushing, Alberta waved a hand in front of her face. "Hardly, I've just helped the police solve a few cases."

"Is that what you're doing now?" Owen questioned. "Does this have anything to do with the brutal and unimaginable horror that took place next door?"

After all the years she'd known her sister, Alberta should have been used to blunt statements, but she was startled by the straightforward tone of Owen's voice. Instantly she chastised herself and remembered that everyone dealt with tragedy in their own way. If someone stated a fact matter-of-factly it didn't mean that someone was unfeeling.

"No, not at all," Alberta said. "I have a question about a clock, and Joyce says you're Tranquility's clock expert, so here we are."

"We won't interrupt your company, Owen," Joyce added. "We have a quick question and then we'll leave."

Smiling, Owen opened the door and waved his arm for the women to enter the shop. "I'm all alone here, as you can see. Come right in."

Once again the phrase—*In bocca chiusa non entrò mai mosca*—flashed through Alberta's mind as she entered the shop with Joyce close behind her. Alberta felt Joyce press a finger into the small of her back as a way for Joyce to convey that she also knew Owen was lying. But why? Could they have already stumbled upon Teri Jo's murderer? Or was lying one of Owen's eccentricities? She almost laughed out loud when she realized she'd been in the man's presence a few short minutes and was already talking to herself. Who was the eccentric?

When she stepped into the store, however, any chance that she might laugh or crack a smile was quickly extinguished because she felt as if she had walked onto an old horror-movie set. The store wasn't filled with knives or evil-looking dolls; it was worse. Everywhere she looked there were clocks.

Grandfather clocks in cherrywood, mahogany, and pine stood all over the shop like guards. The entire right wall was filled with clocks of every shape and size in different types of metal or carved out of wood. Some had weights, pendulums, and winding chimes dangling from their bases, others had elaborate crowns in a variety of shapes.

On either side of the main aisle that led toward the cash register, which itself was a relic from another century, were two glass-enclosed cases that housed everything from stopwatches, to pendant watches, to alarm clocks. Everywhere Alberta looked she saw a clock, and each one was different. She had no idea there could be so many variations on a simple household necessity.

On top of the visual onslaught, there was the overbearing sound. It was like being attacked by an army of crickets. Almost each clock had its own variation on *tick-tock*, *tick-tock* that collectively felt like a cacophony of bombs about to explode. Or a judgmental, spinster aunt tsk-tsking repeatedly while stroking the barrel of a shotgun. The result gave the shop an eerie, creepy aura like nothing Alberta had ever experienced.

"What an . . . adorable shop you have, Owen," Alberta said.

"Thank you, Alberta," he replied, seemingly unaware that she was lying. "I'm quite proud of it. You said you had a question for me. What is it? Time is fleeting, you know."

It might have been the environment, but Owen's chuckle reminded Alberta of one of Vincent Price's many sinister roles, and she felt a tingle shuffle down her spine. She tried to dismiss the foolish thought in order to focus on her mission, but wasn't entirely successful. Owen was one odd bird.

"My sister's birthday is coming up, and I'm looking for a clock that we used to have in our bedroom growing up," Alberta said, repeating the fabricated story she and Joyce came up with as their reason to meet with Owen.

Gesturing with his right hand, Owen said, "As you can see, I have many styles that represent the famous clock trends over the past two centuries. If you look closely, I'm sure you'll find what you're looking for."

"It might be faster if I show you what I'm looking for," Alberta replied.

She held out her phone with a photo of the clock that

was in the box Teri Jo had given them and watched Owen's reaction closely. Once more she felt Joyce's finger press into her lower back as Owen's eyes widened slightly. He could've simply been impressed with the clock or he could have recognized it.

"This specimen is from your childhood?" he asked.

"No, but we had the same kind," Alberta lied. "I found this at an antique store in Lambertville, but it was very expensive so I took a photo of it, hoping that I could find it cheaper somewhere else."

"Unlike you, Owen, some antique dealers have been known to inflate their prices dramatically to make a profit," Joyce purred. "Which is why you've been in business forever."

Owen smiled at Joyce and bowed his head theatrically in appreciation of her compliment. An interesting thought popped into Alberta's head: Owen was more a character than a man. She wasn't sure, however, if he was comic relief or villain. She didn't completely trust him, but she had to admit she enjoyed the fact that at her age she could still be surprised by people. And, in turn, she could surprise them.

"Is there something strange about the clock?" Alberta asked.

"No, not at all," Owen replied. "Rather ordinary, I will say."

"You were studying it so closely, I thought you found something out of the ordinary," Alberta replied.

Owen's green eyes shimmered, but Alberta couldn't tell if it was with delight or disdain. "Clocks such as this, with their ornate carvings, often had figurines on them of country girls or farmers," Owen explained. "This one either didn't have it originally or it broke off at some point in its history."

The women knew that Owen was referencing the Swiss girl figurine Alberta uncovered in the alleyway, but both knew that was a fact that definitely needed to remain undisclosed.

"The one we had as kids didn't have a figurine on it, but that would be a cute touch," Alberta said. "Do you have anything like it in stock?"

"Alas, no, not at the moment," Owen said.

"Have you sold one recently?" Joyce inquired.

Shaking his head, Owen replied, "I don't recall, but you're free to inspect the inventory. I'm sure you'll find that my clocks are much more unique than that one."

"You know what I'd rather do?" Alberta said. "Use your ladies' room. I've been drinking way too much coffee lately."

"You're in luck," Owen replied. "The bathroom's just been fixed. The whole block has had a problem for a week, but the town finally made it a priority and they're starting to make the repairs. It's right back there through the curtain, first door on your right."

"Thank you."

Safely behind the curtain, Alberta opened and closed the bathroom door to make it sound as if she was using the facility and proceeded to snoop around the back room. There wasn't direct light in that portion of the shop so it was hard to see clearly, plus it wasn't very large. Alberta looked to the left and was able to see the window looking out at the alleyway, the same window she and Joyce used to watch Owen interact with Scarface earlier.

Looking around the room she didn't see any drawers

to rifle through, nor was there anything on the one table in the back right-hand corner. So much for taking advantage of an opportunity.

Defeated, Alberta was about to return to the main room when she realized she was supposed to be using the ladies' room, and if she didn't flush, that would seem odd or, at the very least, unsanitary. Abruptly, she turned around and stepped on something that almost made her scream. What felt like a mouse was actually a thick piece of foam. Bending down to inspect it she realized it was nothing worth inspecting and gave it a playful kick, which led to another revelation. Underneath the piece of foam was a prayer card from St. Ann's Church. It wasn't the same church she'd attended while living in Hoboken, but since it was named after same saint, Alberta took it as a sign that a higher power was offering her a clue, and she did what every determined detective would've done— she pocketed the card. She gave the toilet a quick flush, turned on the sink to wash the dirt and dust from the card off her hands, and returned to the main room, where she found Owen and Joyce in mid-conversation.

"That sounds awful, Owen. I'm so sorry."

"What sounds awful?" Alberta asked.

"Owen was telling me about his migraines," Joyce said.

"Ocular migraines, to be precise," Owen corrected. "They can cause me to go blind for days at a time."

"*Dio mio!*" Alberta exclaimed. "That does sound awful."

"As long as it isn't permanent, I find the intestinal fortitude to muddle through," Owen said. "When you've suffered with as many physical ailments as I have, you learn to deal with the pain of life."

A character indeed. Alberta thought Owen sounded like one of those old Italian martyrs she remembered her grandmother talking to on the front porch. The women, all dressed in the same black dresses and sensible shoes, were always complaining about some medical problem and always trying to top each other with who had the most miserable life. Imagine trying to win a contest by being the worst. Luckily, Alberta had shed her pessimistic attitude and had learned to embrace life and all its possibilities instead of focusing on its shortcomings and heartaches. It hadn't been a quick journey to be able to look at life's glass as half full instead of half empty, but she had made the journey and that's what mattered.

The only other thing that mattered now to Alberta was to get the heck out of Owen's creepy clockery.

"Thank you so much for your time, Owen," Alberta said. "If I can't find an exact duplicate for my sister's gift, I'll make sure to come back and look through your inventory and find a worthy substitute."

"It would be my pleasure to help you find the perfect gift," Owen said. "As I always say, if you can't find the clock of your dreams at the Tranqclockery, that clock doesn't exist."

Once again Alberta was stymied for a reply, so once again she lied.

"That is a terrific slogan, Owen!"

In the car, Alberta and Joyce made sure not to say a word until they were safely down the block and there was no way Owen could see them from his window. When they were in the safety zone, they still didn't speak, but instead cracked up laughing.

"I don't know if he's psycho or looney tunes," Alberta said.

"Like I said, he's eccentric," Joyce replied, "but harmless."

"Even though he's a liar?" Alberta asked.

"Well, there is that," Joyce said. "Did you find any clues while you were in the back room?"

"Nothing except the fact that Owen is religious," Alberta conveyed, pulling out the prayer card from her pocket. "But no sign of Scarface. He must've gotten away."

"Also too, he may never have left," Joyce added. "He could've been hiding in the shop the entire time."

"Oh *Madon*! You could be right about that, but I didn't see a hiding place in the back room," Alberta said. "We must find out who this Scarface is and how he's connected to the Clock Man."

"Scarface and the Clock Man?" Joyce said. "Berta, this mystery gets more frightening with every clue."

CHAPTER 8

Colui che aiuta se stesso.

Gina "Jinx" Maldonado hadn't always known that she wanted to be a reporter. For the longest time she'd wanted to be a firefighter because red was her favorite color. Then, after she and her family barely escaped a hurricane, she became fascinated with meteorology and thought being a weather girl on the local TV station would be the coolest job in the whole wide world. It was only when she took a journalism course in college to fulfill an English requirement that she had an epiphany and realized she was meant to uncover truths and tell people's stories. As an added benefit, she hoped to become famous along the way.

That desire to win a Pulitzer Prize or anchor her own nightly news program never faded during her four years of college and traveled with her five bags of luggage and her beloved but beaten up Winnie-the-Pooh stuffed animal when she moved from Eufala, Florida, to Tranquility, New Jersey, after graduation. She told everyone the reason she was moving was because she needed to break into a news market near New York, but her mother, Lisa Marie, knew it was because Jinx wanted to break her mother's heart. Maybe not intentionally, but the result was the same.

Lisa Marie knew the only reason her daughter was moving to New Jersey was to reconnect with her grandmother, from whom Lisa Marie had been estranged for over a decade. The arguments and contentious relationship between Alberta and Lisa Marie were legendary, and after a lifetime of fights and reconciliations and more fights and fewer reconciliations, Lisa Marie had called it quits and moved her family a thousand miles south. When Jinx made the announcement that she was relocating, Lisa Marie wasn't surprised—she had expected it to happen one day—but like every mother in the history of history, when that day came she wished for one more day alone with her daughter.

Experience taught Lisa Marie not to fight with her own child. She gave her some sound advice, let her know that she wasn't going to stand in the way of her reunion with her grandmother, and that she was welcome home anytime she wanted to return. Jinx couldn't have been more grateful. She'd thought for sure that her mother was going to give her a hard time for moving so far away and specifically, so close to her grandmother. It did help that her younger brother, Sergio, had stayed close by and was still living at home, having gone into business with their father, Tommy. But not having to deal with family stress and a relentless mother constantly begging her to move back home where she belonged allowed Jinx to focus on her career.

Now in her second year at *The Herald*, Jinx was evolving into a good reporter, article by article. She was honing her skills, collecting bylines, filling up her virtual Rolodex with sources, and surprisingly, learning that the work itself was more fulfilling than the potential prize. There was no doubt that Jinx was still ambitious, but she understood that ambition without hard work and a track record was, as Alberta liked to say, as foolish as making lasagna for one person; it just didn't make any sense.

Which was why Jinx was thrilled Wyck had given her a solo byline on Teri Jo's murder. Not so she could make a name for herself, but so she could tell Teri Jo's story. In order to do that, she first needed to uncover who Teri Jo was.

"How can she not have any family?" Jinx asked, perplexed. "Everybody's got a family."

The moment Jinx posed the question to Veronica, she realized she was speaking as a lifelong member of the Ferrara clan and not an objective reporter who should know that life is not the same for everyone. There were many people who were orphans or without siblings, parents, or others like Jinx, who had moved far away from their family roots, so they were essentially alone. Then there were the people who were abandoned by their families and had to forge ahead through life on their own. Teri Jo could have been any of those people.

"Sometimes I forget that not everyone is as lucky as I am," Jinx said. "But this isn't about me, it's about Teri Jo, so let me start over. Do you know if she had any relatives?"

Sitting on a stool at the counter next to Jinx, Veronica

twirled a long strand of chestnut-brown hair through her finger and gazed into her coffee cup as if searching for an answer. But none came.

"She didn't have anyone," Veronica said. "She was an only child and her parents died a while back."

"Do you know where they lived?" Jinx asked. "Or even where Teri Jo was born?"

"I wish I could help, but the answers to both your questions are no," Veronica replied.

Jinx paused for a moment and tried to determine if Veronica was telling the truth or deliberately evading her questions. She didn't know the woman very well, so she didn't know what type of relationship she'd had with Teri Jo. Veronica took her employee's murder very hard, but Jinx sensed that Veronica took the fact that Teri Jo was killed while on the job even harder. As if she was stressed out because her business and livelihood had been interrupted instead of the tragedy that a woman she had employed had been killed. *That's it!* Jinx thought. Teri Jo was an employee and every employee had to fill out an application to get a job.

"What about your employment forms? Teri Jo must have filled them out before she started working. May I look at those?" Jinx asked. "They might fill in some of the blanks."

The hair intertwined around Veronica's finger was now being yanked to the side. Veronica smiled nervously in an attempt, Jinx thought, to vamp for time so she could come up with a reasonable answer, but when she spoke Jinx didn't think her answer was reasonable at all.

"We're a diner, we don't have a human resources department," Veronica replied.

"You must have payroll," Jinx insisted.

"Sure, but all the information I need to process a check is Teri Jo's address, which you have, and her social security number, which I can't give to you," Veronica stated. "Listen, I don't know if you've ever worked in a restaurant, but employees come and go like clockwork. I've been lucky that Luis and Teri Jo stayed with me for so long, but everyone else? They're here for a few months or less, and then they're gone, sometimes without a word, they just never show up for work again."

"You're right, I've never been a waitress and I didn't realize it was as transient as you describe," Jinx confessed. "I guess that's why you and Teri Jo became so close."

Again Veronica smiled, but this time there was no awkwardness, only true emotion. Her eyes tried to hold on to the goodness she felt for Teri Jo and all the positive attributes she possessed, but after a few seconds, when the sadness took over, Veronica shook her head in an attempt to ward off the tears.

"It isn't fair," she said quietly. "Teri was a good kid, she was working hard to get her life back on track. Not too long ago she was on food stamps, but she was determined to get off government assistence, and she did."

"My Aunt Helen said Teri Jo had a bit of a difficult upbringing," Jinx conveyed. "Did she confide in you about things that happened to her while growing up?"

"Nothing specific," Veronica said. "Just that she never had a support system and always felt alone. I don't know why she left home, but I know she was on her own for a long time, and when you're by yourself you often find yourself scrambling to live instead of living."

Jinx let Veronica's last words sink in so she would remember them. Yes, she thought they were insightful, but she also thought Veronica unconsciously revealed a part of her own life.

"Thanks so much, Veronica, you've been a great help," Jinx said. "I want my articles to be more about Teri Jo the person instead of Teri Jo the murder victim, so if you think of anything else, please give me a call."

"I'll do that," Veronica said, taking Jinx's card from her outstretched hand. "Though now that I'm back in business and short staffed, I'm not sure how much time I'll have to make a social call."

On her drive to *The Herald*, Jinx didn't have that problem.

"Freddy!" she yelled into the air after she heard her boyfriend's voice. "You will not believe what just happened to me."

"You found another dead body," he replied.

"No! Why would you say that?"

"Dude! Because you and your grandmother are the grim reaper's henchwomen," Freddy cried. "Every time you go outside, another corpse drops out of the sky."

"Freddy! That is so not true!"

"It is too true," Freddy challenged. "It doesn't change how I feel about you, and I figure if I keep you close, the reaper will pass right on by me, so I'll be safe. Despite your name, you're kinda like my good luck charm."

Jinx felt herself smile at the sound of her boyfriend's flirtatious voice, but she didn't want to get sidetracked. She had called him for a reason, and that reason had nothing to do with being flattered.

"Don't you think it's highly suspicious that Veronica,

who was Teri Jo's employer, doesn't have any records of Teri's background?" Jinx asked.

"No," Freddy replied.

"What do you mean, no?"

Clearly, that was the wrong answer, and even someone like Freddy, who was laid-back, knew he had to act quickly to rectify the damage he accidentally caused. What better way to prove that he was worthy of her forgiveness than to remind her he was a terrific entrepreneur.

"Veronica doesn't run a business like I do, Jinx," Freddy began. "Her employees come and go. If she gets a good vibe and thinks she can trust them, she hires them. Here at Freddy's Scuba 'n' Ski Shoppe we do background checks, call references, and in some instances require certification. It's a whole different ball game."

The smile returned to Jinx's face, but this time she didn't let her annoyance with the way her interview with Veronica turned out diminish the pride she had in Freddy for taking on a new business venture. A few months ago, Freddy's boss decided to retire and was looking to sell the business. When Freddy found out, he decided it was time for him to take a few steps up the corporate ladder. He said good-bye to being a mere scuba-diving instructor and said hello to becoming a small business owner.

With help from Sloan and the Ferraras, Freddy revamped the business that up until then only catered to scuba diving and snorkeling, to expand its reach and include winter sports such as skiing, snowboarding, and snow tubing. Like all business ventures, there was a certain amount of risk, but Freddy had told Jinx he wanted to prove to her and, most important, to himself, that he wasn't going to back down from a challenge. Jinx fell in love with him a little more that day.

"I still can't believe I'm dating a CEO," Jinx said.

"Me neither," Freddy said. "Do I know him?"

"Shut up!" Jinx joked. "Thank you for making me feel better. I still find it hard to believe Veronica couldn't be any more help. It makes me wonder if I should trust anything she tells me."

"Wow, you sound just like Aunt Helen," Freddy said. "She doesn't like Veronica very much either. I filled in at the animal hospital and volunteered with her, and that's all she talked about."

"Seriously?"

"Ask her yourself."

Which is exactly what Jinx did.

"Why are you asking me?" Helen said on the other end of the phone.

"Because you seem to have known Teri Jo better than anyone," Jinx explained. "So please meet me at *The Herald.* I'm trying to track down Teri's family, and Veronica was absolutely no help whatsoever. I mean, she was Teri's boss, and she acted like I was asking her about a stranger."

Jinx knew that she was exaggerating, but she also knew her Aunt Helen wouldn't respond unless she thought the situation was dire. If she only thought Jinx was complaining because she didn't like how Veronica answered her questions or was frustrated because she was going to have to do a considerable amount of research to uncover the truth about Teri Jo, Helen would tell her to stop bellyaching and get to work. No, if she wanted Helen's help, she needed to make it sound as if Veronica was concealing facts.

"The only fact Veronica shared is that Teri Jo was an only child," Jinx shared.

When Jinx heard the scream that came through the phone, she was grateful she was using her hands-free device, listening to the call through her car's speaker, and wasn't holding the phone up to her ear.

"Veronica is a liar!" Helen blared. "I'll be at *The Herald* in ten minutes!"

Jinx rushed into the office and zipped past Mary Margaret—a twenty-seven-year veteran who was part receptionist, part office manager, and even part graphic designer—booted up her computer, and entered her password. She was starting to type out her notes from her conversation with Veronica when she heard the front door slam and the *clickety-clack* of very sensible heels on the wooden floor. Aunt Helen had arrived.

Slamming her pocketbook on Jinx's desk, Helen waved a finger at her and shouted, "Jinxie, you cannot trust that woman."

"I assume you're talking about Veronica?"

"Yes! Teri Jo wasn't an only child. She told me only last week while we were helping Dr. Grazioso extract a goiter from Baklava, Mrs. Della Flavia's Irish Setter, that the only real family she still had was her brother."

Momentarily distracted, Jinx couldn't imagine why an Italian woman would name her Irish dog after a Greek pastry. Then she realized Helen had given her yet another reason to distrust Veronica.

"First Veronica tells us she was married, which you later told us was a lie," Jinx described.

"True."

"And second, Veronica tells me that Teri is an only child, when she has a brother, so that's another lie."

"Also true."

"Why all the lies?" Jinx asked no one in particular. "I mean, they're so easy to vet, how does she think she's going to get away with them?"

Helen grabbed the back of a chair, wheeled it close to Jinx's desk, and sat down. "Jinxie, I've been asking myself that question for years. People breathe, people lie. All I can tell you is that Veronica makes the best eggs Benedict on the East Coast, but she's turning out to be a Benedict Arnold."

"What more do you know about Teri Jo's brother?" Jinx asked.

"Only that she hadn't seen him in a while because he lives in Texas," Helen shared. "Where exactly, I'm not sure, but he's out there, somewhere."

"It'll be a longshot, but I'll do an online search for the last name Linbruck and see if there are any matches for men in Texas," Jinx said.

"*Colui che aiuta se stesso*," Helen replied.

"What's that mean?"

"He who helps himself," Helen said. "If Veronica isn't going to help us find out where Teri Jo's family is, we'll help ourselves."

"Helen Ferrara! How nice to see you again!"

Helen stared at Wyck as if she was meeting him for the first time. Which she was.

"Aunt Helen," Jinx said, "this is my boss, Wyck Wycknowski."

"A bit redundant, isn't it?" Helen asked, not rhetorically.

"I guess it is," Wyck replied. "Wyck's a nickname, just like Jinx. My real name is Troy."

"You picked the lesser of two evils," Helen said.

"Exactly!" Wyck cried, delighted by Helen's acerbic banter. "I'm sorry, it's just that I've heard so much about you from Jinx, I feel as if I already know you."

"Are you telling tales about me, Jinxie?" Helen queried.

"Not at all!" Jinx cried. "Well, only the funny stuff."

"The minute someone hears you're a nun, they think you're funny," Helen moaned. "I've never known a funny nun in all my life. Correction, maybe Sister Francisco, because she had a speech impediment and a very deep voice, but in her defense she could never give up her Camels. She loved those cigarettes."

"Helen, you remind me of my Aunt Inga, if that battle-ax only had a sense of humor," Wyck said. "I don't know if this would appeal to you, but if you're interested, there could be a job for you here at *The Herald*."

Jinx and Helen turned to look at each other, and their faces were mirror images of shock.

"This battle-ax doesn't come cheap, you know," Helen replied.

"I'm sure we could work something out," Wyck said. "You give me a call if you want to talk further, or just let Jinx here know. She's on her way to becoming my number-one reporter."

"Why isn't she number one already?" Helen asked.

"There it is! The timing, the wit, I love it!" Wyck cried. "You know what else I love? The fact that ever since Jinx and her grandmother got here, Tranquility has turned into a hotbed of homicide. This was one of the safest places to live, and now every few months somebody gets bumped off."

"I've told you before, Wyck, Tranquility did have its

share of murders before either of us moved here," Jinx protested.

"Once every other year if we were lucky," Wyck claimed. "I make sure all my doors are locked before I go to bed at night, and I increased my life insurance policy, but still, it's terrific for business. Readership is up forty-two percent, thanks to Jinx and her crime reporting. If you're half as good as that, Helen, you'd be worth any price."

After Wyck left, Jinx and Helen needed to decompress for a few moments before continuing their conversation, even though they couldn't remember where they were before Wyck interrupted them.

"I think my boss just made you a job offer, Aunt Helen," Jinx said. "What kind of job I have no idea, but it could be interesting."

"I don't know if I can afford to work," Helen said. "It might get in the way of my pension. The government does believe in the separation of church and state when it wants to."

"The government!" Jinx shrieked. "Oh my God, I completely forgot that Veronica did share one piece of information with me that could help us find out more about Teri Jo."

"Spill it, Jinxie! What piece?"

"She said that for a while Teri was on food stamps."

"There's no shame in that," Helen declared.

"None at all," Jinx replied. "But there should be government records, and on those records might be personal information that will tell us more about Teri Jo than Veronica ever will."

"Sounds like it's time we made an appointment with Uncle Sam," Helen announced.

CHAPTER 9

Senza il tuo nome non hai nulla.

It was time to reintroduce the world to Sister Helen. Once Jinx realized the only way she was going to be able to uncover usable information on where Teri Jo came from was to dig into her past as a food stamps recipient, she knew that Helen was going to be the key to dislodging that data from the clutches of a civil servant. Even the most apathetic, hard-bitten government employee was going to find it hard to resist the pleas of a nun. At least that was Jinx's hope as she and Helen stood on the steps leading up to the Tranquility court house. But even though Helen agreed to that theory, she refused to play her part.

"Sister Helen is dead," Helen declared.

"She is not," Jinx protested, the nun's habit she was holding falling limply in her hand. "She's standing right in front of me."

"This is Aunt Helen, a completely different person," Helen continued. "Sister Helen did her job and did it very well, but she has served her time and moved on. Do not ask her to come out of retirement and do not ask me to make a mockery of my religious order by donning a habit in order to find a clue so we can solve this case."

The passion brimming from her aunt was unprecedented. Jinx, of course, had known her Aunt Helen her entire life, but it was only within the past few years since they both moved to Tranquility that she had gotten to know her as a person and not as a relative mentioned in passing. She only knew bits and pieces of her time as a nun, although she understood that Helen's conviction to serve God and help heal people using His message was deeply rooted. What she, or anyone else for that matter, didn't know was why she'd left the convent suddenly and how that separation was affecting her non-ecclesiastical life. For all Jinx knew, Helen could be suffering some kind of post-traumatic stress disorder now that she had to live outside the cloistered walls of the convent. But then her jaw dropped when she recalled a memory and realized her aunt was simply living a lie.

"Hold on just one minute, Sister!" Jinx cried. "You were the one who suggested I don this habit to play Sister Maria and fool Father Sal into thinking that I was a novitiate. How is that any different than me asking you to revive your role as Sister Helen?"

"You were wearing a costume, but you're asking me to resume a life I walked away from!" Helen barked. "Jinxie, I love you, you know that, and I don't say this as judgment, only observation, but you're not a very religious woman, so you wearing a nun's habit wasn't blasphemous. It would be a very different story for me."

People rushed up and down the steps all around them, but Jinx felt that time stood still. Ever since she had reconnected with her grandmother, and by extension her aunts Helen and Joyce, Jinx had become a witness to a different outlook on life. An older, wiser version that was crafted, both negatively and positively, by a longer life experience. Slowly, she was learning to appreciate those moments and understand that youth wasn't always superior. She could learn a lot from the old ladies around her, especially about herself.

Helen, of course, was a religious woman, as were Alberta and Joyce, but Jinx wasn't brought up in the typical Italian Catholic household. Italian, absolutely—Catholic, not so much. Jinx had been christened, communioned, and confirmed, but more out of requirement than desire by her or her family. Those spiritual events were more pageantry. They were a chance to buy a pretty dress and walk down the aisle with a boy in preparation for what it would be like to walk down the aisle to meet her future husband at the altar. Jinx couldn't remember any of the church's teachings or reasons behind any of those ceremonies except that they were expected of her, and because she had always been a good daughter, she never questioned if she should participate in those rituals. She never even thought she had a choice. She did now.

"You're right, Aunt Helen, and I apologize," Jinx said, stuffing the habit into her bag. "I was being thoughtless. Please forgive me."

Helen reached out to grab Jinx's hands, her pocketbook hanging on her arm swaying in between them like the scales of justice. "Sweetie, we're family, there's nothing to forgive," Helen replied. "And I'm sorry if I came on too harsh. Rumor has it I can do that sometimes."

The women were still laughing when they finally got to the SNAP office and were sitting across from Connie Woo, who according to the name plate on her desk— which was being threatened with demolition by a pile of thick files that both frightened and impressed the women— was the Sussex County SNAP lead coordinator.

"We came here to talk about food stamps," Jinx announced. "What's SNAP?"

Weary but professional, Connie brushed away a stray hair with a long fingernail in a color Jinx couldn't identify but coveted, and explained that the food stamps program, in an effort to reduce some of the stigma that had become associated with the name, had been officially renamed the Supplemental Nutrition Assistance Program, or SNAP.

"We still provide the same benefits and resources to those in need," Connie replied, her voice a rough rasp, "but now with a more progressive acronym."

"Forward thinking is what will propel this country forward, I always say," Helen announced proudly.

From the way Connie's left eyebrow raised, slowly and with very strong opinion, it was obvious that she was not impressed by Helen's comment. If flattery wasn't going to work, facts might.

"Ms. Woo, I'm here on official business," Jinx began.

"Are you a cop?" Connie asked.

"No, I'm a reporter."

"That's not officially official, if you know what I mean," Connie said.

"Honestly, I don't," Jinx replied.

"A cop is official. I have no choice but to answer any questions they might ask," Connie explained. "A reporter has no official authority to make me, as an employee of SNAP, cooperate."

"Then how about we speak to you as Connie, and not as a SNAP coordinator?" Helen asked.

Connie's berry-mauve, matte-finished lipsticked lips formed a perfect O and they weren't sure if the vowel formation was going to lead to an expletive or to a surrender. They did not expect it to lead to a reunion.

"You're a former social worker, aren't you?" Connie asked, directing her question to Helen.

"In a way, yes," Helen replied. "When I was a nun I was many things: teacher, parole officer, and on occasion a social worker."

"I can spot a kindred spirit a mile away," Connie said. "Two miles if I actually wear the glasses my eye doctor prescribed, but I haven't yet found frames that don't squash my false eyelashes."

Ice broken, it was time to get down to business.

"This is my niece, Jinx Maldonado, lead reporter at *The Herald*," Helen conveyed. "She's investigating the murder of my friend, Teri Jo Linbruck."

As expected, Connie's lips formed an even larger O at the mention of Tranquility's most recent murder victim.

"I read about her," Connie said. "Stabbed in broad daylight. Have they found out who did it?"

"Not yet, we . . . I mean, the police are still investigating," Jinx stuttered. "I'm hoping that my journalistic pursuit of Teri Jo's life and background will help bring the culprit to justice."

"Amen to that!" Connie shouted, raising a palm to the heavens. "Anything I can do to help, just ask me."

"Terrific!" Jinx cried. "Could you give me any and all files you have on Teri Jo Linbruck?"

"No can do."

"But you just said you'd do anything you can to help."

"Anything but that," Connie said. "I'll lose my job if I hand over files to anyone who just comes in and asks. You have to know the right way to ask certain questions."

What Connie was asking for did not come naturally to Jinx and Helen. Neither of them could be considered subtle. They were direct, loud, demanding, impatient, and tactless. However, if they wanted to find out who Teri Jo was, they were going to have to switch tactics.

"Why don't we start from the beginning?" Helen suggested, her syrupy voice sounding foreign even to her. "Could you please check to see if you have Teri Jo Linbruck in your system as a SNAP recipient?"

"Why, of course I can, ma'am, that'll only take me two shakes," Connie replied, the syrup in her voice even sweeter than Helen's. But when Connie looked at her computer screen a grimace formed on her face, and when she spoke, the syrupy tone had been doused with vinegar. "Sorry, ladies, I got nothing."

"What do you mean, nothing?" Jinx exclaimed. "You said you'd help."

"I would if I could, but I don't have any records on your friend," Connie explained. "I even tried looking by first names, and there are a few Theresas, but no Teri Jo. I'm sorry, but according to my computer, Teri Jo Linbruck doesn't exist."

"That's impossible. Veronica told me that she had to go on food stamps while she was here," Jinx repeated. "Unless Veronica lied to us again."

"Veronica? As in Veronica's Diner?" Connie asked, and leaned across her desk conspiratorially. "Do you think she's the killer?"

"Not sure," Helen said. "But she is a liar."

"You can't trust anyone these days, can you?" Connie said, accenting her comment with a loud sneeze.

"*Salute*" Helen replied.

Jinx gasped out loud, inspiration rapidly flooding through her veins until it formulated a question she hoped would put an end to this mystery. "Are any of the Theresas on your list Italian?"

"Why do you want to know that, Jinxie?" Helen asked.

"At the diner, the morning of the murder, you sneezed and Teri Jo said *salute* instead of *God bless you* or *Gesundheit*, as a non-Italian might say," Jinx explained. "I figured it was because she had been hanging around you and picked up the word, but maybe it's because she's really Italian."

Connie banged away at her keyboard, which was a feat in itself since her fingernails were at least an inch long, but when she was done it was worth the effort. "Theresa Josefina Rizzoli," she announced triumphantly. "You can't get much more Italian than that."

"I assume you can't give us any more information than that either?" Jinx inquired.

"You would be correct," Connie answered. "As much as I like the two of you, I like my job and my pension even more. Anyway, it's time for my coffee break so you two have to run along now."

Running straight to Alberta's, Jinx and Helen made sure Alberta and Joyce would be there so they could fill them in on their latest bombshell.

"Ah *Madon*!" Alberta cried as she set out a tray of cold cuts, olives, and mozzarella. "All this time we were looking for information on Teri Jo Linbruck and she doesn't even exist."

"I have to say that we've uncovered some surprises before, but this one is the most surprising of all," Joyce said. "Why was this Theresa Josefina posing as a non-ethnic version of herself?"

"Aunt Helen and I talked about that on the drive over, and it could be anything," Jinx said. "She could be running from someone, trying to live incognito."

"She could have committed a crime," Joyce said. "And was avoiding punishment."

"Or she simply wanted a fresh start to life," Helen added.

Only Alberta noticed the wistful tone of Helen's voice. She knew her sister was talking about herself and not merely Teri Jo, but she kept quiet and fought the urge to question her sister further about the true meaning of her statement. It didn't prevent her, however, from making a comment of her own.

"*Senza il tuo nome non hai nulla,*" Alberta said.

"You're right about that, Berta," Joyce agreed. "Without your name you have nothing."

"But now that we know Teri Jo's real name, we still don't know anything about her," Jinx said. "Like where she's from."

"Yes, we do!" Alberta shrieked. "Brooklyn!"

They all turned to look at Alberta as if she had screamed "Fire!" in a crowded bingo hall. But when she demonstrated the logic behind her theory, they felt like they hit the jackpot.

"If her first name was fake, her last name was fake too," Alberta said. "Reverse Linbruck and what do you get?"

"Kcurbnil?" Jinx replied.

"No!" Joyce cried. "The reverse of Lin-bruck is Brook-lyn. That's genius, Berta."

"Now all we have to do is find out where in Brooklyn this Theresa Josefina Rizzoli came from," Alberta said. "And, yes, I know Brooklyn is big, but it's not like it's all of New York, just *un piccolo pezzo*."

"That little piece is still pretty huge, Berta," Joyce declared. "Let's start searching."

Pushing aside the antipasto tray to make way for Jinx's laptop, the women began their search into the newly discovered Theresa Josefina's background. Since Rizzoli is a common Italian name and Brooklyn is populated by thousands of Italians, the search was frustrating, with lots of dashed hopes and dead ends. By the time Jinx wrapped the last piece of prosciutto around the last chunk of provolone, she'd uncovered what could be a break in their investigation.

"Check this out, here's a really old food review of a restaurant in Brooklyn from *The Brooklyn Daily Eagle*," Jinx announced.

"What's that have to do with Teri Io?" Alberta said. "I mean, Theresa Josefina."

"Let's simplify things and call her Teri from now on," Helen suggested. "That's how we all knew her."

"To simplify things even further," Jinx added, "the restaurant in question is Rizzoli's Diner in Brooklyn."

"*Davvero?*" Alberta asked.

"Yes, really, Gram," Jinx confirmed. "According to the review, which is from about twenty years ago, the reviewer's waitress was a teenage girl named Theresa, the daughter of the owner."

"*Bugiarda!*" Helen cried.

"Helen! Don't call Jinx a liar, she's only reading what she found online," Alberta said.

"I'm not calling Jinx a liar, I'm calling Teri a liar," Helen clarified, shaking her head in disbelief. "She told me she had never been a waitress before, but she couldn't find another job so she settled for working at the diner. I thought I knew her, but with all these lies she obviously wasn't the person I thought she was."

"Or maybe she was trying to protect you," Joyce said. "Read this article I found."

Helen took Joyce's phone from her, and the more she read the more her eyes widened.

"What is it, Helen?" Alberta asked.

"Teri wasn't lying, she was trying to stay alive," Helen said.

"What are you talking about?" Jinx asked. "Was she on the lam?"

"Sort of," Joyce interjected. "The Rizzoli family is linked to lots of crime. They're not Mafia per se, but their family members have been arrested and jailed for everything from money laundering to insurance fraud to arson. Even someone named Little Lulu Rizzoli was charged with murder, though she was eventually acquitted."

"If I've learned one thing since we started our new unofficial occupation as undercover detectives," Alberta said, "it's that a coincidence is a clue in disguise. And Rizzoli's Diner is one big fat clue."

"Suddenly I'm having a craving for a BLT and disco fries," Helen announced, grabbing her pocketbook from the kitchen counter. "Who's up for a road trip?"

CHAPTER 10

La familiarità genera disprezzo.

What a difference an hour makes.

It took approximately that long to drive from Tranquility to the Holland Tunnel, but to Alberta it was as if they had driven through an actual time tunnel. Gone was the picturesque enclave she now called home, and in its place were the gritty city streets she was born into and where she started her adult life. Staring out the passenger-side window of Helen's Buick as they approached the tollbooth, Alberta felt like she was a newlywed again.

The Holland Tunnel was in Jersey City, but the landscape of the area was the same as Alberta's hometown of Hoboken, which was walking distance away. The smells, the noises, the gray buildings were all the same, and when Alberta took in the sensory onslaught she was taken back to a much different time in her life. A time when she wasn't in charge, when she was beholden to the people around her, and when her voice didn't matter. She saw a young woman, dressed in workout clothes that were tight fitting and probably built to deflect the cool temperature, jogging down the street pushing a baby stroller in front of her. The woman was a mother, but she hadn't lost her own identity; she was living her life—with her child, not for it. That wasn't an option for Alberta when she was that age.

Sighing lightly, Alberta acknowledged that she had taken part in her own submission, she didn't fight back, she willingly retreated because she thought it wouldn't do any good to speak up. Now, watching this stranger who Alberta assumed without any basis in fact was a strong-willed woman determined to be her husband's equal, she wondered if it would have made a difference if she had started a one-woman revolution when she was first married. Would it have made Sammy look at her differently? Would her children have respected her more? Or would it have made her marriage implode before her first anniversary? She would never know, and, smiling, Alberta knew that was okay because at least she hadn't stayed that same weak woman who was unwilling to take a chance. She had changed, thanks in large part to the women in the car with her. Women who were having their own trips down memory lane.

"I remember Anthony had to drive through this tunnel some nights to pick me up from the office when I had to work late," Joyce remembered. "He didn't want me to take a cab because he said it was expensive and the subway and the trains were too dangerous late at night."

"My brother was a good husband," Alberta said. "For a while."

Joyce laughed and leaned forward to slap Alberta on

the shoulder in mock retaliation. "He was good for a good, long while."

"I still don't understand why the two of you separated, Aunt Joyce," Jinx commented.

"That makes two of us," Alberta added.

Joyce grinned, but this time it was linked to special memories of her husband, private moments that she would never share with anyone, but the existence of which made her happy.

"We grew apart, it's that simple," Joyce started. "We realized that we wanted different things out of the final years of our lives, and neither one of us was willing to compromise. He gets to fish in Florida and I get to solve crimes with some badass ladies in New Jersey. I think I got the better part of the deal."

The women were chattering so much they hardly noticed when Helen parked across the street from Rizzoli's Diner. Helen, however, noticed much more than the restaurant, which took up almost the entire block, and recognized the row of shops across the street that were all in two-story buildings with flat, tarred rooftops. Looking to the left, the ten-story high-rise was clearly an old brick structure that had been updated and modernized to be reinvented as condominiums. Its architecture was sophisticated, but not familiar. The same couldn't be said for the advertisement that had been painted onto the building decades ago.

"Is that Rice-A-Roni sign giving anyone else a sense of déjà vu?" Helen asked.

"It does look similar to the block we grew up on," Alberta said. "Minus the diner, of course."

"No, I mean do you have the feeling that you've been here before?" Helen corrected. "Because I do."

"When were you in Brooklyn, Aunt Helen?" Jinx asked.

"The diocese moved us around to a lot of different places," Helen explained. "We went wherever we were needed."

"I had no idea nuns traveled so much," Jinx commented.

"It's not like we booked a cruise, Jinxie, or hopped a flight to Disney World," Helen said. "Though I wouldn't mind visiting Epcot. I've never been, and it would be cheaper than traveling the globe."

"I'll look for a travel agent when we get home," Alberta promised. "But first, could we do what we came here to do?"

"Order disco fries and grill a waitress for info?" Joyce asked.

"Exactly," Alberta replied. "Stick together, ladies, we're not in Tranquility anymore."

When they were sitting in a booth in Rizzoli's Diner, they didn't feel like they were in Brooklyn either. The interior of the diner didn't look anything like the retro design of Veronica's Diner, but it did resemble the design of most every other diner scattered throughout the tristate area.

Right in the entranceway was a glass case that housed a four-level, rotating dessert display. They watched as tiramisu, then lemon meringue pie, then a chocolate layer cake spun by. To the left was a huge dining hall filled with large round tables, to the right were smaller square tables, and all around the walls on both sides were booths.

On the opposite side of the entrance was the counter, which ran almost the entire length of the diner and was complete with every type of industrial-strength kitchen appliance imaginable, all in high-tech stainless steel. Coffee, espresso, and smoothie machines, a high-speed blender, a dispenser for soft drinks, a fully stocked bar, and a refrigerator with glass doors. Where Veronica's Diner was an homage to the past, Rizzoli's Diner was embracing the future.

The color scheme sought to be tasteful, but resulted in being aggressive because each individual element was vying for attention. Deep navy walls with silver and gold lighting fixtures competed with cherrywood furniture, while the fabric that lined the backs and seats of the booths alternated between burgundy with flecks of gold and emerald green dotted with silver, so it, in essence, competed against itself. The colors hardly melded together, but rather created a tense visual tug-of-war, but it could have been deliberate. If patrons didn't know where to look, they wound up looking at the people they came with. Inadvertently, the décor was bringing people together.

"What brings you ladies here?" the waitress asked. "I don't believe I've ever seen you before. Though I've only been working here for six months, five and a half if you don't count my first two weeks of training as real work."

The women had lucked out. They had been in the diner for less than three minutes and they already knew their waitress. Krista, according to her name tag, was blond, bubbly, and a chatterbox. While filling their glasses with water she informed them that the peas were frozen and the gravy for the open-faced turkey sandwich had so much salt in it she believed it was made in the Dead Sea. Helen was the only one who understood the joke.

They had traveled across state lines for more than culinary tips, however, so when Krista brought over their coffee, Helen took a quick sip and moved their talk in another direction.

"Is there a Mr. Rizzoli?" Helen asked. "Or a Rizzoli family?"

"Yes, there is," Krista replied excitedly. "I've never been formally introduced to them, but they come and go a lot around here, mainly at night. Which is, you know, when they get to do most of their outside work. If you know what I mean."

"I don't," Alberta said.

"Me either," Helen added.

"Also too, are you talking about criminal activity?" Joyce asked.

Krista looked around the diner quickly to see if anyone was within earshot of their chat. There was an older waiter behind the counter; the hostess, two other waitresses on the other side of the diner; and all the patrons were chatting so loudly they could hardly hear themselves, let alone a whispered comment.

"Not real crime, just petty things that don't get you thrown in jail," Krista said. "It's not like they're connected to the mob or anything. They're just loud like most Italians. You know what I mean?"

"Yes, now we understand you perfectly," Alberta said.

"And like most Italians, we're hungry," Jinx said, snapping open the leather-bound menu. "Where are your gluten-free options?"

"I'm sorry, we don't have any," Krista replied.

"Vegan options?"

"How about a salad?" Krista suggested.

"I'll have the Greek salad with lemon vinaigrette dressing," Jinx said, slamming the menu shut.

Alberta ordered a chicken parmigiana sandwich, and Joyce decided on minestrone soup and chicken tenders.

"Disco fries and a BLT," Helen ordered. When she saw the women looking at her with surprised expressions, she replied, "I told you I had a craving."

Halfway through their meal, Krista returned to fill up their water glasses and asked if everything was alright. It was the same question waiters had been asking guests at every restaurant from Chuck E. Cheese to Peter Lugar, and the only answer waiters wanted to hear was *Yes, everything's fine*. Krista didn't get her wish.

"The gravy on the fries was a bit too salty," Helen shared.

"I warned you about the gravy," Krista replied.

"I know, honey," Helen said. "It's just that my friend Theresa and I would always get them so I took the risk. Do you know her? Theresa Rizzoli, she's the owner's daughter."

Alberta watched her sister's face carefully and was impressed that her expression didn't show a sign of breaking. She knew that it must have been hard for Helen to talk about Teri Jo as if she were alive and well in order to find out more information about her, but Helen didn't show any signs of emotional stress. She was like a rock.

"No, the daughter's a bit of a mystery," Krista confided. "Nobody really talks about her except in a whisper, because of the scandal."

In perfect unison all four ladies said the same two words at the same time in the same tone, which was definitely not a whisper. "What scandal?"

Nervously, Krista once again surveyed the room, but the outburst hadn't attracted any attention. It helped that

Dean Martin was crooning about *amore* over the sound system and half of the diners had already left, so very few people were on the premises, but still Krista looked a bit shaken since she was talking about things she probably shouldn't be talking about.

"I'm not entirely sure," Krista hedged. "From what I've, you know, overheard, the best I can piece together is that she ran away or maybe she was, you know, disowned."

"*Dio mio*," Alberta cried. "That's terrible."

"I know," Krista agreed. "To be young and feel that you can't even trust your family so you feel like you have no other choice but to run away."

"What about the brother?" Helen asked. "Do you know anything about him?"

"Dominic?" Krista said. "Not really, he doesn't live around here."

"Are you sure?" Jinx asked.

"Yes," Krista replied. "I remember a customer was trying to pick me up, he was harmless so I wasn't annoyed, but when he found out I was an actress he told me that I better be careful not to wind up like Theresa or Dominic."

"Why would he say something like that?" Joyce asked.

"Because he said they couldn't make it in Brooklyn so they had to pick up and leave town," Krista explained. "He was such a sweet guy."

"Dominic?" Jinx asked.

"No, the customer who tried to pick me up," Krista said. "He didn't want me to leave town either."

"That's nice," Alberta said. "Did he try to ask you out on another date?"

"No, the next morning he died," Krista said. "He wasn't

paying attention crossing the street and got hit by the B64 bus."

"*Oh mio Dio è terribile!*" Alberta cried.

"What would make it less terrible is if you knew where Dominic moved to," Helen said, grabbing the water pitcher from Krista and filling up her glass. "He might not have gone very far. Have you seen him lately?"

"I've never seen either one of them, Theresa or Dominic," Krista said. "They're just names to me, and who can keep track with all the names? Aunts, uncles, cousins, godparents, there are so many Rizzolis I don't even bother trying to remember their names, I'm too busy memorizing my lines."

"Are you in a show now that you're rehearsing for?" Jinx asked.

"No, but I have a big audition tomorrow," Krista said. "For the tour of the musical version of *The Godfather*."

"That sounds like a ticket you can't refuse," Helen joked.

Disregarding Helen's clever spin on the movie's most enduring catchphrase, Krista replied, "I take the show as an omen, because the owners of this diner used to own another one called, get this, Godfather's Diner."

"Oh my God!" Jinx screamed. "It's fate!"

"I know! I'm even willing to dye my hair black for the job!" Krista screamed back. "You ladies have been fab, but I need to go over my lines again. I'll get your check in a sec!"

"Jinxie, you can't possibly be that excited for Krista's career potential," Joyce observed. "What got you so fired up?"

"You don't remember?" Jinx asked.

"No, tell me," Alberta demanded.

"I'll tell you on the drive home," Jinx said. "But we just scored ourselves a major clue."

They quickly paid their bill, left a nice tip for Krista, who wasn't a great waitress but was a terrific, if unwitting, informant, and were heading out of the room when Alberta stopped short, causing the rest of the women to crash into her. Alberta pulled Joyce next to her and whispered, "Scarface is in the house."

Joyce looked in the direction Alberta nodded and was stunned to see the man from the Tranqclockery standing on the other side of the diner. His back was to them, but he was on an angle so they could see the long, jagged scar on the left side of his face. The man he was talking to was over sixty and very Italian looking, so there was a very good chance he was a Rizzoli. Whoever he was, he gave Scarface a manila envelope, which Scarface took and then walked through the swinging kitchen doors and disappeared.

"*La familiarità genera disprezzo,*" Helen muttered.

"Familiarity sure does breed contempt," Alberta translated. "First Owen's store, now here. I don't want to get used to seeing that face, but I suspect if we want to crack this case, we're going to have to."

And Alberta was right.

They sat in Helen's car for a few minutes before pulling away so they could collect their thoughts and resume normal breathing, which had gotten uncontrollable when they were frightened by seeing Scarface. It was more of a shock for Alberta and Joyce, since it was the second time in one week that they had seen the man, but Jinx and Helen were unnerved as well. They were all about to be unnerved one more time.

"Holy Sophia Petrillo!" Alberta cried. "There he is again."

There was no need for Alberta or anyone to point across the street, because Scarface was the only one walking away from the diner, to parts unknown. He was moving quickly, but limping every time he stepped on his right foot. It must have been a slight disability, possibly one from birth, because it didn't slow him down and his movement, while not normal, seemed fluid. In contrast, the Buick was moving at a snail's pace, trying to stay several feet behind Scarface to find out where he was going.

He made a left at the corner and thirty seconds later so did Helen. They didn't have to wait much longer for him to reach his final destination, but when he did they were shocked.

"He's going to church!" Alberta exclaimed.

Scarface grabbed the banister and started walking up the concrete steps that led to the wooden doors of St. Ann's Church. Holding on with his left hand, he stepped up with his left foot and then lifted his right foot, which was unbent and pointing to the right, to reach the next step. He shuffled up the steps again at a quick speed until he reached the top and disappeared inside.

"That's it!" Helen shrieked. "That's why this area is familiar to me. I've been here before."

"What are you talking about, Helen?" Alberta asked. "We've never been here before in our lives."

"Speak for yourself, sister," Helen replied. "Before Father Sal got the plum assignment to join the parish at Tranquility, he worked at St. Ann's, and I remember some of the sisters and I worked here briefly with him until the new pastor arrived. Afterwards we would all go to Rizzoli's Diner."

Surprised by the connection to Brooklyn, Jinx replied, "You and Father Sal go way back, don't you?"

"We have what is commonly referred to as a *history*," Helen said.

"We need to dive into that history," Jinx ordered. "Because I'm not sure what's going on around here, but it is definitely linked to Veronica's Diner and Teri Jo's murder."

CHAPTER 11

C'è un fantasma nel cortile sul retro.

Sitting around her kitchen table with her family by her side, Alberta couldn't believe how relieved she felt to be home. It had been a long time since she'd returned to that part of New Jersey where she was born and spent the early years of her adult life, and she was unprepared for how unsettled it would make her feel.

She'd changed considerably since moving to Tranquility, so the impromptu trip brought some dormant emotions to the forefront. Alberta, however, wasn't one to indulge in a pity party or any kind of meltdown. She was and had always been a practical woman. When she felt such strong emotions of fear, regret, and anger rise up within her, she smiled, because those were all remnants of the past. She had no need for those feelings in her current life. All she needed was her family, a pitcher of Red

Herrings, and two boxes of Entenmann's cakes. Looking around her kitchen, she had all three.

"Sorry, lovey, what did you say?" Alberta asked. "*La mia testa è tra le nuvole.*"

"Your head's been in the clouds the entire drive home," Helen remarked. "Nice of you to finally join us."

Throwing her hands up in the air, Alberta replied, "I was enjoying the scenery, since our driver was such a slowpoke."

"I drive the speed limit, Berta!" Helen exclaimed. "I don't know what math everybody took in school, but fifty-five doesn't mean seventy."

"Ignore them, Jinx," Joyce interrupted. "Tell us again about the diner connection so we can start organizing all the clues."

Jinx pulled her long black hair back from both sides of her face, and with dexterous fingers used an elastic band to gather it into a ponytail. It's what she called a business trick. She loved her long, wavy hair, but noticed that some people—and not just men—didn't take her as seriously when her hair was flowing freely. After some not-so-scientific experiments, she'd discovered that she was observed in a more professional light when her hair was either straightened or pulled back off her face. She didn't have time to blow out her hair, so a ponytail would have to do. It was time to get serious.

"Vinny told us that before Veronica's Diner was Veronica's Diner, it was Godfather's Diner," Jinx conveyed. "If the owners of Rizzoli's Diner once owned a diner named Godfather's Diner, it's more than possible that they owned the Godfather's Diner in Tranquility."

"Which means that Teri Jo wasn't here randomly. She didn't just move to Tranquility because it's a beautiful town," Alberta suggested. "She moved here for the same reason I did, because she had family ties."

"Also too, if the Rizzolis from Brooklyn owned Godfather's Diner, they might be connected to Third Wheel, Inc., the parent company that owns the diner," Joyce added. "That could be the real link that ties all the diners together."

Raising a bloody-red glass, Helen declared, "Veronica's Diner, Rizzoli's Diner, Godfather's Diner, that's a whole lotta diners if you ask me. I don't think the Galloping Gourmet could keep up with all of them."

"Who's the Galloping Gourmet?" Jinx asked.

"He's kind of like the Gordon Ramsay of the late sixties and early seventies," Joyce explained. "If Gordon always prepared a meal with a wineglass surgically attached to his hand."

"I loved the Galloping Gourmet!" Alberta cried. "How do you think I learned to make meatloaf? Not from Mama, that's for sure."

"I'll be sure to YouTube him, but let's remain focused, ladies," Jinx admonished. "If Third Wheel, Inc., connects all the diners, maybe that's why Teri Jo was killed."

"Because she knew something about the parent company?" Joyce asked.

"Possibly," Jinx replied. "Or she somehow got mixed up with shady corporate dealings. I'm not sure if there really is a connection, but I think we need to find out more about this Third Wheel, Inc., before ruling it out."

"We also need to find out more about Veronica," Helen declared.

The mention of the woman's name no longer evoked sighs or cries of adoration for her delicious edible creations like it did before the murder. No more unapolo-

getic confessions about how much they loved her blueberry pie, her pot roast, eggs Benedict, or even the fresh-
ness and smooth taste of her coffee. One fateful morning
changed all of that. Now when the V word was spoken, it
filled the women with a mixture of dread, curiosity, and
distrust.

"Helen's right," Alberta said. "If Veronica's Diner is
somehow linked to Teri Jo's past, then maybe Veronica
herself is linked to her past as well."

"The woman's already lied about being married and
that Teri Jo had no siblings," Helen recounted. "Who
knows what else she's lying about and what other secrets
she's hiding?"

The consensus around the table was that Helen, unfortunately, was right. Veronica was their prime suspect, if
not in the murder itself then in uncovering the truth behind the reason for the murder. But if Veronica had already lied to them and presumably to the police, and if
she had built up a wall between her present and her past
to keep both worlds completely separate, she was crafty
and unscrupulous, which meant she was always on her
guard. If they wanted to pull information out of her, they
needed to figure out a way to do it without making her
suspicious.

"That's going to be tough," Alberta announced, taking
a bite out of an Entenmann's cherry pie. "She already
knows we're amateur detectives."

"Then maybe we use that to our advantage," Jinx suggested.

"What do you mean?" Alberta asked. "Highlight the
fact that we're detectives when we ask her questions?"

"No! That we're amateurs," Jinx clarified. "Let her

think we're four nosy women who like to stick our noses into other people's business."

"Isn't that what we are, Jinxie?" Helen asked.

"Shut up, Helen," Alberta chided. "We're much more than that, and you know it. And I promise you right here and now that whatever tactic we use, we will find out who killed your friend."

Helen looked at her sister, her expression immobile, and nodded her head almost imperceptibly. She acknowledged the comment, but she wasn't yet able to acknowledge the emotions that were wrestling within her. Helen, like her sister, was also on an emotional journey, traveling from childhood to her years spent in the convent to the present day, living the life of a former nun surrounded by friends and family that was filled with purpose and order, but not a recognition of what had led her to this point. That day would come, but it hadn't arrived just yet.

"I know you will," Helen said. "It's the least you could do for me for chauffeuring you people all over the place."

The laughter that erupted around the table almost drowned out the noise outside. It might have gone unnoticed if not for two reasons. It was the second time they'd heard a noise in the backyard in almost as many days, and Lola raced into the kitchen, leapt onto the counter, and tapped a paw against the kitchen window. The women might not be aware, but Lola knew that something or someone was outside.

"Do you think someone is trying to break in again?" Joyce whispered.

"There's only one way to find out," Alberta replied.

Grabbing a frying pan from the drainer next to the sink, Alberta peered out the kitchen window, but didn't see anyone in the darkness. She opened the cabinet door underneath the sink, pulled out a bottle of Mr. Clean, and handed it to Helen.

"You want me to scour down the table in case we're having company?" Helen asked.

"*Non essere stupido,*" Alberta yelled. "Spray it in his eyes."

"Whose eyes?" Helen cried.

"Whoever's out there trying to get in," Alberta replied. "Jinx, hold Lola, and Joyce, take that broom and use it if you have to. I will not be a victim in my own home."

Armed with gumption as well as household products, Alberta led the group to the back door. She hesitated only a moment as she said a quick prayer and touched the gold crucifix around her neck. It was always good to make a spiritual connection before going into battle.

Alberta counted out loud to three, and then yanked opened the door. A cool breeze hit them in their faces and swept inside the kitchen, but nothing more. Once again the backyard was empty.

"Maybe it was one of the cops from the front doing a walk-by in the back?" Jinx suggested.

"I forgot they were doing that," Alberta said. "That could be all it is, but I'd feel better if we checked it out ourselves."

"But isn't that why the police are stationed out front?" Joyce asked.

"God helps those who help themselves, Joyce," Alberta replied, and then added in a much louder voice, "and God help anyone who's in my backyard!"

The four women moved as a group outside, each looking around to see if they could find an intruder, whether that be animal or human. The full moon cast a bright glow over the area, and the reflection off Memory Lake created a shimmering effect that was ethereal, but also allowed for better visibility.

Garnering more courage, each woman spread out in a different direction in their search. Joyce walked past the hydrangea bushes. Jinx went around the right side by the central air unit and a decorative bench that as far as she knew had never been sat on. Alberta walked to the left, getting close to the lake's edge and looking inside the shrubbery and foliage that populated that area; while Helen walked to the right, past the stone memorial to Aunt Carmela and her friend Nettie that led to the more open space around the lake. Before she could even react to the sound of a twig breaking, she came face-to-face with a ghost, who disappeared before Helen fainted and fell to the ground.

"What was that?" Alberta asked.

"I didn't hear anything," Jinx said.

"Me either," Joyce added.

"Helen?" Alberta yelled.

When her sister didn't respond immediately, she screamed her name again. When there was still no response, the women ran to where she had been searching and found her lying in the grass.

"Helen! *Dio mio!*" Alberta cried, kneeling next to her sister and shaking her shoulders. "Helen, wake up!"

"She must have tripped on something," Jinx said, her voice nervous and tight.

"Or she fainted," Joyce said.

Bending down on the soft ground next to the lake, Joyce scooped up some water in both her hands and threw it on Helen's face. Immediately, Helen woke up, her eyes wide, sputtering and gasping for breath.

"*C'è un fantasma nel cortile sul retro,*" she declared.

"A ghost?" Alberta said. "What the hell are you talking about?"

"I saw a ghost in the backyard," Helen said, holding on to Alberta's forearm to hoist herself up into a sitting position and pointing straight ahead. "Right there."

Automatically, the women looked in front of them and didn't see anyone, and then looked at each other and saw the same quizzical expressions. They didn't believe there was a ghost lurking around the bushes or going for a late-night swim, but they also knew that Helen was not prone to lying.

"Was it anyone's ghost in particular that you saw?" Alberta asked, trying hard to keep a sarcastic tone out of her voice.

"Yes," Helen said. "Teri Jo's."

Helen did have a habit of using words and phrases to their maximum benefit, but they were slightly alarmed that she would take such a serious subject as Teri Jo's murder and use it as a punch line. Unless she truly believed what she said. But even if Helen was convinced she saw the ghost of her dearly departed friend, the others would never completely believe her without some proof.

When they got Helen back into the safety of a kitchen chair, there was another noise at the back door that made them jump.

"Ah *Madon*! Not again!" Alberta cried.

Luckily, this time it was the police, armed with the proof they were all hoping they would find.

"Is everything alright in here?" Tambra asked, entering the kitchen. "I heard some commotion out back and wanted to check in on you."

"Tambra Mitchell," Joyce said. "You are an officer

and a gentlewoman. Thank you so much for checking in on us, but it was a false alarm."

"It was not!" Helen cried, wiping her face dry with a towel. "I saw a ghost and I fainted. It was alarming, but hardly false."

"*Basta parlare del fantasma*," Alberta said. "There's no such thing as ghosts."

"I'm not so sure about that," Tambra announced.

"Right after Aunt Joyce gave you such a lovely compliment, you turn on us," Jinx said, shaking her head and Lola along with it.

Tambra had been in the company of the Ferraras long enough now that she was unfazed by their barbs and tangential commentary. In her line of duty as a member of the police force, she had to have compassion, empathy, and understanding. First and foremost, however, she had to have facts. Which she did.

She held up a comic book, and it was the first time they realized she was wearing latex gloves. "I found this out back," Tambra said. "Is it yours, Alberta?"

"I haven't read a comic book in . . . dear Lord, I don't know how long," Alberta said. "And when I did, I preferred *Tarzan* over *Archie.*"

"Can anyone else claim ownership of it?" Tambra asked.

Jinx, Joyce, and Helen all shook their heads in response to Tambra's query.

"Then that means only one thing," the detective said.

"I did see a ghost," Helen declared.

"Close," Tambra replied. "There was someone snooping around on your property again."

Slowly, fear infiltrated the room and started to wrap itself around each of the women. Its tight, unrelenting grip was felt and couldn't be ignored. Ghosts were fanciful and dramatic, but almost certainly unreal, and they didn't pose a threat to the women's safety. An intruder was the exact opposite. And an intruder who paid several visits and displayed a violent tendency was worse. It meant that their lives could be in danger.

It was true that they had been in dangerous situations before, but that was when they were out in the world investigating a case, not when they were within the safety of their own homes. Had they gone too far? Had they misjudged how perilous it could be to investigate crimes? Had they unknowingly done something that had put all their lives at risk?

They had gone into this crime-solving adventure with their eyes wide open, but perhaps they had been too naïve and too foolish to think that at some point they wouldn't bring their work home with them. They didn't have the answers to all the questions they were confronting, but Alberta was certain of one thing.

"You know what else this means?" Alberta asked. She didn't wait for a response before answering her own question. "We really have gotten ourselves our very own stalker."

CHAPTER 12

Toccare il cielo con un dito.

The idea that her life could be in danger hadn't registered in Alberta's mind. She wasn't being naïve, she didn't want to give in to fear. Because if she did, she would abandon all thought of trying to find out who killed Teri Jo or delving into any other mystery that might come her way. Thanks to her granddaughter, she had found a new purpose in life, writing wrongs and exposing criminals who thought they had gotten away with murder. A potential stalker wasn't going to take all that away. If nothing else, Alberta knew she was stronger than that.

However, she was worried for her family. Twice now they'd heard an intruder in her backyard. The person had yet to reveal their face, their motive, or their intention, although on one occasion they took action by throwing Alberta's sundial through her kitchen window. Maybe that act of violence had something to do with the Tranqclockery and was a means of sending a clandestine message to Alberta and her family, but maybe it was just an act of violence and the intruder grabbed the first thing he could find. Both were disturbing for entirely different reasons. One meant their stalker was not the best at dropping clues, the other that he had no desire to offer a clue and was more interested in causing harm.

Alberta's wary nature immediately focused on the latter, since she knew people could be harmful and often lashed out without thinking clearly. But after having worked on several cases involving criminal masterminds, she had begun to adopt the theory that there are no coincidences. That's why she wasn't frantically worried that their stalker was going to step up his game plan and harm them physically. They were investigating a murder that had a link to a clock shop, so a sundial thrown through her window was not a coincidence, but rather a deliberate attempt to gain their attention. Unfortunately, by the next morning it had also gained the attention of the chief of police.

"Why didn't you call me immediately, Alfie?" Vinny yelled from the phone. "Why did I have to hear there was another incident on your property from my own department?"

"I didn't want you to worry," Alberta replied.

"Well, I am worried!"

"That's very sweet of you, Vin," Alberta replied, stirring a pot of pasta sauce that was bubbling in a pot on her stove. "But I'm making gravy."

Coming from the same Sicilian heritage as Alberta, Vinny grew up calling red pasta sauce *gravy*. This sometimes caused confusion, because to most of the world gravy was what was used on turkey, meatloaf, and open-faced roast beef sandwiches. Most of the times Southern

Italians referred to both sauces as gravy, and depending upon the recipe, they knew which kind of gravy they were speaking about. But in deference to those who make a clear distinction between the two, the other gravy was called brown gravy. In an Italian woman's kitchen like Alberta's, there was no doubt which kind of gravy garnered all the attention.

"You're making gravy at seven in the morning?" Vinny asked.

"If I remember correctly, your mother used to make gravy at five a.m. while she was cooking your father's breakfast," Alberta replied.

"You're right about that," Vinny agreed, smiling at the memory. "But that was a long time ago, Alfie."

"So what? If it was good enough for our parents, it's good enough for us," Alberta shared.

Alberta shook the excess gravy off of the wooden ladle and then placed it onto the ceramic spoon rest Jinx picked up for her a while back. It was in the shape of a black cat, complete with a long tail that acted as the handle. Jinx had even used some Wite-Out to draw a streak of white fur over the cat's left eye so it would look just like Lola. Every time Alberta used the spoon rest she smiled and thought of her feline baby. That's when she realized Vinny might be right.

Lola had already gotten out of the house thanks to the escape hatch the intruder created by obliterating her kitchen window. Luckily, Lola was a true Italian and realized there was absolutely no reason to ever leave home. But what if the next time she got a little bit of the gypsy in her and wanted to roam around the area? Or, God forbid, what if the next time the intruder came for a visit he got more brazen and broke in? He might harm Lola to send an even more serious message, or he might kidnap her. When the situation escalated and became perilous, Alberta and her family had proven they could take care of themselves, but Lola would not be able to fend off a cat-napping.

"Are you really worried, Vin?" Alberta asked, her voice now full of concern. "Or are you just being dramatic?"

In response, Vinny's voice blared dramatically into Alberta's ear. "I'm never dramatic!"

"*Non farmi ridere!*" Alberta laughed. "Do I have to remind you that you threatened to kill yourself because Charlene DeFelippo broke up with you?"

"I was seventeen!" Vinny wailed. "I don't think you can really kill yourself by taking an overdose of St. Joseph aspirin."

"I don't know about that, but what I want to know is if you're serious." Alberta asked, "Should we really be worried?"

There was a pause after she posed her question, and if Alberta hadn't been deeply interested in hearing Vinny's response, she would have known what was coming and prepared accordingly. Instead, she got an earful.

"You have a stalker!" Vinny yelled. "Of course I'm worried! You and the rest of your crazy coffee klatch ladies should be worried too!"

Despite the fact that she was irked by his description of their amateur detective group, Alberta could hear the concern in his voice shrouded by the shrieking. When she thought about it logically, she agreed with him. There was someone out there trying to get their attention for most likely bad intentions. However, it also meant that they were getting closer to uncovering important clues that could help solve their case. Despite the risk, they had to press on. Vinny had a completely different point of view.

"I think you should lie low for a while and forget about Teri Jo's murder," Vinny said. "Leave the detective work to the detectives."

"We might not have badges, but we're detectives too," Alberta argued.

Vinny didn't want to get sidetracked from his mission, so he didn't take the bait. He also knew it wouldn't do any good because on several previous occasions he had told Alberta that he needed her family's help in solving a crime. The Ferraras had proven themselves more than capable when it came to criminal investigations, but they were still amateurs and not fully aware of how desperate and downright evil some criminals could be. As the chief of police of Tranquility, and Alberta's longtime friend, it was his job to keep them safe. Unfortunately, he needed their help.

"Regardless of your honorary position in this town and with this police department," Vinny said, hoping his pandering wouldn't sound so obvious, "you need to be careful. This case could be a lot bigger than any of us think."

"You think the Mafia is involved?" Alberta asked.

"No! Why would you even ask that?" Vinny replied.

"We're Italian, Vin!" Alberta cried. "Nothing is bigger or badder than the Mafia."

"They are not involved, but another crime family is," Vinny confirmed.

"Who?" Alberta demanded.

"We did some digging and found out that Third Wheel, Inc. is owned by the Rizzoli family in Brooklyn."

From the other side of the kitchen, Lola, who was lying on the floor, stretched and let out a loud yawn. It was as if Lola was acting out how Alberta felt. Vinny's revelation was shocking news, although they had taken it a step further and connected Teri Jo to the Rizzolis. Alberta wasn't sure if Vinny had discovered that link yet and was deliberately keeping it out of the conversation, or if the Tranquility police force was still in the dark about that important tidbit. She knew that she should share the information she and the ladies had uncovered with Vinny, but she also knew that if she did fill Vinny in, he would use the newfound knowledge to take over the investigation and push their involvement to the sidelines. She was done being a bystander and wanted to be a participant. Still, a tiny part of Alberta wanted to gloat, but the wiser part knew it was smarter to play the fool.

"Really?" Alberta said. "Who are they? I've never heard of them."

"Minor thugs," Vinny replied. "They haven't done anything really bad yet, but they've gotten close. You've got to be careful, Alfie."

"Didn't Tambra say that a cop was positioned outside my house?" Alberta asked.

"Yes, and we'll keep someone on watch, but we can't protect all four of you twenty-four seven," Vinny replied. "You have to help us out a little bit."

"Isn't that what we always do, Vin? Help out the police force," Alberta said. She knew her snarky comment was going to anger Vinny, so she quickly added, "*Non ti preoccupare*. Don't worry, I hear you loud and clear, and will advise the rest of the crazy coffee-klatch ladies to be extra careful until this stalker is caught. Thanks, Vin!"

When Alberta ended the call she didn't even put the phone back into its cradle on the wall, but quickly dialed the other important man in her life.

"Sloan, when do you get in to work?" Alberta asked.

"Well, good morning to you too," Sloan replied, his tone upbeat even at such an early hour.

"Sorry, good morning," Alberta said, her voice sounding much sweeter than a few seconds ago. "But answer me, what time?"

"I'm actually getting ready to leave now. I have to prepare for the big book fair coming up next month," Sloan said. "You wouldn't believe how much work—"

Alberta cut him off. "I'll meet you at the library in ten minutes."

As always, Sloan was delighted to see Alberta waiting for him when he pulled into the library parking lot. Ever since they met, he felt more energized than usual and his life had taken on a new purpose. His life was full before he met Alberta, but now his life had a little more meaning. Plus, a lot more adventure.

"I'd like to think you wanted to see my smiling face this early in the morning," Sloan said, giving Alberta a kiss on the lips. "But I'm sure this has something to do with Teri Jo's murder."

Feigning shock, Alberta placed her hand over her heart and stumbled back into the front door. "*Sono scioccato!*" Alberta cried. "I am shocked that you would think such a thing, Sloan. Utterly and irreversibly shocked!"

Ignoring Alberta's performance, Sloan unlocked the front door and held it open for Alberta to enter "Would Anna Magnani like to make her entrance?"

"Hush up!" Alberta said, walking into the library. "Or I won't let you taste the anisette cookies I brought. Joyce baked them, so you know they're good."

"Culinary bribery will get you everywhere," Sloan joked. "So what lead are we investigating now?"

"Vinny told me this morning that Third Wheel, Inc. is owned by the Rizzoli family," Alberta conveyed.

"That is big news," Sloan replied. "But you were halfway there and made the diner connection."

"I know, but if Vinny found it out that means he's closing in, and the police might soon find out that Teri Jo is actually Theresa Josefina Rizzoli," Alberta stated. "I was hoping you were able to find some more information on Third Wheel that would lead us to Teri Jo's brother, who's still among the missing."

Sloan grinned and Alberta knew he wasn't just happy to be in her presence, which was something she did acknowledge and was learning to embrace; she knew it also meant that he had more information to share.

"Spill it, Sloan!" Alberta demanded. "I know what that smile means."

"It means I can one-up Vinny," Sloan shared.

"This isn't a competition, Sloan," Alberta scolded.

"Maybe not, but I'd rather be the fella who comes to your rescue," Sloan flirted, then quickly retracted his flirt. "Not that you or any of the Ferrara women need rescuing."

"That's true, but a woman always likes to know someone is nearby to rescue her, just in case she needs it," Alberta said. "Tell me what you found out."

Sloan reached for a file on his desk and opened it up. It contained some printouts from the Internet, the first linking Third Wheel to Rusk County Airport in Texas, which was the same state where Helen said Teri Jo's brother, Dominic, was now living. The second page detailed a search for Dominic Rizzoli, showing that he had flown into the airport in Henderson, Texas, multiple times over the last six months.

"This is definitely what Jinx would call a scoop!" Alberta cried. "We have to get in touch with Dominic. He may not even know that his sister is dead. Her family might not care about her, but if Teri was as close to Dominic as she implied when she spoke to Helen, he would definitely want to know what happened to his sister."

"I think I can help make that introduction happen," Sloan said.

Sloan turned the page and showed Alberta that Dominic's flight schedule was almost routine: He traveled on the second and seventeenth of every month.

"The seventeenth is in two days," Sloan said. "You better pack a bag because you're going to Texas."

Later that night, they all gathered at Jinx's apartment to discuss their latest travel plans. Jinx's kitchen table was smaller than Alberta's, so they had to add some folding chairs and squeeze a little closer together so everyone could fit. They also had to use some snack trays to hold the smorgasbord of food, because the array of containers, platters, and bowls wouldn't fit on the table along with everyone's plates. Alberta had brought two trays of lasagna, one vegetarian and the other, as she liked to call it, normal, and a leftover bowl of spaghetti and meatballs. Joyce brought two huge trays of antipasto, and Helen brought three loaves of fresh, crusty Italian bread and three boxes of Entenmann's cakes for dessert.

Sloan came armed with two bottles of cabernet, and Freddy had made the salad himself. He even let everyone know that he mixed his own salad dressing.

"You shouldn't have done that, Freddy," Helen warned.

"Why not, Aunt Helen?" Freddy asked.

"Because if it stinks we'll all know it was your fault," Helen said.

"You know you're gonna love my dressing as much as you've come to love me," Freddy declared.

Silence fell over the apartment as Helen glared at Freddy. How she would respond to outsiders was a variable, an X factor. The truth was that no matter how close Freddy had gotten to the Ferraras and proven his loyalty countless times, until he put a ring on Jinx's finger he would still be classified as an outsider.

Helen broke the end of one of the loaves of bread and dipped it into the bowl filled with Freddy's homemade salad dressing. She plopped the bread into her mouth and chewed for what felt like an eternity.

"It tastes like you made it," Helen said. "Not nearly enough garlic, but good enough." She flashed a quick smile that was just for Freddy's eyes and added, "Just like you, Mr. Frangelico."

Although the evening passed the Helen test, they needed to make sure they could speak openly, since they were going to be talking about classified information.

"Lovey, where's your roommate?" Alberta asked.

"Nola went away with her boyfriend for a few days," Jinx replied. "We have the place to ourselves."

"I'm glad to hear that she's dating again," Alberta said. "Do you like this one?"

Before responding, Jinx made a face and caught Freddy's eyes. Her expression let them all know that she didn't fully approve of Nola's latest beau.

"Ah *Madon!*" Alberta cried. "What's wrong with this one?"

Tilting her head from side to side while opening up the first bottle of cabernet, Jinx replied, "Nothing that involves police intervention, but he's a theatre nerd too, so all the two of them ever talk about is Shakespeare this and Sondheim that. But she seems happy, so I'm keeping my mouth shut."

"Speaking of mouths," Sloan said, "I'm starving. Let's eat."

During dinner no one's mouth stayed shut for more than two seconds. They were either eating or talking or both. First they discussed if they should try and make contact with the Rizzoli family to tell them that Teri Jo had been murdered. They weighed the pros and cons of reaching out or staying silent, including any moral responsibility they might have to share the news, and decided they would, for once, take Vinny's advice and not make any contact with the criminal clan. Trying to find a murderer was one thing; coming face-to-face with a large, corrupt, and potentially deadly Italian family was quite another.

Next on the agenda was arranging travel plans to get to Henderson, Texas, and specifically the Rusk County Airport, in an attempt to make contact with Dominic Rizzoli. Talking to him privately, far away from the rest of the Rizzolis in Brooklyn, was much less scary an alternative.

"I guess I'll need to gas up the Buick," Helen said, biting into a meatball.

"Why drive when you can fly?" Freddy suggested.

"He's right, Helen," Alberta said. "A road trip to Texas would be fun, but it's much quicker to fly. I'll arrange all the tickets."

"You should skip all that and have Owen fly you," Freddy said, chomping on some salad. "You're right, Aunt Helen, next time I won't skimp on the garlic."

"What do you mean, Owen should fly us?" Jinx asked. "Is he a pilot?"

"Mm-hmm," Freddy said, nodding with his mouth full. After he swallowed, he continued, "He used to fly a helicopter at a hospital in Jersey City."

"Christ Hospital?" Joyce asked.

"That's the one," Freddy said. "I thought about getting my pilot's license a few years ago, so I took lessons and Owen was there renewing his license. He's a registered pilot. He even has his own plane. A used one, but still a mighty fine bird."

"As intriguing as that prospect sounds, Freddy, I think we'll need to get to Texas on our own," Alberta stated. "Owen is somehow mixed up in this whole thing. He's connected to Scarface."

"A clock from his store was being sent to Inez, for some unknown reason," Helen added.

"Also too, he knows the brother," Joyce finished.

"Teri Jo's brother, Dominic?" Sloan asked. "How does Owen know him?"

Joyce explained that now that she was embarking on a third career solving crime, she thought it best to brush up on some skills that could come in handy while investigating. Since they were firmly ensconced within the digital age, she thought it wise to learn some hacking skills. Nothing terribly illegal—or at least no skills that she would use for illegal purposes, like stealing someone's online identity or private information for fraudulent use. Just illegal in the way of acquiring data and intel by less than above-board means.

"You astonish me, Aunt Joyce," Jinx said, her voice filled with admiration. "No wonder you were such a Wall Street success story."

"I learned early on, Jinx, that you have to keep learning to keep winning," Joyce said.

"So what have you learned?" Helen asked. "And if I wind up sharing a prison cell with you, I call the bottom bunk. I'm a little afraid of heights."

"I got into the flight schedules for the Rusk County Airport and was able to see the manifests of each plane that landed there within the past three months," Joyce announced.

"That's completely classified information," Sloan declared.

"I know!" Joyce squealed.

"When information is labeled classified, it means it isn't for public knowledge," he pressed.

"Do not steal her joy, Sloan," Alberta admonished. "It's all for a good cause. Continue on, Joyce."

"Thanks, Berta," Joyce said. "It looks like Owen's private plane has made several trips from Henderson that coincide with the dates of the month you said Dominic flew from Texas: the second and the seventeenth."

"Owen knows Dominic!" Jinx cried. "This means he's not just in the thick of things, he might be thick himself." Before anyone could question Jinx, she did it for them. "I know that doesn't make any sense, but you know what I mean."

"It means we have to get to Henderson, Texas, in two days, on the seventeenth, and figure out how to connect with Dominic without Owen getting suspicious," Alberta said. "I'll buy us all first-class tickets when I get home tonight."

"I've already taken care of that," Joyce announced.

"What's this? The rich trying to outdo the richer?" Helen asked.

"Joyce, you didn't have to do that. You know I have enough money thanks to my inheritance from Aunt Carmela, God rest her soul, to buy us all tickets," Alberta said.

"I didn't spend a dime," Joyce announced.

"Which is how the rich get richer," Helen declared, raising her glass of wine.

"Remember my old colleague, Mr. Hurwitz? He passed away, but I'm still friends with his daughter Alison," Joyce explained. "After he died I did a painting of his favorite tree, this huge weeping willow in his backyard, and gave it to Alison. She was so touched she said if I ever needed anything to contact her. So I did, and she's loaning us her family's private plane to fly to Texas."

"*Toccare il cielo con un dito*," Alberta said. "Remember that, Helen? Daddy used to push us in the swing in the park and tell us to do that. Touch the sky with your finger."

Smiling at the memory, Helen replied, "The crazy things we remember from childhood."

"I hope you remember something else from childhood," Sloan said.

"I'm almost afraid to ask what that could be," Alberta replied.

"The story of Icarus," Sloan said. "The boy who flew too close to the sun and fell to his death."

"Your boyfriend's a regular Don Rickles, Berta," Helen snapped.

"He's right, Aunt Helen," Jinx said. "We need to be careful. I have a feeling things are going to heat up in Texas, and if we're not careful we might be the ones who get burned."

CHAPTER 13

Morto che cammina.

Flying in a private plane was yet one more thing Alberta Ferrara Scaglione never thought she would do. It was now one more thing she could check off of her bucket list. Ironically, even though she, along with Jinx, Helen, and Joyce were 41,000 feet in the air, she felt like she was sitting around her kitchen table back in Tranquility.

The layout of the Bombardier Learjet was remarkably similar to Alberta's kitchen. The main cabin consisted of a lacquered mahogany round table with four cushioned buttercream chairs that were made of an impossibly comfortable soft leather, situated on sliding tracks so they could be positioned away from the table and next to the windows for landing and takeoff.

Behind this section was a love seat in the same color and material as the chairs, which faced a small working kitchen complete with a refrigerator, a sink, and a fully stocked bar. Alberta felt right at home.

Jinx surprised them all by bringing along a pitcher of her now famous Red Herrings, and Helen brought some Entenmann's pastries, which were strewn about around the table. Helen played a game of solitaire with her pocketbook resting in her lap, and they truly looked like they were back in New Jersey instead of cruising at 600 mph over western Tennessee. Alberta, Jinx, and Helen were in awe of the surroundings and the latest adventure they were undertaking in a series of long adventures. The only one who seemed unfazed by the luxury and otherworldliness of the private jet was Joyce.

"Fess up, Joyce," Alberta said. "You've flown on one of these things before, haven't you?"

"I cannot tell a lie, Berta," Joyce replied. "During my working-girl days I did fly on a few of these *things*. Once I had to go to London with my team. That was a hoot!"

"You never told us that," Alberta said.

"It was a top secret trip, Berta," Joyce replied. "Had I told you, I would've had to kill you."

"That is insane, Aunt Joyce!" Jinx squealed. "To think that my aunt has flown around the world in the lap of luxury."

"It is quite a perk, but it's not as uncommon as you think," Joyce admitted.

"Says the rich lady to my right," Helen quipped. "Not to be confused with the rich lady to my left."

Alberta looked around the room and realized Helen was talking about her. "Hey, I'm sitting on your left."

"And you're rich, live with it," Helen said.

"There's nothing wrong with being rich," Joyce stated.

"The men who owned the planes I flew in were part of a group. They all chipped in to buy a plane that they shared. Believe it or not, it was less expensive than booking last-minute first-class flights whenever they had to attend a meeting in some far-flung country. They were rich, but also economical."

"I can't believe it looks like a regular house up here," Alberta commented. "I mean, the fixtures and materials are more luxurious, but take away the wings and the cockpit and it reminds me of home."

"That's how Mr. Hurwitz designed it," Joyce said. "He wanted this to be a home away from home for all who traveled with him."

"The way it should be," Alberta concurred.

"You are a rock star, Aunt Joyce."

"There really is no place like home," Helen said. "But a private luxury jet sure comes in as a close second."

"Yes, it does," Joyce agreed.

"Here's to the Fancy Ferrara," Helen said, her glass of Red Herring high overhead. "Long may she reign."

Four crystal glasses clinked, symbolically linking the four women. They didn't need such a gesture to unite them, but it was always important to reaffirm a bond. When they landed in Henderson, Texas, they set out to reaffirm another—the bond they had made with Teri Jo when they agreed to uncover who killed her.

The Rusk County Airport was a one-building facility that catered to small, privately owned planes and the aviation community. To Helen, it was a graveyard.

"*Morto che cammina!*" Helen screamed.

When they saw who Helen was pointing at, they

understood her reaction. Standing five feet in front of them was a man who looked exactly like Teri Jo.

"He might be dead *woman* walking," Alberta corrected.

"Or dead woman's ghost walking," Joyce added.

"Whatever you call it, the dead has come alive," Jinx gasped. "He looks exactly like Teri Jo!"

"You have got to be Dominic Rizzoli," Alberta said.

"And you're Alberta Scaglione," the man replied.

It was then that the women realized introductions weren't necessary. Dominic wasn't surprised by the women because he already knew who they were. They stood for a moment outside the airport terminal, the loud whirl of a propeller filling the silence from somewhere in the distance, and were amazed at how familiar he looked. Despite their gender, Dominic and Teri Jo shared the same facial structure, body size, and even haircut. It was uncanny that they both had an androgynous look to them that was completely natural and not artificially induced.

"You're not just brother and sister," Helen remarked. "You're twins."

"The resemblance always freaked people out," Dominic said. "Theresa and I sometimes wore each other's clothes to see if we could fool people, relatives too. Most of the time we did."

Even their voices sounded alike. The only difference was that Dominic held on to a slight Brooklyn accent that Teri Jo must have worked hard to lose. They wondered if she had to work hard to lose her relationship with her brother, or if that came naturally as well.

"Why haven't you come forward to claim your sister's body?" Helen asked, getting right to the point.

Thrown by the direct questioning, Dominic inhaled

quickly and his expression changed. The jovial spirit gave way to a somber stare.

"And why were you lurking in my sister's backyard?" Helen asked. "You're the ghost I saw snooping around."

Dominic took another deep breath and finally regained control of his voice. "That was me, and I was the one who threw the sundial into your house. I'm sorry if I scared you, I was only trying to get your attention."

"You couldn't just ring the front doorbell?" Alberta asked.

"I don't know who I can trust anymore," Dominic revealed. "I thought the sundial would help you make the connection to the clock shop."

"We have made that connection," Jinx relayed. "But we don't know what the connection really is."

"Or why you've abandoned your sister," Helen added. "Teri Jo said the two of you were close."

An engine roared as a plane behind them took off, the blaring sound making it impossible to hear a word anyone spoke, so it gave Dominic a few seconds to stop his body from shaking and to wipe away the tears that streamed down his face.

"It's very complicated," he said, his voice suffocating with emotion. "I loved my sister, but I knew this would happen someday."

"You knew she'd be murdered?" Alberta asked.

"It's in our family's blood," Dominic replied. "She tried to escape it, we both did, but you can't hide out that long before fate catches up with you."

"You believe it was Teri Jo's fate that she'd be murdered?" Jinx asked.

"If only I had gotten there sooner," Dominic said.

"Gotten where?" Alberta asked.

"It would've been me," Dominic replied. "But . . ."

Dominic was fighting back tears and had to stop talking to pull himself together. The women understood he was upset, but they couldn't allow his emotional state to cost them what might be their only opportunity to question him. They barraged him with more questions about how Owen and the clock shop figured into the mystery, why Teri Jo ran away and changed her name, and why the Rizzolis seemed to abandon one of their own. Dominic looked bewildered, like a little boy facing an angry mob, and even if he could respond and answer each one of their questions fully and without leaving out any details, he didn't have the time.

"Rizzoli! Get over here now! We're already thirty minutes late."

The voice came from behind them, and when the women turned around to see who the voice was attached to, all they saw was a man disappear into a plane that was a bit smaller than the one they had traveled in.

"That's my client," Dominic replied. "I'm a pilot, and I've got to leave."

"Oh no you don't!" Helen cried. "You can't leave without giving us some answers."

"I will, I promise," Dominic said. "I'll answer all your questions, and when I've told you everything, you'll understand why Theresa was killed and who did it."

"Don't leave us hanging!" Jinx screamed. "Tell us."

"Rizzoli! Get your ass on this plane now or you're fired!"

The angry voice once again bellowed over the raging engine. Dominic was torn, and while he seemed loyal to his sister, his loyalty for the moment was elsewhere.

"I'm flying to Connecticut," Dominic said, running toward the plane. "You ladies go back home and I'll call you when I land. I promise I'll explain everything to you tonight."

The women protested loudly, but Dominic ran up the stairs and entered the plane. He grabbed onto a chain and yanked the small flight of stairs upward until the panel was sealed. Thirty seconds later the plane drove toward the runway and in another minute it was airborne. The women had nothing left to do but follow suit and return home, where they'd have to wait until they could see Dominic again and finally get answers that would solve this mystery.

Seven hours later, Alberta's house phone rang and all four women sitting around the table, as well as Lola, who was being cradled in Jinx's arms, jumped at the sound. They had been expecting a call, but were nonetheless startled.

"Hello," Alberta said hopefully.

"It's Dominic. I'm on my way to Tranquility."

"Thank God!" Alberta cried. "How long do you think it'll take you to get here?"

Alberta waited for a reply, but when none came she repeated her question. The response was silence and then a dial tone.

"He hung up," Alberta shared.

"He said he was driving, right?" Joyce asked. "Maybe he put his phone on *do not disturb* so he doesn't get distracted."

"That makes sense, but I'd rather hear him tell me that," Alberta said as she used the old *69 in order to call back the previous number. The call went through, but it went straight to voicemail. Instead of a personalized greeting, however, an automated voice announced that no one was available to take the call and recited the cell phone number. Alberta grabbed a pen and a notepad and jotted down the number so she'd have it to use if necessary and hung up just as the beep sounded for her to leave a message.

The same thing happened when Alberta tried to call the number at half past midnight. Once again she resisted the urge to leave a message because her detective instincts took over. She knew that the police would be able to find her home phone number listed on Dominic's cell phone, but if she didn't leave a message they would never know what they discussed. It wasn't a crime to have a conversation, but she knew Vinny would not be happy if he found out she had made contact with Teri Jo's twin brother without telling him. She would be happy to reveal everything to Vinny after she spoke with Dominic. But that encounter, for now, was put on hold.

All four women crashed at Alberta's house, hoping to be awoken in the middle of the night by Dominic's arrival. Unfortunately, they slept like babies until Helen woke up at 6:45 a.m.

"Berta," Helen whispered loudly, lying next to Alberta in her bed. "Are you up?"

"I am now," Alberta replied, her voice groggy with sleep.

"He never showed," Helen said.

Sitting up in bed, Alberta looked over at the alarm clock and saw the sun pouring through her bedroom window. Lola meowed and jumped onto the bed. She ignored Alberta's waiting arms and scurried next to Helen, where she ran around in a few circles before cuddling next to Helen's head.

"At least we can count on Lola never to disappoint us," Alberta joked.

"Unlike the Rizzoli twins," Helen said. "Looks like they're both liars."

Alberta could see the pain in her sister's eyes, and she wished she could alleviate some of that pain and disagree with her, but Alberta knew Helen was right. Teri Jo had done nothing but lie ever since she came to Tranquility, so it shouldn't come as a shock to know that her brother was a liar as well.

"Maybe he was telling us what we wanted to hear so we wouldn't bother him any longer," Alberta suggested. "Which doesn't explain why he threw a sundial through my window, but obviously he had no real intention of coming to meet us and help us solve his sister's murder."

"Sometimes I really do question mankind," Helen muttered while dragging her fingers through Lola's fur. "And when that happens I get hungry. Let's go get some breakfast."

"Are you sure we should be here?" Jinx asked, as they pulled into the parking lot.

"Where else do you go when you have a craving for eggs Benedict?" Helen asked. "You go to the scene of the crime, so to speak."

They entered Veronica's Diner and were happy to see that there were several patrons seated throughout the restaurant. It wasn't crowded by any stretch of the imagination, but in light of the recent tragedy that took place only a few feet away from the front door, it was good to see that things were slowly getting back to normal.

Veronica disagreed with that assessment.

"It's so good to see you ladies," Veronica said, visibly relieved to see familiar and friendly faces. "A lot of the good folks in town seem to be keeping clear of this place lately."

"It's only a matter of time before everyone separates what took place here from the diner itself," Alberta said.

"I'm not sure that's possible, bad luck seems to be sticking around," Veronica said. "Two more waitresses quit, so I'm working double shifts and the ladies' room is still out of order and won't be repaired until tomorrow. With all the police activity, I'm the last business to get fixed."

"Does that mean I have to use the men's room?" Alberta frowned.

"Sorry, yes," Veronica said. "I put a lock on the door so you can lock it when you enter and at least have privacy among the urinals."

"Be right back, girls, time to see how the other half pees," Alberta said.

Locking the door behind her, Alberta quickly surveyed the men's room and couldn't remember the last time she was in one. She thought back to when her son, Rocco, was a toddler and he refused to use the ladies' room while they were having lunch at a neighborhood restaurant. She'd had to have one of the waiters she knew stand guard at the men's room so she could take Rocco in to do number one. She laughed at the thought and realized it had been too long since she spoke with her son; she'd have to rectify that tonight, but for now she had some other business to attend to.

She walked toward the first stall and was about to open the door when she noticed two feet visible through the opening at the bottom.

"*Mi scusi,*" Alberta gasped. "I thought it was empty."

Alberta turned to leave, but realized the man inside the stall didn't respond in any way to hearing a female voice in a men's room. She called out again, but still no response. Standing in front of the stall, she noticed the door wasn't locked, so with one finger she pushed the door open and gasped in horror at the sight. Dominic was sitting on the toilet, his head hanging forward lifelessly, resting on his chest.

The door continued to swing all the way open and banged into Dominic's knee. The action jostled the man's body and caused him to lurch forward and fall to the ceramic-tiled floor.

This time Alberta shrieked because Dominic was not only identical to his sister in life, but also in death. He was lying face down on the floor, and Alberta saw that a butcher knife had been plunged into his back.

CHAPTER 14

Non puoi fidarti dei tuoi stessi occhi.

For the second time in less than two weeks the police were summoned to Veronica's Diner, and not to partake in a late-night cup of coffee and slice of blueberry pie. They were called to investigate yet another murder. One that was almost identical to the first.

"Looks like we have a copycat, Vin," Alberta declared as Vinny entered the diner, followed closely by Tambra and a team of detectives.

Vinny scrunched up his forehead and lifted his right eyebrow higher than the left as he stared at Alberta. If the situation weren't so dire he would've laughed in her face. What did she know about a copycat killer? Then he realized his former babysitter probably knew just as much about copycat killers as he did.

"How did you come to such a conclusion, Alfie?" Vinny asked.

"See for yourself," she replied, leading Vinny to the men's bathroom, where Dominic was sprawled out, face pressing against the tile floor, butcher knife still rising from the depths of his back.

Vinny pursed his lips and nodded slowly. "Looks like we have a copycat, Alfie."

"Gram already told you that," Jinx said, standing behind them in the entrance to the men's room.

"It's not the knife that killed Teri Jo, of course, but it looks exactly the same," Helen added.

"Also too, the corpses are identical," Joyce added.

"What are you talking about?" Vinny asked, looking at the three women huddled together in the doorway.

"Look at his face," Alberta instructed.

Bending on one knee, Vinny lowered himself until he was face-to-face with Tranquility's latest homicide victim. He could only see the left side of Dominic's face, but it was enough for him to understand what the ladies were talking about. It also was enough for him to understand that this was not a random killing, this was the result of a serial killer, and it was absolutely connected to Teri Jo's murder. There was no question about that. The only question racing through Vinny's mind was, Who in the world was this man that he was looking at?

"He could be Teri Jo's twin," Vinny exclaimed, sitting back on his haunches.

Alberta fought the urge to smile. Not because Vinny was finally coming to the conclusion that she already had come to, but because his expression reminded her of how he looked when they were kids. Innocent, yet filled with curiosity and passion. Despite the tragic circumstances, she was delighted to see that her friend had maintained his sense of wonder after all these years.

"Not *could be*," Helen corrected. "That's *exactly* who Dominic is."

"You know the victim?" Vinny asked.

"Sure, don't you?" Joyce replied. "It's Dominic Ri—"

"Linbruck," Alberta interrupted. "Dominic Linbruck, Teri Jo's twin."

Standing behind Vinny, Alberta looked at Joyce, her eyes wide as she shook her head from side to side and drew a line with her finger underneath her chin. It was the universal sign language which meant, "Shut up immediately and don't say another word." Joyce got the hint.

"The resemblance is uncanny," Joyce said. "Who else could it be?"

Vinny looked at all the faces staring at him and he had a nagging suspicion that they weren't telling him the truth, but when he bent down again to get another look at Dominic's face, he couldn't find a reason to doubt them. This man looked exactly like Teri Jo.

Identifying a physical resemblance was one thing, being 100 percent certain that the corpses were related was another.

"Explain to me how you're certain this is Teri Jo's brother," Vinny demanded. "And do not tell me it's because they look alike."

"We're detectives, Vin," Alberta replied. "It's our job to find out things like this."

Vinny rested on his haunches again, but this time he seemed deflated and weary. "What exactly did you find out?"

Alberta chose her words carefully so she could explain how they came to know Dominic and Teri Jo were related, but leave out what family they were related to. She shared with Vinny that Dominic was the intruder who threw the sundial into her kitchen and that with some digging they found out he had an affiliation with an airport in Texas and tracked him down there. The last they heard from him he was on his way back from Connecticut and was going to tell them who killed his sister and why. He never got the chance because he was murdered in the same way and almost the same spot as his sister.

"You went to Texas?" Vinny asked.

"That's your takeaway from the story?" Helen countered. "My sister handed you prime clues you didn't have, and all you're worried about is our flight schedule."

"I think your sister is handing me a bunch of malarkey, but I know better than to ask questions I'm not going to get the answers to," Vinny said, standing up. "What I do want to know is did Dominic say anything that could point to a motive or to the killer?"

"No," Alberta replied. "He said he knew both and he was going to tell us everything, but he never showed up at my place last night, and we didn't see him again until I had to use the ladies'."

"But you didn't," Vinny said.

"Well, no, I never did get to go because I found a dead man in the bathroom stall," Alberta explained. "It put the kibosh on any urge I had to tinkle."

"No, Gram, that's not what Vinny means," Jinx said. "You never got to the ladies' room because you had to use the men's room instead."

"Veronica!"

Vinny's rough cry made the women jump. His voice bellowed out of the men's room into the diner itself, but produced the results he was after. In a few seconds Veronica was standing in the doorway, almost afraid to enter the men's room. Alberta couldn't tell if she was fearful of the dead body lying on the floor or the questions Vinny was about to ask.

Alberta noticed that despite Veronica's attempt to appear put together and normal, the layers of makeup on her face couldn't hide the stress and anxiety that lay just underneath. She noticed something else clinging to Veronica's face. Anger.

At first this startled Alberta. Shouldn't she be saddened that another dead body was found on her premises? Shouldn't she be scared that her diner was turning into a satellite morgue? Then Alberta looked at it from a business owner's perspective. One dead body is bad for business, two dead bodies within a week means the GONE FISHING sign will permanently hang from the front door. Veronica wasn't only looking at another dead body, she was looking at the death of her livelihood.

"Do you know who he is?" Veronica asked.

"It's Teri Jo's twin brother," Helen said.

Veronica's eyes blinked several times, but that was the only change to her expression. "She had a brother?"

"A twin," Jinx clarified.

"You weren't aware of that?" Vinny asked.

Veronica maintained her stoic expression, the only change was that her eyes moved to look from Jinx to Vinny. She was like a statue, devoid of any emotion. She either wasn't feeling anything or was doing a superb job of concealing her emotions.

"No," Veronica replied. "I didn't know Teri Jo had any family. She never spoke about her personal life, other than to say she had had it rough. I got the sense that she didn't want to talk about it, so I never pried."

A believable response and yet few in the room believed her.

Vinny, for one, was less concerned with the specifics of Veronica and Teri Jo's private conversations or with Veronica's knowledge of Teri Jo's personal life. He wanted to know about the inner workings of the diner.

"How long has the plumbing been a problem?" he asked.

"About two weeks, I guess, maybe a little longer," Veronica replied. "It's the sewer line, and it's affected everyone on the block."

"That's exactly what Owen told us, Berta," Joyce added.

Once again Alberta gave Joyce a look that shut her up immediately. Alberta was surprised by Joyce's slips of the tongue since her sister-in-law was usually quite savvy and understood the power of silence. Possibly being in the presence of her second dead body in a short amount of time had unsettled her. Alberta was getting used to finding fallen corpses littering her path; for Joyce it was a relatively new occurrence, so perhaps she hadn't gotten used to it yet.

Just as Vinny turned to face Alberta, Joyce gave her a look that said, *I'm sorry*. Alberta was unconcerned. She had handled Vinny when he was a boy and she was his babysitter, she could handle him now.

"You were next door at the Tranqclockery?" Vinny asked, although his tone made his question sound more like an accusation.

"I guess the cat's out of the bag," Alberta replied. "I was looking for a gift for my sister. Sorry, Helen, it was going to be a surprise."

"You were going to get me a clock?" Helen asked.

"Like the cuckoo clock we had as kids," Alberta explained, hoping her sister would go along with the ruse.

"The one with the little Swiss girl on the swing?" Helen asked, her eyes lighting up at the faux memory.

"Yes!" Alberta exclaimed, then continued the trip down liar's lane. "The one Daddy said came from some relatives in Sondrio."

"I don't remember you having a cuckoo clock in your house," Vinny announced.

"Because you're not a very good detective," Helen snapped. "Have you even noticed there's something sticking out from underneath that dead body?"

Everyone in the room looked down at Dominic's body, and for the first time they saw that he was lying on top of a piece of paper or possibly a magazine. Vinny took out a pocketknife from his pants and pulled out a pair of tweezers.

"Ah *Madon*!" Alberta exclaimed. "Do not tell me that's the army knife you had when you were a boy?"

"One and the same," Vinny declared. "I got it for passing my wilderness survival test in the Boy Scouts."

"It must've been an easy test," Helen said. "Hoboken wasn't known for its forestry."

"My troop spent the weekend at Camp Hope in Ringwood, smarty pants," Vinny said. "Father Donato, our scout leader, gave me this knife and told me if I took good care of it, it would never let me down. The good father was right."

Using the tweezers, Vinny grabbed hold of the item lodged underneath Dominic's body and pulled it out. It wasn't a magazine, but a comic book.

"It's the same kind of comic book that was found in my backyard," Alberta said. "Why would a grown man be reading about Archie?"

"Comic books are super popular, Gram," Jinx said. "Freddy reads them all the time."

"Doesn't he read the ones about superheroes and caped crusaders?" Joyce pointed out. "Not the kids in Riverdale."

Before they could engage in an in-depth conversation about what type of comic book was appropriate for an adult man, Veronica changed the subject by almost fainting. She leaned to the side and didn't fall to the ground only because she reached out to grab on to a sink.

"Sorry, I haven't eaten today and I guess I'm light-headed," she explained.

Quickly, Vinny placed the comic book on the floor and grabbed Veronica's arm to steady her. He called for Tambra and instructed her to get Veronica something to eat and to stay with her until she felt better. When Veronica left the room, all thoughts of comic books and superheroes were a thing of the past, and they concentrated on the matter at hand, namely the dead body in the room.

"I think Dominic was the real target of the first murder and not Teri Jo," Alberta declared.

"How'd you come to that conclusion, Gram?"

"Isn't it obvious?" Alberta asked. "The poor girl got in the way."

"How did she do that?" Vinny wanted to know.

"Because she must have used the men's room instead of the ladies' room, which was still broken the morning she was killed, and that was a fatal error," Alberta explained. "If she went into the men's room and someone was already in there waiting to kill Dominic, the killer could have easily killed Teri Jo by mistake."

"That's entirely possible, Alfie," Vinny agreed. "If you

were to look at either of them quickly it would be difficult to tell the two of them apart. They have the same slim build, and Teri Jo's pixie haircut wasn't much longer than Dominic's crew cut."

"Plus, Teri Jo was wearing her waitress uniform that day, which not for nothing, is just as unflattering as my old work attire," Helen stated.

Helen was right. Teri Jo's uniform consisted of a men's white, long-sleeved shirt, black slacks, and black sneakers, hardly a frilly, feminine look. From behind she could easily have looked like her brother.

"*Non puoi fidarti dei tuoi stessi occhi*," Alberta muttered.

"I learned that a long time ago, Alfie," Vinny said.

"Learned what?" Jinx asked. "Sorry, the more I learn Italian, the more I learn I need to learn more Italian."

"Say *that* five times fast," Helen quipped.

"I said that you can't trust your own eyes, lovey," Alberta translated. "The murderer had to work quickly and thought he was killing Dominic when he only managed to kill Dominic's sister."

"This is all speculation though," Joyce declared. "We never actually saw Teri Jo go in or come out of the men's room, we just saw her stumbling down the aisle until she fell."

"But, Joyce, the diner was so busy that morning and we were talking. We could've easily missed it," Alberta said. "Just like we could've missed someone else enter the men's room."

"Someone like the killer, you mean?" Vinny asked.

"Exactly," Alberta replied.

"That's because the killer didn't enter the men's room

from inside the diner, he entered from outside," Jinx announced. "Through the window."

They all looked at the closed window at the far end of the bathroom and came to the same conclusion that Alberta and Jinx had determined earlier, that it was large enough for a man to enter—not a man of Vinny's size, but a man the size of Dominic would have no problem entering.

"If someone entered the bathroom from the outside, killed Teri Jo thinking she was Dominic, he could've then escaped unseen by the same route that he used to enter the bathroom," Vinny described.

Shaking her head, Jinx disagreed. "I don't think that's how it happened."

"What do you mean, lovey?" Alberta questioned. "It makes perfect sense."

"It does, but if you look at it from a different angle, it doesn't," Jinx replied cryptically. "Remember when we went snoop . . . I mean, investigating, around the back of the diner? The men's room window was closed."

"Because the killer closed the window behind him when he left," Vinny said.

"Possibly, but think about it from the point of view of the murderer," Jinx said.

Walking toward the window, Jinx positioned herself underneath it and turned to face the group. Jinx held out her hand, mimicking what the killer looked like moments before plunging the knife into Teri Jo's back.

"He just stabbed Teri Jo, and there's a good chance he realized he killed the wrong person because Teri Jo didn't die immediately," Jinx said. "If the killer panicked, even slightly, don't you think he would've looked for the quickest exit to escape?"

"It's a lot easier to leave through the front door than to climb back out the window," Alberta said.

"But you said the window was shut," Vinny repeated.

"That's right," Alberta replied.

"The killer shut the window after he crawled back through it," Vinny deduced. "It was still an active crime scene when you two were *snooping* around the back, so if the window was open the police would've left it that way."

Suddenly, Alberta shuddered. She grabbed for the gold crucifix around her neck and made the sign of the cross.

"Unless it was always his intention to escape by walking out through the diner," Alberta shared.

"Walk right through the door so everyone could see him?" Vinny asked. "That's crazy, that's asking to be caught."

"Not if he knew the diner was absurdly busy that morning," Alberta said. "He wouldn't even be noticed. He would just be another face in the crowd."

"What's so odd about seeing a man walk out of a men's room?" Helen asked.

"Wait a second, ladies," Vinny said, taking a few steps away from them as if they and their suspicions were contaminated. "You're suggesting that someone crawled through that window, deliberately shut it behind him, waited for Dominic to enter the men's room, mistakenly killed Teri Jo, and then just waltzed out the door into the packed diner without anyone seeing him?"

"I think that's exactly what happened," Alberta declared. "I'm just not sure if the murderer knew that he killed the wrong person before he left."

"If he hung around he would've found out," Helen said. "Teri Jo was able to leave the men's room and stumble out into the diner before she died. If the killer waited, or ordered some takeout, he would've seen the whole thing."

Vinny let out a long breath. "I'm not disagreeing with you completely, but if what you're saying is true, we're not dealing with an amateur here, these arc not the actions of someone who's killed for the first time. We're talking about a professional."

"Like an assassin?" Joyce asked.

"Exactly," Vinny replied. "More than likely these were both premeditated murders and not acts of passion."

Tambra entered the men's room with some anxious-looking men standing behind her. "Chief, the team would like to examine the body."

"Of course," Vinny replied. "Time for us to go and let the professionals do their job."

As they all shuffled out of the room, Alberta held back, grabbed Jinx's arm, and whispered in her ear, "I think we know who the other professional is, the one who committed twin homicide."

"We do?" Jinx replied.

"Of course we do."

"Well, tell me what I'm supposed to know."

Alberta took her finger and drew a line down her right cheek. "Oh, lovey, I'm disappointed in you. There's only one possible person we know who could be an assassin."

Jinx's eyes widened and she finally understood what Alberta already knew. Together they spoke the same word. "Scarface."

CHAPTER 15

Omicidio, omicidio ovunque.

Now that the shock of finding a second body had worn off, the truth of the situation had settled in, and it was devastating.

A brother and sister, twins in fact, were dead within weeks of each other, murdered in exactly the same way. But worse than the vicious acts themselves was the fact that their family wasn't in mourning. Alberta knew that the Rizzolis didn't know that Teri Jo, aka Theresa Josefina, had been living in Tranquility and was now dead. She wasn't sure if Dominic was also an abandoned sheep, cast out by the family for some ridiculous reason, but she was certain that his bond with his relatives was tenuous at best. She had no proof other than the fact that she was the mother of an estranged daughter, and she could sense when she was in the presence of a kindred spirit.

Although she had only met Dominic once, he had been on her property trying to catch her attention a few times, and she could see the sadness in his eyes, the desperate longing to connect. Looking back, she realized the same look was brimming in Teri Jo's eyes. The look of a lonely woman trying to fill a void in her life, but unsure how to do it. Alberta closed her eyes and said a quick Hail Mary, not just for Teri Jo's soul, but for her own.

How could she not have seen the woman's emotional pain that flowed underneath the surface of her perfunctory smile and her cordial, but cursory, diner conversation? The woman had been literally staring her in the face, silently asking to be accepted, to be welcomed, and Alberta hadn't noticed or perhaps had even ignored the signs.

Thankfully, Helen had recognized Teri Jo's need to connect with another human being. Then Alberta had a thought that took her breath away: Maybe Helen needed a friend too.

Being Italian, Alberta was always surrounded by people, most of them family members. Not only cousins, aunts, and uncles, but second and third cousins, great aunts and uncles. There were even cousins of relatives by marriage, and then the families of in-laws. Over the years, hundreds of people had hovered around Alberta's kitchen table when she was a young girl, a wife, and now a widow, so she was truly never alone. There were many moments throughout her life, however, when she was lonely. Luckily, those days seemed to be in the past, and she was so happy with her current life that even when she was sitting on the couch by herself with Lola puttering or napping nearby, her heart was full. She was loved and she loved others. When it came to personal relationships, she was fulfilled, but maybe that wasn't the case for her sister.

In Catholic school, Alberta was taught that nuns weren't women. It wasn't an overt education, not explicit, but nuns were described as Brides of Christ, who vowed to live a life of poverty, chastity, and obedience. Even as a child Alberta knew that such a life was a devotion, a true sacrifice, and not something a woman would enter into lightly, but only after much thought and contemplation. In Alberta's mind, the woman had to be strong enough to transcend the chains of gender, had to be more of a spiritual servant than a regular person. How else could nuns accept a life saddled with such harsh limitations and a reward only the truly devout could foresee?

Armed with such an interpretation, Alberta always held Helen in the highest regard. For all of her sister's snarky comments and brusque, no-nonsense attitude, Alberta's love and admiration for her sister never wavered. Alberta could have had the happiest marriage on earth and reared the most successful, life-loving children in the world, and she still wouldn't have accomplished what Helen had, which was to devote her life to one specific purpose without ever asking for or wanting anything in return. There was no way Alberta could match that.

But what if Alberta was wrong? What if there was something that Helen wanted and had never received? What if she had been searching for a connection with someone who wasn't linked to her by blood? What if the only thing Helen wanted was a friend? Could that be one of the reasons Helen suddenly left the convent and quit the only life she had known for forty years? Was the reason as simple as that she no longer wanted to be a nun, but wanted to once again be a woman?

Sitting at her kitchen table, Lola stretched out lazily between a stack of Tupperware yet to be put away and a folded-up skirt that was still waiting to be hemmed, Alberta held her head in her hands and fought back tears and remembered that Helen had said to her that they had to find out who killed Teri Jo, that this would be their most important case. At the time, Alberta didn't really understand the depth of emotion underneath her sister's words, but what if the one friend Helen was able to make had been cruelly taken away from her?

Now that Dominic was added to the body count, another overwhelming truth was added to the mystery, in that it was more than likely that Teri Jo was killed mistakenly. She wasn't the intended victim, she didn't have to die, she was whisked away from this world and Helen's orbit erroneously. Her death didn't have to happen. But it did need to be solved.

Alberta shook off her sadness just in time to greet Helen and Joyce at the door.

"Do you have coffee?" Helen asked as she took off her coat and hung it on the hook over the bench next to the door.

"Also too, some anisette," Joyce added as she did the same with hers.

Alberta smiled at the women and the dichotomy they represented. Glancing at the hutch where their coats hung, Alberta was amused by the tangible representation of their differences. Helen's simple black wool overcoat hung next to Joyce's bright yellow mohair cape. Exact opposites, but somehow the perfect pair.

It was a great relief for Alberta to be reminded that Helen and Joyce had become friends and not just sisters-in-law, but she still knew that Helen's heart ached for the loss of Teri Jo. And for that coffee.

172   *J.D. Griffo*

"Berta!" Helen snapped. "I need coffee."

"*Smetti di urlare per il caffè*!" Alberta yelled, pointing at the kitchen counter. "It's right there in the pot. And the anisette's in the cabinet over the fridge, where it always is."

She watched the two obviously thirsty women maneuver themselves expertly throughout her kitchen until they were sitting at the table, their hands embracing cups of coffee spiked with anisette. Then it dawned on her that she had no idea why they had come over.

"Is this a social visit?" Alberta asked. "Or has there been a break in the case?"

She grabbed Lola, who hadn't moved from the table, and placed her on the floor. Unhappy with being moved and not allowed to maintain her position as the center of attention, Lola let out a long, scratchy meow that Alberta dismissed with a wave of her hand and an Italian expletive that Lola understood meant that she should leave the room without further delay, which is what she did.

"Now that we're alone, tell me what's going on," Alberta demanded.

"I think you got it backwards, sister," Helen said. "You need to fill us in on your conversation with Vinny."

Raising her hands to the sky and throwing her head back, Alberta couldn't believe she had forgotten to fill them in on such pertinent information.

"Ah *Madon*! I'm sorry, I don't know where my head is," Alberta said.

"It's on top of your shoulders, where it usually is," Joyce replied, sipping her alcohol-infused coffee. "Now tell us what Vinny said."

"He agreed," Alberta answered.

After they all had left the men's room at Veronica's Diner so the crime scene investigators could do their job to collect blood samples and DNA evidence, scour the room for finger- and footprints, take detailed information on how the knife entered Dominic's body as well as the knife itself, and, of course, prep the body for its trip to the morgue, Alberta spoke to Vinny privately, old friend to old friend.

"Vin, you have to hold off on announcing Dominic's murder to the public," Alberta had said. "We're closing in on the murderer."

There was so much ruckus and commotion all around them, she didn't need to whisper, but she did in case anyone was eavesdropping.

"You think you know who did this?" Vinny asked, unable to keep the surprise out of his voice.

"I think so, but we don't know his name, just that he has a big scar on his face," Alberta replied.

"That doesn't sound like anybody in Tranquility," Vinny confirmed.

"We think it's an outside job," Alberta said. "Because Dominic wasn't from Tranquility."

"Don't say his name again," Vinny said.

"Dominic?" Alberta replied. "Why?"

"Because if you keep telling me who he is, I won't be able to feign ignorance about the corpse's identity," Vinny explained.

Alberta understood until she didn't.

"But we already told you he was Teri Jo's twin," Alberta said. "And you told Veronica."

"I can handle Veronica. She wants to keep this as quiet as possible, but no one else can find out," Vinny ordered. "I'll say that we found a John Doe sprawled out in the bathroom with no identification on him."

"We won't breathe a word of it," Alberta swore.

"Then no one will find out," Vinny said. "Unless, of course, the DNA tests produce specific results giving me a name, rank, and serial number, so to speak, of the deceased. Then I'll have no choice but to go public."

Alberta stared at her friend for a moment, unsure if she had heard him correctly. She felt like Jinx often did when Alberta spoke in her native tongue. Looking at Vinny, her face a mask of confusion, she translated.

"This means you're going to keep quiet?"

"For as long as I possibly can, Alfie," Vinny replied. "But you and the rest of your senior Scooby gang better work fast."

After Alberta conveyed her conversation to Helen and Joyce, they both raised their coffee cups in appreciation.

"Well done, Berta," Helen said. "Even if that cheeky chief of police called us seniors."

"It's kind of what we are, Helen," Joyce reminded her.

"Speak for yourself," Helen said. "My hair might be a little silver, but I'm still in my golden years."

"Your hair is completely gray!" Alberta shouted. "You're old, we all are. But before we get any older, we have to find out who this Scarface is. I just know that he's our killer."

"You're really sure, Berta?" Joyce asked. "You've never been this certain on a case before."

Alberta avoided catching Helen's eye when she replied, "I guess this case is different."

Doling out slices of Entenmann's strawberry Danish, Alberta informed the women that tomorrow they should meet with Jinx to strategize on how to uncover Scarface's identity. The frightening part was that they weren't sure it was such a wise thing to do. If he'd already killed twice, both times in daylight with witnesses a few feet away, he was not only determined, he was ruthless.

"I hate to say it, ladies," Alberta declared. "But we may have finally met our match."

Sitting across the table from Freddy at Mama Bella's Café, a favorite Italian restaurant on the outskirts of Tranquility, Jinx was delighted that she had found her match. Despite trying to ignore her feelings and tell herself that she was only having fun with Freddy, she was falling in love with him. She had been in love before, or at least felt like she had been, but this was different. The feelings she had for Freddy were deeper, more grounded, and Jinx knew they were the kind of emotions a lifelong commitment could be built upon. For now, however, she just wanted to savor her eggplant rollatini.

"If you repeat what I'm about to say, I swear I will use what I've learned about how to almost get away with murdering people, and kill you," Jinx announced.

"You always say the sweetest things, Jinx," Freddy replied. "What are you going to say that might put me six feet under?"

"This eggplant is better than anything my grandmother has ever made."

Freddy's eyes widened and were almost as big as his floppy ears.

"Dude!" Freddy gasped. "That's like blasphemous."

Ignoring the fact that she had repeatedly asked her boyfriend to stop calling her *dude*, and he repeatedly ignored her request, she had no choice but to agree with him. "I know! Which is why you must take a vow of silence. Girlfriend to boyfriend."

Smiling devilishly, Freddy replied, "If you make a vow to always be my girlfriend."

It was Jinx's turn to smile, although when the long-term ramifications of Freddy's sly comment were fully understood, her smile turned into a blush. "I think that can be arranged."

What was a bit more difficult to arrange was an uninterrupted date night. Just as Jinx took her last delicious bite of eggplant, her cell phone rang. She tried to fight the urge to ignore the call, but lost.

"Sorry, it's work," Jinx said, looking at her phone. "Wyck, what's up?"

"Bingo, Jinxie! There's been another murder."

Jinx's boss's voice was far too gleeful to be conveying such dire news. Lately, however, his exuberance over the rising mortality rate among Tranquility citizens had risen to new heights. As unacceptable as his delight was, Jinx had accepted his tone to be the new normal. She also couldn't berate Wyck too much, because she had discovered that whenever she heard of another murder she shared his excitement.

The loss of life under violent circumstances was nothing to be celebrated, but Jinx was ambitious and determined. And every time a corpse was discovered, it gave her a chance to earn her stripes as an investigative journalist. Morally speaking, she was aware she was working in the shadows. But she also knew that if she continued to be aware of the shadows, she would never fully succumb to the darkness.

"Are you serious, Wyck?" Jinx asked.

"As serious as a heart attack! Or in this case a homicide!" he shouted in reply. "I tell ya, Jinx, since your grandmother came to town, Tranquility has been revitalized. People are talking about us, readership is through the roof! I know murder is wrong, but God bless your grandma, she's single-handedly breathed new life into *The Herald* with all this death she's brought with her."

Jinx opened her mouth to argue with Wyck, but realized that it would be pointless. She knew from experience that when he got into such a feverish, almost manic state, there was no reasoning with him. She even knew without having to see his face that his ears were beet red, the same color as his hair, which always happened when he got excited. The only recourse was to let him continue talking until the fire dissipated.

"A Jane Doe was found in Tranquility Cemetery," he conveyed. "How's that for symbolism? She's being transported to the morgue. Get there now and you'll have the first chance to question the police."

With one look at Freddy's resigned expression, she knew that he knew that their dinner had been cut short.

"I'm on my way, Wyck," Jinx replied.

"That's my girl!" Wyck shouted. "I'm texting you some photos of the body. They border on grisly, so I hope you're not eating."

"Not anymore," Jinx replied, not entirely sure she could handle seeing whatever photos Wyck was going to send her.

"I just sent the pictures of dead Jane," Wyck announced. "Get yourself to the morgue and I want five hundred words to post online by midnight."

Wyck disconnected the call before Jinx could reply, but since she had never been late on a deadline before, there was no need for her to reassure her boss that she would maintain her status quo. When she looked at the photo Wyck texted her, she was unable to maintain any normal expression.

"Oh my God!"

"What's wrong?" Freddy asked.

"It's Scarface, he's struck again," Jinx replied.

She held up one of the photos Wyck sent her, and Freddy immediately understood. It was a photo of a woman, lying face down on the ground, with a butcher knife sticking out of her back.

"*Omicidio, omicidio ovunque*," Freddy said.

The shocks kept coming. "Are you speaking Italian?" Jinx asked.

Nodding, Freddy replied, "If I plan on making you my long-term girlfriend, I thought it would be a necessary asset."

"What does it mean?"

"Murder, murder everywhere," he replied.

"You sound like Wyck, only more poetic," Jinx said.

"I'm taking that as a compliment," Freddy said. "And because I'm the best boyfriend ever in the history of boyfriends, what do you say we finish this date at the morgue?"

"As creepy as that sounds, it's music to my ears."

Incredibly, things got even creepier for the couple on the drive to the morgue. About two blocks from St. Clare's Hospital, Jinx's cell phone rang. She looked down at her phone expecting to see Wyck's name, knowing how anxious he could get whenever they received a juicy tip, but the caller was listed as unknown.

"Hello," Jinx said.

"My sister's been killed."

Jinx didn't recognize the female voice on the other end of the phone, but she understood instinctively that the caller was related to the dead body currently lying on a metal slab in the morgue.

"Who is this?" Jinx asked.

"Gabi Rosales," the woman replied. "You gave me your card when you were looking for my sister Inez. She got herself killed."

A mental picture of the woman staring at her through the crack in the front door flashed through her mind. She also remembered Arturo, the young boy who had answered the door, and a wave of sadness took hold of Jinx as she realized Inez Rosales's son was now without a mother. She silently prayed for the boy and thanked God that she still had a firm hold on her own humanity.

"I'm so sorry to hear that, Gabi," Jinx said

"I told Inez not to get mixed up with those people," Gabi replied.

Her voice was alternating between emotions, so her words were tinged with both sadness and anger. Gabi had more to tell, and Jinx needed to make her talk. The best way to do that was to throw Gabi's words back at her.

"What people, Gabi?" Jinx asked. "How did your sister get herself killed?"

"Because she would never listen to me, she always wanted to take the easy way, and the easy way got her killed!" Gabi cried.

In her short journalistic career, Jinx had already interviewed a wide range of people, from gardening enthusiasts to murder suspects, but they all had one thing in common: They all needed an objective voice to steer the conversation.

"Gabi, how did Inez get herself killed?" Jinx asked.

"She was going to be deported by ICE," Gabi replied.

The full force of a light bulb turned on in her brain. ICE stood for Immigrant and Customs Enforcement, but to a frightened young boy a more relevant way to comprehend the incomprehensible was to call it the Snowman. Which is the person Inez's son told them took her away.

"Was Inez killed in some kind of altercation with ICE?" Jinx asked.

Like most concerned citizens, Jinx knew the immigration situation in the country was heated, and for many like Inez it was frightening. But she also knew that most of the men and women of ICE were doing their job and doing it well.

"No, Inez got mixed up with some other people. I don't know who they were, but it got her killed," Gabi explained. "I saw it happen."

"You saw your sister get killed?" Jinx exclaimed.

"Jinx, who are you talking to?" Freddy asked, one eye on the road and one eye on his girlfriend.

Jinx grabbed Freddy's hand, and with her eyes asked him to be quiet and give her a few more minutes to figure things out. True to his claim of being the best boyfriend ever, Freddy did just that.

"She was stabbed in the back by a man with a scar on his face, the whole right side," Gabi said, now sobbing. "I thought he was going to kill me too, so I ran and he ran after me! I don't know why, maybe because God wouldn't let Arturo be alone without someone to take care of him, but the man with the scar stopped chasing me. I went back later to my sister, but her body was gone."

"I think I might know where she is," Jinx said. "Could you text me a photo of Inez so I can be sure?"

Ten minutes later, as she and Freddy stood over the newest unlucky resident of the morgue at St. Clare's Hospital, Jinx compared the face of the corpse to the photo of Inez Rosales on her cell phone. She wasn't at all surprised to find that the two were a match.

CHAPTER 16

Una bomba a orologeria.

The inside of Alberta's kitchen was almost as cramped as the inside of Inez's cold chamber. A corpse, quite possibly, had more room to stretch its legs. If it could.

As was typical on a Sunday afternoon, the table was filled with plates of food. Alberta's homemade lasagna, made by following her grandma Marie's time-honored family recipe, was in the center of the table surrounded by a bowl of fried meatballs, another bowl overflowing with sausage, braciole, and some more meatballs smothered in tomato sauce, an oversized plate of rigatoni—almost al dente, which was Sloan's preferred way to cook pasta—and two mismatched gravy boats filled to the brim with Alberta's gravy.

Two snack trays had been propped up against the wall to house the many small bowls and trays of cold cuts, olives, peppers, chunks of provolone cheese, three huge

hunks of mozzarella, pickles, and slices of buffalo tomatoes sprinkled with parsley and oregano. There was even
a plate of burrata, an Italian cheese that looked like a ball
of mozzarella, but was softer and creamier in texture and
had more of a buttery taste. Alberta wasn't a fan and
thought it was too milky, but it was Freddy's new favorite, so she made sure she included it in the gastronom-
ically enticing display.

There were also two pitchers of Red Herrings, various
other bottles of soft drinks, and bottles of red and white
wine placed wherever there was space on the table or the
kitchen counter. Looking around the room, Alberta had
no idea where she was going to put the four trays of
dessert that were chilling in the refrigerator, but she
knew, like every Italian woman has known since she
cooked her first meal, she would find room. Food, in an
Italian kitchen, would always find a place.

But the kitchen wasn't only overflowing with mouth-
watering dishes; it was jammed with people too.

Alberta, Helen, Joyce, and Jinx were joined by Sloan,
Freddie, Vinny, Tambra, and even Father Sal, whom Helen
had invited to join them after he presided over morning
mass. And, of course, Lola, never one to miss out on a
chance to socialize, roamed throughout the kitchen, and
between courses was passed around from lap to lap.

It was a joyous, relaxed, and, as expected, loud afternoon filled with laughter and reminiscing and not one
mention of murder or dead bodies. Until Vinny and Tambra had to leave to question a possible suspect in the case
of an illegal import and export business they helped break.
The warehouse was located in Newton, but the driver of
one of the vans was caught speeding in Tranquility, which
was how the local police force got involved.

Armed with two plastic bags filled with cannolis, anisette cookies, and Helen's famous Sicilian cassata cake, Vinny and Tambra thanked Alberta for the delicious meal and said their good-byes before leaving.

"Thank God they're gone," Jinx exclaimed.

"Jinx! That's a terrible thing to say," Alberta admonished.

"It isn't them, Mrs. Scaglione," Freddy said. "It's about the dead body we met last night."

After the gasps, the shrieks, and the chatter in response to this shocking news subsided, Jinx was able to elaborate on Freddy's opening statement.

"I got a call from Wyck last night and he tipped me off that an unidentified woman was found stabbed in Tranquility Cemetery," Jinx explained. "The woman turned out to be Inez Rosales."

Another round of gasps and shrieks filled the room. The ruckus was too much for Lola, as she felt, once again, that the novelty of being in the company of humans had worn off. Head held high, she sauntered out of the kitchen in search of a quieter section of the house to take a nap. Alberta, on the other hand, felt like she needed to take a sedative.

"A third murder?" she said in disbelief. "That makes three dead bodies."

"We can count, Berta," Helen said.

"All found with knives sticking out of their backs," Alberta added.

"Also too, we've made that connection," Joyce said.

"Teri Jo and Dominic's murders are definitely linked to Inez's killing," Freddy declared.

"Which means we have a bona fide serial killer on the loose," Sloan announced.

"You people have the most delightful dinner conversation," Father Sal said, raising his glass of pinot grigio. "Will we be discussing the autopsies over brandy?"

For a moment, Alberta pondered Sal's comment and couldn't disagree with the sentiment. Ever since she and the rest of her family embarked on their career as amateur detectives, their small talk did often navigate toward the macabre and deadly, but they did, after all, have a job to do and it wasn't going to get done by talking about the weather and celebrity gossip. No, they needed to discuss details of the murders, no matter how grisly, as well as the new and curious clues that sometimes fell into their laps. Or in this instance were given to them from one of the corpses themselves.

"This all leads back to the clock," Alberta announced.

"The clock Teri Jo gave us to deliver to Inez?" Joyce asked.

"No, the clock in my bedroom with the lazy second hand," Helen quipped. "Berta, go get it so we can do some further investigation."

While Alberta left the room to retrieve the item in question, the rest of the group cleared the table of most of the remaining dessert dishes and plates. Jinx refilled everyone's glass with what was left of the Red Herring, and once again Father Sal marveled at the post-dinner ritual.

"It's like I'm back on the set of *Law and Order*," he said.

"You were on TV?" Sloan asked.

"No," Sal replied, "I was a consultant for an episode involving the murder of a young priest."

"Can you remember what it was like to be a *young* priest?" Helen asked.

"I was asked to participate because of my expertise in Catholic ceremonial rights and Christian music," Sal replied. "The young man's body was found inside a church organ, and every time the organist played a B-flat there was this squooshy sound, and let me tell you, there are lots of B-flats in our hymns."

"You got paid for this?" Freddy questioned.

"Handsomely," Sal replied. "Bought myself the most comfortable Italian leather loafers. In chestnut. With tassels."

"Maybe when they do an episode about the murder of an *old* priest they can base it on your life," Helen cracked. "Berta, hurry up!"

Perfectly on cue following Helen's plea, Alberta entered the kitchen holding the clock, with Lola in tow. She placed the clock in the center of the table and for a few moments everyone stared at it, expecting it to do something other than just sit there.

"You know what this is?" Freddy asked.

"What?" Jinx replied.

"*Una bomba a orologeria*," he said proudly.

"Listen to him," Sloan said. "Sounds like someone's been brushing up on his Italian too."

"I have," Freddy announced. "Ever since I met Jinx and the rest of you, I've realized I haven't truly embraced my Italian heritage, so I started taking some online classes to learn Italian."

"And one of the first phrases you learned was how to say 'ticking time bomb'? Jinx questioned.

Blushing slightly, Freddy replied, "Dude, I'm on level three."

"We're very proud of you, Freddy," Alberta said. "But

if this clock really is a ticking time bomb, we better figure out what secret it holds before it explodes."

They refocused their gaze on the clock and stared at it as if they were willing the clock to somehow acquire supernatural powers and suddenly speak to them in an otherworldly voice to explain the connection between the Rizzoli twins and Inez Rosales. What reason could there be that resulted in their deadly bond? What was the common denominator among the deceased that linked them together? The clue had to be contained within the clock, but no matter how long they examined it, nothing out of the ordinary jumped out at them. Until Lola jumped onto the table.

Like the rest of the group, the cat wanted to get a closer look at the clock, not to discover an unseen clue, but to play with it. Intrigued by its shape and the way the others in the room were gazing at it, Lola pounded across the table until she was right next to the clock. Purring, she walked counterclockwise around it, rubbing her body against the clock as if it was Alberta's leg and it was an hour past dinner.

"*Dio mio! Scendere dal tavolo!*" Alberta cried.

Lola followed orders and started to jump off the table. At the last second, however, she turned around to avoid landing at Alberta's feet and jumped off the other side of the table, closer to the sink. The quick, spontaneous movement caused Lola's body to teeter and slam into the clock, so when Lola landed on the linoleum she had to scurry out of the way to avoid being hit by the clock, which crashed onto the floor seconds after Lola ran into the safety of the living room.

"Gina Lollobrigida!" Alberta screamed. "You are in so much trouble!"

"Hold on, Gram," Jinx said. "Lola may have just saved the day."

Lying on the floor among the pieces of the broken clock was a small manila envelope. A clue within a clue. Teri Jo may have asked them to deliver the clock to Inez, but the real prize was hidden inside of it.

"Do you have any latex gloves in your pocketbook, Aunt Helen?" Jinx asked.

"I don't leave home without them anymore," she replied, pulling a pair from her purse to prove her point.

When Jinx finished putting on the gloves, she picked up the envelope and placed it on the table. The envelope wasn't sealed, so she simply had to undo the clasp and pour the contents onto the table. What came pouring out were common items found in almost every adult's possession. A social security card, a driver's license, and a passport. Nothing strange about that. Until Jinx read the name on the social security card. It wasn't Inez Rosales, Teri Jo Linbruck, or even Theresa Rizzoli. It was Danielle Ferguson.

"Who in the world is Danielle Ferguson?" Alberta asked.

"I don't know, Gram," Jinx replied. "But she looks exactly like Inez Rosales."

Jinx held up the driver's license and the passport, and the photos on each document were of the same woman. She then took out her phone and showed them the photo Gabi Rosales had texted to her. All three photos were of the same woman, who was currently dead and housed in a cold compartment at St. Clare's morgue.

"Teri Jo was delivering fake documents to Inez because she was an undocumented immigrant," Joyce surmised. "Which is why the Snowman or ICE picked her up."

"What does the clock have to do with any of this?" Freddy asked.

"Because the Tranqclockery is some kind of smuggling ring for the sale of illegal documents," Alberta explained.

"Owen O'Hara's Tranqclockery?" Freddy asked.

"Are there two clock shops in town with the same stupid name?" Helen responded.

"Berta, I follow your logic, but I find it hard to believe that Owen has anything to do with something like this," Joyce said. "I realize you don't know him very well, but you have met him."

"You must have figured out that he's a hypochondriac, nervous, and just a bit eccentric," Sloan added.

"Agreed, he's all of those things," Alberta said.

"I don't think the man has any friends," Sloan said. "How can he be the head of a corrupt operation?"

"The evidence is right here in front of us," Alberta replied. "The documents were well hidden within the clock that Teri Jo was going to deliver to Inez. Teri Jo worked less than fifty feet from the clock shop, so that connects Owen."

"You're right, Alberta," Sloan said. "If Teri Jo was working alone she would've hidden the documents in something she found at the diner, not the shop next door."

"Even if the clock came from the Tranqclockery, there is the possibility Owen knew nothing about it," Jinx mused. "Just because he met with Scarface doesn't mean he was working with him or knew Scarface was using his shop illegally. He could have been an unwitting pawn in this whole operation."

"That makes a lot more sense," Joyce said.

"It doesn't rule him out completely," Alberta argued.

"Not just yet," Jinx said. "But I think I know a way to prove Owen's innocence. Or lack thereof."

The next morning Alberta and Helen went to the Tranqclockery to see if Jinx's plan yielded any results. It did, but not the kind they were expecting.

The women had planned to go to the clock shop and continue the discussion Alberta began with Owen about her phony search to find a clock for Helen's birthday. The ruse would be that Helen found out about Alberta's quest and was so thrilled at the idea of recapturing a piece of her past that she wanted to check out the inventory at the Tranqclockery to see if there was a clock that reminded her of the one that she remembered from so long ago. The real reason they wanted to go was to find out if Owen read Jinx's online article that was posted on *The Herald*'s website late last night.

If Owen didn't mention reading the article, Joyce was going to text Alberta while she was presumably in Owen's presence, to say that she just had to read her granddaughter's latest journalistic masterpiece. The problem was, the Tranqclockery was closed and Owen was nowhere to be found. Veronica, however, was in full view, and she did not look happy.

The women quickly hightailed it from the front steps of Owen's store to the alleyway that separated the Tranqclockery from Veronica's Diner, and found the titular owner staring at her phone and pacing the short distance from the one building to the other. She was so engrossed in whatever she was reading on her phone she didn't even hear the women until Helen coughed, unnecessarily, but loudly.

"Oh for Chrissake, you startled me!" Veronica cried.

"We're so sorry, Veronica," Alberta said. "We were heading into the diner and we saw you pacing back and forth. Is something wrong?"

Veronica stared at Alberta as if she had just asked the owner of the *Titanic* if there was a leak.

"You mean is something *else* wrong," Veronica clarified. "Because ever since Teri Jo was found murdered in my diner, something has gone wrong every single day. If it isn't the plumbing, it's the fact that I have no customers, or sometimes it's a dead body lying on the floor in the men's room."

"What's the problem du jour?" Helen inquired.

"Your granddaughter!" Veronica shouted, waving her cell phone wildly in her hand.

"What?"

Even though Alberta and Helen both knew Veronica must be talking about the article Jinx had written and she wasn't referring to something terrible Jinx had done to Veronica directly, the fact that someone was accusing Jinx of any kind of wrongdoing made them immediately engage in defense mode. They might be women of a certain age, but they were also women of a certain mindset. Being members of a close-knit Italian family, they were not inclined to let anyone get away with accusing one of their own of doing something wrong. They could say whatever they wanted about a family member, but no one outside of the family had that same privilege.

"What are you insinuating about Jinx, Veronica?" Alberta asked.

"No, not her, the article she wrote," Veronica said, her voice much less angry and accusatory. "Didn't you read it?"

Of course they'd read it. They had memorized every word. Jinx wrote that another woman had been murdered in the same way that Teri Jo and the unidentified man were. She identified the woman as Inez Rosales, but didn't reveal any information about the illegal documents she found so she could use that for a follow-up. Indulging in a bit of fanciful writing, Jinx had included the line, *Ticktock, ticktock. Time is running out because the police are close to solving the murders.*

They had all expected Vinny would be upset with such exaggerated prose, but they did not expect Veronica to be so furious. When she explained the reason behind her anger, they realized the woman was justified.

"Now my diner is officially linked to three murders," Veronica said. "How many orders of eggs Benedict do you think I'll be able to sell with that kind of publicity?"

Thankfully, Veronica's cell phone rang before Helen was able to reply.

Then again, the way Veronica was grimacing and grabbing at her hair in response to whatever the person on the other end of the call was saying, it might have been better if Helen had been able to speak. When Veronica pressed a button on her phone to end the call, she muttered something under her breath that was not a phrase that should be spoken in public.

"I'm guessing that was more bad news," Alberta said.

"That was Vinny," Veronica shared. "In light of this third murder, I need to go down to the police station to answer some questions about Inez Rosales. I don't even know who this woman is, but she's helping make my life a living hell!"

"You need to calm down, Veronica," Alberta said. "Tell us what we can do to help."

"Take over the diner for me!" she exclaimed.

Alberta had meant what she said. She did want to help the woman and while it was true that she had enough money to buy the diner, she had no desire to become an entrepreneur at her age.

"I think it's too early to be thinking about selling the place," Alberta said. "This whole 'getting stabbed in the back' thing really is going to blow over."

"I'm not asking you to buy the place, just run it for a few hours while I'm at the police station," Veronica explained. "Luis is in the kitchen, but I don't have anyone to run the front or wait tables. If the two of you could do that while I'm gone, that would save me from having to close up."

"Does a free breakfast come with it?" Helen asked.

"Helen!" Alberta cried. "The woman needs our help."

"And I'm hungry!" Helen cried back.

"You can have Luis make you whatever you want," Veronica assured her. "Including his famous eggs Benedict with my secret recipe. But no, I'm not sharing that. I'd rather close up for the week than give that away."

"I completely understand," Alberta said. "Some secrets were meant to stay secret. Now you go, your diner's in good hands."

Which it was for about an hour, until they had an unexpected customer who didn't want to order anything from the menu. All he wanted was Veronica.

"I'm sorry, but she isn't here," Alberta told the man. "She had to run some errands and I'm not sure when she'll be back."

"Look, I don't have time to wait for her. I have to get back to work," he said. "I'm the plumber who fixed her bathroom the other day. I've been fixing everybody's, but I forgot to take back the certificate I gave Veronica after she signed it, and my boss'll kill me if I don't give it to him. He's got to submit them all to the town this afternoon so we can wrap up this job."

Alberta quickly assessed the man and determined he was telling the truth. He was just trying to do his job; the least she could do was help. "Let me see if I can get her on the phone and ask her where she put it."

"I know where she put it, right in her little office back there," the man said. "I saw her put it in the drawer with the bill I gave her. She handed me the check with the signed invoice and I didn't realize the certificate wasn't included with the papers until I got back to work."

She looked over to the right to a small room, no larger than a closet, between the ladies' room and the kitchen. The door, which Alberta hadn't noticed was open, revealed nothing more than a desk, a chair, and a floor-to-ceiling bookshelf filled with books and files. Alberta knew that snooping around Veronica's personal items was inappropriate, but her detective instincts had been ignited and there was no way she was going to pass up the opportunity to scour through the mysterious diner owner's private office. Plus, she reminded herself, she was going to help out the nice plumber who would otherwise get into trouble, maybe even get fired. There was no way she was going to risk that.

"Which drawer did you say it was?" Alberta queried.

"The top one on the left," the plumber replied.

"Wait right here," Alberta said.

As nonchalantly as possible, Alberta went into the office, making sure Luis was busy in the kitchen cooking up an order and Helen was serving coffee to the young couple who had walked in seconds before the plumber. She opened the drawer, and just as the man said, the certificate was there. She picked it up and noticed it wasn't the only important item in the drawer.

Underneath the certificate and a small stack of papers was a manila envelope, the same standard style and size as the one that tumbled out of the clock. Curious, Alberta pulled it from the pile and was rewarded for her effort when she saw that this envelope was labeled PERSONAL AND CONFIDENTIAL. Alberta only hesitated a moment before taking the envelope out of the drawer along with the certificate. Closing the drawer, she returned to the counter and handed the certificate to the man, while simultaneously placing the envelope on a stack of upturned glasses underneath the counter.

"Ma'am, you are a godsend," the plumber replied.

Startled by his word choice in light of her most recent action, Alberta said, "Not everyone would agree with that, but I'll still take the compliment."

She watched the man leave the diner, and while Helen was socializing with the patrons, relishing her temporary role as waitress, Alberta used a knife to cut through the tape that sealed the envelope. She couldn't believe what she was doing. A few years ago she would never have violated someone's privacy this way; she would consider it to fall in that tempting chasm that lies between a venial and a mortal sin. Now, with the heat in her gut expanding, she knew she had no choice but to find out what Veronica was trying to hide.

When she saw the name that was on the social security card, the driver's license, and the passport that fell out of the envelope, she realized that Veronica Andrews wasn't trying to keep a secret, but someone named Bettina Rizzoli was.

Rizzoli? Alberta gasped out loud when she made the connection. Veronica wasn't upset because Teri Jo and Dominic were murdered in her diner; she was upset because they were part of her family.

CHAPTER 17

È tempo di spezzare il pane con il nemico.

When Alberta saw Veronica walk through the front door, she felt like she was six years old and her grandmother Marie caught her stealing an extra Italian wedding cookie from the jar on her kitchen counter that was always chock-full of Marie's homemade sweets.

Helen, however, was firmly planted in the present. "How's about that free grub?" she queried. "I'm having a craving for Luis's huevos rancheros."

"No eggs Benedict today?" Veronica asked, setting her purse down on the counter.

"I think it's time to spice things up," Helen said.

"I couldn't agree with you more," Veronica replied. "I don't see any broken dishes, so did everything go smoothly?"

"Like Adam and Eve on a raft," Helen replied, refer-

ring to the well-known diner slang waitresses use to refer
to two eggs on toast.

Veronica laughed so genuinely it brought tears to her
eyes.

"Thank you, Helen, thanks to both of you," she said.

She reached out and grabbed both Helen and Alberta
by the hand. Alberta watched her sister willingly accept
Veronica's touch, but for her it was like jabbing her finger
into an electric socket.

"It's nice to know that I still do have some friends in
this town," Veronica confessed. "After spending a few
hours in the chief of police's office being grilled so he
could make some connection between the murders that
took place here and the murder of that poor Rosales
woman, I was starting to get the feeling that maybe I
should pack up and leave. But you two remind me that
this really is my home."

"Take it from someone who's only recently had a
home of her own," Helen said. "Home is where the heart
is. And your heart is right here in this diner. So what do
you say you order me up some breakfast?"

"We don't have time, Helen," Alberta blurted. "I'm so
sorry, Veronica, but we need to leave."

"I completely understand," Veronica replied. "You
didn't expect to have to spend your morning working."

"We actually had fun," Alberta fibbed. "It was good to
help out a friend."

As Alberta took off her apron and folded it, she made
sure she gave Helen a look that hopefully told her to keep
her mouth shut and follow her lead. Family loyalty won
out over hunger, and Helen acted like the obedient sister
and remained quiet until they were in her car.

"What's going on, Berta?" Helen asked as she turned the key in the ignition. "I worked hard for that free breakfast."

"I'll buy you dinner. Just drive me home and I'll explain everything," Alberta replied.

As Helen drove the Buick out of the parking lot, Alberta called Jinx, telling her to leave work and meet them at her house. She then called Joyce and told her to stop whatever she was doing and take the same action. Unfortunately, while Jinx could easily slip out of her office to claim she needed to follow up on a clue or catch an elusive interview subject off guard to snag a quote, Joyce didn't have as flexible a schedule.

"What do you mean, you can't leave?" Alberta asked. "You're retired, you can do what you want."

"Is she in the middle of another painting?" Helen inquired, speaking in a very loud voice to ensure Joyce heard her on the other end of the line. "Tell her Memory Lake will be there tomorrow, it ain't going anywhere."

"Tell Helen I'm not painting today," Joyce replied. "I'm dog-sitting."

"Dog-sitting?" Alberta cried. "Whose dog are you watching?"

"Tambra's. I bumped into her while I was shopping at The Clothes Horse, you know that vintage shop we love," Joyce replied. "She had to go to Trenton to testify against those import/export people she and Vinny arrested, and her usual dog-sitter is sick with the flu. She mentioned she was going to have to put Buster in one of those kennels for the day and I told her I could watch him."

"That's so nice of you, Joyce," Alberta said. "Could you be even nicer and host an impromptu meeting? I stumbled upon a new clue I have to share with everyone."

"Absolutely, come on over," Joyce said. "But bring food if you're hungry. You know my fridge isn't nearly as stocked as yours."

"I'll pick up some pastries and we'll be right over," Alberta said.

Just as she was about to end the call, Helen shouted, "Is Buster people friendly?"

"He's the sweetest boy," Joyce said. "He's a boxer, so he looks tough, but he's a softie."

"Buster, the boxer?" Helen said, contemplating the image. "I know him. He was at the animal hospital after he was found abandoned near the highway. I didn't know Tambra took him in."

"Then it'll be a reunion!" Joyce squealed. "Hurry up, ladies, I'm putting the coffee on."

On their way to the bakery, Alberta texted Jinx to inform her of the change in location, and when she and Helen arrived at Joyce's with two bags filled with assorted fresh pastries, Jinx was already on the floor playing tug-of-war with Buster. When the dog saw Helen he dropped the thick piece of rope he was biting and scrambled to greet his old friend.

"Well, hello, Buster," Helen said, kneeling on the floor to accept Buster's loving embrace. "I wondered where you got to."

Helen giggled as Buster licked her face with his wet tongue and whimpered, clearly excited to see a familiar face. The other three women, Alberta especially, were shocked at seeing such an open display of affection from their normally ornery relative, and while they all had the urge to make a joke or a snide comment about Helen's unusual though thoroughly refreshing behavior, they all knew they would be ruining the experience. Not every

moment needed commentary, some only needed to be witnessed.

The moment Alberta witnessed Veronica's true identity, however, demanded commentary. As well as some
colorful language compliments of Alberta.

"Bugiarda! Imitazione! È la peggior cuoca in città!"

Completely perplexed, Jinx silently vowed to amp up
her Italian language lessons and turned to Joyce with a
silent but physically animated expression that could only
be translated into one word: *Help!*

"Liar, fake, also too, the worst cook in town," Joyce
said.

"I cannot believe that woman has been masquerading
as a poor victim, traipsing around town acting like she's
some innocent bystander who got caught in the crossfire,
when she's been involved with these murders from the
very beginning," Alberta cried.

"I can't believe you don't have half-'n'-half," Helen
said. "What kind of a household are you running here,
Joyce? This kitchen looks like Berta's, but it isn't nearly
as inviting."

The layout of Joyce's house was almost identical to
Alberta's Cape Cod, except Joyce's décor was more modern and the colors tended to lean to more subdued, natural
hues like beige and gray, with pops of navy, deep char-
coal, and in the kitchen, hunter green, which Joyce loved
because it brought a little bit of the lush outside landscape
into the house.

Rushing to the refrigerator, Joyce pulled out a carton
of half-'n'-half that had been hidden from view and
placed it in front of Helen. Now that she solved that mystery for one sister-in-law, she needed her other sister-in-

law to shed light on the other mystery that had brought them all together unexpectedly.

"Berta, do you have proof that Veronica isn't really Veronica?" Joyce asked.

Taking out her cell phone, Alberta told the women to gather around her. They formed a semicircle behind her, with Buster scurrying next to Helen and placing his paws on the kitchen table to get a closer look at what the others found so interesting.

Alberta showed them the photos she took of the incriminating documents she discovered in Veronica's office. The social security card, followed by the driver's license, and then the passport, all attributed to Bettina Rizzoli, showing photos of Veronica.

"I knew that woman was lying ever since she told us she was married," Helen said. "Teri Jo said she never had a husband and if they're related, she would know."

"But how are they related?" Jinx asked. "Do you think Veronica was their mother?"

The three older women all answered with the same single word, "No."

Surprised by their quick and unified response, Jinx pressed on. "How can you be so sure?"

"Lovey, no mother on this planet could sit quietly by after finding out her two children were murdered," Alberta replied. "I haven't spoken to your mother in years, but if I . . . *God forbid* . . . found out something bad happened to her, there's no way I could sit idly by and do nothing."

At the mention of Jinx's mother, the room grew awkwardly silent for a few moments. It wasn't that the air was filled with tension, but with emotion. Everyone had strong feelings about the disintegration of the relationship between Alberta and Lisa Marie, but everyone knew now was not the time to discuss that relationship. They needed to focus on finding out what kind of relationship Veronica, as Bettina, had with the murdered twins.

"There's absolutely nothing on the Internet. I can't find out if Bettina Rizzoli is Theresa and Dominic's mother, big sister, aunt, or a distant cousin," Jinx announced. "It's like Bettina Rizzoli has been wiped clean from the web."

"One thing that isn't clean are her hands," Helen said. "She's obviously mixed up with this whole illegal document scam."

"But is she just a customer, like Inez, someone who wanted to change their identity?" Joyce asked. "Or is she a more willing participant?"

"Do you think it's possible that she's the mastermind behind the whole thing, and not Owen?" Alberta asked. "Maybe she's just using the Tranqclockery to transport documents, and Owen doesn't know a thing about it. It would be the perfect alibi for her."

"What do you mean, Gram?" Jinx asked.

"She could be running the operation from the safety of the diner, but by using the business next door she takes all suspicion off of her and puts it on Owen," Alberta explained.

"I think you missed something," Jinx said.

"Sounds like Berta's covered everything," Joyce replied.

"No, on the photos," Jinx clarified. "Look at this, there's an e-mail address."

Jinx held up Alberta's cell phone to show the women what she was talking about, but none of them could find an e-mail address on the photo in question. Jinx enlarged the photo and then the women saw that underneath the driver's license was a slip of paper with an e-mail address for umbertobottataglia@gmail.com.

"Who's Umberto Bottataglia?" Alberta asked.

"That's sounds like a name fit for a Scarface if I ever heard one," Helen shared.

"Holy Al Pacino, Aunt Helen!" Jinx cried. "You're absolutely right."

"Ah *Madon*, if you're right, that means Veronica is some kind of crime lord working in cahoots with someone as dangerous as Umberto, the Scarface," Alberta deduced.

The women continued to debate the possibility that in addition to Veronica being a restaurant owner, she was also a Mafia princess. They agreed it could be true since they obviously didn't know the real Veronica, and as a Rizzoli she had connections to a minor crime family in Brooklyn. They had no idea, however, if she was the queen bee of the operation, a greedy, low-level employee, or if she was being set up by either Owen or Umberto, or both.

"If Veronica really is a Rizzoli, then it makes perfect sense that Teri Jo would reach out to her and come to Tranquility to start a new life," Jinx began. "Since neither woman ever let on that they were related, they obviously wanted to keep their identities and their relationship a secret."

"If Berta hadn't found those documents, we would never have made the connection," Helen said.

"Yes we would have," Alberta disagreed.

"I don't know, Gram, we're good, but we're not that good," Jinx said.

"We most certainly are," Alberta declared. "Don't you realize that Dominic already revealed Veronica's true identity?"

"He did?" Helen asked. "When?"

"When he died," she replied.

By now the family was used to Alberta's sudden pronouncements, so they weren't terribly startled by this news. However, they were curious as to how a man's death told them about Veronica's past.

"It's all right there in the comic book he was reading when he was fatally stabbed," Alberta said. "Who are Archie's two girlfriends?"

"Betty and Veronica," Jinx replied.

"The Italian version might be *Bettina* and Veronica," Alberta shared. "In this case the two women are one and the same."

"Gram!" Jinx cried. "Wherever Agatha Christie is at this moment, you've made her proud."

"I can make Aggie even prouder," Helen said.

"How can you do that?" Jinx asked.

"Because Archie and the lying, scheming diner owner have the same last name," Helen declared. "Andrews."

"*Mia sorella è un genio*," Alberta said.

"Your sister is a genie?" Jinx asked.

"A genius!" Helen shouted. "As if that wasn't already a well-known fact."

"Also too, another well-known fact is that you should keep your friends close and your enemies closer," Joyce added. "*È tempo di spezzare il pane con il nemico.*"

"That's a brilliant idea!" Alberta cried.

"But let's bring everyone together at Alberta's place," Helen said. "It's homier there and her fridge is more family friendly."

Jinx listened to her grandmother and aunts speak, but she didn't understand a word they were saying. Buster, curled up on the floor at her feet, seemed to follow the thread of the conversation better.

"Sorry, I know we're planning on doing something with the enemy, but what exactly is the plan?" Jinx asked.

"What Italians do better than anyone else," Alberta said. "Have dinner."

The following evening the four women were back in Alberta's kitchen, sitting around the table, another spread of food displayed in front of them, but this time there was a guest of honor. If Veronica realized she had been invited to dinner for no other purpose than for the Ferrara ladies to extract information from her that would get them closer to the truth of who the real killer was, she hid that fact from her hosts. Instead, she focused on the scrumptious meal she was served.

"I can't tell you the last time I had veal piccata," Veronica gushed, savoring the taste of the lemony sauce. "Or broccoli rabe. I can't thank you enough for asking me over, I was going crazy all by myself at home."

Alberta saw an opportunity to finally move the conversation from small talk to something with a bit more substance.

"I don't mean to pry, but I guess that means you never remarried?" she asked.

"No, I was never—" Veronica started, then finished swallowing so she didn't speak with a mouthful. "My first marriage ended so long ago I sometimes forget I was ever married in the first place, but no, I never remarried.

To be perfectly honest, the whole experience soured me from any thought of marriage."

"I hope that doesn't mean you've given up any hope of romance," Joyce said.

Veronica's expression hardened and it was evident she was more comfortable praising Alberta's culinary prowess than discussing her personal life. She was either an incredibly good actress or she believed the women were merely trying to get to know her better, so her features gradually softened and she was able to reveal more about her emotions instead of keeping them safely hidden under lock and key.

"A few years ago I realized that I have a good life," Veronica said. "I'm healthy, I own my own business, I've got a little money tucked away for retirement, and I discovered I don't need a man in my life to make me happy."

"You're absolutely right about that," Helen agreed.

"Of course, no woman needs a man or any other person to make them happy," Alberta said, "but companionship with a special person does bring joy and new meaning to your life."

"I think I'm too old to attract a new companion," Veronica said, laughing as she took a final bite of her dinner.

"That's nonsense," Alberta said. "Look at me. I've found a lovely relationship with Sloan after being widowed. I have enough family and friends around me that without him I'd be fine, but I will admit that I enjoy his company immensely, and he does make a difference in my life."

Sometimes honesty was enough to bring a conversation to a halt. The women looked at Alberta with a variety of expressions—happy, surprised, relieved, even shocked.

Veronica, however, seemed to grow even more comfortable now that she knew Alberta wasn't just a kind older woman, but a vital, emotionally vibrant woman in a relationship with a man. From the look on her face, Alberta couldn't tell if Veronica was dumbfounded or jealous.

"That's . . . well, that's wonderful for you, Alberta," Veronica finally managed to say. "For me, I think time has run out where romance is concerned."

"What about Owen?" Joyce asked. "I know he's got some . . . interesting habits, but he's a very nice man."

"Also too," Helen said, mimicking Joyce's catchphrase, "he's convenient. He lives and works right next door."

At that matchmaking proclamation, Veronica appeared stunned, and she did nothing to conceal her feelings. She stuttered, blushed, and just when it looked like she was going to toss her napkin onto the table and make a hasty exit, she responded to their proposal.

"Owen and I have known each other for a while, but it's purely business," Veronica offered. "He is, as you imply, on the eccentric side, and the only time I really see him is when we have to get together for business meetings because of our family company."

When Veronica uttered the F word, it was Alberta's turn to hide her true feelings.

"Our family?" Alberta asked, trying to sound as disinterested as possible.

"Yes, the, um, parent company that owns some property in town, including the diner and the Tranqolockery, is a family business," Veronica replied.

The next time she spoke it was to announce her exit.

"This has been truly delightful," Veronica said. "I can't thank you enough."

When Veronica reached out to shake Alberta's hand, Alberta was no longer fearful of making contact or dreading the woman's physical touch. In fact, Alberta was so thrilled with what Veronica had inadvertently told them that she turned the handshake into a hug.

"The pleasure was all mine, Veronica," Alberta said, staring the woman directly in her eyes. "You're welcome here anytime."

Once they heard Veronica's car pull away, Jinx, Joyce, and Helen stared at Alberta, trying to figure out why her opinion of Veronica had changed and, if it hadn't, when she'd started taking acting lessons.

"Didn't you hear what she said?" Alberta asked. "She just told us that the parent company, Third Wheel, Inc., is her family-owned business. It's more proof that it must be the Rizzolis."

"To quote you, Gram, *Oh mio Dio in paradise!*" Jinx cried. "I was so focused on finding out if Veronica and Owen were intimately involved, that fact completely went over my head."

"That's why Grandma's here," Alberta joked.

"I guess this means another road trip to Brooklyn," Helen said.

"It sure does, Helen, and don't blow a gasket, but this time we have to bring Father Sal," Alberta said.

"Why?" Helen cried.

"Because Rizzoli's Diner is right around the corner from St. Ann's Church in Brooklyn, and that's Sal's old stomping ground," Alberta reminded them. "If a priest can't get the members of his old congregation to share some gossip about the Rizzoli family business, then I have lost all faith in my religion."

"We can't have that," Joyce said. "I mean, we already

have one heathen in the family in Helen. We can't afford to have two."

Without a word, Helen gathered her coat and her pocketbook. Her face was drawn and expressionless and Joyce was horrified that her remark, which was truly meant to be a joke, had crossed a line.

Just when Joyce was about to apologize profusely for her unintentionally callous remark, Helen turned to face them. She placed her right hand on her hip and held out her left hand, her pocketbook dangling in the crook of her elbow, and did a dead-on impersonation of Bette Davis.

"I'm going to gas up the Buick," Helen announced. "The heathen-mobile will pick you up at nine a.m. sharp. Tell Father Sal not to be late or else it'll be a bumpy ride all the way to Brooklyn."

When she slammed the door behind her, Alberta, Jinx, and Joyce fell into squeals of laughter so loud they woke Lola up from her nap. Once again, Helen had surprised them and, for the time being at least, all was right in their world. Tomorrow, Alberta thought, would be a completely different story.

CHAPTER 18

*Le persone possono morire, ma i ricordi
persistono per sempre.*

When Helen pulled the Buick up to the rectory,
Father Sal was nowhere to be found. Their ride to
Brooklyn had indeed gotten off to a bumpy start.

"We're leaving without him," Helen said, starting to
pull away.

Alberta grabbed the steering wheel and turned it to the
right so the car bumped into the curb instead of heading
out into the street.

"Are you trying to kill us, Berta?" Helen asked.

Ignoring her sister, Alberta replied, "We can't leave
without Sal. He's the reason we're going back to Brooklyn."

"If he doesn't show up, we're not going anywhere,"
Helen declared, turning off the ignition.

She reached for her pocketbook on the seat between
her and Alberta and took out *The Holy Well,* the weekly

newsletter of St. Winifred's Church. "I'll catch up on the spiritual goings-on in town since it looks like we're going to be here until hell freezes over."

"*Basta!*" Alberta shouted as she dialed a number on her cell phone. Before she spoke she put the phone on speaker mode so Helen could hear the conversation. "Sal, come outside, we're here."

"I'm not there," he replied.

"Ah *Madon*! Where are you?"

"I'm at the Tranqclockery with Owen," he said.

"*What?*" Alberta cried. "Listen to me, Sal, do not tell Owen we're going to Brooklyn."

"Why not?" he asked.

"For once in your life, Salvatore DeSoto, be a good Christian and do as you're told," Helen barked. "We're on our way."

Helen shoved the newsletter back into her pocketbook and handed her purse to Alberta. She started the car and revved the engine a few times before pulling away from the curb and into the street. The drive to the Tranqclockery only took seven minutes, but it felt like an eternity because Helen wouldn't stop complaining about Sal. During the short ride she recalled every duplicitous deed and questionable quote that could be attributed to the man Helen declared couldn't be further from what a priest should be. Alberta tried to remain quiet, but as they turned the corner of Main Street she could no longer hold her tongue.

"*Panzana!*" Alberta cried.

"I am not a fibber," Helen protested.

"You are too, Helen, you're full of malarkey," Alberta said. "You and Father Sal are like Cain and Abel. You got some issues between the two of you, but you're both cut from the same cloth. Knock it off and accept the fact that down deep you like the man."

Helen parked in front of the Tranqclockery and turned to stare at her sister. "Do you talk to Sloan this way?"

Smirking, Alberta replied, "No, I save all my sweet talk for you. Wait for me here while I gather up the prodigal son."

"Are you out of your mind?" Helen asked. "If something fishy is going on between Owen and Cain, I want to be a witness."

"What makes you so sure Sal's Cain and you're Abel?" Alberta asked as they walked up the steps to the front door.

"Sal's older than me," Helen replied. "Plus, I wouldn't know the first thing about tending to a farm."

Alberta was about to ring the bell, but she noticed the front door was slightly ajar. Pushing it open, she and Helen stepped into the shop, which was bathed in semi-darkness. It took them a moment to see Father Sal and Owen sitting in the back of the store in front of the curtained partition that separated the shop from Owen's office area and the bathroom. The two men looked identical and were wearing matching black pants, black turtlenecks, and similar black sunglasses.

"Is there a solar eclipse on the calendar that no one told me about?" Helen asked.

"Hello, Helen," Owen said. "Forgive the mood lighting, I'm having one of my ocular migraines and I'm temporarily blind."

"I'm so sorry, Owen," Alberta said. "That sounds terrible every time I hear of it."

"I've gotten used to them, so they've become something akin to a minor inconvenience," Owen said. "But I still like Father Sal to do the eyes for me, just as a precaution."

"The eyes?" Alberta said. "How does an Irishman like you know about the eyes?"

Owen was silent for a moment as Sal continued to mumble some indecipherable words, his hand resting on Owen's shoulder. Owen's sunglass were dark and the sides were enlarged to avoid any light coming in from the periphery, so Alberta couldn't tell if he was looking at her, Helen, surveying the room, or if his eyes were shut. It was a disquieting feeling not being able to make a visual connection and it added to Owen's overall mystery.

He was quirky, introverted, and a man living among relics of time who was something of a relic himself. But Alberta's gut instinct told her that Owen was also dangerous, and she had made a vow to herself not to ignore her suspicions. She could, however, consciously compartmentalize and push those nagging thoughts to the side. Because looking at him now, a prisoner of darkness, she knew Owen might be mysterious, he might be dangerous, he might be living a life of crime, but for the moment he wasn't any different than any other human on the planet. Right now he needed a friend.

"I grew up around a lot of Italian families and they always did the eyes," Owen explained. "I know it's an old wives' tale and nothing more than a prayer to ease someone's pain and suffering, but I find it comforting."

"Sometimes all you need is a friend to share your pain with you," Alberta said.

When Owen moved his head, Alberta knew for certain that he was looking right at her. He might not be able to see her, but they had made a connection. She was suddenly consumed with guilt that in her next breath she was going to break that connection by lying to him. Unfortunately, she had no choice. Owen might be worthy of her sympathy, but he had not yet earned her trust.

Father Sal made the sign of the cross, took a deep breath, and folded his hands in his lap. The ritual was over and it was time for reality to take over. Or a slightly altered version of reality.

"We need to leave, Sal," Alberta said. "The children are waiting."

As should have been expected, Sal had absolutely no idea what Alberta was talking about. Since his amateur sleuthing skills had not been finely tuned like those of the women in the unofficial Ferrara Family Detective Agency, he didn't realize he was supposed to play along with Alberta's comment and not take her words as gospel.

"What children?" he asked, taking off his sunglasses.

"The ones waiting for you," Alberta answered.

She immediately realized her vague reply was not going to satisfy Sal's curiosity or get him to understand that he was part of a ruse. Sal might not have been a true member of their makeshift group of detectives, but he'd been around them long enough to know when they were investigating a crime. He knew they were trying to solve this string of murders and he knew their trip to Brooklyn wasn't a joyride, so he should've understood that Alberta's comments were nothing more than a means to an exit. Watching his confused expression, Alberta simultaneously felt sorry for the priest while resisting the urge to slap him on the side of his head. Frustrated, Alberta did what she typically did when she didn't know what else to do—she looked to her sister for help.

"Helen, would you like to remind Sal of our mission?" Alberta asked.

Helen glared at her sister for a few long moments, but finally turned to face Sal with a fake smile plastered on her face.

"The children at Sacred Heart Academy, Sal," Helen said. "They're expecting you to bless their pets today. So let's get a move on, because a room full of third-graders and gerbils can go off the rails quicker than you can say Saint Eligius, and you don't want him to find out the truth about why you were late, do you?"

Alberta watched a transformation take place as Sal morphed from bewildered to obedient. "Oh no, Helen, we mustn't have that," Sal said, rising from his chair. "Will you be okay on your own, Owen?"

The temporarily blind man turned toward Sal and smiled. "I am now, thank you."

"Should we call for someone to stay with you until you get your sight back?" Alberta asked. "Maybe Veronica next door."

"No," Owen said, his voice stronger than it had ever been. "I've been on my own a long time, I'll manage. I know how to use the voice commands on my phone if I need any help, but there's really nothing I can do but ride this out."

"Speaking of rides," Helen said, "I'll start the car. Feel better, Owen."

"Thank you, Helen," Owen replied. He reached out to his right where Sal stood and, understanding the reason for the gesture, Sal grabbed it. "I don't know that one very well, but I get the sense you shouldn't keep her waiting."

Despite her misgivings about the man, Alberta was impressed. Owen might not be able to see, but he was insightful.

In the car, as Helen crossed the Tranquility city limits, Alberta was eager to learn what cryptic clue Helen sprinkled into her dialogue to make Sal understand they were lying and simply needed to make a hasty exit.

"St. Eligius," Sal replied.

"The patron saint of animals?" Alberta asked.

"That's just it, St. Eligius has nothing to do with animals or pets, he's the patron saint of clockmakers," Sal informed her.

"There's a patron saint of clockmakers?" Alberta questioned.

"Berta, you're Catholic," Helen said. "You should know there's a patron saint for everything."

"Once I heard Eligius's name, I knew I was being a *stunod* and you were trying to leave without giving Owen a hint as to where we're going," Sal said. "By the way, where are we going?"

"We told you, Brooklyn," Helen answered.

"I know that, Helen, but where exactly in Brooklyn?" he asked.

"To your old stomping ground," Helen replied. "Get ready to return to your past."

During the ride, Alberta explained that they were heading to Brooklyn to search for more clues into the murders, since both Teri Jo and Dominic grew up there. She also conveyed the importance of keeping their road trip a secret from Owen, and even Veronica, because the Tranqclockery was somehow involved in the mystery surrounding the murders. They weren't sure if Owen was a willing or unknowing participant, but until they found out some more details they couldn't risk him finding out they were suspicious.

Sal understood that the facts pointed toward Owen being involved in some way, but he said that for as long as he'd known Owen, he'd been an upstanding citizen. "His only crimes are that he's odd and aloof," Sal said. "Owen likes to keep to himself. He isn't the social butterfly inside and outside the pulpit like I am."

Definitely not, Alberta thought, but he could be masquerading as an innocent man when he's really a homicidal maniac. She and the others would dig deeper into Owen's history later. First she was hoping to find out more details on the background of Bettina Rizzoli, aka the owner of Veronica's Diner. With Sal's help, of course.

The priest, however, didn't understand how he could aid them in uncovering the truth about a woman he barely knew, until he saw St. Ann's Church looming in the distance.

"You think this Bettina person was once a member of my old parish," Sal deduced.

"Since Rizzoli's Diner is around the corner, we figured it's a very good chance this was the family's church," Helen said.

"I was only the pastor here for a few months," Sal reminded them. "When Father Timothy passed away so suddenly, the archdiocese transferred me to Tranquility and St. Winifred's. I don't remember any of the parishioners, and I doubt anyone is going to remember me."

The moment the rectory door was opened the priest was proven wrong.

"*Ah Madonna mia!*" the woman cried. "The prodigal son has returned."

Evidently, Helen had been right about Father Sal all along.

Filomena Sammartino had been the rectory house-keeper at St. Ann's Church for the past thirty-six years. It was her first and only job and one that she never applied for. When her children were in nearby St. Ann's High School, Filomena had extra time on her hands, so she started volunteering at the rectory. After a while she began keeping regular hours, and after a few months she was finally put on the books. Father Sal was the first pastor she worked for in an official capacity, and a woman always remembered her first.

"I can't believe you remember me, Filomena," Father Sal gushed. "It's been so long."

"Besides being my first boss, you're the only priest I've ever met who wears such flashy eyeglasses and shoes," Filomena said. "Come in, I just put a pot of coffee on the stove and I have a bottle of Sambuca to top it off the way you like."

As they entered the rectory, Helen whispered to Alberta, "I think we hit pay dirt, Berta. If she can remember that, she's got to remember Bettina."

Looking around the kitchen, all Alberta could think of was her childhood and the countless happy memories she had of spending Saturdays in her grandma Marie's kitchen, watching her cook and learning what it meant to feed a family. This kitchen, like Marie's, was spotless, not a trace of dirt, grease stains, or the remnants of spilled food could be found anywhere, and yet it had the lived-in quality of a well-worn and well-loved room.

They sat around the chrome and Formica table and it was like sitting down for dinner in 1955. The rectangular tabletop was a raspberry color, in a cracked-ice pattern with a white stripe going down the length of the table. The soft vinyl chairs matched the vibrant color, but were imprinted with a white floral design on the backs. Even though the set was decades old, it looked like it came out of the store yesterday; there wasn't a scratch on the table or a tear on the seat cushions.

The cabinetry was all white with simple black hardware, and one of the cabinets over the counter had a glass sliding door so it could be used as a display case. Mixed in with some religious pieces, like a chalice and a beautifully carved Ankh cross that Alberta remembered were popular in the 1970s, were knickknacks you'd find in a typical home.

A small stuffed bear holding an American flag, crystal vases and decanters, but it was a blue and white porcelain clock that brought Alberta back to the present day and the reason they were sitting in the Brooklyn kitchen drinking coffee with a stranger. Well, at least Filomena was a stranger to Alberta and Helen—the way she was chatting with Sal it looked like they were lifelong friends.

"Do you remember Father Augusto?" Filomena asked.

Sal took a long sip of his Sambuca-laced coffee and contemplated the question. "Was he the one who wore the hot water bottle underneath his robes?"

"One and the same!" Filomena howled.

"Why on earth would he do that?" Helen asked.

"It was during a freezing cold spell and the pipes burst, so we had no heat," Sal explained. "Augusto was from Brazil, so he wasn't used to the cold. He thought a hot water bottle would stop him from shivering during mass."

"He was standing in front of the entire congregation

when the bottle broke and from the pews it looked like he was peeing himself," Filomena shared. "*Le persone possono morire, ma i ricordi persistono per sempre.*"

The Italian proverb was like a light bulb that went off in both Alberta and Helen's minds. They mentally translated the phrase and agreed that people may die, but memories linger on forever. It was time to find out what other memories were still dawdling in Filomena's mind.

"You seem to have an excellent memory, Filomena," Alberta said.

"I'll be seventy-six next month and the old noggin still seems to be working," she replied.

"When one does the Lord's work, one is rewarded," Father Sal said as he poured a tad more Sambuca into his half-drunk cup of coffee.

"Truer words were never spoken, Father," Filomena said, crossing herself three times before kissing her fingers and offering them up to the heavens.

Unimpressed with what she considered to be an ostentatious display of devotion, Helen wanted to zero in on more practical matters. So she went in for the kill.

"Prove it," she said. "Do you remember a woman named Bettina who lived in the neighborhood years ago?"

Sal almost choked on his coffee trying to respond to Helen's query. "Holy Virna Lisi! How's Filomena supposed to remember a woman from over thirty years ago?"

"She remembered you," Alberta offered.

"I'm memorable," Sal declared.

"So's Bettina Rizzoli."

Alberta and Helen couldn't believe what Filomena just said. She confirmed that Veronica really was a fake persona and the woman running the diner was Bettina Rizzoli and was somehow related to the two murder victims who were found dead on her property. Suppressing a huge smile, Alberta felt excitement and energy travel throughout her body. Once again, she, with the help of her family, had followed the clues and wound up with answers. All she had to do was follow where this road led and she might discover who murdered the victims.

"Why is Bettina Rizzoli so memorable?" Alberta asked.

A chatterbox by nature, Filomena didn't detect an ulterior motive in Alberta's question and was more than happy to answer.

"Because Bettina was the only person on this block who left and never came back," the housekeeper stated. "This place is like a boomerang, you can leave, stay away for a few years, but eventually you come back, everyone does. Except Bettina."

"How long ago did she leave?" Helen asked.

Filomena leaned back in her chair, crossed her arms, and gazed up at the ceiling. "I think it was the early eighties, because Bettina was about eighteen years old and the last time I saw her she had really big, teased-up hair, blue eye shadow, and was wearing an overcoat with those huge padded shoulders."

"God, I miss the good old days," Sal declared. "People knew how to make a statement with fashion back then."

While Sal mused about the styles of the '80s, Alberta did some quick math in her head and confirmed that Bettina would be the same age as Veronica. No doubt about it, they were one and the same. But why?

"Do you know why Bettina left?" Alberta asked.

"Do you even have to ask?" Filomena replied. "It's the same sad story from the beginning of time, because of a man."

As Filomena told the story of Bettina's sorry past, Alberta was enveloped by a strange sense of déjà vu. When Bettina was still a teenager she was supposed to marry a man—not an Italian, which would have been expected of her, but a foreigner. Filomena couldn't remember if he was Scottish or Irish, but he spoke with a brogue.

Whatever the boy's nationality, he was a good, respected kid, but had one major flaw: He wanted to please his family.

"How could that be considered a character flaw?" Helen asked.

"Family is a beautiful thing," Filomena said. "Until it suffocates you."

Alberta felt heat rise in her cheeks. It was like Filomena was speaking directly to her. She took a bite of the crumb cake to avoid having to speak. Luckily, Filomena was delighted to keep on sharing her story.

"The fact was that Bettina couldn't have children. She had the same problem my sister Rosie had, but Rosie and her Joe adopted," Filomena conveyed. "Bettina never had the chance."

It turned out that Bettina's boyfriend came from a large family who wanted each member to have their own large family, and the only way to do that was to reproduce. Infertile women need not apply. Once the boyfriend's family found out that Bettina couldn't have children, they wedged themselves in between the couple and refused to allow them to marry. To ensure they would be victorious in their quest, they pooled their money and paid Bettina to leave town.

"I guess Bettina saw this as an opportunity to start over, and she took the bribe, left Brooklyn, and never came back," Filomena said.

"I can't believe a young girl would choose to leave her family," Alberta muttered, shaking her head.

"It's sort of what I did," Helen said.

"Entering the convent, Helen, is completely different than taking the money and running off for parts unknown," Sal declared.

While Filomena got up and refilled their coffee cups and put some more cookies on the table, Alberta suddenly remembered a dream she'd had recently about an old family painting and its link to a piece of Ferrara family history. Bettina and her boyfriend reminded her of her ill-fated relative, Viola, and her paramour, Marcello. Just like Bettina, Viola was jilted and it altered the course of her life forever. Alberta then realized she had this dream the night before Teri Jo was killed and before this mystery began. Had she had a premonition? She would have to ponder that later when she was home with Lola and a nice cup of citrus green tea. For now, she needed to concentrate on what Filomena was saying about Bettina's family.

"The Rizzolis aren't what you'd call *amorevole*. No one's ever accused them of being loving and affectionate," Filomena explained. "Criminals, sure, but not one big happy family."

"Do you know what happened to the boy?" Alberta asked.

Sitting down, Filomena responded, "No, he was from another part of town, so he didn't go to St. Ann's. Plus he was studious and didn't play stickball, so he didn't pal around with the other boys on the block. The only reason he ever came around was Bettina, and when she was gone so was he."

Alberta caught Filomena looking at the clock next to the door, and she realized that as hospitable a hostess as Filomena was, they may have overstayed their welcome. It was nearing lunchtime and she did have work to do. But so did Alberta. As they were collecting themselves to leave, Alberta had one more very important question to ask.

"Since you seem to be the memory keeper of the neighborhood and not just the rectory housekeeper, I wonder if you know of a man named Umberto Bottataglia."

Filomena's olive complexion turned white and she fumbled with the cup and saucer she was carrying to the sink.

"Please don't ever say his name again," Filomena urged.

"Why?" Alberta asked. "It's only a name."

"There are good men and there are bad men and then there are men like Umberto Bottataglia," Filomena said. "You need to all promise me that you'll stay away from him."

Alberta and Helen mumbled a promise to Filomena that neither one of them had any intention of keeping. Father Sal thanked her for her sharing her time and memories with them, and blessed her. His invocation seemed to return her to her good spirits, but it wasn't enough to allow her visitors to remain.

"This has been a lovely diversion, but I'm behind schedule now and have to get back to work," Filomena said. Just as she was about to close the door, she paused to address Alberta, and added, "Please remember what I said and don't go near Umberto."

Before Alberta could respond, Filomena closed the door.

"At least you didn't have to lie to her," Helen said, fishing for her car keys in her pocketbook.

"What do you mean?" Father Sal asked. "Alberta's sensible, she wouldn't go against such a stern warning as that."

"Just when I thought you weren't as dumb as you look," Helen groused. "Umberto is the key to this whole mystery. If you think Berta, or any of us for that matter, are going to stay away from him, you don't know us very well."

Alberta grinned from ear to ear when she got into the Buick. She had no idea how dangerous the situation was going to be when she met up with Umberto, but she knew she'd be safe because her sister and the rest of her family would be by her side.

CHAPTER 19

Sono solo soldi.

A few days later, when Alberta and Sloan entered Joyce's house, it felt like a frigid wind accompanied them despite the crisp fall temperature outside. Joyce examined their expressions and surveyed their body language and came to the only possible conclusion: The happy couple had had their first fight.

"Do I have to play marriage counselor for you two?" Joyce asked.

"Why would you ask that?" Alberta scoffed, hanging her coat on the back of one of the kitchen chairs.

"Because the two of you look like you came in from the battlefield," Joyce replied.

"It was only a skirmish," Sloan said, his voice cheery. "Nothing like the Battle of Chickamauga."

"Chicka who?" Joyce asked.

"One of the deadliest battles during the Civil War,"

Sloan said. "And one of the few victories for the Confederates."

Joyce placed a pitcher of iced tea and carafe of coffee onto the table and asked, "Who's the victor of *this* civil war?"

"You'll have to ask him," Alberta said. She didn't look at anyone, but poured coffee into her cup. "Everything I say is apparently stupid."

"Alberta Marie Teresa Ferrara Scaglione!" Sloan cried.

"Watch out, Sloan's using your full name," Joyce joked.

"I never said any such thing," Sloan said.

"You told me this running around after a criminal was a stupid idea and I should stop entertaining such thoughts," Alberta said.

"Yes, I did," Sloan agreed. "Because it is a stupid idea, but I never said everything you say is stupid nor would I ever say such a thing, you know that."

Alberta did know that, she was annoyed because nothing Sloan had said to her was wrong or unjustified. Her pursuit of Umberto *was* stupid. He was a dangerous criminal, and a woman she hardly knew had begged her to steer clear of him. What was her response to all this advice? Ignore it.

"Alberta, if you want to track this Umberto down, I'll help you," Sloan said. "I think it's the dumbest idea since New Coke, but I'm not going to let you investigate him on your own."

This time when Sloan spoke, Alberta listened to every word he said and then she replayed it silently in her mind, and she was stunned. She couldn't recall another man in her life speaking to her in the same way. He disagreed with her and yet he wasn't forbidding her to do the thing she wanted to do. He wasn't berating her for what he con-

sidered to be a foolish action. Every time she looked a little closer at Sloan McLelland, she liked the man that
much more.

"I have a compromise that I think you'll both like and
will go a long way to saving your relationship," Joyce
said.

"You really need to audition for the next Tranquility
Players production, Joyce," Alberta said. "You are a total
drama queen."

"I have several monologues already prepared," Joyce
replied. "Until I get my big break, why don't we e-mail
Umberto? We have his e-mail address from the documents you photographed, and I spent last night setting up
a fake e-mail account."

"You did?" Alberta and Sloan asked in unison.

"Once we discovered a way to communicate with Umberto, I knew it was a matter of time before we would
want to contact him," Joyce explained. "So last night it
was me, a bottle of rosé, and my laptop. Within an hour
LizGargiulo@gmail.com was born."

Once again Alberta and Sloan asked a question simultaneously. "Who's Liz Gargiulo?"

"My husband Anthony's girlfriend before he met me,"
Joyce replied.

"Oh my God, Joyce, is she still alive?" Alberta asked.

"Does it matter?" Joyce replied. "I figure if Umberto
somehow tracks her down—dead or alive—I won't lose
any sleep over it. I've never forgotten that she made some
rather unsubtle plays for Anthony while we were engaged."

While Alberta cracked up laughing, Sloan's jaw dropped.
Noticing Sloan's shock and mild discomfort, Joyce tried
to put him at ease.

"Don't worry, Sloan, revenge is more of a woman's thing," she said. "Isn't that right, Berta?"

Before Alberta could reply, Sloan interrupted her. "I don't think I want to hear your answer."

"Then let's summon up the spirit of Umberto Bottataglia the twenty-first-century way," Joyce declared, "with technology."

Joyce led Alberta and Sloan into her living room, and as usual Alberta was struck by the tasteful décor. It wasn't her style, but it suited Joyce perfectly, and Alberta always felt more sophisticated when she was in her sister-in-law's home.

The gray wool couch was set against a navy wall on which hung a huge gold-framed mirror. On either side of the couch were two small gray leather club chairs, and on the opposite wall hung a sixty-inch flat-screen television. A glass cocktail table was in the center of the room atop a rug in a navy, gray, and yellow abstract design. A triumph in minimalism, and a place Alberta loved to visit, but wouldn't want to live in.

On top of the cocktail table was Joyce's opened laptop. She sat in the middle of the couch with Alberta and Sloan on either side and typed in her password until an e-mail account appeared on screen. Not Joyce's, but the newly created one for Liz Gargiulo.

Joyce hit a few keys and a blank e-mail message popped up onto the screen. She typed in Umberto's e-mail address in the To line, and *Hello* in the Subject line, but after that she turned to Alberta and Sloan with a blank stare.

"What do I say to a possible three-time murderer?" she asked.

"I've actually been thinking about this," Alberta

replied, "and we have to concoct a story to make it look like we need fake documents."

"I don't know if I'm impressed or scared, but that's a terrific idea." Sloan beamed.

"Thank you," Alberta said, all thoughts of any discord between them already forgotten. "How about this? I'll dictate and you type."

Joyce positioned her manicured nails over the keyboard. "I'm ready when you are."

As Alberta spoke, Joyce typed, and Sloan stared at his girlfriend, smiling in disbelief. He couldn't believe the words that were coming out of her mouth so effortlessly as if they were truth.

She had created a story about her Aunt Regina living in Isernia, Italy, and in need of a fake passport. Regina needed to travel to Lowell, Massachusetts, in the United States to take care of her dying mother. Regina's sister, Carla, lived nearby, but was useless and only thought of herself, so their mother was not getting the attention she deserved. The problem was that in her youth, Regina did a lot of dumb things and got into trouble, eventually getting arrested. As part of her plea deal, she had to give up her passport so she couldn't travel outside of Italy.

Joyce finished the e-mail, adding that her close friends here in New Jersey told her that Umberto could help her and had a solution to her problem, so she hoped to hear from him soon, as she didn't know how much longer her mother could hold on.

"Sincerely, Liz Gargiulo," Joyce said.

"Would she sign off using her last name?" Alberta asked.

"I do when it's a formal e-mail," Joyce replied.

"I'm not sure an e-mail to a man who's an expert in

forgery and murder can be considered formal," Alberta said. "Sloan, what do you think?"

Momentarily speechless, Sloan's jaw dropped for the second time in less than an hour. "I have no idea. This, I am very happy to say, is uncharted territory for me."

"For me too," Alberta said. "I hardly ever write e-mails."

"I think he means who we're writing this e-mail to," Joyce clarified. "I'm going to go with formal. And I'm hitting Send . . . and it's sent."

Like three Pavlovian dogs in an experimental lab waiting for a light to flash to indicate a door would open and a treat would be revealed, Alberta, Joyce, and Sloan sat transfixed by the computer screen. They had just e-mailed Umberto—why hadn't he e-mailed them back?

"Did you use the right address?" Alberta asked.

"Yes, I checked it three times," Joyce replied.

"Maybe he's busy," Sloan suggested.

"Killing someone else?" Alberta asked.

Her question floated uninterrupted in the air for a few moments until they all realized the seriousness of what they had just done. They had willingly reached out to a man who they suspected had killed three innocent people.

"Are we crazy?" Alberta cried. "Umberto is dangerous."

"Alberta, calm down," Sloan said. "It's only an e-mail."

"Also too, it's a fake name and a fake account," Joyce reminded her.

"What if he tracks down Liz Gargiulo and kills her too?" Alberta questioned.

"Then she'll get what she deserves for trying to sleep with my husband," Joyce asserted.

Alberta let out a gasp. "Joyce Perkins Ferrara! You say a dozen Hail Marys right now for that comment."

"You know I'm only kidding," Joyce said. She took a

dramatic pause that would definitely land her a role with the Tranquility Players and added, "Sort of."

Energized by the rash, reckless action they had taken, the three of them began to pace around Joyce's living room. Alberta thought it was lucky that they were in Joyce's house instead of her own because Joyce had less furniture than Alberta, which meant there was more room to walk around. They all stopped moving the second they heard Joyce's laptop chime, indicating that a new e-mail had been received.

Screaming like schoolgirls, they ran to the couch, resumed their positions, and screamed even louder when they saw that Umberto had indeed returned their e-mail.

"*Dio mio!*" Alberta cried. "It's an e-mail from the killer!"

"What does it say, Joyce?" Sloan asked. "I can't see that far away without my glasses."

Leaning closer to the laptop, Joyce read aloud, "'Dear Liz, I understand your situation and I can help you. Please send me a photo of Regina and wire ten thousand dollars to the below account. Once I receive the money I can give you the documents in forty-eight hours. At which time I'll send you information on where we can meet.'"

"Ten thousand dollars?" Sloan asked. "Who has ten thousand dollars to spare?"

"I do!" Alberta shouted. "I have lots of ten thousand dollars that I'm dying to use for a good cause, and I think I just found one."

"Are you sure about this, Alberta?" Joyce asked. "I know you have millions now, but ten thousand dollars is still a lot of money."

"*Sono solo soldi,*" Alberta said. "It's only money.

Plus, if this will get us closer to finding out who killed Teri Jo, her brother, and that innocent Rosales woman, it'll be money well spent."

It took less than an hour for Joyce to open up a bank account in Liz Gargiulo's name, transfer the funds from Alberta's bank account into Liz's, and then transfer the money again into the account Umberto gave them. Alberta was stunned that nothing Joyce did with her money was illegal.

"What we did was all on the up-and-up," Joyce declared. "Now the only thing left for us to do is wait for Umberto to e-mail us instructions on where to meet and pick up our documents."

"I feel like this is going to be a long twenty-four hours," Alberta said.

"I don't know about you ladies, but all this skullduggery has made me hungry," Sloan announced. "Let's go to that new Japanese restaurant in Sparta, my treat."

Joyce closed up her laptop and started to clear things from the cocktail table. "You two go. I've got some of Alberta's leftover ravioli in the fridge."

"Nonsense. When do you choose leftovers over a free meal?" Alberta asked. "Never!"

"Thank you, but I'm too old to be a third wheel," Joyce declared.

"You're half right," Alberta said. "You're too old, but you could never be a third wheel." Alberta grabbed Joyce by the shoulders to prevent her from walking into the kitchen, and looked her in the eyes. "Do you hear me?"

Joyce felt tears unexpectedly well up in her eyes and she blinked several times in a failed attempt to stop them from running down her face. "I hear you loud and clear, Berta."

Sloan held out his hands and each woman took one. "Now let's go prove to the world that three is never a crowd."

The next day in the offices of *The Herald*, that lesson had not been properly learned.

Fingers flying over her keyboard, Jinx was banging out a quick follow-up article to Inez Rosales's murder. It was part profile on Inez and her struggles after illegally immigrating here from Guatemala, and part exposé on how violence against illegal immigrants goes largely unreported.

As she took a pause to review what she had already written, she was interrupted by Eric, the new intern, who was well meaning but not incredibly bright and only got the position because he was Wyck's nephew. Jinx had no problem with the hire because she understood and believed in nepotism, but she did have a problem with the fact that he always delivered the wrong mail.

"Eric!" she cried from her desk.

She was going to continue her tirade, but Eric never returned. Looking through the mail she saw that she had four letters for Wyck, three for Calhoun, and one for her. She opened up the letter addressed to her and it was, of course, from a manufacturer asking her if they could help satisfy her fax machine needs.

"Yes, you could . . . if this were 1987!"

Furious, Jinx grabbed the rest of the mail not addressed to her and marched to Wyck's office. It was her lucky day because he and Calhoun were having a meeting, so she would only have to make one stop to deliver both men's mail.

She knocked on the door, but didn't wait for either man to acknowledge her presence before entering. "Excuse me."

Calhoun whipped around in his chair and scowled at Jinx. "Can't you see we're busy in here?"

He placed his cell phone on top of some files and nervously switched the pencil holder and the stapler on Wyck's desk.

"You're having a dumb-jock conversation about fantasy football," Jinx replied. "I can see the stat card you shoved underneath your cell phone."

Calhoun and Wyck both looked at the cell phone and had completely different reactions. Wyck howled with laughter, Calhoun just howled.

"You need to learn to knock, Maldonado!" he cried.

"You need to learn to close the door, Calhoun, if you're going to play games at work," Jinx cried back.

"Like you don't play games all day with your grandma, trying to solve murders!" he shouted.

"We do solve murders!" she shouted back. "Which I then write articles about."

"And those articles have increased our circulation," Wyck added. "Jinx, you're welcome in my office anytime."

"When there isn't already a meeting in place," Calhoun corrected.

"Simmer down, Calhoun," Wyck placated. "Don't take it out on Jinx because she's got the most read articles online. Your turn will come."

"This should be my turn! I have seniority," Calhoun yelled.

"She's got the gift," Wyck said.

"What gift?" Jinx asked.

"She's always in the right place at the right time—no matter where Jinx goes, tragedy strikes," Wyck explained. "Keep it up, kiddo."

"I'll, um, do my best," Jinx said, turning to leave.

"Wait, what did you come in here for?" Wyck asked.

Turning back around, Jinx tossed Wyck's mail onto his desk. "Your nephew needs to learn how to read. He keeps giving me the wrong mail."

She handed Calhoun his letters and the both of them began to leave the room. "Ever since you became a father, you've gotten a lot crankier," Jinx said.

"It's because I never get to sleep," he replied. "Then I get here and I have to take your hand-me-downs."

Just as their fight was positioning itself to explode, a literal explosion took place behind them. They turned around and saw that Wyck had flipped over the back of his chair and was sprawled out on the floor. On his desk was an open envelope with smoke still emanating from the inside.

"Call the police!" Jinx said as she rushed around the side of Wyck's desk. "Wyck, are you alright? Can you hear me?"

Slowly, Wyck opened his eyes and started to move from side to side, grabbing at the floor in an attempt to stand up.

"Take it easy, try and sit up," Jinx said.

"The police are on their way," Calhoun advised.

"The police? Why did you call the police?" Wyck asked.

"Because someone sent you a letter bomb," Jinx said.

Inexplicably, a grin appeared on Wyck's face and his eyes twinkled with pride. "I've never gotten one of those," he declared. "I owe it all to you, Jinx."

"Me!"

"Yes, you!" Wyck cried. "What was I just saying, wherever Jinx roams, danger will surely follow. You're not going to tell me it's a coincidence that you deliver my mail and one of the letters explodes when I open it. It's proof. You're a jinx, Jinx, but a good one, at least for our readership numbers."

He grabbed on to the edge of his desk and with Jinx's help pulled himself up until he was standing. For a moment it appeared as if he was going to collapse on the floor again, but he held his hands in front of his chest, palms up, and didn't teeter.

"Look, Ma, no hands," Wyck said. "Now leave me alone so I can write this article." He started typing on his keyboard and read his words out loud. "Editor-in-chief attacked by an anonymous bomber. Just listen to that, it writes itself."

Vinny arrived while Wyck was finishing up his article, and he brought with him an unlikely sidekick.

"Freddy!" Jinx cried. "What are you doing here?"

"I was doing some business with Vinny when he got the call, so I hitched a ride with him," Freddy explained.

"What kind of business?" Jinx asked.

"Background checks on new employees," Freddy said. "Vinny's helping me out with that stuff."

Freddy looked around the office and couldn't immediately see why the police had been summoned. Until the policeman in the room explained.

"I'll have them examine this closer, but it looks like a simple c-lock bomb," Vinny said.

"What's that?" Jinx asked.

"A cylinder lock, c-lock for short," Vinny explained. "Not very powerful, but still lucky it didn't hurt anyone."

"No chance of that with my good luck charm a few feet away," Wyck said. "Isn't that right, Jinx?"

"You are so right, Wyck," Jinx replied sarcastically.

"She's brought more action to this paper than we've had in years," Wyck boasted. "We never had random acts of violence like this before she got here."

Freddy tugged on Jinx's arm and pulled her to a corner of the room. He turned his back on the rest of the men in the room so only Jinx could see his face. He was scared.

"This wasn't random, Jinx," Freddy said. "This incident is definitely involved with all the crazy goings on surrounding the Tranqclockery."

"How can you be so sure?" she asked.

"The bomb the person used, it's a c-lock," Freddy said. "Spell it out, it's clock."

Jinx instantly covered her mouth with her hand so no one could hear her gasp. "Oh my God, Freddy, you're right. Do you think Owen sent the bomb?"

"If it wasn't him, it was someone who has a connection to the clock shop," Freddy said. "And to the illegal document operation."

"If that's true, Freddy, you know what this means, right?"

"What?"

"That whoever's in charge of this whole thing knows we're getting closer to the truth and they're getting scared," Jinx said. "It's only a matter of time before we solve this mystery, Freddy."

Her boyfriend didn't look nearly as optimistic as Jinx did.

"Or it's only a matter of time before the killer strikes again."

CHAPTER 20

Guarda oltre ciò che vedi.

Wherever Alberta looked she was surrounded by family. Her living room was no different.

She was sitting on her couch, her feet propped up on the ottoman, drinking a cup of green tea with a dollop of honey like Jinx recommended, with Lola snuggled into a ball resting against her hip. No one else was in the room with her and yet she felt generations of love embrace her as tightly as her father used to when she would hurt herself as a young girl, and after her confirmation ceremony, and even on her wedding day. Alberta knew her father had no idea she had mixed feelings about marrying Sammy; he thought it was a celebration, so she couldn't hold his exuberance against him. What she held close to her heart was his unconditional love. It's what she felt about her entire family as she looked around the room.

Unlike Joyce, Alberta was not a minimalist. She wasn't

by any means a hoarder, but she subscribed to the theory
that a home should represent the person or people who
lived there. Despite her rocky marriage, Alberta was a
homebody, a woman who believed in family but who also
understood that everyone's definition of family was different. Like most women her age, her family unit living
under one roof had dwindled to one—well, one and a half
if Lola was part of the census count—but she considered
herself one of the lucky ones to still be in close contact
with her family and see them on a regular basis. Even if
she didn't see Jinx, Helen, and Joyce almost daily, she
only needed to look on the walls of her living room, the
mantel, and the glass-and-brass étagère to see their smiling faces.

On the mantel over the fireplace, which was catty-
cornered to the left, near the entrance to the kitchen, were
photos of Alberta's immediate family. Even before
Sammy died, she had decided that the shelf life of her
wedding photo had expired and it had been relegated to
one of the plastic storage boxes in the back of a closet.
The photo she chose to display was from her son Rocco's
wedding, because it was one of the rare photos where Alberta and Sammy were both smiling. She didn't know
how much longer she would keep it out and knew it had
remained on the mantel primarily out of wifely guilt.
With Sloan becoming a more permanent fixture in her
life, it might be time that photo joined the others in storage, but for now she left it where it was.

Surrounding that photo was one of Lisa Marie and
Tommy at Christmas, another of Rocco and his son, Gregory, on a random fishing trip in California where they
lived, Jinx at her college graduation, and Jinx's brother
Sergio's high school graduation photo.

Across from the couch was Alberta's television, which was a flat-screen like Joyce's, but instead of being mounted on the wall it stood on top of the cherrywood media center Alberta bought on sale in 1998. All these years later it still looked brand-new. To the left of the TV was an almost floor-to-ceiling montage of framed photos of Alberta's parents, grandparents, Helen as a novitiate on the day she became a nun, her brother Anthony and Joyce and their twins, Bobby and Billy, more photos of Jinx, Lisa Marie, Tommy, Rocco, Sergio, various cousins, aunts, and uncles, even two portraits of Lola, one when she first arrived in Alberta's life as a kitten and the other several years later, fully grown.

Looking at decades of her life captured in photographs, Alberta's heart broke for Teri Jo. Alberta couldn't imagine feeling so alone and abandoned that her only recourse, her only viable solution would be to run away and never return home. Despite the misgivings she'd had walking down the aisle to greet Sammy at the altar, her life had turned out fine. Sammy may not have been the best husband in the world, and if Alberta was being completely honest with herself she had not been the best wife, but he provided for her and their family and he never once was physically abusive. He didn't speak to her the way she dreamed her husband would, sometimes he didn't speak to her at all, but Alberta didn't always try to make the relationship work. Their marriage wasn't a fairy-tale romance because neither one of them were perfect.

Even still, if she had divorced Sammy or run from the church before saying *I do*, she would have had her family, they would never have abandoned her. But the thought of running away wouldn't have crossed her mind. Even

Viola, her distant cousin, had remained with her family after being publicly humiliated by Marcello. If running away had been an option for her, she never chose it. She knew her life would continue even without the love of her life.

Alberta started to cry, thinking about how lonely Teri Jo must have been all these years, knowing her family was a short drive away, but also knowing that she could never make that journey. Hopefully, she found some solace reconnecting with Veronica, who was most likely her aunt or her cousin. Veronica couldn't be Teri Jo and Dominic's mother because she couldn't have children. Whatever the title, she was Teri Jo's blood relative, and Alberta desperately wanted to believe that Veronica gave Teri Jo the kind of unconditional love she deserved.

In turn, maybe Teri Jo gave Veronica the same kind of support. How could two women in the same family in two different generations feel so isolated that they both decided their only chance of a good life was to turn their backs on the only life they knew? Then Alberta thought that maybe Teri Jo was inspired by Veronica's bravery. She most certainly had heard stories of what Veronica— or Bettina, as she was known by the Rizzolis—had done, and instead of considering it blasphemy like most of the Rizzolis assuredly did, Teri Jo perceived it to be a stunning victory. At her darkest moment, Bettina Rizzoli may have saved Theresa Rizzoli's life by leading by example and giving her the strength to move away.

Or Veronica was simply the one who got Teri Jo killed.

Alberta shook her head and sighed. There was something illegal and deadly going on between the Tranqclockery and Veronica's Diner, and she was determined to find out what it was. When Joyce called to tell her Umberto had made contact, she knew she was getting much closer to uncovering what that connection was.

This time when the threesome comprised of Alberta, Joyce, and Sloan met, it was in Sloan's office.

"Close the door, Joyce," Sloan said as he took the laptop from her.

"Do you think that's a smart idea, Sloan?" Alberta asked.

"I want to make sure we're not interrupted," Sloan said. "I'd rather not have to explain why I'm e-mailing a criminal from my office."

"At least you're not using library equipment," Joyce reminded him. "All of our communication with Umberto has been on my laptop with Liz Gargiulo's e-mail account."

"I was only thinking of your reputation," Alberta said, pulling the extra chair in Sloan's office around to the other side of the desk, next to his. "One man, two women in his office, that's how rumors start."

Sloan smiled and Alberta could tell he was trying to decide if he should answer her sincerely or come up with a quick comeback. Much to her delight, he chose the former.

"Anyone who knows me knows I only have eyes for you, Alberta," Sloan replied. "Sorry, Joyce."

"Don't you dare apologize," Joyce said. "I know my place. And it's right in between the two of you, scoot over."

Sloan and Alberta shimmied their chairs in opposite directions so Joyce could stand between them. She opened her laptop, booted it up, hit some keys to bring up the fake e-mail account, and then knelt down as she brought up Umberto's e-mail.

"I got this e-mail this morning," she conveyed. "Umberto has the documents and told us to meet him in Tranquility, New Jersey, specifically in the alleyway between the Tranqclockery and Veronica's Diner at midnight tonight."

"*Dio mio!*" Alberta cried. "This is solid proof that both Owen and Veronica are somehow involved."

"But how are they involved?" Sloan asked, his frustration building. "That's still the sixty-four-thousand-dollar question."

"Once we make contact, maybe we'll get some answers," Alberta suggested.

"Speaking of contact," Joyce interjected. "How exactly are we going to handle the drop-off with Umberto?"

"First of all, there's no 'we' about this," Sloan stated. "I'm going to meet with Umberto alone."

"You can't do that," Joyce said. "You look nothing like Liz Garguilo."

"I'll tell him I'm Liz Garguilo's husband," Sloan replied.

"Are you *pazzo*?" Alberta asked. "You're crazy if you think we're letting you meet a murderer at midnight, alone."

"Well you're *pazzo* if you think I'm going to let you or any of your detective troupe put themselves in danger by meeting this psycho in the dark!" Sloan exclaimed.

Alberta was not at all offended by the harsh tone of Sloan's voice. On the contrary, she was amused. She admitted to herself that she liked this side of Sloan. Normally, he was mild-mannered and gentlemanly, but he was passionate, and every once in a while that passion bubbled up to the surface and exploded. It was different from the way Sammy yelled. His voice had been filled with anger and irritation, he had wanted to win an argument regardless of how it made Alberta feel. Sloan was protecting her, and within his yelling there was always compromise. There was also an incorrect use of Italian grammar. As a woman she couldn't be *pazzo*, but *pazza*. However, Alberta didn't think it was the appropriate time to point that out. Now was the time for compromise, not a lecture.

"You can meet Umberto alone if we get to drive the getaway car," Alberta said. "It has become Helen's forte, after all."

For a few moments they were at a standstill, no one moving or changing their expression to give away what they were thinking, until Sloan extended his hand to Alberta so they could shake on it.

"Deal," Sloan said as if he had just finalized a business transaction.

"Deal," Alberta agreed. "Now all that's left to do is wait."

"I know you're not going to like this, but I think there's something else we should do," Joyce said. "I think it's time we told Vinny what we know and what we're about to do."

"Normally I would agree with you, Joyce," Sloan said. "But Umberto is savvy, he's going to know if the police are lurking around, ready to nab him. I think in this instance we need to go rogue for the time being. Once we have the proof of the illegal documents in hand, then we turn it all over to the police for them to catch him."

"Do you think they'll be able to do that, Sloan?" Alberta asked.

"Of course. Look how easy it was for us to fish him

out," Sloan said. "Let's focus on collecting the evidence and then the police can focus on bringing this *malfatorre* to justice."

Alberta sighed deeply. "I'd be lying if I said I wasn't worried, but I agree with Sloan—no police."

"You're right," Joyce said. "It's risky, but it's really the only way to move forward. Who knows? Maybe Umberto isn't so bad after all."

"Joyce! How can you say that?" Alberta asked. "He's a murderer."

"Don't you remember *The Godfather*? They all have a code of ethics," Joyce declared. "So far Umberto has responded to us in a timely fashion, he's giving us the documents we want within the aforementioned time frame, and also too, he thanked us for the money and even signed his e-mail, *Cheers, Umberto*."

"He is awfully polite for a criminal," Alberta noted.

"You cannot judge a book by its rap sheet, Berta," Joyce said.

A person also couldn't be judged by their age. Alberta, Helen, Joyce, and even Sloan were not in what would generally be considered the prime of their lives. They were in their golden years, and as such were expected to act in a certain way. No one would expect them to be sitting in Helen's Buick a block away from the Tranqclockery, waiting for the stroke of midnight when Sloan would enter an alleyway to meet a hardened criminal. It wasn't something old folks did. This group did not comprise typical old folk.

Two blocks away on the other side of the Tranqclockery, Jinx and Freddy were parked in her red Chevy Cruze. The plan was for them to follow Umberto once he left his clandestine meeting with Sloan. By having cars on either side of the drop-off point, they hoped that Umberto wouldn't be able to get away and they'd track him back to his home base. They wouldn't go inside to apprehend him, that would be a fool's errand, but they would call Vinny and keep lookout to make sure Umberto didn't escape before the police arrived to arrest him. It was a sound plan, but they had learned from previous experience that very few plans actually go as planned.

In the back seat of the Buick, Sloan looked at his watch and said, "The witching hour is upon us, ladies."

Alberta, sitting next to him, and Helen and Joyce in the front seat, all looked at their watches and saw that it was five minutes to midnight. The time had come for Sloan's rendezvous.

"Are you sure you want to do this?" Alberta asked.

Sloan could see fear in Alberta's eyes and the sight made him catch his breath. "Don't you worry about me," he said, making sure he kept all trace of doubt and apprehension out of his voice. "This is going to be over in a few minutes. Even if he refuses to give Liz Garguilo's husband the documents and leaves, Jinx and Freddy will be right behind him. Once he's caught we can put this mystery behind us and get back to more important things."

"Like what?" Alberta asked.

"Like you and me," Sloan replied.

Sloan held Alberta's face with his hands and felt her warmth. He kissed her softly, then firmly, and she kissed him back with equal measures of surprise and concern. She almost felt like she was seeing her beau off to war.

As quietly as possible, Sloan got out of the car and walked down the block. He didn't look back, but that wasn't because he didn't want to steal another glance at

Alberta. On the off chance that Umberto was watching him, Sloan didn't want to give Umberto a hint that he wasn't traveling solo.

"Are you alright back there?" Helen asked.

Lying, Alberta replied, "I'm fine." She wiped away some tears with a stray tissue she found in her jacket pocket and continued, "No, I'm not fine at all. This is insane. We can't let Sloan go in that alleyway by himself, what if this is a trap?"

"Then Sloan's about to become the sacrificial lamb," Helen said.

"We have to follow him," Alberta ordered. "We have to be his backup."

"Okay, I'll drive up slowly and maybe he won't notice us," Helen said.

Just as she was about to turn the key in the ignition, Joyce grabbed her hand. "No, Umberto will hear the car and if he does, who knows how he'll respond?" she said. "We need to do this on foot."

The three women got out of the Buick, closing the doors as quietly as they could, and then scurried down the block huddled together like one oversized pedestrian taking a late night stroll.

Joyce had to walk on her toes so her heels didn't make noise on the sidewalk, and when possible they stepped on patches of grass to silence their footsteps. Finally, they came to the entrance of the alleyway. They stopped and got into a position so they could all peek out around the wall to see what was happening at the same time. Helen crouched down as low as she could, Alberta straddled her and bent over, and Joyce, the tallest, held on to Alberta's back and leaned forward. It was a miracle not one of them gasped out loud when they looked down the alleyway and saw Sloan and Umberto face-to-face.

The lights from the diner and the Tranqclockery shone in the distance, so it brought some illumination into the alley, but it was still quite dark. Both businesses were closed—the diner used to stay open into the early morning hours to cater to the late-night crowd, but ever since the multiple murders that plagued it, business had dropped so badly that it no longer made sense to stay open after the dinner rush dissipated.

The women couldn't see Umberto clearly and if he had looked past Sloan, it was doubtful that he would have seen their faces, one on top of the other. It was more realistic that they would appear to be shadows or even the back of a sign protruding out from the wall. Unfortunately, his actions told them that he didn't care if he was being observed or not.

The first swing was so unexpected and swift that if Sloan hadn't stumbled to the right, the women would have thought a bird flew by or one of the lights in the distance flickered. When Umberto struck Sloan a second time, this time with a punch right across his face that made him careen into the side of the Tranqclockery before crashing to the gravelly ground, they knew what they were witnessing: They were watching someone they loved be attacked.

"NO!"

Alberta's cry raced down the alleyway, and the way Umberto looked up from his victim to the voice in the darkness, they knew he hadn't noticed them before. He was caught off guard and the women hoped to use it to their advantage.

Without any thought for their own safety, Alberta, Helen, and Joyce charged down the alley, screaming as loud as they could. They each knew they were no physical match for Umberto, but they also knew they were not going to allow him to lay another hand on Sloan. They had no idea what they were going to do when they came face-to-face with Umberto; they would think about that when the moment arrived. It never did.

Seeing the three women running toward him, Umberto stood motionless for a few seconds. It was as if the wheels in his brain were turning. Should he stay and fight off three crazy women or hightail it out of there? He chose the latter and ran in the opposite direction. It was more like a fast-paced limp, but he clearly had experience fleeing the scene of many a crime, so he was moving at a very quick speed.

Alberta was first to reach Sloan's unmoving body, and when she knelt next to him and saw the blood running down the side of his face, his pale complexion, and his closed eyes, she thought Umberto had claimed a fourth victim. Somehow she managed to work through her growing panic and ignore the loud thumping of her heart, and she reached for Sloan's hand to check for a pulse. It was faint, but it was there.

"Call an ambulance!" Alberta cried.

"They're on their way," Joyce said, raising her cell phone to indicate that she had already made the call.

Helen knelt on the opposite side of Sloan, and Alberta could see her sister trying to maintain her composure. She knew Helen was forcing herself to remain calm to let Alberta maintain the hope that Sloan's bruises and situation weren't as grave as they appeared. She'd never loved her sister more deeply than she did at that moment.

Joining them, Joyce knelt near Sloan's head and the three women held hands in silent prayer. They remained that way until the paramedics arrived a few minutes later.

Like zombies, the women stood up and parted ways so the medics could do their job and save Sloan's life. They offered reassuring but vague words as they hoisted Sloan's body onto a stretcher and began to roll him out of the alleyway. Joyce told Alberta to ride in the ambulance with Sloan and she and Helen would meet her at the hospital.

Nodding absentmindedly, Alberta turned to go and then turned back. "Don't forget to tell Jinx."

"I've been texting her," Joyce said. "She and Freddy drove around trying to find Umberto, but came up empty. She's going to call Vinny and bring him up to speed."

"Thank you," Alberta said, the tears finally given permission to appear. "Thank you both."

Joyce gave Alberta a quick hug and Helen followed suit. When Helen was holding her sister tight, she whispered in her ear, *"Guarda oltre ciò che vedi."*

Alberta's expression became very serious. She understood what Helen had told her, she had to look beyond what she saw. It was exactly what she had to do.

Jinx knew exactly what she had to do too. She rounded the corner just as she saw the ambulance and Helen's Buick speed away. Perfect timing, she thought, to pick up the investigation when the major players might think the evening's activity had ended.

She parked on the side of Veronica's Diner and she and Freddy got out and walked around the corner to Main Street so they could enter the front door of the Tranqclockery. It was time to inform Owen that another attempted murder had taken place on his property. Down deep, Jinx was hoping the elusive clock store owner would say or do something that would finally give them a hint as to his role in the latest string of crimes. All she discovered was that Owen was as elusive as ever.

After the fourth knock they were about to give up and go around the back of the store to search for clues, when Owen suddenly opened the door. He was wearing a blue-and-gold paisley silk robe over navy-blue pajamas, classic black bedroom slippers, and his blackout sunglasses. He looked like a character out of an old Clark Gable movie or a Noël Coward play. Debonair, soigné . . . but deadly?

"Who's there?" Owen said.

"It's Jinx Maldonado and Freddy Frangelico," Jinx replied. "Are you, um, okay?"

"If you're referring to my odd choice in eyewear, yes, I'm fine," Owen informed them. "I'm having one of my ocular migraines, and it causes me to go temporarily blind."

"Dude! Really?" Freddy exclaimed.

"Yes . . . *dude* . . . really," Owen replied. "Do not fret. I will admit the headaches are coming more frequently than usual. I suppose it's because of the shenanigans of late."

"Shenanigans?" Jinx questioned. "You mean the murders?"

"Yes, well, put another, cruder way, one may label them as such," Owen agreed.

"Speaking of shenanigans, there's been another attempt on someone's life," Jinx shared. "Just tonight in the alleyway."

"Dear me, please tell me that everyone is alright," Owen said.

"We don't know yet. We were hoping you might be able to fill us in on what happened," Freddy said. "The event did take place a few yards from here. You must have heard or seen something."

Smiling indulgently, Owen raised his hand to his glasses and held the frame. "Like I said, I can't see anything, and when the migraines come over me I've learned it's best to shut out the world, past, present, and future," Owen said. "I've had my headset on, listening to Vivaldi. Very soothing Vivaldi is, so I haven't heard a thing."

"That's convenient," Freddy replied.

Jinx agreed with him, but slapped him in the chest for being so honest about his thoughts while interrogating a potential witness.

"More like a necessary tactic for me to maintain my sanity in the midst of an uncontrollable symptom of my affliction," Owen said. Then, without waiting for Jinx or Freddy to answer any more questions, he said, "I'm sorry I can't be of more help." And proceeded to close and lock the door.

"He might be sort of blind and kind of pathetic, but I don't trust that guy," Freddy declared.

"Dude, I couldn't agree with you more," Jinx said. "But there's nothing else we can do here. Let's head over to the hospital to see how Sloan's doing."

By the time they arrived at St. Clare's, Sloan was thankfully out of danger. No one was throwing a party yet or breaking out the champagne, but Sloan was conscious and the doctor assured Alberta there would be no permanent damage. Alberta's relief was tremendous and she openly wept at Sloan's bedside. She held her gold crucifix in her hands as she gave her thanks to God for sparing Sloan's life. In her emotional state she didn't know if Sloan was her friend, her boyfriend, or her next husband, but none of that mattered. He was someone she truly cared for, and the fact that his life was spared and he was able to come out of this vicious attack unscathed, renewed her faith in prayer and the fact that there was still good in the world. Sloan seemed to agree.

As one of the nurses informed Alberta that she needed to leave so they could transfer Sloan to a regular room, he opened his eyes and had enough strength to give Alberta the universal sign for okay with his fingers and then made the peace sign. Greatly relieved, Alberta burst into another round of tears, grabbed Sloan's hand and pressed it close to her face. She kissed the palm of his hand, then his lips, and told him to rest and she would see him soon. He was already drifting off to sleep when she left the room.

She went from viewing one incredible sight to another. First, Sloan's recovery, and then Helen and Sal sitting next to each other in the waiting room, seemingly recovering the friendship that they'd had decades ago. When Helen saw Alberta she reacted as if she got caught eating the Eucharist like it was a late-night snack.

"What's going on here?" Alberta asked.

"Nothing," Helen replied a bit too quickly. "I called Sal and asked him to come here . . . just in case."

"In case Sloan passed, you mean," Alberta said, finishing the sentence for her sister. "Crisis averted. Sloan is going to need his rest, but the doctors gave him a clean bill of health. He's going to be fine."

"Thank God," Helen said, making the sign of the cross.

"I mean no disrespect, Sal," Alberta started, "but if Sloan did need last rites, Helen could have administered them, like she did for Teri Jo at the diner."

Sal and Helen exchanged a glance that Alberta found to be very curious and suspect. Whatever they were telepathically conveying to each other was making Helen nervous as well, which was odd. Alberta had seen Helen experience many emotions in Sal's presence—anger and frustration mainly—but never anxiety.

"If Helen had done that, I have no doubt Sloan would have been escorted directly to the Pearly Gates, just as Teri Jo was," Father Sal said.

It was a beautiful sentiment and it filled Alberta's heart with joy to hear Sal talk about Helen with such reverence. It made Helen cry.

Alberta was dumbfounded. She had seen her sister cry before, of course, but this was different. She wasn't sobbing, she wasn't reacting to an immediate occurrence, she seemed to be reacting to the truth that lay behind Father Sal's words. Worse, she looked ashamed. What in the world could Helen have done to be ashamed of?

Father Sal clasped Helen's hand in an attempt to give her back some of the strength that seemed to have escaped her body and said, "I think it's time you sisters had a talk."

CHAPTER 21

Il Signore sia con tutti tranne te.

Ever since Helen was a child she'd had an innate desire to help others. Collect cans of food for hungry children, read to the blind, listen to them talk about their problems. By the time she was eleven years old she'd accepted that she had found her purpose. It wasn't until she was about to graduate high school that she shared her vision with her parents.

"I want to be a nun."

Her mother cried and her father looked confused.

"Why would anyone want to become a nun?" her father had asked.

"I can't speak for anyone else," Helen had replied. "But for me it isn't a choice, it's a need."

With her parents' approval, if not their blessing, Helen Marie Ferrara set out on her journey to devote her life to Christ one month after graduating Immaculate Conception High School. Forty-four years later, she reversed her decision and left the convent. She'd never explained her reasons for leaving the church, until now.

"What does Sal mean, we have to talk?" Alberta asked, concern filling her voice. "Is something wrong? Are you alright?"

"I'm fine," Helen assured.

She took a few moments to compose herself to speak again. When she did, her voice was stronger, but still fueled by long-suppressed emotions. The time had come, however, for Helen to share her truth with her baby sister.

"It's about why I left the convent," Helen said.

"Sal knows?" Alberta asked.

"If you haven't noticed, Sal knows a little bit about everything," Helen replied. "And despite what I might say about the man, he knows how to keep his mouth shut. But he's right, I owe you an explanation."

"Helen, you don't owe me or anyone anything," Alberta said.

"You're my family, you're all I have, Berta, you deserve to know," Helen replied.

The simplicity and grace of Helen's comment stunned Alberta and left her speechless. The depths of her sister's heart and her ability to use words as a tool to communicate what lay there, marveled Alberta. She was too anxious to hear what Helen had to say and knew she wouldn't be able to emulate Helen's facility for saying the right thing, so she kept silent and listened.

"I was working with an outreach program run by the Basilica of the Sacred Heart in Newark that was specifically created to help single mothers and their children," Helen began. "We tried to give them alternatives to lives of selling and using drugs and show them that they could resist the pressure of joining a gang. We wanted to give them options.

"We also helped the mothers navigate the maze of government funding for social programs, food stamps, welfare, financial aid for housing, school lunches, all the resources that lift some of the burden of raising a family on your own," Helen said.

"One day I was visiting a single mother, Nadia. She lived just a block away from the church and we were starting to look through applications for private high schools for her son, Emmanuel, even a few boarding schools," Helen explained. "Manny was very bright and an exceptional artist. We thought he had a really good shot to get into one of the more prestigious schools in the area, maybe in all of Jersey, if the funding came through for him to live on campus.

"From her window, Nadia saw Manny walking down the street," Helen said. "He was carrying a painting that had won first prize in a city-wide contest, not just for students, but any aspiring artist. We heard the gunshot and his mother saw him fall to the ground."

"Oh my God," Alberta gasped.

She resisted the urge to say anything more or embrace her sister so Helen would have the freedom to tell the story she needed to share.

"By the time we got downstairs, Manny was in a pool of blood," Helen said. "I saw two groups of kids running in opposite directions and I knew immediately that it was a drug deal gone wrong or some act of gang revenge, and Manny got caught in the crossfire.

"Nadia was holding her son and I was sitting there doing nothing, until Manny asked me to pray with him," she recalled. "I had taught Manny some prayers and he told me that he would say them when he felt he needed some extra help to get through the day or a particular situation. Together we recited the Lord's Prayer, but he wasn't able to finish a Hail Mary. He was slipping away."

Helen looked away and stared down the hall, at nothing and everything at the same time. Alberta turned her focus to the floor to give her sister the space and time she needed to continue.

"Nadia asked me to perform last rites on her son because she knew he wasn't going to survive much longer," Helen said. "And I did. She was grateful, she said it gave her peace to know her son's soul would have a better chance in heaven than it ever had on earth. The diocese didn't feel the same way."

"What are you talking about?" Alberta asked. "What you did was beautiful. It's what you did for Teri Jo."

Helen looked at her sister like she used to when they were children and Alberta would state with utter conviction that Santa Claus was real and at that very moment could be heard outside their window. Her eyes then and now were filled with love, but also the knowledge that Alberta had so much more to learn about life.

"I told Father Matthew, the pastor at Sacred Heart, what I had done, and he didn't respond in any way that prepared me for what he did next," Helen said. "On Sunday, in front of the whole congregation, he told the story of what I had done as an example of hubris against God, as an illustration of a woman who doesn't know her place on earth. *Il Signore sia con tutti tranne te* The Lord be with everyone except you. In front of everyone, he said that I had shamed God because I assumed I knew better than He what I was intended to do."

"*Bastardo,*" Alberta said.

"Yes, well, he was indeed that," Helen replied. "It didn't matter that Nadia and most of the rest of the congregation disagreed with him. His words hurt me deeply. I wasn't embarrassed by what he said, but I knew he wasn't the only priest who felt that way. For quite a while I had been disillusioned with the church's practice and public statements, but I knew right there, sitting in that pew listening to Father Matthew's words, I could no longer serve an institution that could be so closed-minded and unforgiving," Helen said. "The very next day I quit."

Alberta inhaled deeply and let the breath slowly leave her body. She always knew there was an underlying reason for why Helen left the convent, and she never believed Helen's vague, blasé explanations that it was time for her to go or that she had done everything she could. She never imagined anything as profound or life changing as this. It was no secret that Alberta had always admired her sister, but now, after hearing the secret that she had kept hidden for so long, she understood her. That was much more important.

"You have always been the strongest person I have ever known," Alberta said. "I don't have to tell you that you did the right thing, you already know that, but I will tell you that I have never loved you more than I do right now."

Helen turned to face Alberta and smiled. "I already knew that too."

The sisters embraced and cried a few more tears, and then Alberta asked a question that brought their conversation full circle.

"Did Father Sal know all about this when it was happening?"

Nodding her head decisively, Helen replied, "That son of a b had my back every step of the way."

Obviously Helen wasn't the only person Alberta saw in a completely new light. Father Sal had more layers to his character than he did shoes.

After all these years, Alberta finally knew why her sister left the convent. Her heart ached for the turmoil and pain Helen went through, and although she understood why Helen chose to work through her anguish alone, Alberta wanted Helen to know there shouldn't be any secrets between them. They were sisters and should be confidants.

"Promise me one thing, Helen," Alberta said.

"What's that?" Helen asked.

"No more secrets."

"I promise."

Alberta stood up and extended her hand toward Helen. "I don't know about you, sis, but I'm exhausted. Let's get out of here."

After a brief nap on her couch, Alberta fed Lola, took a shower, and drove back to the hospital to see how Sloan was doing. Although the doctors assured her that he would have a full recovery, he wasn't out of the woods yet, and Alberta wasn't going to stop worrying until he was discharged. Even then she doubted that she would ever stop feeling guilty. She blamed herself for him getting attacked. If it wasn't for her desire to contact Umberto, he wouldn't be lying on a hospital bed.

She paused before the entrance to St. Clare's because she wasn't going to aid in Sloan's recovery if she was riddled with guilt and self-loathing. This wasn't about her, it was about Sloan. What was more certain, she didn't control him, he was a grown man and he made his own decisions. He knew what he was getting into when he walked down that alley. She knew that if she uttered her thoughts she would be perceived as cold and harsh, but that couldn't be further from the truth. Guilt was not concern, and shame was not sympathy. Alberta raised her chin and entered the hospital and smiled proudly—some days it wasn't so hard being an adult.

But it wasn't always so easy being right.

When Alberta got to the waiting room she saw that Jinx and Joyce were already there, sitting and drinking coffee out of paper cups.

"I don't know why everyone always complains about the coffee in hospitals," Jinx said. "This isn't so bad."

"Also too, the machine has nondairy creamer so I'm having a little hazelnut this morning," Joyce added.

"I'm happy to see that you two are having a grand old time here at good ole St. Clare's," Alberta joked.

"You make do with what you got, Berta," Joyce said. "And before you ask, Sloan is fine. They gave him a sedative so he could sleep, but all his tests came back normal. There's no cause for alarm."

"Thank you," Alberta replied. "I kind of knew that from last night, or I guess it was early this morning. Anyway, as they were wheeling Sloan out, he gave me the peace sign. He wasn't able to speak, but he wanted me to know he was okay."

Jinx and Joyce looked at each other with expressions that clearly disagreed with Alberta's interpretation of Sloan's attempt at sign language.

"You mean this sign, Gram?" Jinx asked, holding up her index and middle fingers to create a V.

"Yes, exactly," Alberta confirmed. "The peace sign, V for victory."

"Or V for Veronica," Joyce said.

"Ah *Madon*! I am a *stunod*!" Alberta cried. "How could I not have made that connection?"

"Cut yourself some slack, Gram, you were worried sick about Sloan," Jinx said. "You were praying for a sign that he was okay and you thought you got one."

"But I thought wrong!" Alberta cried. "Maybe he was trying to tell me something about Veronica."

"He was attacked in the alleyway, which is right outside of the diner," Joyce pointed out.

"What could Sloan have been trying to tell me?" Alberta asked. "We saw Umberto attack Sloan. Veronica had nothing to do with that."

"She might not have been the one throwing the punches, but she could very well be the one pulling the strings," Jinx said. "I don't know exactly what role Veronica is playing in this whole illegal-document operation, but she is definitely not an innocent bystander."

"We need to figure out how not-so-innocent she is," Joyce said.

"Or we need to find out how guilty Umberto is," Alberta replied. "He looks dangerous, we keep hearing that he's dangerous, but just how dangerous is he? I mean, what has he truly done?"

"Do you think it's time to bring Vinny in on what we know?" Joyce asked. "If Umberto is a criminal, he's got to be in the police system. Vinny could probably answer our questions in a few minutes."

"Not before he asks a ton of questions of his own," Jinx said. "Along with a very stern lecture about a woman knowing her place and maybe a thing or two about sidestepping the law."

Immediately, Alberta was reminded of her conversation with Helen a few hours ago. The age-old story of men thinking they knew what was best for women. Whether their misogynistic monologues stemmed from a place that simply wanted to protect the women in their lives, or control them, Alberta didn't know. It was a complicated issue. As with many complicated issues, a resolution was simple. A woman needed to take action and make a stand.

"There's no need to ask Vinny for help when Jinx has the resources to find out about Umberto's criminal past at her disposal," Alberta announced. "That's right, lovey, isn't it?"

"One hundred percent. Let me do some digging at work, which I'm late for," Jinx said, looking at the clock on the wall. "I'll call you later."

As Jinx dashed out of the waiting room, her long black hair bouncing with each step, another woman entered the room. She looked like Jinx's photo negative. She had the same long, wavy hair, but hers was platinum blond. Being somewhat of an expert on hair coloring, Alberta could tell that this woman's hair color was natural. Coming from a southern Italian family, almost every one of Alberta's relatives had black or dark brown hair. The only member of her very large family tree to be a true blonde was her third cousin Nicolletta, and rumor had it that her father was actually a Norwegian businessman on holiday, so she didn't really count. Alberta had no clue if blondes had more fun, but for her, they were always persons of interest.

This blonde was more interesting because she was also a doctor.

"Are you Alberta Scaglione?" she asked.

"Yes," Alberta replied as she and Joyce stood up. "Are you one of Sloan's doctors?"

"Yes, I'm Doctor Manzini, Kylie for short," she replied.

"I thought I looked odd for an Italian," Joyce said, "but you look downright Scandinavian."

"That's because I am," Kylie confirmed. "My father was born in Oslo."

For a moment Alberta wanted to ask Kylie if her father had been a traveling salesman who made house calls, but Alberta didn't think she could stand the shock of finding out that her family tree was even larger than she originally thought. Best to deal with the matter at hand: Sloan.

"Is he alright?" Alberta asked.

"He's had a minor setback," Kylie informed.

"What?" Alberta asked. "How minor?"

"He has an infection from his wound, but it's nothing to be alarmed about, I promise you," Kylie assured her. "We have it under control, but it means that he's going to be under sedation for a few more hours, so you might want to take a break and come back later this afternoon."

"If you think it's best," Alberta said.

"I do," Kylie replied. "He's going to sleep the day away."

"I guess we might as well go then," Alberta said. She looked at Joyce and they started to turn to go, when Alberta abruptly turned around and called after the doctor, "I almost forgot, were you able to contact Sloan's daughter?"

"Not yet," Kylie said. "I did receive an out-of-office

e-mail from her though. She's apparently with her family on an African safari, so it might be a few days before I hear from her."

"Sloan did mention that Shannon was a globetrotter," Alberta replied.

"I'm sure once she hears how attentive you've been, she'll be grateful her father wasn't alone," Kylie said.

Alberta wasn't sure if Shannon and her family would be so grateful to find out why she and Sloan were together at the time of the incident, but she thought it best to keep her mouth shut about that.

As Joyce drove them to have lunch at any restaurant other than Veronica's Diner, she couldn't help but ask more questions about Sloan's family.

"Are you planning to meet with Shannon?" Joyce asked.

"I'm sure I will whenever she's able to get here. I'd love to get to know her better. Sloan adores her, and from what I've gathered, she feels the same way about him," Alberta replied. "Which reminds me, I finally spoke with Rocco last night. Can you believe it's been almost six months since I heard his voice?"

"How's he doing?" Joyce asked.

"I think he's back to his old self," Alberta replied. "It took him a long time to get over the divorce and Annmarie has not been a very good ex-wife."

"Is the new wife any better?" Joyce asked.

"Rocco said Cecilia is the best thing that ever happened to him," Alberta said. "And he adores Gregory. They go fishing, they play ball, just last week Rocco took him to the natural history museum to see the dinosaurs. He's made some mistakes, my Rocco, but he's a good man."

"Yes, he is. And so is Sloan McLelland," Joyce stated. "Sloan picked a good woman too."

"Oh shush," Alberta said, playfully slapping Joyce's arm. "I just wish I wasn't going to meet Sloan's family under such unpleasant circumstances."

"Speaking of unpleasant," Joyce said. "I've been thinking about Scarface or Umberto or whatever his name is, and I agree that he's most likely the killer. But if the illegal-document operation is somehow tied to Third Wheel, Inc., that means the Rizzoli family is involved."

"You really can connect the dots, can't you?" Alberta observed.

"It comes from years of trying to predict the unpredictable stock market," Joyce explained.

"If what you say is true, the Rizzolis are a lot more ruthless than we thought," Alberta said.

"Do you think they could have put a hit out on members of their own family and hired Umberto to kill Teri Jo and Dominic?" Joyce questioned. "I've heard of cold-blooded before, but that's glacial."

Looking at the scenery passing by her from the passenger seat of Joyce's car, Alberta wondered if such a scenario could be possible. Not every family is a group of individuals who love, support, and protect each other. Even her own immediate family was broken and splintered. But she couldn't imagine that her own daughter, at the height of her fury with Alberta, would ever entertain the idea of killing her. Such things were the tales of fiction and not reality. Yet, Alberta had learned recently that the truth could be very strange indeed.

"Anything is possible, Joyce," Alberta admitted. "I'm starting to believe that those twins were killed by their family's own hands. That they hired Umberto to do the unthinkable."

Alberta might have thought that, but she would be wrong.

Her phone buzzed and she saw that the caller was Jinx. "Do you think Jinx got dirt on Umberto's past already?"

"Don't ask me, ask her," Joyce advised.

"Lovey, what did you find out?" Alberta asked, putting the phone on speaker so Joyce could hear the conversation as well.

"Are you sitting down, Gram?"

"Yes, I'm in the car."

"Are you driving?" Jinx asked. "You may want to pull over for this."

"No, Joyce is driving."

"Good, you don't need to stop then."

"Why does Joyce get to keep driving, when you wanted me to pull over?" Alberta asked.

"Because Joyce handles bombshells better than you do, Gram."

"She's right about that, Berta," Joyce said.

"Not for nothing, but I am very good under pressure," Alberta protested.

"We can agree to disagree," Joyce interrupted. "Can we please let Jinx speak so she can tell us what she found out about Umberto?"

"Fine," Alberta said, clearly not fine. "How hardened a criminal is he?"

"Hard as the cement blocks he's tied to the feet of whistleblowers before he's dumped them in the river," Jinx announced.

"*Dio mio!*" Alberta and Joyce exclaimed, one scream louder than the other.

"He's also been arrested for arson, breaking and entering, grand theft auto, and he owes thousands in parking violations," Jinx conveyed.

"Those tickets really do add up," Alberta said.

"Focus, Gram!" Jinx cried. "Umberto has a seriously long and violent rap sheet."

"So that proves he's our killer," Alberta declared.

"We were right all along," Joyce added.

"Wrong!" Jinx cried. "There's no way that Umberto killed anyone. Not Teri Jo, not Dominic, not even Inez."

"Lovey, you're not making sense," Alberta said. "You gave us the profile of a serial killer."

"Who's serving a very long sentence for his crimes," Jinx said. "Umberto Bottataglia can't be our killer because he's been in jail for the past two months."

CHAPTER 22

*L'unico crimine che vale la pena commettere
è un crimine di passione.*

Alberta never imagined she would one day go to
prison, but that's exactly what she and Jinx were
planning to do. While other grandmothers and granddaughters would set up lunch dates or take in a matinee,
Alberta and Jinx scheduled a trip to Riker's Island. For
them as investigators it was inevitable; for others, like
their loved ones, it was downright frightening.

Holding Lola in her lap and letting her cat lick some
cannoli custard off her fingers, Alberta sat at her kitchen
table and listened while Freddy tried to persuade Jinx to
rethink her decision to make such a dangerous trip.

"Since Sloan is still unconscious, I'm speaking for him
as well," Freddy said. "You ladies are out of your minds."

"Freddy, I know you're concerned, but what other
choice do we have?" Jinx asked.

"Stay home and let Vinny and his police force handle

this," Freddy replied. "Those people are trained to deal with crazy, homicidal inmates. What are you and your grandmother going to do? Bring Umberto a tray of lasagna?"

"Now, that is a smart idea!" Alberta said. "The best way to a man is through his stomach. It's a cliché because it's true."

"You can't bring food to Riker's Island," Helen said. "Trust me, I've tried."

"Dude! I mean, Aunt Helen! You've been to Riker's Island?" Freddy asked.

"Many times. I was part of a group made up of nuns, some clergy, social workers, and politicians that visited inmates who were preparing for release," she explained. "I mainly met with women who had made some really bad choices, and I tried to help them figure out how to survive in the real world."

"That's amazing!" Freddy squealed. "I had no idea you had such street cred."

"Where do you think the rest of them get their chutzpah from?" Helen asked. "It all starts with the nuns, Freddy, remember that."

"Chutzpah actually started with the rabbis," Joyce corrected. "It's a Hebrew word and its original meaning isn't as complimentary as it is today or by American standards."

"Chutzpah means something different in Hebrew?" Alberta asked.

"Most certainly," Joyce replied. "It means overstepping your boundaries, acting in a morally unacceptable way, and describes a person who lacks total common sense."

"That doesn't sound like something the nuns would approve of, Helen," Alberta said.

"They're an evolving group, Berta," Helen said. "Regardless of the word's origin, in this country it means having the guts and courage to practice what you preach. You want to solve this crime? You have to make an appointment with Umberto."

"Unfortunately, Umberto's ability to receive guests is strictly limited," Joyce said.

"Luckily, Aunt Helen's already been a guest at Riker's, so she's going to show us the ropes," Jinx declared. "Doesn't that make you feel better, Freddy?"

"As strange as it sounds, it does," Freddy replied, shoving an éclair in his mouth. "With Aunt Helen acting as your very own tour guide, what could possibly go wrong?"

The only reason Freddy was able to believe such a statement was because he had never visited a prison before. And Riker's Island made the cells at the Tranquility police station resemble a country club in comparison. As New York City's main correctional facility, Riker's was located on a four-hundred-acre island between Queens and the Bronx and housed more than ten thousand prisoners. Thousands more people worked there to run the place, and thousands more visited each day.

Helen explained that getting to Riker's Island was no picnic. First they had to drive from Tranquility to Queens, New York, which would be about a two-hour trip. Then they had to catch the Q100 bus, which would take them over the Riker's Island Bridge, which was the only way to get to the prison complex, and then deal with the myriad checkpoints and security procedures all visitors had to endure. She also prepared them for the smell.

Since Riker's was built over a giant landfill, as the garbage decomposed it produced methane gas, which, unfortunately, has the same aroma as rotting eggs. It was going to be a long, complicated, and smelly trip.

Even though Jinx's day job as a reporter for *The Herald* meant that she was able to tell the guards and administrators that she and Alberta, who was posing as a consultant, were visiting the prison for professional reasons, they were not offered any preferential treatment. There was no discrimination there, and Jinx and Alberta had to wait in line like every other visitor.

Helen was going to wait for them in the Benjamin Ward visitors' center while they met with Umberto. She said she had learned from her experience working with inmates that three was most definitely a crowd and often made them nervous and unwilling to talk, which is why Helen was sitting at a table in the visitors' center reading an old Danielle Steel novel, while Jinx and Alberta were sitting in front of a thick plastic partition waiting for Umberto to take his seat on the other side.

After ten minutes of waiting, Jinx started to get anxious.

"We only have an hour, Gram, what if he doesn't show?"

"Lovey, there really isn't anything we can do about it," Alberta said. "It isn't like we can go back there and force him to come out and talk to us. As difficult as it is, we're going to have to be patient."

"I know, but this place doesn't exactly make me all Zen and calm," Jinx replied. "I honestly don't know how people survive in a place like this."

Looking straight ahead, Alberta replied, "We're about to find out."

Walking toward them was the man they had seen multiple times in the past few weeks in both Tranquility and Brooklyn. But how could that be, if during that time he was locked up here behind bars? Contemplation on that question would have to wait. For the moment, Alberta and Jinx needed to harness every ounce of their strength to remain seated and not bolt from the room. They had been in hazardous, hair-raising situations before, they understood what it was like to be in jeopardy, they had even come face-to-face with heinous human beings, but watching Umberto limp slowly toward them was an entirely new experience. They were coming face-to-face with evil.

Umberto looked like something out of a movie, and not the kind Alberta and Jinx liked to watch on the Hallmark Channel. His limp seemed more pronounced, and he dragged his right leg every other step in an exaggerated motion because his ankles were shackled and connected by a long metal chain, which limited his movement. A similar manacle bound his wrists, so he kept his hands clasped in front of him, making it appear as though he was attempting to pray.

He wore loose-fitting gray pants, a short-sleeved V-neck shirt over a long-sleeved white undershirt, and black sneakers. If it weren't for the shackles, he would have looked like a doctor after a long shift in the emergency room. Unless you looked at his face, and then you'd see him for what he really was—a criminal who deserved to be behind bars. *Joyce was wrong*, Alberta thought. *You can judge a book by its cover.* Especially if the cover of that book was written by Umberto Bottataglia.

He possessed a thick head of hair that they hadn't noticed before, because every time they saw him he was wearing a hat: a mass of black waves with some gray at the temples that reminded Alberta of every man she'd ever met walking down the street in Hoboken, New Jersey. His eyes were coal black, so the pupils and the irises melded together to create one dark, ominous circle, and his nose was bent to the left, most certainly the result of being on the receiving end of some thug's left hook.

He had a five o'clock shadow, even though it was barely eleven, bags under his eyes as if he had just woken up, deep wrinkles on his forehead and around his mouth, and the telltale scar running down the left side of his face. He was a character out of a dime-store novel, a creature from a horror film, and someone the women would never forget.

When he sat down across from Alberta and Jinx, they pressed their knees into each other and fought the urge to grab hands. They were frightened, but they were committed not to show how they truly felt. They were determined to act as if they were truly reporters investigating a lead for an article and not a grandmother and granddaughter who knew, without a doubt, that they were completely out of their league.

He placed his hands on the ledge with a clang and smiled. His teeth were remarkably straight and white, making his smile both inviting and deadly. It was easy to imagine how despite his rough exterior he could charm his victims into a false sense of security. When Alberta remembered that Sloan was somehow his latest victim, her heart started to race. She reminded herself that if this meeting was going to be successful, she couldn't make it personal. Umberto didn't get the memo.

"Well, well, well," Umberto said, his smile lengthening. "This must be my lucky day. Two beautiful ladies for the price of one visit."

He leaned closer to the partition and the women willed themselves not to lean back.

"You must be Jinx," he said, pointing at Jinx. "And you, *bellissima*, must be Alberta."

Again, Alberta was reminded of Sloan. He would often use that word to describe her, and although his accent was atrocious, it was a sound she loved. Hearing Umberto say the word, even in his perfect pronunciation, made her sick. She knew they had to take control of the conversation immediately, or else the entire trip would be a waste of time.

"You would be correct," Alberta said. "And you must be the one and only Umberto Bottataglia."

"I broke the mold when God made me," he said.

It was difficult to comprehend that God had any involvement in the creation of the man they were looking at, but He did work in mysterious ways, so anything was possible. Even the fact that Umberto was responsible for three deaths while being incarcerated.

"Thank you so much for agreeing to meet with us, Mr. Bottataglia," Jinx started.

"I'm no mister," Umberto interrupted. "Call me Umberto."

"Alright, Umberto," Jinx said. "It seems that you've been spending more time out of prison lately than you have in your cell. How did you make that happen?"

"Why do you think that?" he asked.

"Because we've seen you in Brooklyn and Tranquility, New Jersey," Alberta said. "Walking in broad daylight, acting like you're an innocent man."

"Innocence is in the eye of the beholder, *bella*," Umberto mused.

"So you admit that you somehow broke out of your cell several times over the past few weeks?" Jinx asked.

"I can't give away all my secrets," Umberto said. "But it's a known fact that some of the guards here can be . . . *persuaded* . . . to help a man find a temporary retreat from this place."

"A retreat like Rizzoli's Diner?" Alberta asked.

Umberto's black eyes widened. "Have you tried their sausage and peppers? You must, *la salsiccia è deliziosa*."

A shiver ran down Alberta's spine when Umberto kissed his fingers and raised his hand to the sky. For a second it was like watching a flashback of her father after tasting one of her mother's meals.

"Why did you go to Rizzoli's?" Jinx asked. "Did they hire you to take care of some business for them?"

"Those Rizzolis do a lot of business, some good, some not so good," Umberto replied. "I assume you ladies know all about the brothers."

Out of the corner of her eye, Alberta saw that Jinx was about to answer his question, and she knew Jinx was going to respond like the hard-hitting reporter she was becoming. Unfortunately, Alberta had already sensed that Umberto didn't want to talk to reporters, he wanted to talk to women. Although it disgusted her, Alberta understood that it was important to use the appropriate arsenal when in combat with an opponent.

Sitting up straight and pushing her chest out, Alberta smiled and said, "You know what they say about a lady, Umberto? She needs a man to help her become a woman. Why don't you help us out and tell us what you know about the Rizzoli brothers?"

Both Jinx and Umberto stared at Alberta, Jinx in shock and Umberto in delight. She knew her granddaughter was appalled by her brazen talk, succumbing to the common misconception that a woman needed to use her gender to succeed, but the clock was ticking, and if Alberta had to flirt with Umberto to get him to spill the beans on the Rizzolis, so be it.

"What do you want to know about Giuseppe and Enrico?" Umberto asked.

"Everything," Alberta replied. "Why not start with their business?"

"The two brothers own Third Wheel, Inc., along with a family friend, Shamus MacNamara," Umberto said. "The three of them were literally partners in crime since they all met in the school playground. When they grew up they kinda went legit, bought some real estate, and opened up the diner. Everybody thought they'd kill each other within a year, but they proved us all wrong, they're still together. In name anyway."

"What do you mean by that?" Jinx asked.

"They're not friends no more, haven't been for years, business partners only," Umberto explained.

"What happened to their friendship?" Alberta asked.

"What always breaks up the friendship among men?" Umberto asked back. "A woman."

"One of them had an affair with someone else's wife?" Jinx asked.

"No, if that had happened somebody would've wound up dead. This had to do with Giuseppe's daughter, Bettina," Umberto replied. "She fell in love with Shamus's nephew and they were set to be married, but Bettina wasn't all woman, if you know what I mean?"

Remembering the story Filomena told them about Bettina, Alberta did know what Umberto meant. "She couldn't have children?" she asked.

"*Sì,* as barren as the Mojave," Umberto replied. "There was no way a proud Irishman was going to let one of his own marry a woman who wouldn't be able to contribute a branch to the family tree. It would have been . . . *sacrilego* . . . so they called off the engagement, paid her off, and she left town."

It was working. They were getting the information they needed to corroborate what they already knew. It was time to push further and find out things they didn't already know.

"What can you tell us about the twins, Theresa and Dominic?" Alberta asked.

"Ah, those *stronzos,*" Umberto said. "Enrico's grandchildren never stood a chance."

Alberta felt half victorious and half defeated. Umberto's reply explained that Veronica was the twins' aunt, but she didn't understand why they were schmucks or why they never had a chance. Neither did Jinx.

"What do you mean by that?" Jinx asked.

"They got their roles reversed. Theresa was the tough one and Dominic was weak," Umberto said. "Theresa was never going to be satisfied to play the role the family expected of her, and Dominic wasn't strong enough to be a real man. They both left home, just like Bettina, but they were nothing like that one, let me tell you."

"How can you say that?" Jinx asked. "The three of them did the exact same thing, they all fled their family."

"Sure, when they were young, but when they got older the twins stayed away, they didn't want anything else to do with Brooklyn or the Rizzolis," Umberto explained. "But Bettina, that one is *un'arpia vendicativa,* she wanted revenge."

Both Alberta and Jinx had to remind themselves that Umberto wasn't only speaking about Bettina, he was giving them information on Veronica too.

"How do you know Bettina was a vindictive harpy, Umberto?" Alberta asked.

"Because who, *cara signora,* do you think Bettina called to help her get revenge for being dumped and abandoned all those years ago? Me, that's who," Umberto said, proudly. "I hadn't heard from her for years and then *improvviso* . . . how do you say? Out of the blue she contacts me for my services. I was more than happy to help her out."

"What did you do?" Jinx asked.

"She wanted me to frame him so the cops would go after him," Umberto started. "But then I realized her *drudo* could help me more than I could hurt him."

"How could Veronica's *drudo* help you?" Alberta asked.

"I'm sorry, what's a *drudo*?" Jinx asked.

"The man who jilted Veronica," Alberta said. "Answer me Umberto, how could he help you?"

Umberto didn't feel like answering any more questions, he was more in the mood to reminisce about the past and fantasize about the future.

"It's always easy when you deal with strong women and foolish men," Umberto said. "Do you know what's better? A strong woman and a stronger man, like you and me, Alberta."

"What?" Alberta cried.

"*È la forza del destino*," Umberto replied. "Berta and Berto, sounds like a match made in heaven, no?"

Absolutely not, Alberta thought. But she couldn't say that out loud; she needed Umberto to tell them exactly who Veronica as Bettina wanted revenge on. Unfortunately, the guard who approached Umberto had other ideas.

"Time's up," the guard said.

"We're almost done with our interview. Could we just have a few more minutes?" Alberta asked.

The guard looked down at Alberta and she thought he had a very kind disposition. She was wrong.

"No," he replied. "C'mon, Bottataglia, back to your cell."

"What crime did Bettina want you to commit?" Jinx asked. When Umberto didn't respond, she grew more desperate to get answers. "Did you kill Theresa and Dominic Rizzoli? And Inez Rosales?"

"Alberta, next time come by yourself and leave the kid at home. She asks too many questions," Umberto said. "*Anche,* she's too young and innocent to know the truth. *L'unico crimine che vale la pena commettere è un crimine di passione.*"

They watched Umberto limp away, more uncertain than ever. They had gained some clarity, but garnered even more confusion. Could he be right? Was the only crime worth committing, a crime of passion? And if so, how many passionate crimes did Veronica commit?

CHAPTER 23

Salva l'anima davanti al corpo.

The moment Alberta saw Dr. Manzini's face as she stood at Sloan's bedside, she knew the next words she heard were not going to be words she wanted to hear. They were going to be unpleasant and difficult to comprehend, and she was going to feel angry, then scared, and then an unsettling combination of the two. Once again Alberta proved to be prophetic, because all of those things came to be.

"What do you mean he's in a coma?" Alberta asked. "You said he was going to be alright."

"He is, but—" Kylie started.

"No! No buts!" Alberta said. "I don't want to hear anything other than Sloan is awake and conscious and perfectly fine. You told me that all he had was a minor infection. Now you tell me he's in a coma!"

"A medically induced coma," Kylie corrected.

"What's the difference?" Alberta cried. "A coma's a coma!"

"Not precisely," Kylie replied. "Coma just means a deep state of unconsciousness. The difference is how someone gets there, either naturally or with medical intervention."

"Which is what you did to Sloan?" Alberta asked.

"Yes, because his brain started to swell," Kylie explained.

"Oh dear Lord!" Alberta exclaimed.

"It's a normal reaction to the kind of trauma Sloan sustained. The only anomaly is that his brain didn't swell immediately," Kylie said. "We thought things were under control, but it seems the infection triggered an adverse reaction."

In her mind, Alberta no longer saw Kylie. She was standing in front of another doctor, a much older white-haired man, and he was jabbering on, offering her information that she did not understand. All she remembered hearing was something about a severe stroke, massive damage to the brain and heart, and little to no chance of survival. It all added up to one simple fact: Sammy was going to die.

She never thought she'd have to live through such an experience again. As a widow she thought she'd be spared, and yet here she was. Alberta knew that she should be hoping for the best, but after spending a lifetime preparing for the worst, it was hard to shift her mindset.

"Do you know how long he'll be like this?" Alberta asked.

"It's hard to tell, but the delayed swelling that I've seen in the past usually takes a few days to rectify," Kylie replied.

"Once he wakes up, what are the repercussions?"

"Usually none, but we'll know better in a few days."

"Have you been able to reach Sloan's daughter yet?" Alberta asked.

"Not yet, but we'll keep trying."

There was nothing more for Kylie to say, so she clasped Alberta's hands, smiled, and went on to see her next patient. Alberta remained standing in the hallway, unsure of what to do next. She knew that she should go into Sloan's room and sit by his bedside so he could feel her presence, but she didn't move. Her mind, however, was racing.

Why was she behaving like this? She had been through medical crises before with friends and family and had been on the receiving end of more than her share of bad news. This was not a pleasant situation, but it wasn't unique. So what was the difference? Was it merely her fear of losing Sloan before their relationship truly started, or was it the guilt she felt because she was finding it harder to let go of Sloan than it had been to say good-bye to Sammy?

The realization struck her in the chest like a bolt of lightning. Was she a widow or a girlfriend? Was she ending or starting her life? Did she belong to Sammy or Sloan?

Standing motionless in the hospital, activity bustling all around her, she understood that the truth was, she was all of the above. She would always be part of Sammy's life and she was currently part of Sloan's. Would she continue to be a fixture in Sloan's life forever? She didn't know, but for now they meant a great deal to each other.

Her life wasn't ending or beginning, it was continuing, from the past to the future, from being a wife and mother to being an independent woman who happened to be in a relationship with a new man. When she cried, she wasn't crying for loss or out of fear that Sloan wouldn't recover; she was crying because she had found the answers by herself, all the strength she needed was inside of her, she just needed to be reminded of it every once in a while.

It also reminded her that she should go to the hospital chapel and light a candle for Sloan. It didn't hurt to give medical science some extra help. While she was there she also wanted to give thanks to God, and some angels and saints as well, for giving her the insight into her own personal capabilities. Knowing that God dwelled somewhere deep inside of her, filled Alberta with more optimism than she ever thought she could handle.

The chapel was not elaborately decorated, which Alberta liked. It didn't promote the pomp and circumstance of religion, but rather the essence of spiritual healing. Inside the small room was everything that was needed to pray. Four rows of pews made out of simple pinewood stained a dark brown, with matching kneeling benches that were topped with a burgundy cushion. The gold and red tabernacle sat on top of a wooden altar that stood behind a three-tiered wrought-iron candleholder that consisted of rows of red votives, long matches, and a container of sand to extinguish the flames.

To the left of the front door was a holy water font, on the right wall was a stained-glass depiction of the pietà in the same primary colors as the one on the front door, and

on the right wall was a small confessional with two isolated compartments, one for a priest to hear a confession
and another for the sinner to confess. Alberta thought it
was a perfectly crafted room, devoted to personal healing
and not meant to be an ostentatious display of wealth or
power.

After lighting her candles, Alberta prayed silently for a
few minutes, kissed the gold crucifix around her neck,
made the sign of the cross, and started to leave. Just as
she placed her hand on the doorknob, she saw through the
stained-glass window the distorted images of Father Sal
and Owen walking toward her. She wanted to confront
each of them for very different reasons, but she made a
split-second decision based on the fact that her curiosity
would be quelled quicker if she listened to their conversation instead of participating in it.

She pulled the curtain of the confessional closed and
lifted her feet above the hemline just as Sal and Owen entered the chapel. She made another sign of the cross, asking for forgiveness, when she realized she was defying
the basic teachings of the nuns from her grammar school.
She was in hiding so Sal and Owen could be heard and
not seen, rather than the other way around. Hopefully, she
would overhear something worthwhile that would make
the morally ambiguous action she was undertaking worth
the risk.

"I guess it's the curse of the Irish, Father," Owen said.
"To go to a priest before a doctor."

"*Salva l'anima davanti al corpo,*" Sal replied.

Silently Alberta agreed with Sal that it was more important to save the soul before the body.

"Like I've told you before, and I think your doctors

agree with me, your migraines are the result of too much stress," Sal added.

"You may be right," Owen said. "The Tranqclockery doesn't get much business anymore, so keeping the shop financially solvent is a daunting exercise."

"Isn't most of your income derived from private collectors?" Sal asked.

"Yes, very demanding, impatient private collectors," Owen replied. "They expect to have what they want, when they want it, and not a moment later. Let us not forget that I also have to contend with my bosses."

"Third Wheel, Inc.?" Sal asked.

"One wheel is worse than the other," Owen said. "Greedy, duplicitous, untrustworthy, and after all these years still treating me like a hired hand instead of a vital piece of the enterprise."

"Not everyone has as forgiving a boss as I do," Sal joked. When the response from Owen was silence, Sal apologized. "I'm sorry, I did not mean to make light of your situation."

"That's alright, I should apologize. I'm taking up your time with my petty problems when there are sick people who need your attention, like Sloan," Owen said. "I do hope he recovers soon."

Alberta felt violated when she heard Owen mention Sloan's name. How dare he bring up Sloan's condition and use it as some kind of comparison to his own predicament? He shouldn't even be allowed to bring it up in conversation. It was because of whatever illegal scheme he had going on with Veronica and Umberto that Sloan was in the dire straits he was in.

"Sloan's prognosis is good," Sal said. "He's had what

is considered a setback, but the doctors look at it as necessary intervention. Life really can be viewed from more than one angle."

"That's reassuring," Owen said. "Maybe by the time I'm back he'll be fully recovered."

"Where are you going?" Sal asked.

"To Texas to heed the bosses' call," Owen replied.

"When are you leaving?"

"Tomorrow morning," Owen said.

"Is this a wise move on your part?" Sal asked.

"Perhaps not, but when Third Wheel requests your attendance at a business powwow, you drop everything to comply," Owen explained. "My private plane is gassed up and ready to leave tomorrow morning, nine a.m. sharp."

"You still have your plane even though you're having financial hardships?" Sal asked. "Trust me, I understand the need for luxury, but why don't you sell it?"

"Bite your tongue, Father," Owen reprimanded. "I will not throw the baby out with the bathwater simply because I'm going through a bit of a slump."

"You're also going through a bit of a medical crisis. How are you going to fly your plane if you could go blind in mid-flight?" Sal asked.

"Thank you for your concern, but I've hired a pilot," Owen confirmed. "And Veronica is going with me."

"The two of you? Alone on a plane?" Sal asked. "I thought you said she hasn't been acting very neighborly lately."

"You are correct, but the truth is we've never been very close other than geographically, and I'm sure she's been less friendly than usual because of the tragedies that have occurred on her premises, which is completely understandable," Owen said. "I have an idea. Why don't you join us? I could use a buffer if the tension gets too thick."

"Owen, I'm a man of the cloth and I don't give in to superstition, but I have a bad feeling about this trip," Sal confessed. "I really wish you would take my advice and cancel. I can strongly recommend to your doctor that he admit you. Your bosses can't expect you to check yourself out of a hospital just for some meeting."

"Thank you, Father," Owen replied. His voice sounded different to Alberta, pared down and genuine. "I appreciate your concern more than you could ever know. You really are the only friend I have. However, this trip is essential and serves a dual purpose. I'm meeting a new client to hand deliver a very expensive grandfather clock to him. He's paying extra for it to be hand delivered, so not only would I lose the respect of my bosses if I cancelled, I'd lose a lot of money."

Laughing derisively, Sal replied, "Business always gets in the way of salvation, doesn't it?"

Sal led Owen in prayer for a few moments and Alberta, with little else to do, prayed along. However, her heart almost stopped beating for a few seconds when she heard Sal ask Owen if he would like Sal to hear his confession. Her heart didn't start beating again until she heard Owen decline the offer.

"I should be going now, Father," Owen said. "I need to make sure that grandfather clock is packaged correctly. It's so large, I ordered a few crates in different sizes so I have one that fits properly."

"Travel safe, Owen."

"Cheers."

After the front door closed, Alberta heard Father Sal return the kneeling bench to its upright position. She began to relax her legs, but made sure they didn't drop below the curtain so she wouldn't be exposed. She needn't have wasted any time thinking she would expose herself, since Father Sal was more than willing to do that for her.

Whipping the curtain open, Father Sal hovered over Alberta and struck a stern, priestly pose brimming with heavenly disapproval.

"Oh my God!" Alberta shrieked.

"Only one of His servants," Father Sal replied. "What on earth are you doing in there?"

"How on earth did you know that I was in here?" Alberta asked.

She was stunned that she had been discovered. Nothing that Sal or Owen said had given her any indication that they knew someone was eavesdropping on their conversation. She hadn't made a sound, even though she was starting to get a cramp in her leg from sitting in a crouched position for so long. But it wasn't a sound that gave her away, it was a smell.

"I can detect Shalimar perfume a mile away," Sal said. "At first I thought it was the lingering scent of a patient's wife, but when it didn't fade and only got stronger, I knew it meant you finally crossed the line of decency and were holding a stakeout in the confessional. What's next? Hide-and-seek in the tabernacle?"

"I'd love to say I'd fit in there, but we both know that's a lie," Alberta quipped.

"Alberta Ferrara Scaglione, I'm serious!" Sal shouted. "One thing's for certain—you are your sister's sister."

"I know you're upset with me, but understand that you helped me so much, and it's because of you that I'm going to be able to solve this mystery," Alberta declared.

"From what Owen and I discussed?" Father Sal replied. "We didn't say anything important."

"Oh yes, you did," Alberta corrected. "You were just listening to the conversation from the wrong angle."

Alberta was so excited she couldn't even wait until she got home to call Joyce, Helen, and Jinx, so she sat in her BMW and placed the calls one after the other. Each conversation was short and to the point. She told them to meet her at her house at seven p.m. because they needed to make plans for tomorrow. Joyce and Helen didn't ask any questions—they heard the power in Alberta's voice and they knew they would learn everything they needed to know in a few hours. Jinx, however, was filled with too much youthful energy not to bombard her grandmother with requests for more details.

"Gram, what's this all about? You sound like you're going to explode, but, like, in a good way," Jinx said, sitting at her desk at work.

"Lovey, I'll explain all the details later, but tomorrow we're finally going to be able to reveal to everyone who the murderer is," Alberta declared.

"You figured it out?" Jinx exclaimed.

"Yes, I know who killed Teri Jo, Dominic, and Inez," Alberta declared. "And, lovey, you need to brace yourself because you're not going to believe who it is."

CHAPTER 24

Un voto fatto non può mai essere infranto.

By the time the women arrived at Alberta's house, she had a vegetable lasagna warming in the oven, antipasto on the table, and a pitcher of Red Herrings waiting to be poured into four empty glasses. When Jinx, Joyce, and Helen noticed that the glasses were Alberta's fine crystal given to her by her parents as a wedding present, and not the typical jelly jars she used on a daily basis, they knew this was going to be an important meeting.

Even Lola sensed this was more than a typical gathering. Instead of lying on the floor in the doorway that led into the living room, where she usually camped out so she could take a nap if the human entertainment grew boring, she was perched on top of the side table next to the doorway so she could have a perfect view of the goings-on.

Alberta stood in front of her family and smiled. Once

again they had done it, they had been confronted with a horrible truth—the murders of innocent people—and together they worked tirelessly to uncover the culprit and the reasons why blood was spilled in their town. They had followed leads and gathered clues and finally Alberta had connected all the dots and solved the mystery. At least she was 99 percent certain she had solved it. She wouldn't be absolutely, positively sure until she confronted the suspect.

She wasn't going to let that infinitesimal possibility of failure dampen her spirits, or make her second-guess her and her family's achievements. It was a time for celebration for all their hard work. Alberta was the only one who wanted to celebrate, however. The rest of the Ferrara ladies wanted answers.

"Spill it, Gram! Who's the murderer?"

"If I just tell you, you're not going to believe me," Alberta said. "What I need you all to do is trust me."

"Of course we trust you, Berta," Joyce said. "But you brought us here to tell us who killed Teri Jo, Dominic, and Inez, so tell us."

"I brought you here so we could make plans for tomorrow," Alberta corrected. "That's when we'll know for certain if I'm right."

"What's so special about tomorrow?" Helen asked.

"Owen and Veronica have been summoned by the bosses of Third Wheel, Inc.," Alberta started.

"Giuseppe and Enrico Rizzoli and Shamus MacNamara?" Jinx interrupted.

"Yes, the three men who run the parent company," Alberta confirmed. "There's some kind of business meeting in Texas, and Owen and Veronica are being forced to attend."

"Do you think they're going to Henderson, Texas, where we found Dominic?" Joyce asked.

"That's my guess," Alberta answered. "Tomorrow, when we stow away on Owen's plane, we'll know for sure."

Slowly, Helen, Joyce, and Jinx drained their glasses of Red Herring, doubtful that they heard Alberta correctly.

"Gram, I think you've lost your mind," Jinx said.

"The four of us are never going to be able to hide on that small plane," Helen added.

Acting as if she heard every word Alberta said but couldn't fathom how any of it could be plausible, Lola meowed loudly and rolled onto her back, stretching her body so she resembled a long, black, furry snake.

"Don't be so dramatic, Lola," Alberta said. "The same goes for the rest of you. We're not all going to stow away on the plane, just me and Joyce."

"Well, that makes much more sense," Helen said. "Thank you for clarifying and forgive us for ever doubting you, Oh Grand Poobah."

Jinx grabbed the pitcher and refilled their glasses. "No, Aunt Helen, that would be Oh *Gram* Poobah!"

"Laugh all you want, but I have a plan," Alberta said. "And if we all play our parts, it's going to work."

"Berta, how did you find out that Owen and Veronica were going on a trip?" Joyce asked. "None of us heard about it."

"I accidentally overheard Father Sal and Owen discussing it at the chapel at the hospital while I was visiting Sloan," Alberta said.

"Accidentally?" Jinx asked.

"How did they not see you?" Joyce asked. "That chapel's almost as small as the inside of Owen's plane."

"You hid in the confessional, didn't you?" Helen asked.

"Gram, you did not!" Jinx squealed.

"Lovey, I saw an opportunity and I took it," Alberta confessed, taking the lasagna out of the oven.

"I have never been more proud of you than I am right now," Jinx said.

"Helen, you have more in common with Father Sal than you know," Alberta said. "He knew I was there the entire time, even though I didn't make a sound. He didn't give me away, but after Owen left, he pulled back the curtain and scared me half to death."

"How'd he know you were there, Gram?"

"I bet it was the Shalimar," Joyce said.

"Yes, he smelled it!" Alberta exclaimed. "How did you know that?"

"You lean toward a heavy spray," Joyce replied.

"I do?" Alberta exclaimed. "*Dio mio!* I'm like Aunt Nancy and her Emeraude. You must be able to smell me a mile away."

"Just a few feet," Joyce said. "But I love Shalimar! Every time I'm near you I feel like I'm walking in a garden."

"It's your signature, Gram," Jinx said. "Don't ever stop wearing it! Or spraying heavy."

"Can you please stop talking about Berta's perfume and let her tell us about this alleged plan?" Helen barked.

"Helen's right," Alberta said. "Jinx, honey, cut everybody a piece of lasagna and I'll explain how we're going to expose what's been going on in town the past few weeks. God willing, tomorrow it'll all be over."

The next morning, Joyce picked up Alberta at seven a.m. and drove them to the Tranqclockery. They were headed to the same destination, but looking at them they appeared to have been given separate dress codes.

Joyce was decked out in a red collarless car coat, a black silk taffeta dress that was exactly one-and-a-half inches longer than her coat, and red patent leather pumps. Her accessories were equally fashionable. She wore her trademark gold hoop earrings, a pin fastened to her coat in the shape of Salvador Dali's melting clock, which she chose for the irony, a red silk scarf, and black patent leather driving gloves. Alberta, in contrast, was dressed like she was going for a morning run and was clad in a navy-blue tracksuit and sneakers. And not an ounce of Shalimar.

Alberta went through her plan from start to finish once again to make sure Joyce hadn't forgotten anything. They discussed what they would do in case of a snafu or if there was an unexpected glitch, and by the time Joyce pulled into the clock shop's parking lot, they felt comfortable that they had considered every possible problem that could arise. There was nothing more to say, which was good, because from here on out, Alberta had to remain silent for their plan to work.

Joyce looked at Alberta and nodded her head, giving her the signal to open her door. They each stood on opposite sides of Joyce's Mercedes held their door handles, and didn't close their doors until Joyce once again nodded her head. If anyone was listening, it sounded as if only one person had exited the car, which is exactly what the women wanted.

They walked across the asphalt and only one set of footsteps could be heard because while Joyce's pumps clicked loudly each time her feet hit the ground, the extra cushiony soles of Alberta's sneakers prevented her from making any noise while she walked.

Before Joyce rang the doorbell, she looked at Alberta

and crossed her fingers. If Owen answered the door and wasn't in the throes of an ocular migraine, they were going to have to switch to plan B, because he would see that Joyce had company. In that case, there was nothing they could do to sway the odds in their favor. They would have to think quick, on their feet.

When the door opened to reveal Owen wearing his dark sunglasses with the thick frames that blocked out light from all sides, they knew they had passed their first hurdle.

"Good morning, Owen, it's me, Joyce."

"Joyce, what a pleasant surprise," Owen said.

"I had a very early appointment to meet with a potential buyer for one of my paintings, and on my way back I thought I'd pop in and see how you're doing," Joyce lied.

"How thoughtful," Owen said. "Did you make a sale?"

"What?" Joyce replied.

Alberta poked Joyce in the shoulder as a way to remind her that Owen's question was in response to Joyce's fabricated story.

"The painting," Owen said. "Did your potential buyer come through and buy the piece?"

"Yes, he most certainly did and also too, he commissioned a new piece!" Joyce said, making her lie even more elaborate.

Joyce saw Alberta's stern glare and knew she needed to get back on track and get them inside before anyone saw the two of them standing on the front stairs.

"It's been a very successful morning so far," Joyce added. "But I heard from Father Sal that you're not having much success with your headaches and they've become relentless lately. I wanted to see if I could help in any way."

Owen stared at Joyce, and she prayed he couldn't see that her expression was the complete opposite of the calmness of her voice.

"Isn't that neighborly of you," Owen said. "Here I had all but given up on being on the receiving end of acts of kindness. Please come in."

As Joyce entered she told Owen she would close the door and held his left hand, forcing him to turn to the right. This allowed Joyce to open the door wide enough so Alberta could enter behind her.

Once inside, Alberta realized she was going to have to move very slowly because some of the floorboards in the shop were old and squeaky. She hoped that Joyce's incessant chatter would conceal any noise she might make and Owen would attribute it to the creaks of an old store.

"I apologize for barging in like this, Owen," Joyce said. "But as someone who lives alone, I know that it can be challenging to get certain things done if you're not feeling well."

"Please don't apologize, Joyce, you're one of the very few visitors I have had," Owen shared. "Honestly, I'm the one who should apologize."

"Why would you have to do any such thing?" Joyce asked.

"Because I have an appointment this morning, as well, which is going to prevent me from being a proper host," Owen explained. "I do have time for one cup of tea, if you'd like to join me."

"Owen O'Hara, you should know by now that I will never pass up a chance to have a cup of Earl Grey," Joyce said.

"Then this, milady, is your lucky day," Owen said. "If you could steer me to the hotplate, I'll make us a cuppa."

While Joyce was simultaneously keeping Owen engaged in conversation and navigating him to the back of the store, Alberta was slowly making her way down to the back room of the Tranqclockery, where she had last seen the grandfather clock. According to what Owen had told Father Sal, he was getting ready to transport the clock with him on his morning flight to Texas to deliver it to a customer, so it should be on the premises, waiting to be moved. She entered the back room, leaving the curtain open so she and Joyce would be able to see each other, and was thrilled that she was correct. There was a large wooden crate with the grandfather clock's certificate of authenticity taped to it. What delighted Alberta even more was to see a second, slightly smaller crate, standing next to it, just as Owen told Father Sal there would be.

A few feet away Owen was boiling water on the small hotplate he kept in the back corner of the shop on top of an old-fashioned metal cabinet.

"Why don't I take care of the tea?" Joyce suggested.

"Thank you, dear," Owen replied. "You'll find everything you need within arm's reach."

Joyce guided Owen to sit in the chair, deliberately turning it around so his back faced Alberta. Joyce rummaged through the cabinet until she found two cups and a box of teabags. While she was setting everything out on the surface of the cabinet, she continued making small talk with Owen and let him explain to her, yet again, how his ocular migraines had developed and worsened through the years. She also stole glances at Alberta to make sure she knew what her sister-in-law was up to. Thankfully, she had become a whiz at multitasking while working on Wall Street. She never realized she'd need to utilize her skills in her retirement.

Alberta caught Joyce's eye and pointed to herself and then pointed to the empty crate, to indicate that this was how Alberta was going to sneak onto Owen's plane. Joyce nodded that she understood, but had to turn away because the water started to boil. While Joyce was busy pouring tea, Alberta took the certificate of authenticity off the large crate and taped it onto the smaller one. Now came the hard part. Alberta had to get into the crate without being heard.

Once again, Alberta waited until she caught Joyce's eye. When she did, she opened the door to the crate and released a silent sigh of relief that it didn't make a sound. Joyce grabbed hold of the handle to the cabinet, and just as they did when exiting the Mercedes, they timed it so they each closed their door at the same time.

Breathing deeply, Alberta felt a small wave of panic start to rise from the pit of her stomach. Another way to describe the crate, which was her temporary home, was to call it a coffin. Or a casket. Or one of those metal compartments in the morgue. Alberta fought to control her breathing and not think about the fact that she was actually in the type of confinement that would be her final resting place. It was a morbid thought, but it was the truth. Even though death seemed to be all around her lately, she didn't spend copious amounts of time thinking of her own mortality. She had her ailments, but she wasn't infirm, she was old, but not elderly, and thanks to Jinx and the rest of her family she had a lot of living left to do. She never spent time thinking about her departure from this world. Until now.

Part of her thought she was making a huge mistake or, more accurately, the stupidest decision of her life. The other part of her remembered that she vowed to her sister

Helen that she would bring Teri Jo's killer to justice, and she wasn't going to let her down. She remembered something her grandfather would always tell her: *Un voto fatto non può mai essere infranto*. A vow made can never be broken. If she had to hide out in a crate for a few hours and fight back the fears about her own eventual death in order to get the prime suspects alone and in a place where they didn't have a chance of escaping, that was the price she would have to pay. If the rest of her plan went as smoothly as the first part had, Alberta wouldn't have any further problems.

Wishful thinking.

From inside the crate, Alberta couldn't see anything, but she heard every word of the conversation Owen had with the moving men he hired to transport the grandfather clock to his plane. She did not like what she heard.

"Which crate are we taking, Mr. O'Hara?"

"The one with the certificate of authenticity on it," Owen replied.

"Got it," the man said. "I'll just lock it up and it'll be on the plane waiting for you before you take off."

"Thank you so much," Owen said. "Tell the pilot we'll be there shortly. We'll leave for the airport once Veronica arrives."

Alberta held her breath, and she knew Joyce was doing exactly the same on the other side of the crate. They both realized that they weren't as smart as they thought they were, because they had not planned on the crate having to be locked. But why wouldn't it be secured? Owen was transporting an expensive item and he couldn't risk the door to the crate opening up during the flight and having the grandfather clock fall to the airplane floor. His lucrative sale would be ruined.

Alberta heard the mover attach a padlock to the crate and snap it shut. Then she heard him repeat the process not once, but twice more. She was now stuck in a crate with three padlocks keeping it locked and secure. How in the world was she ever going to get to confront the suspect and solve this mystery?

Once again, fate was on her side. Sort of.

"The three locks have the same combination, Mr. O'Hara," the man said. "I've written it down on this piece of paper."

Owen reached his hand out, but he underestimated the distance between him and the deliveryman, so his fingers were clutching at the empty air. Joyce quickly stepped in and took the paper for him.

"Thank you," Joyce said. "I'll make sure Owen has the combination so he can unlock his precious cargo when he lands."

The next thing Alberta knew, she was being jostled as the deliverymen prepared to move the crate from the shop onto their truck. Slowly she turned counterclockwise until she was horizontal, resting on her right shoulder, and then the men tipped the crate so Alberta was on her back. The men adjusted their grip, which gave Alberta a moment to get used to the new position and she happily realized she was physically comfortable.

"This must be some clock you got in here, Mr. O'Hara," the man said. "It's heavier than I thought."

Emotionally, however, Alberta had just gotten bruised.

As the men were walking down the steps that led to the alleyway, they were greeted by Owen's traveling companion.

"Owen, move it!" Veronica bellowed. "Let's get on with this charade."

Alberta wasn't sure if the men stopped in their tracks because Veronica was blocking their exit, or because of the nasty tone of her voice. Once Veronica noticed Joyce, however, she corrected herself and Veronica sounded like she always did. Hearing this other side of Veronica made Alberta wonder which one was the real person, and to use Veronica's word, which one was the charade.

"Joyce, good morning," Veronica said. "I didn't expect to see you here."

"I stopped over to check in on Owen," Joyce replied. "I didn't realize the two of you were jetting out of town. How glamorous!"

"Hardly. It's an unavoidable business trip, we'll be back by tonight," Veronica said. "Unless we miss our flight, which we cannot do. Owen, are you ready to leave?"

"I am, but there's been a change of plans," Owen said.

Alberta grabbed her crucifix and said a quick prayer that she hadn't been discovered or that Owen hadn't decided to transport the grandfather clock in a cargo plane. She needn't have worried, because Owen was doing exactly what she thought he would do.

"We don't have time to make any changes, Owen," Veronica said, her voice once again unpleasant and irritated. "They're expecting us."

"Don't fret, Veronica, we'll get there on time," Owen said. "I'm not changing the flight plan, only the passenger list. Joyce, please say you'll join us for the ride."

"Owen, are you out of your mind?"

Alberta didn't need to see Veronica's face or body language, she could tell from her voice that she had abandoned all pretense. She wasn't trying to appear friendly and cooperative; she was angry and she didn't care who noticed. Alberta wasn't sure if this was the real Veronica, but she knew it was a side of her that came naturally.

"I'm sorry, Joyce, but this is a business trip," Veronica said. "We're not flying down to Rio."

"Maybe we will after we get done with our meeting," Owen said, chuckling. "It's my plane and I want Joyce to join us."

"This is ridiculous!" Veronica cried. "Shamus and the others aren't going to be pleased when they see that you've brought company to a company meeting!"

"Veronica, stop being such a prickly pear," Owen demanded. "Don't pay any attention to her, Joyce—honestly, I never do. Our meeting won't be long, and you can relax on the plane until we're done. Please say that you'll take a ride with us, Joyce. It's so rare that I get to share the friendly skies with, well, friends."

Alberta was beaming inside the crate. Everything was going according to plan. She knew from the conversation she overheard between Father Sal and Owen that he and Veronica weren't on the friendliest of terms and that Owen was hoping for a third wheel to join him on his trip to meet with the literal Third Wheel. She also knew that Owen had very few friends in town, and Joyce was one of the few people he liked. So Alberta had figured if she placed Joyce in the right place at the right time, Owen would take the bait. And she was right. She didn't have to hear Joyce's response to know that the second part of their plan was intact. Joyce would be on the plane and be Alberta's witness when she revealed who the killer was.

"What do you say, Joyce?" Owen asked. "Are you up for a little adventure?"

"Owen, adventure is my middle name," Joyce declared. "Texas, here we come!"

CHAPTER 25

L'aereo! L'aereo!

The third part of Alberta's plan was unfolding at the airport without her. She didn't worry that it wouldn't be executed precisely as she had instructed, because Jinx, who was sitting in Helen's Buick parked at the Morristown Airport, was leading the effort. Jinx was in the passenger seat, Freddy was in the back, and Helen, as usual, was in the driver's seat, her hands gripping the steering wheel even though the engine was turned off. From where they sat they could see Owen's Cessna Denali getting fueled up for their upcoming flight. A flight that, if Jinx did her job, would never get off the ground.

"You realize your grandmother has lost her mind," Helen stated.

"I think Gram's got a better hold of her mind than all of us," Jinx replied. "She's the one who figured this whole thing out."

"I'm not talking about her smarts. My habit's off to her," Helen said. "I'm talking about her mental state. She's crazy to think she can get away with this."

"She isn't doing it alone," Jinx corrected. "She's with Joyce and she has us, and once I get ahold of Vinny, she's going to have the cops on her side too."

"He still hasn't called you back?" Freddy asked.

"No, and I've left three messages," Jinx complained.

They watched the maintenance men disengage the fuel lines from the top of the wings and return them to their stationary positions. By the time they were finished with their job, Freddy had Vinny on the line.

"Dude, it's Vinny," Freddy said.

"How did you get him on the line?" Jinx asked.

"I called his cell," Freddy answered.

"And he picked up?" Jinx asked, her voice about an octave higher.

"We've kind of become tennis buddies," Freddy confessed.

"You play tennis with Vinny?" This time Jinx's voice was so high it pierced Helen's ears.

"Answer the phone already before we get attacked by a pack of wild dogs!" Helen shouted.

Yanking the phone out of Freddy's hands, Jinx started the call in a fashion that could only be described as inappropriate, especially if you wanted the person you were speaking with to follow your orders.

"Why didn't you call me back?"

"I've been busy investigating three unsolved murders, Vinny barked.

"What do you think I've been doing?" Jinx cried.

"I'm doing my job. You're having fun and getting in the way."

"Really? I'll have you know that I'm sitting in the Morristown Airport waiting for the killer to fly out of town," Jinx said. "So there!"

"You figured out who the murderer is?" Vinny asked.

"Yes! Well, no, my grandmother did, but what does that matter?" Jinx said. "You need to help us."

"You Ferraras have been doing God knows what on your own since Teri Jo was murdered, and all of a sudden you need my help?" Vinny asked.

Vinny was shouting so loudly his voice echoed throughout the car. Helen, who could bicker with the best of them, had had enough of the bickering and knew that time was running out if she wanted to help her sister. She grabbed the phone from Jinx and told Vinny exactly what he had to do.

"Vinny, this is Helen, so don't give me any back talk," she said. "Get in your squad car and get to this airport now so you can stop Owen and Veronica from taking off in his plane. Otherwise, you're letting a murderer escape."

"One of them is the murderer?" Vinny asked.

"Stop talking and start driving!" Helen yelled.

"I'm on my way," Vinny said.

Helen handed the cell phone back to Freddy. She turned to face forward and keep an eye on the plane, "He's on his way."

"Riddle me this, people," Jinx said. "Freddy calls Vinny and he picks up immediately. Helen gives him an order and he complies. Correct me if I'm wrong, but I don't think Vinny likes me."

"He doesn't, sweetie," Helen said.

"He's used the words *entitled* and *hothead* when he talks about you," Freddy said. "I've told him those are

only *parts* of your personality. The whole Jinx is like a totally different person, and he's starting to come around."

"Dude! You are so lucky we're on a stakeout right now
or there would be hell to pay!" Jinx screamed.

"Keep your voice down, Jinxie," Helen said. "We've
got company."

From their vantage point they saw Joyce's Mercedes
pull up near Owen's Cessna, followed by a white van.
They watched in silence as Joyce and Veronica got out of
the car and they followed Joyce with their eyes as she
walked around the car to help Owen out of the passenger
seat. Veronica approached Owen and she could be seen
saying something to him, but she must not have liked his
response because she turned her back on him, crossed her
arms in front of her chest, and started pacing back and
forth between the vehicles.

They heard the side door of the van open up, but since
it was facing the opposite direction they didn't see the
two men carrying the crate until they were a few feet from
the plane.

"That's Gram!" Jinx shouted.

"Keep your voice down, Jinx," Helen said. "You don't
want to give us away."

"Sorry, I'm starting to freak out a little," Jinx said.

They then heard a ping from Freddy's cell phone, indicating that he received a text message.

"Is that Vinny?" Jinx asked.

"Tambra," Freddy replied. "They're about ten minutes
away."

"Tell them to hurry," Jinx said. "They're boarding the
plane now."

Veronica ran up the stairs into the plane, followed by
Owen and Joyce, who were moving much slower. Joyce

entered the plane last and waited while the staircase was
wheeled away to pan the parking lot for Helen's car. As
the door was lowered into place, she held her hand up as
a signal that she saw them. The next second the door
closed and Joyce disappeared from view.

"Vinny's not going to make it in time to stop the plane,
Aunt Helen," Jinx announced. "What are we gonna do?"

"The only thing we can do, Jinxie," Helen said. "Stop
it ourselves."

Helen turned the key in the ignition and the Buick
revved up. It was by no means a sports car, but it had
served them well and had become an integral part of their
detective work. She was praying the old baby wouldn't
let them down now, because she was going to take it—
and herself, for that matter—out of its comfort zone. If
David could stop Goliath, Helen thought, why couldn't a
Buick stop a Cessna?

They watched as the propeller began to spin until it
was whirling so quickly they could no longer see the
blades. When the plane started to turn to the right toward
the small runway, Helen knew that she had to take action.
If she was going to prevent Alberta and Joyce from being
whisked away with someone who had already killed
three times, she had to act now.

Helen slammed her foot on the gas pedal with such
force that it threw them all back against their seats.
"Buckle up!" she cried.

"Too late!" Freddy yelled from the floor of the back
seat.

Doing her best imitation of Paul Newman crashing the
Indy 500, she sped down the runway, gaining on the
plane in the hopes of getting in front of it to block it from
being able to take off. She wasn't alone.

Freddy's phone pinged again, signaling the receipt of another text from Tambra. "She says look to the left," Freddy said.

They did and saw Vinny's police car racing down the runway on the opposite side of the plane. Two cars on either side of a plane all careened down the runway, each trying to outrun the other, but as the Buick's speedometer crept toward 100 miles per hour, the car started making odd sounds similar to what can be heard in the belly of a ship. White smoke that quickly turned black emerged from underneath the hood, and despite Helen's foot being pressed firmly on the gas pedal, the car decided it had had enough and started to slow down.

They looked to the left and saw that the police car was still riding neck and neck with the Cessna, but before it could overtake the plane and turn to the right to prevent it from taking off, the plane became airborne.

"*L'aereo! L'aereo!*" Freddy shouted.

"You mean the plane is gone, Freddy," Helen corrected. "So's any chance of us helping Berta and Joyce."

Rabid, Jinx got out of the car and stormed over to Vinny, who was running his hands through his hair. He was just as angry, and when Jinx confronted him with her own fury, it was like a fireworks display. The wind started to rustle around them and combined with the airport noise it made normal conversation difficult to hear. Luckily both Vinny and Jinx were in the mood to shout.

"This is how you help the citizens of your town!" Jinx exclaimed.

"If the citizens of my town would follow the rules, I wouldn't have to try and stop a speeding plane from taking off!" Vinny shouted.

"Well, if you did your job right, we wouldn't have to break the rules!"

"For your information, we have been doing our job!" Vinny bellowed. "We are this close to making an arrest."

"You couldn't make an arrest if somebody committed a crime right in front of your face!"

Vinny looked at Tambra, Helen, and Freddy, who were all standing around watching the confrontation, in disbelief. Sometimes his job was easy and other times it was like today.

"We've been looking into Owen and Veronica's business relationship with the Rizzoli family and Third Wheel, Inc., and had you told me that they were flying to Texas more than ten minutes before takeoff, I could've hauled them in for questioning," Vinny said. "We also know that Umberto Bottataglia is connected to Third Wheel, and although he's been in jail for several months, we've been investigating some dirty cops at Riker's to find out if he could have possibly escaped."

Jinx opened her mouth to speak, but Vinny closed it for her.

"Shut up and let me finish!" he cried. "We also know that Inez Rosales's murder is linked to Teri Jo's and Dominic's, because when I talked to Inez's sister Gabi, she showed me the card you gave her. The real question is when are you and your family going to trust me and my police officers and stop trying to do this all on your own?"

"When are you going to trust us enough to bring us in on your investigations from the very beginning?" Jinx asked. "Not just when you've hit a brick wall."

"Enough!"

Helen's cry was stern enough to make Vinny and Jinx stop their argument and clear their heads. The wind was getting even stronger, so Helen grabbed Freddy's arm for support.

"Three people are dead, Sloan is in a coma, Alberta and Joyce are on a runaway plane, and all you two can do is argue?" Helen said. "You make the Catholic Church look like a well-oiled machine!"

Shaking his head and throwing his hands up in the air, Vinny replied, "We'll continue this discussion later, but for now we have work to do."

"Boss, I've already alerted the Rusk County Airport in Henderson not to let anyone off of that plane," Tambra said.

"Good work," Vinny said. "Now all we have to do is pray that plane lands safe and sound."

"Did I see a car on the runway?" Veronica asked.

"I may be blind, Veronica," Owen said, "but you must be seeing things."

"Joyce, what about you?" Veronica asked. "Did you see a car on the runway?"

Joyce not only saw one car, but two, on the runway. She decided, however, that it was best not to reveal that information, considering who her travel companions were.

"No," she replied. "I always close my eyes during take-off and say a little prayer, just in case."

"Because, Joyce, you are a wise woman," Owen said. "If only the rest of your gender were your equal."

"Like you would know anything about women, Owen," Veronica sniped.

Ever since she'd arrived at the Tranqclockery earlier, Veronica had been trying to contain her foul mood. Trapped on the plane, she had given up any attempt to be polite, cordial, or cooperative. She wanted to be anywhere other than in a plane the size of a tour bus, flying thirty thousand feet in the air with people she obviously did not like.

Thanks to her career in a male-dominated industry, Joyce could spar with the best of them, and if she chose, she could take Veronica down with a few choice words, but she needed to maintain the illusion that she wasn't taking sides. She wasn't Team Veronica or Team Owen, she was Team Alberta all the way. And Joyce needed to bide her time until she could unlock the crate to free Alberta without creating any suspicion. Since the interior of the plane wasn't much larger than Alberta's kitchen, it was not going to prove easy. What she needed was some help, but it appeared, for the moment, that she was on her own.

Until Mother Nature stepped in.

Without warning, the plane dipped as if the sky had parted underneath them. They couldn't tell if the plane descended two feet or twenty, but it felt like they were about to plunge back down to the ground. Just when the plane started to gain altitude, it shook from side to side. The contents of the overhead cabinets were jostled, but the cabinets themselves remained closed.

Joyce turned around and saw that even though the crate had been propped up against the back wall and was secured in place with a bungee cord fastened to hooks on either side of the crate, it was still teetering like a metronome. She cringed to think that Alberta was getting banged up inside and was about to get out of her chair and run to the crate before her sister-in-law broke an arm or got a concussion, when the turbulence stopped as suddenly as it started.

Immediately, Veronica complained about this being the worst plane ride of her life, when she was cut off by the pilot's voice coming over the intercom.

"Sorry about that takeoff, Mr. O'Hara," the pilot said. "There's a storm directly in front of us, nothing too serious, but we are going to experience some more turbulence."

"That's alright, Eugene," Owen said. "I know that we are safe in your hands and you'll get us to our meeting in one piece."

"Like hell he will!" Veronica shouted. "Turn this plane around, Eugene, and do it now!"

"Ignore the shrieking banshee, Eugene," Owen said, a smirk on his lips. "You've been given your orders, now do as you're told."

"Oh my God! You treat everyone like they're a possession!" Veronica yelled. "After all these years, you still don't know how to treat a person like a human being!"

Owen's smirk grew into a smile and he patted Joyce's hand. "How she prattles on. Maybe she'll jump out of the plane so we can talk in peace."

Joyce watched as Veronica headed toward the cockpit, and knew this might be her only chance to free Alberta.

"Excuse me, I need to use the ladies' room before we get tossed around again."

With one eye on Veronica pounding on the cockpit door, Joyce unhooked the bungee cord from its hook on the wall and quietly placed it on the floor. She then took out the piece of paper with the combinations to the locks printed on it and started to unlock one of the three pad-locks.

"Are you alright, Berta?" Joyce whispered.

"I'm fine, but what the hell is going on?"

"Veronica is throwing a tantrum and Owen seems to be enjoying the show even though he can't see a thing," Joyce replied.

She finished entering the three numbers, pulled on the padlock, and opened it.

"One down!"

"Hurry up, Joyce, I think I'm developing claustropho-bia," Alberta said.

"Hold on, only two more to go."

On the other side of the cabin, Veronica was just as de-termined to get into the cockpit as Joyce was to get Al-berta out of her crate.

"Eugene! I will break this door down with my bare hands, and if you don't think I can do it, you're in for a rude awakening!"

Veronica continued to pound on the door and scream wildly until the door opened to reveal Eugene standing there. He pulled the door open so abruptly, Veronica fell into his arms.

"Sorry, Berta, we got company," Joyce said. "I have to try later."

Joyce walked back toward her seat and watched the al-tercation between Eugene and Veronica. She quickly re-alized that if Eugene was arguing with Veronica, there was no one at the controls.

"Pardon me, but who's flying this plane?" Joyce asked.

"I have it on autopilot," Eugene replied. "We're per-fectly safe, but, Veronica, I must insist you get back to

your seat and stop banging on the door or I'm going to
have to restrain you."

"Are you kidding me?!" Veronica shouted.

Alberta grabbed her head and wanted to pound it on
the crate. This was not how the plan was supposed to go.
They were not supposed to be in midair. She was not supposed to be locked in a crate. When was she going to
learn that she couldn't control everything? And when did
she get such a big ego?

Standing in the darkness, hopeless to escape without
outside help, Alberta had time to think, and she wasn't
pleased with herself. Why didn't she present her thoughts
to Vinny? Lay out for him all the clues that she and her
family followed that had brought her to her conclusions?
Was she hungry for attention after decades of living in the
shadows? Had she allowed her own growing notoriety to
become more important than bringing criminals to justice
and righting the wrongs done against innocent victims?

She promised herself that once she got out of this crate
and this plane, and was back in her kitchen with her family, where she belonged, she would do better. Until then
she had to do something to end this nightmare. She just
had no idea what that something was going to be.

"Veronica, will you please shut up!"

Owen's cry appeared to be the figurative slap in the
face that Veronica needed to end her verbal tirade. She remained silent long enough to be thrown against the wall
when the plane hit another pocket of turbulence, this time
much more severe and longer than the first. Joyce managed to grab hold of her seat, so when she fell into the
window she only slid down the wall and wasn't tossed vi-
olently across the plane like Veronica was. Alberta wasn't
so lucky.

The crate banged into the bathroom door and then the wall a few times before hurtling forward and crashing to the floor. The landing was so rough it broke the hasp and staple at the top of the crate, releasing the padlock's hold. With the top two locks removed, Alberta was able to lift the back of the crate and crawl to freedom. She didn't care that the plane was still jerking back and forth—it could act like the inside of a washing machine all the way to Texas. All she cared about was that she was no longer trapped in darkness.

"Alberta!" Joyce cried. "Thank God."

The women crawled toward each other and embraced. They held on to each other even after the plan was flying smoothly again and didn't let go until they heard Owen's voice.

"Alberta? What in the world are you doing here?"

"Can I interest anyone in a grandmother clock?" she said.

Owen turned toward her voice and repeated his question. "Did you stow away on my plane?"

"Yes, Owen, with Joyce's help I did just that," Alberta replied.

"If you wanted to come along as my guest, I would have gladly allowed it," Owen said.

"I doubt you'd be so accommodating if you knew why I was really here," Alberta said.

"Why is that?" Veronica asked.

She struggled to stand up, but finally did. Leaning against the wall of the plane to steady herself, Veronica wiped blood from the gash in her forehead and absent-mindedly smeared it on her dress. She made the action look natural, and it reminded Alberta of a waitress wiping kitchen grease on her apron, a waitress like Teri Jo.

"To tell the murderer that I figured out this whole mystery," Alberta replied.

"I think that can wait, Berta," Joyce said.

"We've waited long enough, Joyce," Alberta said.

"We can wait a little longer," she insisted.

"What could possibly be more important than this?" Alberta asked.

"Finding someone to fly this plane," Joyce said. "The pilot's been knocked out cold."

CHAPTER 26

Nascondersi in bella vista.

Sprawled out in the narrow aisle of the cockpit was Eugene Dalrymple. He was hard to see because the door was halfway closed and only remained open because it kept hitting his foot. For the moment, the Cessna was flying itself.

"Dammit, Eugene!" Owen shouted. "I command you to fly this plane."

"He's unconscious, you idiot!" Veronica yelled.

"Wake him up," Owen said. "Pour cold water on his face, kick him, do whatever it takes to revive his uncooperative body, or else we will eventually run out of fuel and crash. From what I've read, it is not a pleasant death."

"It can't be any worse than being stabbed in the back!" Veronica shouted.

"*Basta!*" Alberta cried. "Owen's right, we have to revive Eugene."

Joyce ran to the small kitchen area located behind the seats and turned on the cold water. As it ran she rummaged through the cabinets underneath the sink and found some glasses. She filled two of them with water, ran to Eugene, and threw the water in his face. He didn't respond.

"Wake up, you bastard!" Veronica screamed while kicking Eugene in the leg.

"Stop! You'll hurt him," Alberta said.

"He's half dead," Veronica replied. "How can I hurt him any more than he's already been hurt?"

Joyce refilled the glasses and once again threw water in Eugene's face, but he still didn't respond. None of them were doctors, but they all knew he was unconscious and he was going to stay that way for several hours.

"Eugene, if you don't get up right now and fly this plane, I'm going to garnish your wages!" Owen yelled.

"I can't believe anyone so stupid could be a murderer," Veronica said.

"Must you always speak nonsense and lies?" Owen asked. "I'm not the murderer, you are. Isn't that what you've come to pronounce, Alberta?"

"One of you did commit all three of those murders, and I've figured out how and why," Alberta said. "But none of that matters now because we need to gain control of this plane! Unless I'm mistaken, the only one here who's conscious and a registered pilot is Owen."

"You would be correct, Alberta," Owen confirmed.

"Also too, he's blind," Joyce said.

"You would also be correct, Joyce," Owen said. "At least for the moment."

"You can sit next to me and tell me what to do so I can land this plane safely," Alberta said.

"What makes you so sure I'll do as you wish?" Owen asked.

"Because you want to know how I figured out that you've been impersonating Umberto Bottataglia for weeks," Alberta declared. "And how you tried to frame Umberto for the murders you committed."

"Oh my God!" Joyce cried. "That's incredible."

"That's ridiculous!" Veronica screamed. "Umberto and Owen are nothing alike!"

"Then you admit that you know Umberto too?" Alberta asked.

Veronica's eyes widened and her nostrils flared. It was the classic facial expression of someone who got caught saying something they shouldn't have said. She was about to do something she shouldn't have contemplated.

She reached under the seat and pulled out a parachute and began putting it over her head. It was obvious that she didn't know how to securely fasten it to her body, but she wasn't thinking clearly. All she wanted was to get off the plane.

"I have had enough of this!" Veronica shouted. "I'm getting out of here."

"Now who's the idiot?" Owen asked. "Where do you think you're going?"

"I'm going to jump," she declared.

Veronica grabbed the door handle on the cabin door, but before she could pull it or start to unlock it in any way, Joyce and Alberta ran to her, each grabbing an arm, and pulled her to the other side of the plane. By this point she was hysterical, and there was only one way she was going to stop screaming and crying. Alberta and Joyce had the same idea at the same time, so Veronica wound up receiving slaps across both sides of her face. The slaps hurt, but they snapped Veronica back to reality.

"I'm sorry," she said, taking off the parachute and tossing it aside. "I've been under a lot of stress lately."

"Now where were we?" Alberta asked. "Oh yes, Owen was going to be a gentleman and help me turn this plane around so we can go home."

"I'd rather hear the campfire tale about Umberto Bottataglia and me being one and the same," Owen added.

"Don't twist my words, Owen," Alberta advised. "I didn't say you two were the same, I said you've been masquerading around town as Umberto. *Nascondersi in bella vista.* Hiding in plain sight."

"I know what it means, Alberta," Owen hissed. "I've been around the Eye-talians most of my life. Now if someone would help me into the cockpit, I'll try to prevent us all from dying an agonizing, fiery death."

Joyce grabbed Owen's arm and followed Alberta into the small compartment, careful to step over Eugene, and helped Owen sit in the chair next to Alberta. Joyce stood behind Owen, and Veronica hovered in the aisle. They were desperate to hear how Alberta came to the startling revelation that Owen was impersonating Umberto while Umberto was incarcerated in Riker's Island, but first they needed Owen to teach Alberta how she could impersonate a pilot.

He described how the instruments on the panel were similar to the tools she used while driving a car, so very few of them should be foreign to her. He was right. There was the airspeed indicator; the altimeter, which displayed the altitude the plane was flying at; the vertical speed indicator, which indicated the airplane's rate of climb and descent; and the artificial horizon, which was primarily used when visual flying was compromised. There was the control wheel, which was the plane's steering wheel, and the thrust, or the plane's gas pedal and brake pad combined in one device. Most important was the turn coordinator, which would be crucial to allow them to make a U-turn and change direction, which was what they wanted to do.

"Before you do any flying, you must call air traffic control and let them know that you need to change your flight plan," Owen instructed.

"How do I do that?" Alberta asked.

"There's a yellow switch at five o'clock in front of you, "Owen said. "That's your lower right-hand corner. Do you see it?"

Alberta looked down and saw the switch. She focused her eyes on the instrument in front of her and not out the window, because she thought she might pass out if she looked out at the clouds. "Yes."

"Flip it up and you'll be connected to the air traffic controller," Owen said. "I can do the talking."

Instantly, a voice boomed through the speaker, joined by a great deal of static. "This is air traffic control, go ahead."

"Air traffic control, this is Owen O'Hara, owner of Cessna Denali X72439. Our pilot has suffered an injury from turbulence and is unconscious," Owen conveyed.

If the controller was surprised by this information, he didn't show it. He responded like a veteran 9-1-1 caller, calm and professional.

"Is there anyone on board who can fly a plane?" he asked.

"Yes, me," Owen replied. "Regrettably, I am suffering from a temporary loss of my vision."

There was a pause before the man replied. "Seems like you have a bit of a problem."

"It is an obstacle. However, I'm instructing untrained personnel on how to turn this plane around so we can return to land at Morristown Airport," Owen advised. "There's a storm in front of us with quite a lot of turbulence, and she won't be able to control the plane with that much interference."

"Roger that, the wind's picking up here as well," the man said. "You have permission to land. Stick to the reverse flight plan and you'll be fine. We're advising all aircraft in the area of the situation to steer clear of your craft."

"Thank you," Owen said.

"We'll keep this frequency open and check back with you," the man said.

"That's most kind," Owen said. He tilted his head so his next comment was directed at Joyce and Veronica. "The two of you should go back to your seats and buckle up. This might not be the smoothest of maneuvers."

Not surprisingly, both women refused to leave the cockpit. They sat on the floor and held on to the base of the chairs in front of them, which they hoped would prevent them from getting knocked around and winding up like Eugene. They did hold on tighter when Owen told Alberta to turn off the autopilot and advised her that she was now flying the plane all on her own.

"Berta, I can't believe what you're doing!" Joyce squealed. "I should really take a photo of this."

Alberta couldn't believe it either. Instead of shaking and hyperventilating, she felt like she was outside of her body, watching a stranger fly the plane. The thought of what she was doing, that the lives of everyone on the plane were in her hands, was so overwhelming that it was as if her mind and her body separated. She had a job to do, and if she gave in to fear and anxiety, she would fail. And failure, in this instance, was definitely not an option.

"Let Owen help me get us turned around and back on track so I can put the autopilot back on," Alberta said. "We can have a photo shoot later."

Owen expertly coached Alberta on how to bank the wings without losing altitude, how to maintain climbing and acceleration speeds, and how to keep the turn coordinator at the appropriate levels. When the plane was back on the original flight plan, except in the other direction, Owen asked Alberta to read all the numbers back to him from the various instruments on the panel. He instructed her so she could make some minor adjustments, and when he was satisfied he told her to switch on the autopilot button.

"Finally!" Veronica exclaimed. "Now explain this cockamamie story about Owen being Umberto."

Alberta took a deep breath and looked out the window. They were flying above the clouds, closer maybe to heaven than earth, and it was all her doing. She acknowledged her accomplishment, thanked God silently, and then swiveled around in her chair to face everyone. She had a story to tell.

Even though Owen kept his sunglasses on and stared straight ahead so she couldn't see his eyes, Alberta directed most of her story to him. He was, after all, the leading man.

"It took me a while to connect all the dots, but when Jinx and I went to see Umberto at Riker's Island, we realized that there was no way he could have escaped that prison," Alberta said. "There are too many checkpoints and guards, and the only way off the island is that one bridge, and each vehicle that enters and exits is examined.

"Even if he did somehow convince a guard to help him escape, Umberto would still have had to walk freely around both Tranquility and Brooklyn to murder three people without anyone noticing him," Alberta explained. "The only answer was that there had to be someone impersonating him, and that someone was you, Owen."

"Alberta, I understand that it's an incredible longshot that the real Umberto got out of jail," Veronica said. "But Owen looks nothing like him."

"That's true, Owen and Umberto look nothing alike," Alberta conceded. "Umberto is wider across the shoulders, but they are the same height and with the right toupee, makeup, and costuming, they could easily be mistaken for each other."

"Wait a second, Berta, we saw them together in the Tranqclockery when we only knew Umberto as Scarface," Joyce said.

"We saw them together because that's what Owen wanted us to see," Alberta said. "In order for his scheme to work, he knew there had to be witnesses who saw Umberto and Owen together to make it look like they were two different people. Owen must have known we were in the alleyway, so he turned his back to us, dressed as Umberto, and acted like he was shaking hands with someone else, who we would assume was Owen."

"Damn, that's clever," Joyce said.

"If you remember that night, Joyce, I went into the back room of the Tranqclockery to see if I could find Scarface hiding out," Alberta said.

"I do remember, but you came up empty," Joyce replied.

"Not really," Alberta said. "I didn't find Scarface, but I found a piece of foam, which I realized later was like the foam from the shoulder pads that we used to wear in the '80s. Put them underneath an oversized coat and a man looks a lot larger than he really is."

"That's the oldest fashion trick in the book," Joyce said.

"That night I also found a prayer card for St. Gemma that had a St. Ann's Church stamp on the back," Alberta explained. "I thought it might belong to Umberto, until I did some research and found out that St. Gemma is the patron saint of migraine sufferers, so the card belonged to Owen. He must have picked it up when he visited St. Ann's Church in Brooklyn, as Umberto."

"Now you're the clever one!" Joyce squealed.

"No, she isn't," Veronica corrected. "She's forgetting an important detail about the very first murder."

"What's that?" Alberta said.

"Owen was in the diner the morning Teri Jo was murdered," Veronica said. "He was sitting at the front counter having breakfast with Father Sal."

"You have many faults, Veronica, but at least you have a very good memory," Owen said. "Father Sal had the French toast and I had an egg white omelet with broccoli and mushrooms."

"You seem to have a pretty good memory too, Owen," Veronica replied. "When it suits you."

"You're both only remembering half of what happened that morning," Alberta said. "Owen was there, but not the entire time. He joined Father Sal, ordered breakfast, and

J.D. Griffo

then left, leaving his tweed jacket on the stool, the same one he's wearing right now in fact. He went around to the alleyway, crawled through the window of the men's bathroom, and killed Teri Jo. Then he rejoined Father Sal to finish his meal."

"I must also be able to impersonate an invisible man if no one saw me do that," Owen said.

"People saw you, it just never registered that it was an odd thing to see a man leave to tend to his business next door," Alberta explained. "I didn't even know the Tranqclockery existed before all this began and Joyce explained it was because I didn't need to know about it. Since I never had any use for the shop, it was invisible to me. Our mind plays tricks on our eyesight. You should know all about that, Owen, with the ocular migraines you suffer from."

Owen smiled slowly at the reference to his persistent ailment. "Why didn't Father Sal ever question my absence from our meal?"

"He mentioned more than once that he has come to accept your eccentricities," Alberta said. "He was fully aware that you left, but he considered it normal activity from you. Father Sal also thinks you're a good person and could never imagine you're a cold-blooded killer."

"Berta, are you saying that after Owen realized he killed Teri Jo by mistake, he walked right back into the diner from the men's room?" Joyce asked.

"Exactly," Alberta said. "He didn't change into his Umberto disguise, because he wouldn't have had time to change back and it would've been too risky to leave his clothes in a bathroom stall or a garbage can."

"This is all fascinating, but how did he kill Teri Jo by

mistake?" Veronica asked. "He knew she was working that day."

"Because he was expecting to meet with Dominic," Alberta replied.

"Really?" Joyce asked. "How do you know that?"

"When we talked to Dominic in Texas he said 'If only I had gotten there sooner, it would've been me,'" Alberta said.

"I don't remember that at all," Joyce said.

"We were all talking so quickly and the plane was about to take off; there was a lot going on," Alberta explained. "I didn't remember it until much later, but it means that Dominic was meant to be at the diner that morning—more than likely to meet with Owen. He had no idea that Owen's real reason for the meeting was to kill him. When Owen saw Teri Jo from the back, he thought it was Dominic and killed her instead."

"You killed Teri Jo by mistake?" Veronica asked. "How could you be so vile?"

"My guess is that once you knew that you were going to have to murder again in order to kill off Dominic, who was your intended target in the first place, you got the idea to make it look like someone else was terrorizing the town," Alberta said. "You knew Umberto had a sinister past, so you picked him. He would've been your perfect alibi except you didn't know he was currently serving time."

"You realize this is all circumstantial evidence, don't you?" Owen asked.

"Circumstantial evidence adds up," Alberta said. "Like the fact that Gabi Rosales said Umberto's scar was on the right side and not the left, and that he ran away from her. She didn't mention a thing about Umberto having a limp."

"Then there was the e-mail we received from Umberto," Alberta said. "It struck me odd that a lowlife criminal would be so polite and sign an e-mail 'Cheers,' until you said the same thing when you left Father Sal in the chapel yesterday."

"You were there?" Owen said, turning to face Alberta for the first time.

"She was hiding out in the confessional and heard every word of your conversation," Joyce said.

Owen stared at Alberta for quite a long time. It was unnerving because she could only stare back at black sunglasses, but she refused to turn away. If he was trying to intimidate her, he was going to lose.

"Even if you convince the police of your . . . *theory*, what's my motive?" Owen asked, turning his head back to face the cockpit window. "Why would a quiet clockshop owner suddenly go on a killing spree?"

"Because you're more than a shop owner, Owen, you're involved in selling illegal documents," Alberta said. "The Tranqclockery is nothing more than a cover for your far more lucrative side business."

"That's ludicrous," Owen said. "I've never been involved in anything illegal in my life."

"What about that scandal with the fake birth certificates at Christ Hospital, where you used to work flying their helicopter?" Joyce asked. "Is that where you got the idea?"

"Or did you get it from Bettina?" Alberta asked.

This time when Owen turned to face Alberta, Veronica did the same thing.

"The next time you have illegal paperwork that you

don't want anyone to see, Veronica, you should keep it in a safe and not in a drawer at work," Alberta said. "Anyone could accidentally stumble upon it."

Veronica's lips started to form a protest, but suddenly stopped. She dropped her head to her chest and took several breaths. When she looked up, she seemed relieved.

"I had no idea when I asked Umberto all those years ago to help me get fake documentation so I could start my life over, it would lead to the deaths of my niece and nephew, you've got to believe me," Veronica said.

"I do," Alberta said. "Sadly, it means that you set this whole thing into motion. If you hadn't reached out to Umberto for the documents and then years later to get revenge on the man who jilted you when you were a young woman, the man whose family paid you to leave town, Owen and Umberto would never have met."

"Owen is Veronica's ex?" Joyce asked.

"Yes, he's her weak-willed Irishman," Alberta said. "Their story is just like Viola and Marcello's."

"Who?" Joyce asked.

"From our family history, Marcello abandoned Viola the same way Owen abandoned Veronica. The only difference is that Viola was able to find some happiness in her life," Alberta explained. "I dreamt about the two of them just before Teri Jo was killed. The painting in my bedroom is an heirloom from Viola and it always reminds me that love comes in many forms."

"Anthony told me about that story when we were dating," Joyce reminisced. "He said nothing like that would ever happen to us. You can't always trust men, can you, Veronica?"

"No, you can't," she replied. "You can't always trust your family either. All I wanted was to marry Owen, but his family wouldn't hear of it and my family was more interested in preserving their business relationship, so they refused to interfere."

"Is that why you relocated to Tranquility, Veronica, to rekindle your romance with Owen?" Alberta asked.

"I thought after all this time we could have the happiness we should've had years ago, but Owen didn't even recognize me when I came to town," Veronica said. "He abandoned me when I was young and he rejected me decades later. So yes, I wanted revenge. I got in touch with Umberto and told him to do whatever he wanted to frame Owen for something that would put him in jail."

"You didn't count on Umberto and Owen working together to funnel illegal documents through the Tranq-clockery," Alberta said. "Or for him to recruit Teri Jo to do his dirty work for him."

"I should've put a stop to it," Veronica said, "but I thought she would do one job and Owen would finally get caught."

"That's because you've always underestimated me," Owen said. "My parents gave you money and you took it and ran away. You just assumed I was in on the scheme. You never gave me a chance to persuade them to let us marry."

"You wanted to marry me?" Veronica asked. "Even though I couldn't have children?"

"Did I ever get married? Did I ever have any children? No!" Owen cried. "I didn't care about that, all I cared about was you, and you took the easy way out. The truth, Veronica, is that you abandoned me, not the other way around!"

The words slapped against Veronica's flesh harder than any physical attack ever could.

"When Umberto came to me, he told me that you sent him and that you wanted revenge to get back at me for deserting you all those years ago," Owen explained. "I told him that he had been duped and that you were the one who deserted me. Together, we devised a strategy to make a little money off of your idea."

"So you and Umberto were partners," Joyce declared.

"At first," Owen confirmed. "But then he got bored and I took over the operation. We went our separate ways, you could say."

"Which is why you didn't know he was back in jail," Alberta said.

"No I didn't, which was a fatal error," Owen admitted. "I had begun to believe I really was invisible, untouchable. Everything was going so smoothly until Teri Jo told Dominic about our arrangement and he demanded she stop. I was doing the girl a favor! I was helping her make some extra money because she was always strapped but Dominic was a scared little boy and he threatened to tell my Uncle Shamus and the rest of the Rizzolis, so he left me no choice."

"But to kill him?" Alberta asked.

"Yes!" Owen cried. "You were right, Alberta, he was supposed to meet me at the diner that morning to discuss business, and Teri Jo . . . got in the way! I didn't know it wasn't Dominic until she turned to try and look at me and I saw her profile."

"What did you feel when you realized you killed an innocent woman?" Veronica asked.

"Numb," Owen replied. "I couldn't move, but then suddenly I remembered exactly who I was, the Invisible Man. I knew I could follow Teri Jo out into the crowded diner and take my seat next to Father Sal before the poor woman fell to her death."

"You were taking an extraordinary risk," Alberta said. "If even one person had seen you leave the men's room, you would've been caught."

"I had no other choice but to take that risk," Owen explained. "I must admit I loved it. The rush of adrenaline I felt was almost overwhelming. I felt alive for the first time in years."

"You felt alive because you killed someone?" Joyce asked, her voice filled with both shock and disgust.

"That's a simplified, though succinct way to put it," Owen replied. "And the answer is yes."

"I cannot believe I ever loved you," Veronica said.

Once again Owen smiled, but this time it was wistful and filled with memories. "Neither can I."

"What about Inez?" Alberta asked. "Why did you kill her?"

"She was asking too many questions and said she was going to tell ICE where she got her fake documents!" Owen cried. "I tried to convince her that I would give her enough money to run away, but she refused and said she was going to tell."

"So you just had to kill her too," Veronica said.

"Yes, I did! But I let her sister live," Owen said. "I should have killed her, she saw me, but I knew Inez had a son and I couldn't leave him without anyone. I am not heartless!"

"No, Owen, you're just a coward and always have been," Veronica said. "Maybe I ran away, but you never looked for me. Then when you found me again, you treated me like a stranger."

"Because that's what you are to me," Owen said.

"So are you!" Veronica cried. "The sweet, funny young man I fell in love with could never have grown up to become a murderer. I don't understand this, what turned you into such a monster?"

"You did," Owen replied.

He turned away from Veronica to stare straight ahead and out the cockpit window. Suddenly, he took off his sunglasses and gasped, "Oh my God."

"You can *see*?" Alberta screamed. "You were faking your blindness all this time?"

"It returned when I hit my head against the back of my seat during the turbulence," Owen said. "But I wish I were still blind."

"Why?"

"You see that mountain range in the distance?" Owen asked. "We're about to crash right into it."

CHAPTER 27

Un tempo codardo, sempre codardo.

The Appalachian Mountains are usually a beautiful sight. Looking at them from the cockpit of the plane, inching closer every second, brought terror into everyone's hearts. If they didn't do something soon they were going to crash into the mountains and become part of the landscape.

"We must've lost altitude," Owen announced. "Air traffic control should've warned us."

"Owen, take over the controls," Alberta commanded.

Even though he was no longer wearing his sunglasses, Alberta couldn't detect any emotion by looking at him. His face was stoic, expressionless, despite the fact that he was looking at the same mountains they all were and drew the same conclusions they did. Inaction equaled death.

"Owen!" Veronica cried. "Do what she said! Take control of the plane and fly us over those mountains."

His one-word answer rendered them speechless.

"No."

"Are you insane?" Alberta asked. "If you don't do something we're all going to die. You said you weren't heartless, now prove it."

The only sound that could be heard in the cabin was the occasional static coming from the radio. The women were afraid to speak and held their breath, waiting for Owen to respond. He might be a murderer, but he wouldn't put his own life at risk after doing so much to avoid being caught. The survival instinct was too great.

When Owen turned to Alberta, she realized the instinct to surrender could sometimes be stronger. There was nothing behind his eyes, no emotion of any kind, not love or hate or anger or fear. It was like she was staring at a mannequin.

"Why should I?" he asked. "I've already killed three people, maybe four if Sloan doesn't pull through."

At the mention of Sloan's name Alberta felt rage rise from her belly to her throat and it took every ounce of strength she had not to lunge forward and attack Owen. As much as she wanted to lash out at the man for hurting Sloan, she needed him to save their lives.

"The courts have been known to show mercy," Alberta said.

"I am many things, Alberta, but I am not an idiot," Owen said. "The second we get back home I'll be arrested and with your help the police will put together a case against me that will have only one result, a lifetime in prison. Look at me, Alberta, do you think a man like me can survive a day in prison, let alone a lifetime?"

"You'd be surprised how strong you can be when you're tested," Alberta said.

She tried to focus her attention on Owen, but she kept stealing glances out the window. Her heart thumped louder as she watched the mountains get closer. She felt sweat start to accumulate on her brow and the radio static was becoming deafening.

"Think of the time you'll have to reflect on your life," Alberta said. "Prison might be good for your soul."

"My soul?" Owen scoffed. "Do you really think there's any chance of redemption for my soul?"

Alberta didn't have to think over the question, she instinctively knew the answer. Owen had done some heinous things, and despite his claims that he had a heart—which was questionable—Alberta had come to believe that if a person truly wanted salvation, despite their previous actions, they could receive it. The path wouldn't be easy, and forgiveness from the people and families that were destroyed might not ever come, but where there was remorse, there was hope.

"Yes," Alberta replied.

Finally, Owen showed some emotion. He smiled and his eyes filled with tears. "Then you, my dear Alberta, are a disappointment," Owen said, his smile disappearing. "You may be clever, but you're quite a stupid woman. There's nothing left for me here on Earth, or wherever I'll go to when this plane hits those jagged mountains just up ahead."

Stunned by such a cruel sentiment, it took Alberta a moment to regain control of her voice and her body, but when she did she wasn't going to let her fate rest in the hands of a man who had given up.

"You might have nothing left to fight for, Owen, but I've got a life to live and I'm not going to let it end be-

cause of you!" Alberta declared. "I should've known . . .
Un tempo codardo, sempre codardo."

"I could've told you that," Veronica said. "Once a
coward, always a coward."

"Berta, what are we going to do?" Joyce asked.
"Owen's the only one who knows how to fly a plane."

"Alberta! Can you hear me?"

The voice broke through the constant pulse of the
radio static like a life preserver, and Alberta held on for
dear life. She turned to Joyce and smiled. "Looks like I'm
going to learn how."

"Alberta!" the voice cried.

"Yes I'm right here," Alberta replied. "In the driver's
seat."

"We lost contact with you for a while," the man said.
"You need to remain calm, but the plane has lost altitude
and you're flying directly into the mountains."

"You don't have to tell me that," Alberta replied. "I
can see them right in front of me."

"I need you to take hold of the thrust and slowly pull it
toward you, not too fast and not too slow," the man said.
"Make like you're Goldilocks, Alfie."

"Vinny!" Alberta cried. "Is that you?"

"It's me," Vinny confirmed. "I'm here with Jinx,
Helen, and Freddy, and we heard every word you said.
That's damn fine detective work, Alfie, I'm proud of
you."

"We're all proud of you, Berta," Helen said.

"Keep pulling that thrust back, Alberta," the air traffic
controller said. "You're doing fine, but I need you to raise
your altitude a little more."

"You got this, Gram!" Jinx cried. "You were right,

Owen, the only thing you have to look forward to is a lifetime in jail."

Owen's head snapped toward Jinx's voice on the radio and he exhibited the strength and fury he had unleashed while he was masquerading as Umberto. He reached out and grabbed Alberta's hand, pushing the thrust away from her so the plane tilted forward and started to descend.

"No!" Alberta cried.

"What's happening?!" Jinx shouted.

"You're descending, Alberta," the ATC said. "You need to keep climbing."

"That's what I'm trying to do!" Alberta shouted. "Ladies, get him off of me!"

Working like a team that shared a long history, Veronica and Joyce banded together and attacked Owen. First, Veronica punched Owen in the jaw, which caused him to fall into the instrument panel on his side of the plane. With his hand off the thrust, Alberta was able to resume her attempt to increase the plane's altitude and fly over the mountains instead of into them. But Owen wasn't giving up so easily on his attempt to kill them all.

He lunged forward and threw himself on top of Alberta, the force of his body pushing Alberta to the left, but she was right, the survival instinct was far too strong, and never once did she let go of the thrust. Owen might have wanted them to die, but she was more determined to make sure they all lived.

Joyce grabbed Owen's shirt collar and yanked him back, but Owen was fighting to remain on top of Alberta in an attempt to block her view and pull her hand off of the thrust. He might have been successful, but Joyce had a partner. Veronica grabbed Owen's arm and pried his hand free from the grip he had on Alberta, and once they were separated, Veronica and Joyce were able to wrestle him to the ground.

Still, he squirmed and rocked back and forth, trying to get free. He had come this far, there was no way he was going to stop until he was victorious.

"Hold him down," Joyce commanded.

Veronica straddled Owen and pinned his arms down. She was using every ounce of strength that she had, but instead of growing tired, Owen was getting stronger. Meanwhile, Joyce was looking for something to use to knock Owen out. She grabbed the fire extinguisher, but was afraid she would kill him if she hit him with it. She looked around the cockpit for a substitute and came upon the perfect solution. If the pilot couldn't do his job, the pilot's shoe would suffice.

Joyce grabbed the loafer off of Eugene's unmoving foot, whipped around, and bashed Owen in the head with it. One more wallop for good measure and Owen wouldn't cause them any more problems. Just to be safe, they took off his belt and tied his hands around his back and used Joyce's scarf to bind his feet together. Even if he did wake up before they landed, he would be powerless to stop them.

"You're doing great, Alberta," the ATC said. "Just a little bit more and you'll clear the top of the mountain."

A profound silence filled the cockpit as Alberta, Joyce, and Veronica watched in awe and admiration as the majestic mountain disappeared underneath them. They had made it. Despite the efforts to thwart them, they had survived. No one was more grateful than Alberta.

"Karen Black is giving you a thumbs-up, Berta," Joyce said. "You just starred in your own *Airport* movie."

"It isn't over yet, Joyce," Alberta said. "I still have to land this thing."

"I'll be with you every step of the way from here on out, Alberta," the ATC said. "I'm going to guide you on the new course, and then you'll turn on the autopilot. When you begin the descent, you'll just push the thrust away from you, press the button to let the landing gear release, maintain your horizon, and hit the brakes. It's like driving a car."

"I drive a BMW," Alberta said. "That car can drive without me."

"Imagine you're driving a big old Buick," the ATC said. "Takes skill to maneuver one of those classics."

Helen's voice came over the radio loud and clear. "That's what I've been trying to tell you people for years!"

When the time came to land the plane, it wasn't as easy as the ATC predicted, but with his guidance and the prayers of all those around Alberta in the cockpit and on the ground, she somehow managed to land the plane on the airstrip, if not smoothly, then safely.

Once the plane was at a full stop, Alberta bowed her head and said her own prayer. She prayed to God for forgiveness for putting others in danger and thanked him for giving her the strength to lead them to safety. She was rattled, but far from broken. Her plan might not have worked out entirely as she had envisioned, but the result she hoped for was achieved. Teri Jo, Dominic, and Inez's killer would be brought to justice.

An ambulance whisked the pilot to the hospital and

Vinny greeted Owen with handcuffs and a police escort. In contrast, Alberta and Joyce were greeted with hugs, yelps, and tears by Helen, Jinx, and Freddy.

"Gram, you are absolutely amazing," Jinx gushed. "If I'm going to be the journalist I want to be, I better start following in your footsteps."

"Lovey, you're an amazing reporter," Alberta said. "You follow your own footsteps, they'll take you as far as you want to go."

Fighting back tears, Jinx said, "For right now there's no other place I want to be other than with you and my family."

"Dude!" Freddy shouted.

"And Freddy," Jinx added.

Standing alone a few feet away from the group, Veronica watched the reunion. She was alone, but couldn't blame anyone else for that except herself. She fled her family, stayed as far away from them as possible, and took their money and a business opportunity instead of their love and companionship. Teri Jo was the only family member she'd ever truly had a relationship with, and she was gone.

In an odd way, Helen understood Veronica's motive. She too left her family because they couldn't provide her with the life she knew she had to experience. She felt a connection to Veronica, a kinship of sorts, which compelled her to reach out.

"How are you?" Helen asked.

"Alive, thanks to your sister," Veronica said. "This all started because of me, because I wanted to become someone else."

"I know the feeling," Helen replied.

"Teri Jo spoke so highly of you," Veronica said.

"She was a good person," Helen said. "I considered her a friend."

Veronica fought the urge to look away, but knew that if she did she would be running from her own truth, so as hard as it was, she looked Helen in the eye.

"Can you ever forgive me for what I've done?" Veronica asked.

Helen knew what Veronica wanted to hear, but she was not one to sugarcoat the truth. If she was going to help Veronica heal, she couldn't start with a lie.

"My forgiveness is irrelevant," Helen said. "You have to find some way to forgive yourself, and that isn't going to be easy."

"I know," Veronica replied. "I think I'm going to need some help."

Helen held out her hand and Veronica quickly took it in hers. "When you're ready to ask, you know where to find me."

Alberta looked around at the commotion and the spectacle and didn't know if she wanted to laugh or cry or scream. She looked up to the heavens and silently told God that He'd have to wait a little while longer for her arrival. Right now she was exactly where she wanted to be, surrounded by friends and family.

And safely and securely on the ground.

EPILOGUE

Un dono di Dio.

After the verdict came in, finding Owen guilty of being the serial killer terrorizing Tranquility, he was sentenced to multiple life sentences in prison. Veronica was cleared of any criminal charges, but her past and the role she played in the deaths haunted her. She sold the diner and true to form, and much to Helen's disappointment, she left town for parts unknown.

Theirs weren't the only lives greatly affected by the tragedies, but thankfully the terrible events that took so many lives also had a positive impact on even more.

"This is too generous," Gabi said.

Joyce completely disagreed. "It's only money. You're going to have to do the rest."

Gabi understood what Joyce meant. She thanked Joyce for the check that would cover the expenses to pay for Arturo's education, even if he decided he wanted a

PhD. The boy's financial worries were over, but he was going to need Gabi's strength, guidance, and love to heal the emotional wounds caused by the death of his mother.

The flowers Helen placed on Teri Jo's grave were the same color as the ones she'd put there a few days ago. Pink was Teri's favorite color, and while Helen was never fond of the shade, it's what her friend loved, so she put her own thoughts aside.

Having spent so many years in the convent, living in different parishes and with other nuns who came and went, Helen hadn't formed many long-lasting friendships. She had her family, whom she treasured, but Teri Jo, despite their differences in age and background, had offered the opportunity to experience something new and fulfilling. That chance was taken away from Helen, but even though Teri Jo had moved on, Helen wanted to honor their friendship. It might have been brief, but it would always be remembered.

Jinx didn't care if it looked like she was flaunting her success. She placed the award she received from the New Jersey Society of Professional Journalists for Best Crime Reporting on her desk, right next to her nameplate, so no one could miss it. Her series of articles profiling Owen, Veronica, Umberto, and all three of Owen's victims had garnered critical acclaim for their sensitivity and insight, while presenting the facts objectively and without judgment. The public loved them too, and *The Herald*'s readership went up another 5 percent, leading Wyck to give Jinx a raise.

She was proud of her accomplishment, and every time she looked at it she was reminded that the goal she set for herself when she moved to Tranquility—to become a serious investigative reporter—had been achieved. She also knew that she was going to have to work even harder to prove to everyone, including herself, that she was worthy of the award and it wasn't a fluke.

Whether it was cockiness or confidence, she knew that was another goal she would eventually achieve.

Lola sat on the kitchen counter and pawed at the window. It was a gorgeous day with a picture-perfect cloudless blue sky that almost melted into the shimmering blue surface of Memory Lake. She couldn't be blamed for wanting to be a part of it, but Alberta and Sloan were long overdue for some private time.

While Alberta was learning how to fly a plane, Sloan had woken from his coma fully healed and thinking that no time had elapsed. He wasn't surprised to be told by his doctor that Alberta had solved the mystery and brought the criminal to justice.

"I don't think there's anything that you can't do, Alberta," Sloan said.

They were sitting on the wicker love seat in Alberta's backyard, Sloan's arm around Alberta's shoulders, so they, like the sky and the lake, gave the appearance that they were inseparable.

"A few years ago I would have laughed at that comment," Alberta said. "Now I think you might be right."

"I am right," he said. "What more proof do you need? You landed a plane all by yourself."

"I did have a little help," Alberta replied. "If I've

learned one thing about my life, and from this crazy experience. You can try to do things on your own and you
might succeed, but life is so much better when you share
it with someone."

"I like sharing my life with you Alberta," Sloan said.
"And I can't wait to show you off to my daughter. The
doctors finally got in touch with Shannon and she and her
family are flying in from Africa. I told her not to, but of
course she wouldn't listen to me."

"I can't wait to meet her," Alberta said. "It'll be like
seeing a whole new side of you."

The sun grew brighter in the sky, casting a glow onto
Memory Lake and the surrounding lush landscape. It also
lit up Sloan's face, although the fact that he was staring at
Alberta might have had something to do with that.

Ever since Sloan was attacked and lapsed into a coma,
Alberta could no longer ignore the depth of her feelings
for him. He was a surprise gift from God, *un dono di Dio*,
and it was time she acknowledged it.

"I love you, Sloan McLelland," Alberta said.

She didn't wait for Sloan to respond because she saw
the answer in his eyes. Instead, Alberta did what she had
learned she was fully capable of doing. She took action
and kissed her man.

Please turn the page for recipes from Alberta's kitchen!

Alberta's Italian Eggs Benedict with Pesto Hollandaise Sauce

Alberta swears this tastes better than Veronica's secret recipe, but Helen disagrees. You be the judge.

Ingredients
$\frac{1}{2}$ cup butter, cubed
1 tablespoon prepared pesto
4 large egg yolks
2 cold eggs
2 tablespoons water
1 tablespoon lemon juice
2 teaspoons white vinegar
Thin slices of prosciutto
Basil
Toast

Directions
1. In a small saucepan, melt the butter and stir in the pesto.
2. In a separate saucepan over a high flame, whisk the egg yolks, water, and lemon juice until it's all blended. Cook until the mixture is thick enough to stick to a spoon and the temperature reaches 160° and then reduce the heat to very low.
3. Slowly, add in the warm butter and pesto, making sure you keep whisking it constantly.
4. Transfer the contents to a small bowl, then place that bowl into a larger bowl that's filled with warm water.
5. Keep the sauce warm and stir it occasionally until

it's ready to serve. You're going to need someone to help you do this while you finish the recipe.

6. Use a large saucepan with high sides and pour in 2–3 inches of water.

7. Add vinegar and bring to a boil, then quickly reduce to a simmer.

8. Break cold eggs into a small bowl, then hold the bowl close to the surface of the water and let each egg slip into the pan.

9. Cook uncovered for 3 to 5 minutes or until the whites are completely set and the yolks start to thicken.

10. Use a slotted spoon to lift the eggs out of the water and place them on toast.

11. Layer on the prosciutto and basil, then top with the hollandaise sauce and serve it right away.

12. Then tell Helen it's the best eggs Benedict you've ever tasted!

Jinx's Gluten-Free Breakfast Pizza

Ingredients
For the Crust

6 cups frozen hash browns, thawed
1 large egg
2 tablespoons butter, melted
½ teaspoon salt
¼ teaspoon pepper

For the Pizza

1 tablespoon butter
5 large eggs
¼ cup milk—Don't substitute soy or almond milk be
    cause they don't mix well
6 slices dry aged bacon, cooked and crumbled
6 sausage links, sliced
1½ cups shredded cheddar cheese
½ cup tomatoes, diced

Instructions
For the Crust

1. Preheat the oven to 425°.
2. In a large bowl, combine the hash browns, egg,
   melted butter, salt and pepper.
3. Mix well and shape it into a 12-inch circle, pressing
   down on it firmly.
4. Place it on a pizza stone (if you have one like my
   grandma does) or (if you're like me) on a baking
   sheet lined with parchment paper.

5. Bake 20–25 minutes or until the edges are starting to brown. Do not get distracted or else the pizza will burn and you'll have to start all over again. Trust me!
6. Remove and reduce the oven temperature to 350°.

For the Pizza

1. In a large pan over medium-ish heat, melt the butter.
2. While the butter is heating, whisk the eggs and milk in a large bowl and season as little or as much as you'd like, but remember that you're cooking for others and not just yourself.
3. Pour the contents of the bowl into the pan and wait about 30 seconds before stirring.
4. Use a spatula to stir, lifting and folding from the bottom until the eggs are cooked thoroughly.
5. Sprinkle the scrambled eggs over the pie crust, add the crumbled bacon and sliced sausage, and top with the shredded cheese.
6. Bake for 20 minutes
7. Top with diced tomatoes and it's ready to serve.

Helen's Favorite Jersey-Style Disco Fries

Ingredients

2 pounds seasoned crinkle fries—from a package.
Alberta may want to make her own fries, but that's
pazzo!

8 ounces shredded mozzarella cheese

Brown gravy—for this Alberta's right, don't use a jar,
make your own!

Parsley

For the Gravy

3 cups beef stock

1 small shallot, minced

1 garlic clove, minced

4 tablespoons unsalted butter

¼ cup flour (Use gluten-free flour if someone like Jinx is
sharing your food with you.)

2 teaspoons Worcestershire sauce

Sea salt and pepper

Instructions

1. Preheat the oven to 425°.
2. Spread the fries in one single layer on a large parchment-lined baking sheet.
3. Cook the fries according to the package instructions, but remember sometimes those instructions are wrong, so keep an eye on the fries and take them out when they're golden and crispy. If you burn the fries, you'll have to start all over again!
4. While the fries are cooking, make the gravy.

5. Melt the butter in a saucepan and add the shallot and garlic—don't get carried away with the garlic like my sister can.
6. Season with sea salt and pepper.
7. Cook until the shallot and garlic are softened and then sprinkle in the flour and cook for another 3 minutes.
8. Whisk in the beef stock, but keep stirring to avoid lumps.
9. Add the Worcestershire sauce.
10. Bring the gravy to a boil and simmer 5–7 minutes until thickened.
11. When the fries are done, take them out of the oven and sprinkle them with the shredded mozz. Put the tray back into the oven for 2–3 minutes until the cheese is melted.
12. Pour the warm gravy on top and *buon appetito!*

Optional Twist

Make it really Italian and use marinara sauce instead of brown gravy!

Alberta & Jinx's Neapolitan
Non-Dairy Milkshake

Ingredients
2 frozen bananas

3 scoops dairy-free vanilla ice cream (If you can't find non-dairy, try Breyer's Lactose-Free Vanilla—it's *delicioso*, as my grandma would say.)

⅔ cup dairy-free milk—Jinx's favorite is vanilla-flavored almond milk

¼ cup ice cubes

1 cup strawberries

1 tablespoon cocoa powder

Instructions
1. In a blender, combine the frozen bananas, the dairy-free vanilla ice cream, the dairy-free milk, and the ice cubes.
2. Pour the mixture into 3 small bowls and set 1 bowl to the side—this is bowl #1.
3. Add one mixture back into the blender and add the strawberries. Mix it until it's thoroughly blended and then set it aside—this is bowl #2.
4. Add the last mixture into the blender and add the cocoa powder. Mix that one really well and set it aside—this is bowl #3.
5. In a serving glass, pour bowl #3 in first.
6. Using a spoon, pour bowl #2 in next, spreading it all over.
7. Then pour bowl #1 on top.
8. Enjoy—it's as easy as 1-2-3!

Connect with Us

Visit us online at
KensingtonBooks.com
to read more from your favorite authors, see books
by series, view reading group guides, and more.

Join us on social media

for sneak peeks, chances to win books and prize packs,
and to share your thoughts with other readers.

facebook.com/kensingtonpublishing
twitter.com/kensingtonbooks

Tell us what you think!

To share your thoughts, submit a review,
or sign up for our eNewsletters, please visit:
KensingtonBooks.com/TellUs.

Grab These Cozy Mysteries from
Kensington Books